THE LION WAKES

Also by Robert Low

The Whale Road
The Wolf Sea
The White Raven
The Prow Beast

ROBERT LOW

The Lion Wakes

HarperCollins*Publishers*

HarperCollins*Publishers*
77–85 Fulham Palace Road,
Hammersmith, London W6 8JB

www.harpercollins.co.uk

Published by HarperCollins*Publishers* 2011
1

A catalogue record for this book
is available from the British Library

ISBN 978 0 00 733791 0

Set in Sabon by Palimpsest Book Production Limited,
Falkirk, Stirlingshire

Printed and bound in Great Britain by Clays Ltd, St Ives plc

Mixed Sources
Product group from well-managed
forests and other controlled sources
www.fsc.org   Cert no. SW-COC-001806
© 1996 Forest Stewardship Council
FSC

FSC is a non-profit international organisation established to promote the
responsible management of the world's forests. Products carrying the FSC
label are independently certified to assure consumers that they come
from forests that are managed to meet the social, economic and
ecological needs of present and future generations.

Find out more about HarperCollins and the environment at
www.harpercollins.co.uk/green

To my wife, who is the sun on my
shiny water: without her, I don't sparkle

Being a chronicle of the Kingdom in the Years of Trouble, written at Greyfriars Priory on the octave of Septuagisma, in the year of Our Lord one thousand three hundred and twenty-nine, 23rd year of the reign of King Robert I, God save and keep him.

In the year of Our Lord one thousand two hundred and ninety-six, the Scots decided they had had enough of King Edward lording it over them with his appointed Balliol king and so declared. The English came north with fire and sword and the Law of Deuteronomy at Berwick, so that the slaughter caused the name of that town to be used as a watchword and rallying cry for ever after.

The defeated King John Balliol was brought to Edward's feet, to be stripped of crown and regalia, the proud heraldry of his rank torn from his surcote, so that he was known as Toom Tabard – Empty Cote – ever after. The coronation regalia of Scotland – the Holy Rood and the Stone of Scone – was seized, while the Great Seal was ceremonially snapped in half.

Then King Edward rode south, giving control of what he now thought of as his own lands to a governor, to keep the Scots in thrall to him.

'A man does good work,' he declared, washing his hands of the place, 'when he rids himself of such a turd.'

But the Scots would not bow the knee . . . there was rebellion in the north under Moray, the east under Frazier, in the west under a brigand called Wallace. Scotland's bishops were defiant. Sir William Douglas, who was called The Hardy for his boldness, and had defended Berwick against King Edward, was captured and then pardoned into the king's peace on his promise to serve in the English army in France. Not long after, he slipped his bonds of oath and came to join the rebels.

Stung to action by this last, King Edward ordered his loyal subjects in Scotland to oppose these rebels and Robert Bruce the Younger, Earl of Carrick, was sent to Douglas Castle, to slight the fortress and take Sir William's wife and bairns hostage.

But when the lion wakes, everyone must beware its fangs . . .

PROLOGUE

Douglas, Lanark
Feast of St Drostan the Hermit, July 11, 1296

The worst part had been the dark. No moon, no stars, just the whispering of lost souls searching the wind for a way home, or a body to slither into for the memories of warm blood and life. There had been owls and he did not like owls, for they shrieked like Cyhiraeth, goddess of woodland streams, who wraiths through the dark screaming at those about to die.

Gozelo knew he should not allow himself to believe in such matters, being a good Christian, but his grandmother, old Frisian that she had been, had stuffed his head with such tales when he'd been younger. It only came out when he was ruffled and fretted and even God would have to admit that this country He had clearly forsaken did ruffle and fret.

Not the country so much as the Cloaked Man. Gozelo shivered and dragged his own cloak tighter round him, moving on into the silvered dawn and happy to see the light. He had been heading for Carnwath, held by the Lord Somerville – English or not, he was at least light and heat and, above all, safety – but the dark had put paid to that

3

and Gozelo was now certain he had missed that place and was headed for Douglas.

He worried that a man limping in on foot would be sent away with a curse and a waved spear. A man on a horse had status while one slithering through the wet summer dawn on ripped shoes, with a cloak and tunic stained with hard travel, was nothing at all, even if he was a Flemish Master Mason from Scone. Not only that, Gozelo knew that Douglas was home to a nest of former rebels, who could not be trusted to keep out the ones he was sure now hunted him.

Something whirred and Gozelo started, looked wildly round and hurried on. He should never have taken the task but that old mastiff-faced Bishop Wishart had cozened him into it with flattery and promises of a fat purse. Not that making the piece had been difficult and Manon had seen to the carvings; Gozelo did not doubt now that the poor stone worker was dead.

Then the Cloaked Man had appeared with a cart and a worn horse for it and the Fleming realised that they were taking the original and leaving the cuckoo in its place. Manon, he had been told, was paid and gone already; that was when the chill, cold as altar stone, had sunk into his very soul.

'We take this to Roslin,' the Cloaked Man had said in French. 'There you will be paid, both for your skill and to keep your mouth closed on this matter.'

If it had just been the Cloaked Man who had schemed all this, Gozelo would never have countenanced it at all − but it had been a bishop, no less, who had broached the subject of it. Gozelo thought Bishop Wishart a singular churchman at the time, had basked in the warm flattery and the promise of riches until the long struggle after the cart, the relentless wet − Christ in Heaven, was there no other weather in this Scotland? − and the gibber of his own fears had melted his resolve like gold in the assay. The Cloaked Man, grim as a wet cliff, became more and more sinister with each passing mile until, no more than

4

a good walk from Roslin, the last of Gozelo's courage crumbled and he ran.

The Cloaked Man had thought hard about it. Gone off without the fat purse and in a panic for his life, having finally worked out the possibilities. Aye, well – smart wee man that he was, he would work out more when his legs stopped long enough to let his mind start running. Like how to make up the lack of fat purse. He would head for Lanark and the English sheriff, Heselrig, where he would tell all he knew.

It was, the Cloaked Man noted, just as Wishart had said, calling him aside with a quiet: 'If you trust *os vulvae*, then you are a fool. Go with God, my son.'

The Cloaked Man had to admit the bishop had been right, both about the Fleming's character and how his mouth, wet-lipped and surrounded by a silly fringe of beard and moustache, did look like a woman's part if you turned your head sideways. The Latin of it, *os vulvae*, the Cloaked Man decided, sounded better than the English – cunt face.

Of course, the Cloaked Man reasoned, clucking the weary pony up to the castle at Roslin, this Fleming may just head on to Dumfries and the English border. He was a Master Mason, after all, and would not be short of work for long.

Sir William Sientcler, the Auld Templar of Roslin, gave him a good, fast hobin horse and a sharp, meaningful glance when this had all been laid out to him.

'Mak' siccar,' he said and the Cloaked Man nodded. He would make sure.

Gozelo could see the faint lights in the dark and almost sobbed with the relief of it, for he was now close to Douglas and could find shelter there before going on to Lanark. He would tell all he knew, he thought viciously, for what the Cloaked Man had put him through. He had convinced himself that he had been right to run before he had been black murdered in the dark. He would never return to this country again and would tell all he knew to the English, even after what they had done to the Flemings – some of them kin – in Berwick. They would pay, too and offset the loss of the promised purse. What was a silly stone to him, after all?

The shape rose up from behind the last fringe of trees leading to the water meadow that ran down to the shrouded bulk of the fortress and the so-near lights. Gozelo screamed, high as an owl, but it was all too late.

'You went off without your due,' the Cloaked Man said mildly and Gozelo fell back, babbling wildly, in French, English – any language that came to him. He was only vaguely aware of his bowels running down his leg, his mind a mad whirl of pleas that his mouth could not get out quickly enough.

'You'll say nothing?' the Cloaked Man repeated, catching one of them as it spewed out, and saw the Fleming nod so wildly it seemed his head would fly off.

The Cloaked Man nodded sympathetically, then reached up with both hands to draw back the hood and show himself to the moon. The pallid light of it did nothing for his face and made the four-sided sliver of steel in one fist wink; Gozelo shrieked so high only dogs could hear him.

'Best mak' siccar,' said the Cloaked Man into the Fleming's bewilderment, stepping close and punching once; Gozelo leaned against him like a spent lover, then was gently slid to the mulch and the undergrowth.

The Cloaked Man wiped the dagger clean on the Fleming's cloak, took what he needed from the unresisting corpse and left, leading the horse until he was sure he was clear away.

It was, he suddenly realised, the day after Longshanks had decreed for all Scotland's community of the realm to meet at Brechin and witness what happened to a king who defied English Edward.

There had been, no doubt, humiliation and lies and viciousness. Edward would already have packed up the Rood and the Seal and the Stone as he had threatened, stripping both King John Balliol and kingdom of authority.

But Longshanks did not have all of Scotland in his grasp – one small part of the Kingdom had been taken from his fist.

The Cloaked Man smiled, warmed by the thought even as the summer mirr soaked him.

CHAPTER ONE

Douglas Castle, almost a year later
Vigil of St Brendan the Voyager, May 1297

The hounds woke Dog Boy as they always did, stirring and snuffing round him. Where there had been heat was suddenly cool and growing colder until it hooked him, shivering, from sleep.

At his movement, the dogs were round him, tongues lolling, panting fetid breath in his face, whining with hopeful looks and fawning eyes to be fed. They knew the routine of the day as well as Dog Boy – better, according to the Berner's right-hand, Malk.

Dog Boy struggled up, speeding the process as the cold air chewed him. He pulled straw from his hair and clothes, fumbled for his pattens and stumbled in the half-dark of the kennels, a long, low building of wattle and daub with timber pillars. There was no light for fear of fire and the rear wall was solid, cold stone, part of the brewhouse; the only light dappled through the chinks in the daub on to the straw floor, which stank as it did every morning.

He found a rough wool over-tunic on a hook near the leashes, pulled it over his head and fumbled his arms through the holes, blowing on his hands for it was cold just before the dawn. Someone coughed; heads appeared, dark knobs surfacing through the straw and the other kennel-lads struggled into a new day. The dogs whined and whimpered, wriggled and circled endlessly, tails working furiously, wanting fed.

'Soft, soft,' Dog Boy soothed. 'Quietly. It won't be long.'

Unless there was a hunt, of course, in which case the dogs would not be fed, for full bellies made poor runners and the runners were the hounds he, with a handful of other lads, was responsible for. Raches and limiers, they were, about thirty all told, and they circled and whined while the other hounds, partitioned off to keep them from each other's throat, started up a hoarse, howling bark.

'Swef, swef,' Gib called out to silence them, showing off the French he had learned from Berner Philippe. The dogs ignored him and Dog Boy smiled to himself – the limiers were English Talbots, white sleuthhounds, all nose and no stamina; Dog Boy thought it unlikely they would know any French. The raches were all colours, Silesian-bred hounds forming the bulk of the pack and made for long running. Once the limiers marked the trail, the raches would follow relentlessly until they brought the prey to bay or dropped.

He thought it unlikely any of them would understand French – if dogs understood any language at all – but France was the place thought to be the home of hunting and so all the hounds were given their French names and the head houndsman was a Frenchman, given his title in French – *berner*. Yet the prey they hunted here was the same – hart, hind and boar, all the preserve of the Dale, the Water and beyond, the lands given by God and King into the hands of the Douglas.

Beyond the thin partition, the other boys stirred as the alaunts and levriers bayed and howled. Dog Boy shivered and it was not from the cold: there were twenty levriers in there, fighting grey gazehounds with cold eyes and snarls. Yet even they balked and put their tails down when the strangers, two great rough-coated and huge deerhounds, curled a leathery lip.

The levriers were capable of running down and tackling a young, velvet-horned hart or a doe, the alaunts could tackle a good stag if it had been brought to bay, but only the deerhounds could run a prime stag into the ground and still have the wind left to drag it down.

Douglas had no deerhounds, so it came as a shock to see this pair arriving with Sir Hal of Herdmanston and his riders. It had seemed to Dog Boy that there were a lot of riders for a simple hunting party, but he had been put right on that by Jamie and others – Sir Hal had come in the guise of a hunting party, sent by his father to hold to the promise they'd made to the Douglas fortalice to defend it in time of threat. There was no larger a threat, it had seemed, than the Lord Bruce of Carrick and his men, come to punish the Lady and her sons for her husband's rebellion against the English King Edward.

It had come as a shock to Dog Boy to see all those men – more folk than he had ever seen in his life before – flowing round the castle like spilled oil. It was even more a shock to see how unruly the Herdmanston dogs were, so that the wolf-howls of them set every hound in Douglasdale off. Berner Philippe had been furious – but, to everyone's surprise, the sight and smell of Dog Boy had calmed the two great beasts almost at once.

'This one is Mykel,' Master Hal had told him, and the dog had looked at Dog Boy with great, limpid eyes. 'It means great, an old Lothian word. The other is called Veldi, which means power in the same tongue.'

Dog Boy nodded, breathless with the attention of the towering, smiling Hal and his towering, smiling crew, with names like Bangtail Hob and Ill Made Jock. Veldi, pink tongue lolling from between the white reefs of its teeth, looked at Dog Boy, the blue-brown eyes unwinking, and he felt the sheer heartleap of surety that these dogs were angels in disguise.

He tried to say as much, but could only manage 'angels', which made the giants laugh. One clapped him on the shoulder, almost driving him into the ground with the strength of it.

'Angels, is it? Wee lad of pairts you, are ye not?' this one said – Dog Boy had heard the others call him Tod's Wattie. 'Ye'll chirrup different first time these hoonds of hell mak' ye birl yer hocks in the glaur.'

From his bitterness, Dog Boy knew the dogs had somer-saulted Tod's Wattie into mud at least once; he could have sworn Mykel winked at him and he laughed, which made Tod's Wattie scowl and all the others slap their thighs at his expense.

Sir Hal, grinning, had told him to take good care of his pets and Dog Boy had looked up into the old-young face, bearded and with eyes like sea haar, and loved the man from that moment; Mykel nudged a rough muzzle under his arm and stared at him with huge blue-brown eyes.

Once, on the day he had arrived in Douglas, Dog Boy had seen a hound as big as Mykel. A wolfhound, he had learned, rough-coated and big as a pony it seemed – but Dog Boy knew that he had been smaller then and had an idea that the deerhounds were even longer in the leg.

That animal had died when Dog Boy was eight, two years after his mother, walking proud and desperate, had shep-herded him through the gatehouse of this place, which had been wooden then. On it had hung the Douglas shield, with its three silver stars – mullets, Dog Boy had been told, though he could not see that they looked like fish. He now knew – because Jamie Douglas had told him – that it came from the French, *molette*, which was a six-arrayed star.

Jamie, despite their differences in rank, was his friend and could read and knew where France lay. Dog Boy could not read at all and had no idea even where England was and a vague idea that Scotland lay fairly close to Douglasdale.

He knew that the English of England had come to Douglasdale, all the same, for Jamie spoke of little else these days, bitter that his mother had given in without a fight; now the Carrick men swarmed inside and outside Douglas Castle and the Lord Bruce, young and certain of himself to the point of arrogance, had politely taken over, in the name of the English – even though he was not one.

The one certainty in Dog Boy's life, the thing that he hugged to himself when everything else seemed to whirl like russet leaves in a high wind, was his age – eleven. He knew this because he heard his mother say it, knew her voice better than he did her face.

He could not remember his father, though he had a rag-edged memory of stumbling in the plough ruts behind a man making kissing sounds to two oxen which were not his own, watching the plough blade curve a wave out of the earth.

He could feel it yet between his naked toes, see the birds wheel and cry at the exposed beetles and worms. It had been his job to get to the worms first and tuck them safely back in the torn ground, for they were ploughers of the earth every bit as much as Man. He heard a voice say that and thought it might have been his father – but all that was gone, save for the moment when the great slab face of his da came down to his level, the crack-thumbed hands on either of his thin shoulders.

It had come at the moment after he had run across the fields clutching the rough bag with a slab of day-old porridge and two bannocks in it. Run like a deer to where his da stood with the oxen he was so proud of owning. No-one else had such a prize.

His da had looked at him for a long time and then crouched down into his face.

'Tha runs fast as a wee dug,' he said sadly. 'Fast as any wee dug.'

The day after that his ma had walked him into the castle and stood looking at Berner. Dog Boy was ashamed these days that he could not quite remember his own ma's face now, but he remembered her voice and the feel of her hand on the top of his combed head.

'I have brung him,' she said. 'As Sire said I could, when he could run fast as the dugs. He is six.'

Since then, there had only been those stones and the dogs.

Malk, the Berner's assistant, reckoned up Dog Boy's age and marked it in the Rolls along with the birthing dates of all the hounds and their pedigrees. It did not matter to Dog Boy, for he did not know, that Malk could trace a hound's lineage back through several generations and recorded Dog Boy only as a scion of 'bound tenants' from a huddle of cruck houses twenty miles away.

It would have been a surprise to Dog Boy to know that he had a name, too − Aleysandir, same as the king who fell off a Fife cliff and plunged the whole of Scotland into chaos in the year Dog Boy was born − but Dog Boy did not know any of that and had been Dog Boy for so long that he knew no other name now.

'Get aff me, ye dungbags!'

The voice jerked Dog Boy guiltily back to the kennels; Gib was pushing dogs away and, beyond him, The Worm stretched and yawned noisily, straw sticking out from his unruly hair. Dog Boy scratched a fleabite and then half-crouched, his habitual pose at sudden noises and surprises, as the heavy door banged open, flooding in cold light and chill air.

'Avaunt, whelps.'

Silhouetted briefly in the pale square light of the doorway, the figure paused slightly, then stepped in, flicking his dogwhip; the hounds knew him well and circled away from him, yet kept coming back, tails down, fawning and whimpering.

Berner Philippe had to stoop to avoid the low roof, though he was not tall. He wore a battered leather jack to protect the plain, stained-wool robe, itself worn to keep the pale-grey tunic clean from the dogs. He also wore his habitual sour sneer, which bristled his trimmed black beard.

'Come on, come on, stir yourselves,' he growled. 'There's work to be done – where is Gib?'

Gib stumbled forward, picking straw off himself and rubbing sleep from his eyes. He swept a bow, almost mocking, as he showed off his little command of French.

'*A votre service, Berner Philippe.*'

The scowl deepened a little as Philippe looked at him. This one was becoming too familiar by half. It wouldn't do. He tongued the stump of a tooth, then forced a smile and patted the boy on the cheek.

'Ah, lordling,' he said lightly. 'Such manners, eh?'

The others watched him caress Gib as he would do the dogs, chucking him under the chin, fondling behind one ear; it was as much part of the ritual of morning as waking, for Gib was the berner's favourite.

There were six houndsmen under Berner Philippe. Together with the six piqueurs, the huntsmen, they considered themselves the true Disciples of Douglas, not the strutting men-at-arms, who numbered the same. If that were so, then Berner Philippe was St Peter, White Tam, the head *piqueur* was James, brother of Jesus, the Lady Eleanor was the Virgin Herself – and The Hardy was Christ in Person.

Thus was life arranged by Law and Custom, which is to say, by God.

'Take five lads and clean this cesspit,' said Philippe and looked from Dog Boy to Gib and back again. Then he nodded to Gib and watched as the boy shambled off to obey. He was getting bigger . . . too big, God's Wounds. What had once been soft flesh was filling and hardening and, even to a nose used to stinks, Gib reeked more and more positively of dog every day.

Dog Boy stood, looking at the fetid straw as if there was

a cunning picture in it, and Philippe wondered, as he had always done, why he had never taken to the lad. Too scrawny, probably. There was a new lad − Philippe's head swung this way and that like a questing hound on a scent. What was his name . . . ? Hew, that was it. That was the name his parents had given him, but he was on the Rolls with an easily remembered nickname − a dog name, Falo, which meant 'yellow', and Philippe picked him out from the others by his cap of golden hair.

Disappointment. Too young − still, that blond hair, which spoke of decent ancestry implanted in the mongrel Scots, fell over the boy's face as he gathered armfuls of stinking straw and Philippe's groin tightened a little. Worth waiting for . . .

He caught sight of Dog Boy, edging, as always, into the shadows. Dog Boy felt more than saw the eyes fall on him and stopped, dull with despair.

'You,' Philippe said shortly, eyeing the thin-limbed, dark-eyed boy with the distaste he gave to all runts. 'Mews. Gutterbluid wants you.'

Outside, the cold bit Dog Boy and he hugged himself, dragging himself to the mews across the expanse of Ward in a cold wind out of the charcoal sky. Dog Boy eyed the glowing coals where Winnie the smithwife was blowing life into the forge fire, sparks flying dangerously up to the stiffened thatch of the wagon shed and the great stretch of stables. Beyond was the palisade and ditch, the gatehouse, newly done in stone, and the wooden dovecote etched blackly against the slow, souring milk of a new dawn. Behind, the bulked towers and stone walls of the Keep humped up and lurked over him.

The forge flames flared and danced brief eldritch shadows up the wall of one tower, to the narrow cross-slit window of the chapel, where light glowed, the honey-yellow of tallow candles; Brother Benedictus, the Chaplain, was already at his devotions, murmuring so that Dog Boy was almost sure he heard the words he knew so well:

16

Domine labia mea aperies. Et os meum annunciabit laudem tuam. Deus in adiutorium meum intende.

Dog Boy, hurrying on past the bakehouse, already spewing stomach-gripping smells and smoke, muttered the expected response without thinking – *Ave Maria, gracia plena.* The rest of it followed him, circling faintly like a chill wind off the river – *Gloria patri et filio et spiritui sancto. Sicut erat in principio et nunc et semper et in secula seculorum. Amen. Alleuya.*

He went past the dovecote, with its steep little roof surmounted by a strange bird pecking its own chest, and saw Ferg the scullion fetching new loaves and grinning at him, for he knew the Latin words as well. Neither had a clear idea of what they meant and knew them by rote only.

Next to the bakehouse, the kitchen sheds were quiet and coldly pale, as were most of the buildings within the rough palisade separating the Ward from the Keep, where lay the Great Hall, the stables and barracks and some little gardens.

Somewhere, high up on the *hourds*, watchmen stamped and blew on their hands. Soon those wooden hoardings would be dismantled, for the need for them was gone now that the Lady had given in to the Carrick men.

There had been a moment of confusion a few days later when a new host appeared, smaller but no less fierce. Dog Boy had heard the leader of it hailed as the Earl of Buchan and Jamie had muttered that no-one was sure whether this Comyn lord was for or against King Edward.

Dog Boy had watched them arrive, with their banners and their shouting; it had been exciting for a while and he wondered if he would see fighting – but then it had all ended, just like that. It was a puzzle that the Lady of Douglas now treated the Invaders as Friends and the castle was crowded with them, while more were huddled in makeshift shelters all over the Ward and beyond.

'Dog Boy,' called a voice, and he turned to see Jamie

stepping from the shadows. Dog Boy bowed and Jamie accepted it as his due, since he was The Hardy's eldest, with black braies and a dagged hood, a fine knife in a sheath on his belt, good leather boots and a warm surcote.

He was of ages with Dog Boy, yet bigger and stronger because he trained with weapons and would one day take the three vows and become a knight. One day, too, he would become Jesus Christ, Dog Boy thought, when his father, The Hardy, died and left him the lordship of Douglas. Even now he was able to fly a *tiercel gentle,* a male peregrine, if he chose – the memory of where that bird roosted brought misery crashing back on Dog Boy.

'Cold,' Jamie offered with a grin. 'Cold as a witch's tit.'

Dog Boy grinned back at him. They were friends of a sort – even if Dog Boy wore worn, mud-coloured clothing and was of no consequence at all – because Jamie liked the dogs and had no mother, like Dog Boy. Dog Boy had questioned this once, because he had thought the Lady Eleanor was Jamie's mother, but Jamie had put him on the straight road of that one.

'My real mother was sent away,' he said bluntly. 'To a convent. This one is my father's new woman and the sons he pupped on her are my stepbrothers.'

He turned and looked at Dog Boy then, savage as his tiercel.

'But I am the heir and one day this will be mine,' he added and Dog Boy had no doubt of it. It was what they shared, what cut through their stations. The same age, the same colouring, the same abandonment by ma and da. The same loneliness. It had all brought them together from the moment they could toddle and they had rattled around like two stones in a pouch ever since.

Both of them knew that changes were happening, all the same, as much to their rank as their bodies, and that unseen pressures were forcing them further and further apart. Dog Boy would never be anything more than he was now – Jamie would become a knight, like his father.

There had been no knights other than The Hardy in Douglas, though there had once been twenty men-at-arms, with stout jacks, swords and polearms. Now there were only six, for the rest were gone and Dog Boy felt the cold unease slide into him, the way it had done the year before when the four surviving men had carried a fifth in through the gate.

They also carried the news that The Hardy was imprisoned and all the other Douglas men were dead, together with some thousands of folk who had been living in Berwick when English Edward had captured it.

'The blood came up ower the tops of my shoes,' Thomas the Sergeant had told them, and he should know, for some of it was his and he wore the scar, raw as memory, down one side of his face. He had been the fifth man and, for a while, it looked as if he would die – but he was tough, folk said, hard as Sir William Douglas himself.

Jamie loved and feared his father in equal measure and the fact that Sir William had survived the siege and slaughter at Berwick and was fighting still, flooded his world – though Dog Boy did not quite understand all of it and Jamie explained it, as if schooling a hound.

It seemed that the Earl of Carrick, who was a young, dark Bruce called Robert, had arrived on orders from the English to punish the Lady because of her man's siding with the uprisen Scots. The Lothian lord, the hard-eyed man with the big hounds, had come in the last drip of the candle to help the Lady defy this earl.

For reasons the Dog Boy could not quite grasp, he and the Lady had then surrendered to Earl Robert – but none of the dire consequences everyone else said was certain if you gave into Invaders had happened. Nothing much had happened at all, save that the Castle grew crowded.

Not long after that, another Earl had arrived at the gate, this one called Buchan. It seemed he and the Earl Robert did not care much for each other, but seemed to be on the same side. Which was not the one Sir William Douglas stood on.

Dog Boy had no clear idea why this Earl Buchan had arrived at all, but was surprised to find that the fox-haired Countess who had arrived with Earl Robert was, in fact, the wife of the Earl called Buchan. It was a whirl of leaves in a high wind to the Dog Boy and, finally, Jamie saw his audience's interest slipping. He spasmed with childish irritation.

'From your point of view, I suppose this war is only an annoyance of rolling maille in a barrel of sand to clean it, or having to practise archery.'

Dog Boy said nothing, aware his friend was angry and not quite sure why. There was guilt, too – he was supposed to attend archery practice like all the lower orders, but seldom did and no-one cared if the runty Dog Boy never turned up.

It didn't bother him, missing out on the butts, for there had never been an enemy here until the Invaders – and they had ended up Friends. Yet, slowly, Dog Boy was becoming aware of a tremble in the fabric of life, could hear the cracking of the stones of Douglas Keep.

'Faugh – you stink today,' Jamie said suddenly, wrinkling his nose as the wind changed. 'When did you wash last?'

'Fair Day,' Dog Boy replied indignantly. 'Same as the rest, wi' real soap and rose petals in the watter.'

'Fair Day,' Jamie exploded. 'That was months since – I had a wash only last week, in a tub of piping hot water with Saracen scented soap.'

He winked what he thought was in knowing, lecherous fashion.

'And a wench to scrub my back – eh?'

'I dinna think your lady mother would suffer that,' Dog Boy answered doubtfully, aware of the mysteries of dog and bitch but not yet sure how it translated to the mumblings and groans he heard sometimes in the night. He was aware, too, that there was a Rule about women. In Douglas there was a Rule about almost everything.

'The Lady Eleanor is not my mother,' Jamie answered, stiff and haughty. 'She is my father's wife.'

He frowned, all the same, for Dog Boy was right and yet Jamie had seen matters and heard more which only confused him about what was permitted and what was not. There were women in the castle − notably Agnes in the castle kitchen and some tirewomen for his stepmother and now the Countess of Buchan, who laughed a lot and had wild hair a wimple could not keep in check. She stayed in her own tower rooms, though, while her husband scowled in his proud, striped panoply in the Ward, and that was strange.

'I'm off to get some bread,' Jamie decided, throwing the matter over his shoulder. 'Do you want some?'

Dog Boy's mouth watered. The birds could wait; the smell of baking bread, newly turned from the ovens, brought both their heads up, sniffing and salivating.

'Dog Boy!'

The voice slashed them apart, a soft rasp of sound like a blade drawn down a rough wall. Both boys shrank at the sound and turned to where the Falconer had appeared, as if sprung from the ground. He gathered his marten coat round him, wore his marten hat with its single eagle feather and if there were three other items of value in the entire world, it was said, Falconer did not know of them.

Those who said that did not call him Gutterbluid where he could hear it, since it meant 'low-born whelp'. His real name was Sib, according to some, and he had the name Gutterbluid because it was one you gave to folk born in Peebles when you wanted to annoy them. No-one wanted to annoy Sib, so they simply called him Falconer and no-one liked him; Dog Boy liked him least of all.

'You are dallying, boy,' Falconer sibilated. Jamie, recovering, struck a shaky air of nonchalance, aware that he should try to conquer his fears if he was to be a knight.

'I was addressing him, Falconer,' he declared, then wilted beneath the black gaze of the man, whose eyes burned from his lean, brown face. No wonder, Jamie thought wildly, folk think he is a Saracen.

Falconer looked the boy up and down. Lisping pup, he thought. Falconer had more skills, more intelligence and more right to dignity – yet this little upstart was noble born and Falconer could only aspire to looking after what mean birds they could afford.

He wanted to cuff the boy round the ear but knew his place and the price for stepping out of it. So he bowed instead.

'Your pardon, young master. When you are done, I will have my lure.'

Dog Boy saved Jamie from further torture by bobbing a bow to him and scuttling past Falconer towards the mews, where he slipped on the badger-skin gloves, and hunched, waiting. Jamie and Falconer stared at each other for a moment longer until the last of Jamie's courage melted like rendered grease. Falconer, satisfied, curled a smile on one lip, bowed again and strode after Dog Boy.

The mews was dark, fetid with droppings, filled with a sound like great hanging banners fluttering faintly in a wide hall; the birds, a dozen or so, moving softly on their perches, claws scraping. Each bird stood in its own niche, or on a perch, motionless as a corbel carving, blind knights in plumed hoods. Dog Boy stepped in, basket held in the crook of one arm, a bloody little feathered body in one gloved hand.

He drew in a breath, heavy with the rank must of the birds, they scented him, exploding in a frenzy of frantic hunger, shrieking and screaming. The air was filled with the mad beating of wings and a sleet of feathers. They screeched and leaped to the furthest ends of the jesses, flinging themselves in desperate desire at Dog Boy, red-eyed and wild, battering him furiously.

Dog Boy winced and shoved the food at them, staggering down the passage between them, unable to strike back for fear of what Falconer would do, trying to protect himself from the wind and the storm of hate. Jamie's gerfalcon careered off its perch and could not find its way back. One frenzied bird lashed out with a talon and scored a hit on the back of Dog Boy's wrist as the glove slipped.

A hand fell on the blizzard-blinded youth, gripping him by the shoulder and pulling him from the whirl of feathers and claws and endless, endless shrieks. He was flung out the door to land in a sobbing heap and, after a while, got enough breath back to sit up, wiping tears and feathers from his face. There was a long, scarlet trail on the back of one hand and he sucked it, then slithered off the gloves, seeing the new, tufted rents in them.

He heard Falconer – soft, soft, he was saying. My beauties, all over now. Soft, soft, my children.

A shadow fell on Dog Boy and he jerked, started to wriggle away. Falconer . . .

It was Jamie, his mouth set in a stitched line. He held out a piece of bread without a word and Dog Boy took it. It steamed, fresh from the oven and was hot in Dog Boy's mouth.

'Finished?'

Dog Boy nodded, unable to speak, and Jamie held out his hand, took Dog Boy's wrist and hauled him up. Together, they sprinted for the smithy, wriggling up to the forge block, picking metal shavings and bent nails from under their bodies.

Winnie the Smithwife, short, stocky and dark as a north dwarf, stuck her fire-reddened face, hair braided into thick plaits against flying sparks, down into their corner and grinned. She passed them down some small beer without a word, for she liked their being there, like little mice, while she pounded metal into shape. Warmed by the food and the fire, Dog Boy began to feel better.

'Not much,' Jamie said, studying Dog Boy's new wound.

'When I am lord here,' he added, 'this will end.'

Neither of them spoke after that, for there was nothing to say. This was Dog Boy's other task in life – the birds were starved and then fed by him and only him. If they hunted and one was lost, Dog Boy was sent out to find it. No matter how much it had eaten, or whether the exultant joy of freedom gripped it, the sight and smell of Dog Boy, whirling bait on the end of a line, would make the bird stoop and be recaptured.

Hal saw them scamper as he passed, padding silent, on his way to see to the Herdmanston men and make sure they toggled their lips on any mention of what they had seen or heard about the Countess Isabel of Buchan and the young Bruce.

He did not like Gutterbluid, or the lure he made of the kennel laddie, and knew it for a punishment he suspected had been ordered by the Lady Eleanor. He suspected he knew why, too – but such was the way of the world, decreed by Law and Custom and, therefore, by God.

It did not help that the world was birling in ever more strange jigs these days, none stranger than finding that he had been sent to defend Douglas rights only to find his Roslin kin – and liege lord the Auld Templar Sir William Sientcler – riding with Bruce.

Hal had known that before he had set off, scraping almost every man Herdmanston possessed on the orders of his father and despite protests. There was scarce a man left to guard the yett of their own wee tower fortalice, but his father, rheumy eyed and grit-voiced, had thumped his shoulder when he had voiced this.

'I hold to the promise made that the Sientclers of

Herdmanston would defend the rights of the Douglas. There was no wee notary's writing in it concerning gate guards or our kin's involvement, lad.'

There was considerable relief, then, when the Lady Eleanor took Hal's advice and surrendered to The Bruce and his Carrick men without demure, though she had scowled and all but accused him of treachery because the Auld Templar stood on the other side.

Hal had swallowed that and convinced her, sighing with relief when the gates were opened and young Bruce, the Earl of Carrick rode in and never so much as cocked an eye at the Lady's truculence.

'I was sent by my father,' he told her, his bottom lip stuck out like a petulant shelf, 'who was himself instructed by King Edward to punish Douglas for the rebellion of Sir William.'

He leaned forward on the crupper of the great horse while the Ward milled and fumed with men, some of them only half aware of the Lady Eleanor's straight-backed defiance and the young Bruce's attempts to be polite and reasonable.

'Your man quit Edward's army without permission, first chance he had,' he declared flatly. 'Now God alone knows where he is – but you could pick Sir Andrew Moray's north rebellion as a likely destination. I have come from Annandale to take this place and slight it, Lady, as punishment. That I have not knocked it about too much, while putting you in my protection, means my duty is done, while you and your weans are safe.'

The rebel Scots may cry Bruce an Englishman, Hal thought, but the real thing would not have been so gentle with the Lady Eleanor of Douglas – but she was a fiery beacon of a woman and not yet raked to ashes by this sprig of a Bruce.

'You do it because my husband's wrath would chase ye to Hell if ye did other. As well young Hal Sientcler's kinsman was with you, my lord Earl. A Templar guarantee. My boys and I thank you for it.'

The Auld Templar, his white beard like a fleece on his face, merely nodded but the young Bruce's handsome face was spoiled by the pet of his lip at this implication that the Bruce word alone was suspect; seeing the scowl, the Lady of Douglas smiled benignly for the first time.

It was not a winsome look, all the same. The Lady Eleanor, Hal thought, has a face like a mastiff chewing a wasp, which was not a good look for someone whose love life was lauded in song and poem.

She was a virgin – Hal knew this because the harridan swore she was pure as snow on The Mounth. He didn't argue, for the besom was as mad as a basket of leaping frogs – but if God Himself asked him to pick out the sole maiden in a line of women he would never, ever, have chosen Eleanor Douglas, wife of Sir William The Hardy.

Her fierce claim was supposed to make her legitimately bairned. That, Hal thought, would also make her two sons, Hugh and Archie, children of miracle and magic since she and The Hardy had been lovers long before they were kinched by the Church. Then The Hardy had abducted her, sent his existing wife to a convent and married Eleanor, risking the wrath of everyone to do it.

Not least her son, Hal thought, seeing the young Jamie standing, chin up and shoulders back beside his stepmother. Hal watched him holding his tremble as still as could and felt the jolt of it, that loss. Like his John, he thought bleakly. If Johnnie had lived he would be the age this boy is now.

The memory dragged him back to the Ward and the sight of Jamie and the kennel lad scurrying for the smithy, and he felt the familiar ache.

Sim Craw, following Hal into the blued morning, also saw the boys slip across the Ward – and the cloud in Hal's eyes, like haar swirling over a grey-blue sea. He knew it for what it was at once, since every boy Hal glanced at reminded him of his dead son. Aye, and every dark-haired, laughing-eyed woman reminded him of his Jean. Bad enough to lose a son to the ague, but the mother as well was too much punishment from God for any man, and the two years since had not balmed the rawness much.

Sim had little time for boys. He liked Jamie Douglas, all the same, admired the fire in the lad the way he liked to see it in good hound pups. No signs and portents in the sky on the night James Douglas was born, he thought, just a mother suddenly sent away and a life at the hands of The Hardy, hard-mouthed, hard-handed and hard-headed. Unlike his step-siblings, quiet wee bairns that they were, James had inherited a lisp from his ma and the dark anger of his da, which he showed in sudden twists of rage.

Sim recalled the day before, when Buchan had arrived and everyone flew into a panic, for here was the main Comyn rival to the Bruces standing at the gates and no-one was sure whether he was in rebellion, since he should not be here at all.

Worse still, his wife was here, thinking her husband a few hundred or more good Scotch miles away with English Edward's army heading for the French wars, so leaving her free for dalliance with the young Bruce.

So there had been a long minute or two when matters might have bubbled up and Sim had spanned his monstrous latchbow. The young Jamie, caught up in the moment, had raised himself on the tips of his toes and lost entirely the usual lisp that affected him when he roared, his boy's body shaking with the fury in it, his child's face red.

'Ye are not getting in. Ye'll all hang. We will hang you, so we will.'

'Weesht,' Sim had ordered and slapped the boy's shoulder, only to get a glare in return.

'Ye cannot speak to me like that,' he spat back at Sim. 'One day I will be a belted knight.'

There was a sharp slap and the boy yelped and held his ear. Sim put his gauntlet back on and rested his hand on the stock of his latchbow, unconcerned.

'Now I have made ye a belted knight. If ye give your elders mair lip, Jamie Douglas, ye'll be a twice belted knight.'

He mentioned the moment now to Hal, just to break the man's gaze on the place where the boys had been. Jerked from the gaff of it, Hal managed a wan smile at Sim's memory.

'Bigod, I hope he has no good remembrance of it when he comes into his own,' he said to Sim. 'You'll need that bliddy big bow to stop him giving ye a hard reply to that ear boxing.'

A sudden blare of raucous shouting snapped both their heads round and the great slab face of Sim Craw creased into one large frown.

'Whit does he require here?' he asked, and Hal did not need to ask the who of it, for the most noise came from in and around the great striped tent of the Earl of Buchan.

'His wife, I shouldn't wonder,' Hal answered dryly, and Sim laughed, soft as sifting ashes. Somewhere up there, Hal thought, glancing up to the dark tower, is the Countess of Buchan, the bold and beautiful Isabel MacDuff, keeping to the lie that she had coincidentally turned up to visit Eleanor Douglas.

Buchan, it seemed, was the one man in all Scotland who did not know for sure that the young Bruce and Isabel were rattling each other like stoats and had been lovers, as Sim said, since the young Bruce's stones had properly dropped.

For all the humour in it, this was no laughing matter. The Earl of Buchan was a Comyn, a friend to the Balliols of Galloway, who were Bruce's arch-rivals. A Balliol king had been appointed four years before by Edward of England – and then stripped of his regalia only last year when he proved less than biddable. Now the kingdom was in turmoil, ostensibly ruled directly from Westminster.

But all the old kingdom rivalries bubbled in the cauldron of it and it would not take much for it all to boil over. Finding an unfaithful wife with her legs in the air would do it, Hal thought.

A piece of the dark detached itself and made both men start; a wry chuckle made them drop their hands from hilts, half ashamed.

'Aye, lads, it is reassuring to a man's goodwill of himself that he can make two such doughty young warriors afraid still.'

The dark-clothed shape of the Auld Templar resolved into the familiar, his white beard trembling as he chuckled. Hal nodded, polite and cautious all the same for the Auld Templar represented Roslin and the Sientclers of Herdmanston owed them fealty.

'Sir William. God be praised.'

'For ever and ever,' replied the Templar. 'If ye have a moment, the pair of ye are requested.'

'Aye? Who does so?'

Sim's voice was light enough, but held no deference to rank. The Auld Templar did not seem put out by it.

'The Earl of Carrick,' he declared, which capped matters neatly enough. Meekly, they followed the Auld Templar into the weak, guttering lights of hall and tower.

The chamber they arrived in was well furnished, with a chest and a bench and a chair as well as fresh rushes, and perfumed with a scatter of summer flowers. Wax tapers burned honey into the dark, making the shadows tall and menacing – which, Hal thought, suited the mood of that place well enough.

'Did you see him?' demanded Bruce, pacing backwards and forwards, his bottom lip thrust out and his hands wild and waving. 'Did you see the man? God's Wounds, it took me all of my patience not to break my knuckles on his bloody smile.'

'Very laudable, lord,' answered a shadowed figure, sorting clothing with an expert touch. Hal had seen this one before, a dark shadow at the Bruce back. Kirkpatrick, he recalled.

Bruce kicked rushes and violets up in a shower.

'Him with his silver *nef* and his serpent's tongue,' he spat. 'Did he think the salt poisoned, then, that he brings that tooth out? An insult to the Lady Douglas, that – but there is the way of it, right enough. An insult on legs is Buchan. Him and his in-law, the Empty Cote king himself. *Leam-leat*. Did you hear him telling me how none of us would have done any better than John Balliol? Buchan – *tha thu cho duaichnidh ri èarr àirde de a' coisich deas damh*.'

'I did, my lord,' Kirkpatrick replied quietly. 'May I make so bold as to note that yourself has also a *nef*, a fine one of silver, with garnet and carnelian, and a fine eating knife and spoon snugged up in it. Nor does calling the Earl of Buchan two-faced, or – if I have the right of it – "as ugly as the north end of a south-facing ox" particularly helpful diplomacy. At least you did not do it to his face, even in the *gaelic*. I take it from this fine orchil-dyed linen I am laying out that your lordship is planning nocturnals.'

'What?'

Bruce whirled, caught out by the casual drop of the last part into Kirkpatrick's dry, wry flow. He caught the man's eye, then looked away and waved his hands again.

'Aye. No. Perchance . . . ach, man, did I flaunt my garnet and carnelian *nef* at him? Nor have I a serpent's tongue taster, which is not an honourable thing.'

'I have a poor grasp o' the French,' Sim hissed in Hal's ear. 'Whit in the name of all the saints is a bliddy *nef*?'

'A wee fancy geegaw for holding your table doings,' Hal whispered back out of the side of his mouth, while Bruce rampaged up and down. 'Shaped like a boatie, for the high *nobiles* to show how grand they are.'

It was clear that Bruce was recalling the dinner earlier,

when he and Buchan and all their entourage had smiled politely at one another while the undercurrents, thick as twisted ropes, flowed round and between them all.

'And there he was, talking about having Balliol back,' Bruce raged, throwing his arms wide and high with incredulity. 'Balliol, bigod. Him who has abdicated. Was publicly stripped of his regalia and honour.'

'A shame-day for the community of the realm,' growled the Auld Templar from the shadows, heralding the eldritch-lit face that shoved out of them. It was grim and worn, that face, etched by things seen and matters done, honed by loss to a runestone draped with snow.

'From wee baron to King of the Scots in one day,' Sir William Sientcler added broadly, stroking his white-wool beard. 'Had more good opinion of himself than a bishop has wee crosses – now he is reduced to ten hounds, a huntsman and a manor at Hitchin. He'll no' be back, if what he ranted and raved when he left is ony guide. John Balliol thinks himself well quit of Scotland, mark me.'

'I am bettering,' Bruce said with a wan smile. 'I understood almost all of that.'

'Aye, weel,' replied Sir William blithely. 'Try this – if ye don't want the same to choke in your thrapple, mind that it was MacDuff an' his fine conceit of himself that ruined King John Balliol, with his appeals for Edward to grant him his rights when King John blank refusit.'

Bruce waved one hand, the white sleeve of his *bliaut* flapping dangerously near a candle and setting all the shadows dancing.

'Aye, I got the gist of that fine – but MacDuff of Fife was not the only one who used Edward like a fealtied lord and undermined the throne of Scotland. Others carried grievances to him as if he was king and not Balliol.'

Sir William nodded, his white-bearded blade of a face set hard.

'Aye well – the Bruces never did swear fealty to John Balliol,

31

if I recall, and I mention MacDuff,' he replied, 'less because he has raised rebellion in Fife, and more because ye are trailing the weeng with his niece and about to creep out into the dark to be at her beck an' call, with her own man so close ye could spit on him.'

He met Bruce's glower with a dark look of his own.

'Doon that road is a pith of hemp, lord.'

The silence stretched, thick and dark. Then Bruce sucked his bottom lip in and sighed.

'Trailing the weeng?' he asked.

'Swiving . . .' began Sir William, and Kirkpatrick cleared his throat.

'Indulging in an illicit liaison,' he said blandly, and Sir William shrugged.

Bruce nodded, then cocked his head to one side.

'Pith of hemp?'

'A hangman's noose,' Sir William declared in a voice like a knell.

'Serpent's tongue?' asked Sim, who had been bursting to ask about it since he had heard it mentioned earlier; Hal closed his eyes with the shock of it, felt all the eyes swing round and sear him.

After a moment, Bruce sat down sullenly on the bench and the tension misted to shreds.

'A tooth for testing salt for poison,' Kirkpatrick answered finally. He had a face the shadows did not treat kindly, long and lean as an edge with straight black hair on either side to his ears and eyes like gimlets. There was greyness and harsh lines like knifed clay in that face, which he used as a weapon.

'From a serpent?' Sim persisted.

'A shark, usually,' Bruce answered, grinning ruefully, 'but folk like Buchan pay a fortune for it in the belief it came from the one in Eden.'

'We are in the wrong business, sure,' Sim declared, and Hal laid a hand along his forearm to silence him. Kirkpatrick saw it and studied the Herdmanston man, taking in the breadth of shoulder and chest, the broad, slightly flat face, neat-bearded and crop-haired.

Yet there were lines snaking from the edge of those grey-blue eyes that spoke of things seen and made him older. What was he – twenty and five? And nine, perhaps? With callouses on his palms that never came from plough or spade.

Kirkpatrick knew he was only the son of a minor knight from an impoverished manor, an offshoot of nearby Roslin, which was why Sir William was vouching for him. The Auld Templar of Roslin had lost his son and grandson both at the battle near Dunbar last year. Captured and held, they were luckier than others who had faced the English, fresh from bloody slaughter at Berwick and not inclined to hold their hand.

Neither Sientcler had yet been ransomed, so the Auld Templar had gained permission to come out of his austere, near-monkish life to take control of Roslin until one or both were returned.

'Sir William tells me you are like a son to him, the last Sientcler who is young, free, with a strong arm and a sensible head,' Bruce said in French.

Hal looked at Sir William and nodded his thanks, though the truth was that he was unsure whether he should be thankful at all. There were children still at Roslin – two boys and a girl, none of them older than eight, but sprigs from the Sientcler tree. Whatever the Auld Templar thought of Hal of Herdmanston it was not as an heir to supplant his great-grandchildren at Roslin.

'It is because of him I bring you into this circle,' Bruce went on. 'He tells me you and your father esteem me, even though you are Patrick of Dunbar's men.'

Hal glanced daggers at Sir William, for he did not like the sound of that at all. The Sientclers were fealtied to Patrick of Dunbar, Earl of March and firm supporter of King Edward – yet, while the Roslin branch rebelled, Hal had persuaded his father to give it lip service, yet do nothing.

33

He heard his father telling him, yet again, that people who sat on the fence only ended up with a ridge along their arse; but Bruce and the Balliols were expert fence-sitters and only expected everyone else to jump one side or the other.

'My faither,' Hal began, then switched to French. 'My father was with Sir William and your grandfather in the Crusade, with King Edward when he was a young Prince.'

'Aye,' answered Bruce, 'I recall Sir John. The Auld Sire of Herdmanston they call him now, I believe, and still with a deal of the lion's snarl he had when younger.'

He stopped, plucking at some loose threads on his tight sleeve.

'My grandfather only joined the crusade because my own father had no spine for it,' he added bitterly.

'Honour thy father,' Sir William offered up gruffly. 'Your grand-da was a man who loved a good fecht − one reason they cried him The Competitor. Captured by that rebellious lord Montfort at Lewes. It was fortunate Montfort was ended at Evesham, else the ransom your father had to negotiate would have been crippling. Had little thanks for his effort, if I recall.'

Bruce apologised with a weary flap of one hand; to Hal this seemed an old rigg of an argument, much ploughed.

'You came here with two marvellous hounds,' Bruce said suddenly.

'Hunting, lord,' Hal managed, and the lie stuck in his teeth a moment before he got it out. Bruce and Sir William both laughed, while Kirkpatrick watched, still as a waiting stoat.

'Two dogs and thirty riders with Jeddart staffs and swords and latch-bows,' Sir William replied wryly. 'What were ye huntin', young Hal − pachyderms from the heathen lands?'

'It was a fine enough ruse to get you into Douglas the day before me,' Bruce interrupted, 'and I am glad you saw sense in obeying your fealtied lord over it, so that we did not have to come to blows. Now I need your dogs.'

Hal looked at Sir William and wanted to say that, simply

because he had seen sense and trusted to the Auld Templar's promises, he was not following after Sir William in the train of Robert Bruce. That's what he wanted to say, but could not find the courage to defy both the Auld Templar and the Earl of Carrick at one and the same time.

'The dugs – hounds, lord?' he spluttered eventually and looked to Sim for help, though all he had there was the great empty barrel of his face, a vacant sea with bemused eyes.

Bruce nodded. 'For hunting,' he added with a smile. 'Tomorrow.'

'To what end?' Sir William demanded, and Bruce turned fish-cold eyes on him, speaking in precise, clipped English.

'The kingdom is on fire, Sir William, and I have word that Bishop Wishart is come to Irvine. That old mastiff is looking to fan the flames in this part of the realm, be sure of it. The Hardy has absconded from Edward's army and now I find Buchan has done the same.'

'He has a writ from King Edward to be here,' Kirkpatrick reminded Bruce, who gave a dismissive wave.

'He is here. A Comyn of Buchan is back. Can you not feel the hot wind of it? Things are changing.'

Hal felt the cold sink of that in his belly. Rebellion. Again. Another Berwick; Hal caught Sim's eye and they both remembered the bloody moments dissuading Edward's foragers away from the squat square of Herdmanston following the Scots defeat at nearby Dunbar.

'So we hunt?' Sir William demanded with a snort, hauling his own tunic to a more comfortable position as he sat – Hal caught the small red cross on the breast that revealed the old warrior's Templar attachment.

'We do,' Bruce answered. 'All smiles and politeness, whilst Buchan tries to find out which way I will jump and I try not to let on. I know he will not jump at all if he can arrange it – but if he does it will be at the best moment he can manage to discomfort the Bruces.'

35

'Aye, weel, your own leap is badly marked – but you may have to jump sooner than you think,' Sir William pointed out sharply, and Bruce thrust out his lip and scowled.

'We will see. My father is the one with the claim to the throne, though Longshanks saw fit to appoint another. It is how my father jumps that matters and he does not so much as shift in his seat at Carlisle.'

'Which gives you a deal of freedom to find trouble,' Hal added, only realising he had spoken aloud when the words were out.

He swallowed as Bruce turned the cold eyes on him; it was well known that the tourney-loving, spendthrift Earl of Carrick was in debt to King Edward, who had so plainly taken a liking to the young Bruce that he had been prepared to lavish loans on him. There was a moment of iced glare – then the dark eyes sparked into warmth as Bruce smiled.

'Aye. To get into trouble as a wayward young son, which will let me get out of it again as easily. More freedom than Sir William here, who has all the weight of the Order bearing down on him – and the Order takes instruction from England.'

'Clifton is a fair Chaplain in Ballantrodoch,' the Auld Templar growled. 'He gave me leave to return to Roslin until my bairns are released, though the new Scottish Master, John of Sawtrey, will follow what the English Master De Jay tells him. The pair are Englishmen first and Templars second. It was De Jay put my boy in the Tower.'

'I follow that well enough,' Bruce said and put one hand on the old Templar's shoulder. He knew, as did everyone in the room, that those held in the Tower seldom came out alive.

'If God is on the side of the right, then you will be rewarded . . . how is it you say it? At the hinter end?'

'Not bad, Lord,' Sir William answered. 'We'll mak' a Scot of you yet.'

For a moment, the air thickened and Bruce went still and quiet.

'I am a Scot, Sir William,' he said eventually, his voice thin.

The moment perched there like a crow in a tree – but this was Sir William, who had taught Bruce to fight from the moment his wee hand could properly close round a hilt, and Bruce knew the old man would not be cowed by a scowling youth, earl or not.

He had sympathy for the Auld Templar. The Order was adrift since the loss of the Holy Land and, though it owed allegiance only to the Pope, Sir Brian de Jay was a *tulchan*, at the beck of King Edward.

Eventually, Bruce eased a little and smiled into the blank, fearless face.

'Anyway – tomorrow we hunt and find out if we are hunted in turn,' he said.

'Aye, there's smart for ye,' Sim burst out admiringly. 'Och, ye kin strop yer wits sharper listenin' to yer lordship and no mistake. There's a kinch in the rope of it, all the same. Yon Buchan might try and salt yer broth – a hunt is a fine place for it.'

'What did he say – a kinch? Rope?' demanded Bruce.

'He congratulates you on your dagger-like mind, lord,' Kirkpatrick translated sarcastically into French, 'but declares a snag. Buchan may try and spoil matters – salt your broth.'

Bruce ignored Kirkpatrick's tone and Hal saw that the man, more than servant, less than equal, was permitted such liberties. A dark, close-hugged man of ages with himself, this Roger Kirkpatrick was a cousin of the young Bruce and a landless knight from Closeburn, where his namesake was lord. This one had nothing at all and was tied to the fortunes of the Carrick earl as an ox to the plough. And as ugly, Hal noted, a dark, brooding hood of a man whose eyes were never still.

'Salt my broth,' Bruce repeated and laughed, adding in English, 'Aye, Buchan could arrange that at a hunt – a sprinkle of arrow, a shake of wee latchbow bolts, carelessly placed. Which is why I would have a wee parcel of your riders, Hal of Herdmanston.'

'You have a wheen of yer own,' Hal pointed out and Bruce smiled, sharp-faced as a weasel.

'I do. Annandale men, who belong to my father and will not follow me entire. My own Carrick men – good footmen, a handful of archers and some loyal men-at-arms. None with the skills your rogues have and, more importantly, all recognisable as my own. I want the Comyn made uneasy as to who is who – especially Buchan's man, the one called Malise.'

'Him with the face like a weasel,' Kirkpatrick said.

'Malise,' Sir William answered. 'Bellejambe. Brother of Farquhar, the one English Edward made archdeacon at Caithness this year.'

'An ill-favoured swine,' Kirkpatrick said from a face like a mummer's mask, a moment that almost made Hal burst with loud laughing; wisely, he bit his lip on it, his thoughts reeling.

'Slayings in secret,' he said aloud, while he was thinking, suddenly, that he did not know whether his father would leap with Bruce or Balliol. It was possible he would hold to King John Balliol, the Toom Tabard – Empty Cote – as still the rightful king of Scots, which would put him in the Balliol and Comyn camp. It seemed – how he had managed it was a mystery all the same – Hal had landed in the Bruce one.

Sir William saw Hal's stricken face. He liked the boy, this kinsman namesake for his shackled grandson, and had hopes for him. The thought of his grandson brought back a surge of anger against Sir Brian de Jay, who had been instrumental in making sure that his son had been sent to the Tower. He would have had grandson Henry in there, too, the Auld Templar thought, but was foiled – the man hates the Sientclers because they wield influence in the Order.

Thanks be to God, he offered, that grandson Henry is held in a decent English manor, waiting for the day Roslin pays for his release. In the winter that was his heart, he knew his son would never return alive from the Tower.

Yet that was not the greatest weight on his soul. That concerned the Order and how – Christ forbid it – De Jay might bring it to the service of Longshanks. The day Poor Knights marched against fellow Christians was the day they were ruined; the thought made him shake his snowed head.

'War is a sore matter at best,' he said, to no-one in particular. 'War atween folk of the same kingdom is worst.'

Bruce stirred a little from looking at the violet tunic, then nodded to Kirkpatrick, who sighed blackly and handed it over. Linen fit for trailing the weeng, Hal thought savagely. I have lashed myself to a man who thinks with his loins.

The day Buchan and Bruce had come to Douglas, he recalled, had been a feast dedicated to Saint Dympna.

Patron saint of the mad.

CHAPTER TWO

Douglas Castle, later that day
Vigil of St Brendan the Voyager, May 1297

They waited for the Lady, knights, servants, hounds, huntsmen and all, milling madly as they circled horses already excited. The dogs strained at the leashes and leaped and turned, so that the hound-boys, cursing, had to untangle the leashes to load them in their wooden cages on the carts.

Gib had the two great deerhounds like statues on either side of him and turned to sneer at Dog Boy. The Berner had given the stranger's dogs into Gib's care because Dog Boy was less than nothing and now Gib thought himself above all the sweat and confusion and that the two great hounds leashed in either fist were stone-patient because of him. Dog Boy knew better, knew that it was the presence of the big Tod's Wattie nearby.

Hal frowned, because the deerhounds, if they had chosen, could leap into the mad affray and four men would not hold them if their blood was up, never mind a tall, scowling boy with the beginning of muscle and a round face fringed with sandy hair. With his lashes and brows and snub nose, it all contrived to make him look like an annoyed piglet; he was not the one with the charm over the deerhounds and Hal knew the Berner had arranged this deliberately, as a snub, or to huff and puff up his authority.

The one with the hound-skill − Hal sought him out, caught his breath at the stillness, the stitched fury in the hem of his lips, the violet dark under his hooded eyes and the dags of black hair. Darker than Johnnie, he thought . . . as he had thought last night, the lad had the colouring and look of Jamie and might well be one of The Hardy's byblows, handed in to the French hound-master of Douglas for keeping. Hal switched his gaze to fasten on Berner Philippe, standing on the fringes of the maelstrom and directing his underlings with short barks of French.

The weight of those eyes brought the Berner's head up and he found the grey stare of the Lothian man, blanched, flushed and looked away, feeling anger and . . . yes, fear. He knew this Sientcler had been given the Dog Boy by the Lady, passed to him without so much as a 'by your leave, Berner', and that had rankled.

When told − told, by God's Wounds − that the Dog Boy would look after the deerhounds he had decided, obstinately, to hand them to Gib. It was, he knew, no more than a cocked leg marking his territory − all dogs in Douglas were his responsibility, no matter if they were visitors or not − and he did not like being dictated to by some minor lordling of the Sientclers, who all thought themselves far too fine for ordinary folk.

He liked less the feel of that skewering stare on him, all the same, busied himself with leashes and orders, all the time feeling the grey eyes on him, like an itch he could not scratch.

Buchan sat Bradacus expertly and fumed with a false smile. The hunt had been the Bruce's idea at table the night before and he had spent all night twisting the sense of it to try to the Bruce advantage in it. Short of a plot to kill him from a covert, he had failed to unravel it, but since he'd had nothing else to occupy him the time wasted had scarcely mattered. The bitterness of that welled up with last night's brawn in mustard, a nauseous gas that tasted as vile as his marriage to the MacDuff bitch.

It had seemed an advantageous match, to him and the MacDuff of Fife. Yet Isabel's own kin, bywords for greed and viciousness, had slain her father, which was no great incentive for joing the family. Even at the handseling of it, Red John Comyn of Badenoch had tilted his head to one side and smeared a twisted grin on his face.

'I hope the lands are worth it, cousin,' he had said savagely to Buchan, 'for ye'll be sleeping with a she-wolf to own them.'

Buchan shivered at the claw-nailed memory of the marriage night, when he had broken into Isabel MacDuff. He had done it since − every time she was returned from her wanderings − and it was now part of the bit, as much as lock, key and forbiddings to make her a dutiful wife, fit for the title of Countess of Buchan. That and the getting of an heir, which she had so far failed to do; Buchan was still not sure whether she used wile to prevent it or was barren.

Now here she was, supposedly ridden to Douglas on an innocent visit and using Bradacus' stablemate, Balius, to do it. Christ's Wounds, it was bad enough that she was unchaperoned − though she claimed such from the Douglas woman − but without so much as a servant and riding a prime Andalusian warhorse in a country lurking with brigands was beyond apology.

She could be dead and the horse a rickle of chewed bones . . . he did not know whether he desired the first more than he feared the second, but here she was, snugged up in a tower, refusing him his rights while he languished in his striped panoply in the outer ward, too conscious of his dignity to make a fuss over it.

That dropped the measure of her closer to the nunnery he was considering. He was wondering, too, if she and Bruce . . .

He shook that thought away. He did not think she would dare – but he had set Malise to scout it out.

Now he sat and fretted, waiting for her to appear so they could begin this accursed hunt, though if matters went as well as the plans laid, the Gordian knot of the Bruces would be cut. Preferably, he thought moodily, before Bruce's secret blade.

Which, of course, was why he and his men chosen for this hunt were armed as if for war, in maille and blazoned surcoats; he noted that the Bruce was resplendent in chevroned jupon, bareheaded and smiling at the warbling attempts of young Jamie Douglas to sing and play while controlling a restive mount. Yet he had men with him, unmarked by Carrick livery so that no-one could be sure who they belonged to.

He looked them over; well armed and mounted on decent garrons. They looked like they had bitten hard on life and broken no teeth – none more so than their leader, the young lord from Herdmanston.

Hal felt the eyes on him and turned to where the Earl sat on his great, sweating *destrier*, swathed in a black, marten-trimmed cloak and wearing maille under it. The face framed by a quilted arming cap was broad, had been handsome before the fat had colonised extra chins, was clean-shaven and sweating pink as a baby's backside.

The Earl of Buchan was a dozen years older than Bruce, but what advantage in strength that gave the younger man was offset, Hal thought, by the cunning concealed in those hooded Comyn eyes.

Buchan acknowledged the Herdmanston's polite neck-bow with one of his own. Bradacus pawed grass and snorted, making Buchan pat him idly, feeling the sweat-slick of his neck even through the leather glove.

He should have begged a palfrey instead of riding a *destrier* to a hunt, he thought moodily, but could not bring himself to beg for anything from the Douglases or Bruces. Now a good 25 merks of prime warhorse was foundering – not to mention the one his wife had appropriated, and he was not sure whether he fretted more for her taking a warhorse on a jaunt or for her clear, rolling-eyed flirting with Bruce at table the night before.

Brawn in mustard and a casserole of wheat berries, pigeon, mushrooms, carrots, onions and leaves – violet leaves and lilac flowers, the Lady Douglas had said proudly. With rose petals. Buchan could still feel the pressure of it in his bowels and had been farting as badly as the warhorse was sweating.

It had been a strange meal, to say the least. Old Brother Benedictus had graced the provender and that was the last he said before he fell asleep with his head in his rose petals and gravy. The high table – himself, Bruce, the ladies, wee Jamie Douglas, the Inchmartins, Davey Siward and others – had been stiffly cautious.

All save Isabel, that is. The lesser lights had yapped among themselves, friendly enough save for those close to the salt, when the glowering and scowling began at who had been placed above and below it.

Conversation had been muted, shadowed by the distant cloud that was King Edward – even in France, Buchan thought moodily, Longshanks casts a long shadow. He had put Bruce right on a few points and been pleased about it, while giving nothing away to clumsy probings about his intentions regarding the rebelling Moray.

'*Exitus acta probat*,' he had answered thickly, choking on Isabel's smiles and soft conversation with the Lady, talking right across him and ignoring him calculatedly.

'I hope the result does validate the deeds,' a cold-eyed Bruce had answered in French, 'but that's a wonderful wide and double-edged blade you wield there.'

Hal would have been surprised to find that he and Buchan shared the same thoughts, though his had been prompted by the sight of the Dog Boy, whose life had been wrenched apart and reformed at last night's feast as casually as tossing a bone to a dog.

'Your hounds are settled?' Eleanor Douglas had called out to Hal, who had been placed – to his astonishment – at the top of the lesser trestle and within touching distance of the high table. He thought she was trying to unlatch the tension round her and went willing with it. Then he found she only added to it.

'Yon lad is a soothe to them, mistress,' he had replied, one ear bent to the grim, clipped exchanges between Buchan and Bruce.

'It pleases me, then, to give you the boy,' the Lady said, smiling. Hal saw the sudden, stricken look from Jamie, spoon halfway to his mouth, and realised that the Lady knew it, too.

'Jamie will have me a wicked stepma from the stories,' she went on, not looking at her stepson, 'but he spends ower much time with that low-born chiel, so it is time they were parted and he learns the way of his station.'

Hal had felt the cleft of the stick and, with it, a spring of savage realisation – the hound-boy is a byblow of The Hardy, he thought to himself, and the wummin finds every chance to have revenge on wayward husband and her increasingly fretting stepson. Gutterbluid was one and now I am another – a dangerous game, mistress. He glanced at Jamie, seeing the stiff line of the boy, the cliff he made of his face.

'I shall take careful care of the laddie,' he had said, pointedly looking at Jamie and not her, 'for if he quietens those imps of mine, he is worth his weight.'

He realised the worth of his gift only later and, staring at the scrawny lad, marvelled at the calm he brought to those great beasts; the Berner's mean spirit came back to make Hal frown harder and he suddenly became aware that he was doing it while glaring at the Earl of Buchan.

Hastily, he formed a weak smile of apology, then turned away, but he realised later that Buchan had not been aware of him at all, had been concentrating, like a snake on a vole, on the arrival of his wife.

She appeared, a spot of blood on the *vert* of the day,

smiling brightly and inclining her head graciously to her scowling husband, the huntsmen and hound boys. She sat astraddle, on a caparisoned palfrey – at least she is not riding my other warhorse this time, Buchan thought viciously – while the Lady of Douglas, demure and aware of her rank, rode sidesaddle and was led by Gutterbluid, who had her hawk on his wrist.

Isabel wore russet and gold and, incongruously to Hal, worn, travel-stained half-boots more suited to a man than a Countess, but the hooded cloak was bright as a Christmas berry. Hal realised all of it was borrowed from the Lady Douglas – save the boots, which were her own and all she had arrived with bar a green dress, an old travel cloak and a fine pair of slippers.

Jamie rode alongside her, a lute in one hand; he winked at Dog Boy, who managed a wan smile and the pair of them shared the sadness of this, their final moments together in all their lives to this point.

'Wife,' growled Buchan with a nod of grudged greeting and had back a cool smile.

'La,' she then said loudly, cutting through all the noise of dogs and horses and men. 'Lord Robert – finches.'

Buchan brooded from under the lowered lintel of his brows at Bruce and his wife, playing the same silly game they had played all through last night at table. He felt the temper in him rising like a turd in a drain.

'Easy. A chirmyng,' Bruce replied. 'Now one for you – herons.'

Hal saw the way Isabel pouted, her eyes sapphire fire and her hair all sheened with copper lights; he felt his mouth grow dry and stared. Buchan saw that too, and that irked him like a bad summer groin itch that only inflamed the more you scratched it.

'A siege,' she answered after only a short pause. 'My throw – boys.'

Bruce frowned and squinted while the hunt whirled round them like leaves, not touching the pair of them, as if they sat in a maelstrom which did not ruffle a hair on either head. But Hal watched Buchan watching them and saw the hatred there, so that when Bruce gave in and Isabel clapped her hands with delight, Hal saw the Comyn lord almost lift off his saddle with rage.

'Ha,' she declared, triumphantly. 'I have come out on top again.'

Then, as Bruce's face flamed, Hal heard her add, 'A blush of boys.'

'If ye are done with your games,' White Tam growled from the knotted root of his face, 'we may commence the hunt.

'My lord,' he added, seeing Bruce's scowl and managing to invest the term with more scathe than a scold's bridle. Since White Tam was the Douglas head huntsman and more valued than even Gutterbluid the Falconer, Bruce could only smile and acknowledge the man with a polite inclination of his head.

'Now we will begin,' White Tam declared and flapped one hand; the cavalcade moved laboriously off, throwing clots up over the grass from the track that led into the forest alongside the Douglas Water. Dog Boy watched Gib being pulled into the wake of the hound cart by the deerhounds.

'*Peace, o my stricken lute,*' warbled Jamie shakily and plucked one or two notes, though the effect was spoiled by his having to break off and steer the horse.

'Bloody queer *battue* this,' Sim Craw growled, coming up to Hal's elbow. Buchan and Bruce were armed and mailled, though they had left helms behind as a sop to false friendship and because what they wore was already a trial in the damp May warmth.

Buchan even rode his expensive warhorse, Sim pointed out, as if he expected trouble, while the shadow of Malise Bellejambe jounced at his back on a rouncey fitted with fat saddle-packs on either side.

'Or would mak' trouble,' Hal answered and Sim stroked his grizzled chin and touched the stock of the great bow slung to one side of his rough-coated horse, watching the constantly shifting eyes of Bellejambe. Kirkpatrick, he noted, was nowhere to be seen and the entire fouled affair made him more savage at the mouth of the barrel-chested Griff, a foul-tempered garron, small, hairy and strong.

All his men rode the same mounts, small horses ideally suited for rough trod and long rides in the dark and the wet, with only a handful of oats and rainwater at the end of it. They could run for hours and sleep in snowdrifts, but would not stand up to a mass of men on horses the like of Buchan's Bradacus – but Hal was Christ-damned if he would be caught in a fight on a mere gelded ambler.

Sim and two hands of riders, wearing as much protection as they could strap on, followed him and they were not sure whether they were here for hunt or *herschip*, since they were armed with long knives and Jeddart staffs.

Bruce's smile was wry when he looked at them. It was hardly a hunting weapon, the Jeddart, an eight-foot shaft reinforced with iron for the last third, fitted with polearm spearpoint, a thin sliver of blade on one side and a hook like a shepherd's crook on the other. Men skilled with it could lance from horseback, or dismount and form a small huddle of points, capable of hooking a rider out of the saddle, or slicing his expensive horse to ruin. Bruce, for all he thought they looked like mounted ruffians, saw the strength and use of them.

'*If you were April's lad-ee and I were Lord of May*,' Jamie twittered as they scowled along the river road, the sun shining like a jest on their mockery.

They swung off the road, the carts lurching and the caged dogs whining eagerly. Dog Boy saw the forest, dark and musked, pearled with dawn rain. The trees, so darkly green they looked black, sprawled over hills alive with hidden life, tangled with bracken and scrub.

A place of red caps, dunters and powries, Sim Craw thought to himself and shivered at the idea of those Faeries. He liked the flat, long roll of Merse and March, bleak as an old whore's heart; forests made him hunch his shoulders and draw in his neck.

The trees closed in and the road vanished behind them as the sun turned faint, staining the woods with dapple; the flies closed in, whirring and nipping, so that horses fretted and twitched.

'What do they eat when we're elsewhere?' Bangtail whined, slapping his neck, but no-one wanted to open his mouth enough to answer, in case he closed it on cleg.

The Lady smiled at Hal and he remembered her turning to him in the Ward after Buchan and Bruce had gone off, arm in arm like returned brothers. He remembered it particularly for the astonishment in seeing her snub-nosed, chap-cheeked pig of a face softened by concern.

'I know what this day has cost,' she had murmured in gentle, courtly French and both the language and the sentiment had shocked him even more. Then she'd added, in gruff Scots, 'Not me nor the boy here will be after forgetting, either. Ye'll be sae cantie as a sou in glaur whenever ye come to Douglas after this.'

Sae cantie as a sou in glaur – happy as a pig in muck – and not the best offer Hal had ever had; for all her courtly French and De Lovaine breeding, the Lady of Douglas had the mouth of a shawled washerwoman when she chose. Hal thanked her all the same, while watching Buchan watching Bruce and the pair breaking off only to watch Isabel MacDuff.

The Lady of Douglas turned and spoke to White Tam, waving flies from her face. The old huntsman was like some gnarled tree, Buchan thought, but he knew the business well enough still. White Tam signalled and the whole cavalcade stopped; the hounds milled in their cages, yelping and whining.

A nod from the huntsman to Malk, and the houndsmen struck off the road and up into the trees with the carts, the dog boys leaning in to push over the scrub and rough; everyone followed and in a few steps it seemed to everyone as if the forest had moved, stepped closer and loomed over them, sucking up all noise until even Jamie gave up on his love dirges.

White Tam stood up slightly in the stirrups, a bulky, redfaced figure with a cockerel shock of dirty-snow hair which gave him his name. He had a beard which reminded Hal of an old goat and had one eye; the other, Hal had heard, had been lost fighting men from Galloway, in a struggle with a bear and in a tavern brawl. Any one, Hal thought, was possible.

The head hunstman rode like a half-empty bag of grain perched on a saddle. His back hurt and his limbs ached so much nowadays that even what sun there was in these times did nothing for him. It would have astonished everyone who thought they knew the old hunter to learn that he did not like this forest and the more he had discovered about it, the less he cared for it. He liked it least at this time of year and, at this moment, actively detested it, for the stags were coming into their best and the hunt would be long, hot and tiring.

The huntsman thought this whole farce the worst idea anyone had come up with, for a *battue* usually achieved little, spoiled the game for miles around for months and foundered good horses and dogs. He drew the ratty fur collar of his stained cloak tighter round him – he had another slung on the back of the horse, for experience had taught him that, on a hunt, you never knew where your bed might be – and prayed to the Virgin that he would not have to spend the dark of night in this place. Distantly, he heard the halloo and thrash of the beaters.

White Tam glanced sideways at the Sientclers, the Auld Templar of Roslin and the younger Sientcler from somewhere Tam had never heard of. His hounds, mind you, were a pretty pair and he wondered if they could hunt as well as they looked.

He watched the Lady Eleanor cooing to her hooded tiercel and exchanging pleasantries with Buchan and saw – because he knew her well now – that she was as sincere as poor gilt with the earl. That yin was an oaf, White Tam thought, who rides a quality mount to a hunt and would regret it when his muscled stallion turned into an expensive founder. An Andalusian cross with Frisian, he noted with expert eye, worth seven times the price of the mount he rode himself. Bliddy erse.

He considered the young Bruce, easy and laughing with Buchan's wife. If she was mine, White Tam thought, I'd have gralloched the pair of them for makin' the beast with two backs. It seemed that Buchan was blind or, White Tam thought to himself with years of observation behind it, behaving like most *nobiles* – biding his time, pretending nothing was happening to his dignity and honour, then striking from the dark and behind.

White Tam knew that men come to a *battue* armed as if for war was no unusual matter, for that style of hunt was designed for the very purpose of training young knights and squires for battle. Still, the old hunter had spoored out the air of the thing and could taste taint in it. The young Sientcler had confirmed it when he had come to Tam, enquiring about aspects of the hunt and frowning over them.

'So we will lose each other, then,' he had said almost wearily. 'In the trees. Folk will scatter like chaff.'

'Just so,' White Tam had agreed, seeing the worry in the man and growing concerned himself; he did not want rival lords stalking one another in Douglas forests. So he spilled his fears to the Herdmanston lord, telling the man how there was always something went wrong on a hunt if people did not hark to the Rule of it all. Foundered horses, careless arrows – there had been injuries in the past and especially in a *battue*. Beside that, a bad shot, a wild spear throw, a stroke of ill luck, all frequently left an animal wounded and running and it was a matter of honour for the person who had inflicted the damage to pursue it, so that it did not suffer for longer than necessary. Alone, if necessary, and whether he was a magnate of the Kingdom or a wee Lothian lord.

'Provided it is stag or boar,' White Tam had added, wiping sweat drips from his nose. 'Stag, as it is the noblest of God's creations next to Man and boar for they are the most vicious of God's creations next to Man and the worst when sair hurt.'

Anything else, he had told Hal pointedly, can be left to die.

Now he rose in the stirrups and held up a hand like a knotted red furze root, mottled as a trout's belly. Then he turned to Malk, who was *valet de limier* for the day.

'Roland,' he said quietly and the dog was hauled out of one cartload. White Tam dismounted stiffly and, grunting, levered himself to kneel by the hound; they regarded each other sombrely and White Tam stroked the grey muzzle of it with a tenderness which surprised Hal.

'Old man,' he said. '*Beau chien*, go with God. Seek. Seek.'

He handed the leash to the grim-faced Malk and Roland darted off, tongue lolling, moving swiftly from point to point, bush to root, head down and snuffling impatiently as he hauled Malk after him. He paused, stiffened, loped a few feet, then determinedly pushed through the scrub and off into the trees at a fast, lumbering lope. The houndsmen and dog boys followed after, struggling with the carts.

Hal turned to Tod's Wattie, who merely grinned and jerked his head: Gib came up on foot, the two deerhounds loping steadily ahead and hauling him along like a wagon. Hal returned the grin and knew that Tod's Wattie would keep a close eye on the boy and, with a sudden sharpness deep in him, saw the dark dog boy slogging through the bracken.

Sim Craw saw it too and caught his breath – wee Jamie's likeness, just as Hal had pointed out. Now there is a mystery . . .

'Follow Sir Wullie and stay the gither,' Hal said loudly, so that his men could hear. 'Spread the word – bide together. If something happens, follow me or Sim. I do not want folk scattered, eechie-ochie. Do this badly and I will think shame to be seen with you.'

The men grunted and growled their assent and Sim urged his horse close to Hal.

'What of the wummin, then?' he asked, babe innocent. 'Mayhap ye would rather chase the hurdies of the Coontess of Buchan?'

Hal shot him daggers and felt his face flame. God's curses, had he been so obviously smit with Isabel MacDuff's charms?

'Let that flea stick to the wall,' he warned and Sim held up a placatory hand.

'I only ask what's to be done,' he said with a slight smile and the mock of it in his eyes. 'Leave the Coontess to her husband – or Bruce, who is sookin' in with her, as any can spy but the blind man wed on to her?'

Hal shot a look at the Countess, a flame in the dim light under the green-black trees, remembering how she had shone in the dark, too.

He had been fumbling his way to the jakes after the awkward feast, flitting as mouse-quiet as he could through the chill, grey, shadowed castle to the latrine hole. Halfway up the turn of a stair he had heard voices and stopped, knowing one was hers almost before the sound had cleared his ear. He moved on, so that he could peer over the top step along the darkened passage.

She was at the door of her room, barefoot and bundled in a great bearskin bedcover and clearly naked underneath it. Her hair was a russet ember in the shadows, tumbling in tendrils down white shoulders.

At the side of her door hung a shield, a little affair glowing unnaturally white in the grey dim, with a bar of blue across the top and the Douglas mullets bright on it. A gauntlet hung over it.

'Young Jamie's shield,' she explained to the shadow, who clasped her close. 'He hung it there with the metal glove, look there. He has sworn to be my knight and champion and hangs that there to prove it. If any refuse to admit that I am the most beauteous maid in all the world, they must strike the shield with the glove and be prepared to fight.'

The shadow shifted and laughed softly at this flummery while Isabel pouted hotly up into his mouth. For a moment, Hal's breath had caught in his throat and he wished he was looking down, feeling that warmth on his lips.

'Shall I strike it for you?' she'd asked archly, and raised her long, white fingers, which spilled the fur from her shoulders and one impossible white breast, ruby-tipped like flame in the grey; Hal's breath caught in his throat. 'A tap, perhaps, just to see if he storms along the corridor.'

'No need,' the shadow declared, moving closer to the heat of her. 'I have no argument with what he defends.'

She reached and he grunted. She smiled up into his eyes, moved a hand.

'Nevertheless, Sir Knight,' she said, slightly breathy. 'It seems your lance is raised.'

'Raised,' the shadow agreed, guiding her into the doorway, so that the firelight fell on his face.

'But not yet couched,' Bruce added and the door closed on the pair of them.

A low, hackle-prickling bay snapped Hal from his revery and the caged hounds went wild.

'Wind, wind!' White Tam called out hoarsely – and unnecessarily, for everyone was heading towards the sound; Hal saw that Isabel had handed her hawk to the loping, hunched figure of the Falconer and was now spurring her horse away. Bruce, who had been admiring Eleanor's hawk, now thrust it back at the Falconer and followed, the pair of them forging ahead. Hal heard her laugh as Bruce blew a long, rasping discordance on a horn.

The limiers, hauling against their leashes as the luckless dog boys panted after, forged stealthily off in the eerie silence bred into them, the scent Roland had spoored for them strong in their snouts.

Malk appeared with Roland, the hound panting and trembling with excitement. He struggled at the leash and sounded a long, rolling cry from his outstretched throat that was choked off as Malk hauled savagely on the leash.

'Enough!' growled White Tam and shot Philippe a harsh look, which carried censure and poison in equal measure. He saw the Berner's mouth grow tight and then he was bellowing invective at the luckless Malk.

'Hand him up,' demanded White Tam and Malk, scowling, hauled the squirming Roland off the ground and up on to the front of the old huntsman's saddle.

'Swef, swef, my beauty. Good boy.'

White Tam suffered the frantic face licks and fawning of the hound, then tucked it under one arm and turned to Hal with a wry smile.

'What a pity that when the nose is perfect, the legs have to go, eh?'

Roland was returned to Malk, who took him as if he were gold and carried him gently back to the cage. White Tam, frowning, looked down at the berner.

'We will have Belle, Crocard, Sanspeur and Malfoisin,' he declared. 'Release the *rapprocheurs.*'

The hounds were drawn out and let slip, flying off like thrown darts, coursing left and right. Dog Boy saw Gib stagger a little under the slight strain of the two deerhounds, but a word from Tod's Wattie made them turn their heads reproachfully and whine.

Dog Boy saw Falo start to run after the speeding dogs, leashes flapping in his sweating hands and remembered all the times he had been the one with that thankless, exhausting task. Now he had been handed to this new lord and it was no longer part of his life. He realised, with a sudden leap of joy, so hard it was almost rage, that he was done with Gutterbluid and his birds, too.

Behind Falo the peasant beaters struggled to keep up, locals rounded up for the purpose and, in the mid-summer famine between harvests, weak with hunger and finding the going hard on foot; the *rapprocheurs'* sudden distant baying was wolfen.

Cursing, Hal saw the whole hunt fragment and stuck to the plan of following the Auld Templar, knowing Sir William would stick close to the Bruce and that Isabel would be tight-locked to the earl as well. If any Buchan treachery was visited, it would fall on that trio and Hal was determined to save the Auld Templar, if no-one else.

He forced through the nag of branches, looking right and left to make sure his men did the same. He urged Griff after the disappearing arse of Bruce's mare, growling irritatedly as one of the Inchmartins loomed up, his stallion caught in the madness, plunging and fighting for the bit.

White Tam sounded a horn, but others blared, confusing just where the true line of the hunt lay; Hal heard the huntsman berate anyone who could hear about 'tootling fools' and suspected the culprit was Bruce.

A sweating horse crashed through some hazel scrub near Dog Boy and almost scattered Gib from the deerhounds, who sprang and growled. Alarmed and barely hanging on, Jamie Douglas had time to wave before the horse drove on through the trees.

A few chaotic, exhausting yards further on, Hal burst through the undergrowth to see Jamie sliding from the back of the sweat-streaked rouncey, which stood with flanks heaving.

The boy examined it swiftly, then turned as Hal and the riders came up.

'Lame,' he declared mournfully, then stroked the animal's muzzle and grinned a bright, sweaty grin.

'Good while it lasted,' he shouted and started to lead the horse slowly from the wood. Hal drove on; a thin branch whipped blood from his cheek and a series of short horn blasts brought his head round, for he knew that was the signal for the 'vue', that the quarry was in sight of the body of the hunt – and that he was heading in the wrong direction. Which, because he had been following the distant sight of red, made him angry.

'Ach, ye shouffleing, hot-arsed, hollow-ee'ed, belled harlot,' he bellowed, and men laughed.

'The quine will not be happy at that,' Sim Craw noted, but Hal's scowl was black and withering, so he wisely fastened his lip and followed after. Two or three plunges later, Hal reined in and sent Bangtail Hob and Thom Bell after the Countess, to make sure she found her way safely back to join the hunt.

They forged on, ducking branches – something smacked hard on Hal's forehead, wrenching his head back; stars whirled and he felt himself reel in the saddle. When he recovered himself, Sim Craw was grinning wildly at him.

'Are ye done duntin' trees?' he demanded and looked critically at Hal. 'No damage. Yer still as braw as the sun on shiny watter.'

Tod's Wattie came up, shepherding a panting Gib and the running deerhounds, who were not even out of breath – but they were on long leashes now, held by Tod's Wattie from the back of his horse, and starting to dance and whine with the smell of the blood, begging to be let loose. Dog Boy trotted up and Hal saw that, because he was not being hauled at breakneck pace by dogs, he was breathing even and clean; they grinned at one another.

Tod's Wattie threw the leashes to Gib, who wrapped them determinedly in his fists, truculent as a boar pig. Horsemen milled in a sweating group; a few peasants stumbled to the boles of trees and sank down, exhaustion rising from them like haze. Horse slaver frothed on unseen breezes.

'*Bien aller*,' bellowed White Tam and raised the horn to his blue, fleshy lips, the haroo, haroo of it springing the whole crowd into frantic movement again. Berner Philippe, breathing ragged, gasped out a desperate plea for space for his hounds and White Tam rasped out another blast on his horn.

'Hark to the line,' he bellowed. 'Oyez! Ware hounds. Ware hounds.'

The stag burst from the undergrowth and, a moment later, a tangled trail of baying hounds followed, skidding in confusion as the beast changed direction and bounded away.

It stank and steamed, rippling with muscle and sheened like a copper statuette, the great horned crown of it soaring away into the trees as it sprang, scattering hounds and leaping majestically, leaving the dogs floundering in its wake. The powerful *alaunts* had been released too soon, White Tam saw, and had already been left behind, for they had no stamina, only massive strength.

'*Il est hault*,' he roared, purple-faced. '*Il est hault, il est hault, il est hault.*'

'Tallyho to you, too,' muttered Hal and then tipped a nod to Tod's Wattie, who grinned and nudged Gib.

White Tam cursed and banged the horn furiously on the cantle, for he could see the stag dashing away – then two grey streaks shot swiftly past on either side of him, silent as graveshrouds. They overtook the running stag, barging in on one side and forcing it to turn at bay. The deerhounds . . . White Tam almost cried out with the delight of it.

Dog Boy gawped. He had never seen such speed, nor such brave savagery. Mykel dashed for the rear; the stag spun. Veldi darted in; the stag spun – the hound seized it by the nose and the stag shook it off, spraying furious blood. But Mykel had a hock in his jaws and the back end of the beast sank as the rest of the pack came up and piled on it.

Even then the stag was not done. It bellowed, fearful and desperate, swung the massive antlered head and a dog yelped and rolled out like a black and tan ball, so that Dog Boy felt a kick in him, sure that it had been Sanspeur.

Tod's Wattie shouted once, twice, three times but the grey deerhounds clung on and the stag hurled itself off into the forest, staggering, stumbling, dragging the deerhounds and the rest of the pack in a whirling ball. Hal bellowed with annoyance when he saw Mykel ripped free from the hind-quarters of the beast, the leash that should have been removed before he'd been released snagged on something in the undergrowth.

Choking, the hound floundered, trying to get back into the fray, gasping for breath and doing itself no good by its own frantic, lunging efforts. Tod's Wattie lashed out at Gib, who knew he had erred but was too afraid of the hound to go forward and release it – but a small shape barrelled past him, right to where the gagging deerhound whirled and snarled.

Dog Boy ignored the sight of the fangs, sprang out his eating knife and sawed the cord free from the dog's neck, the white, sharp teeth rasping, snapping close to his face and wrists. Released, Mykel sprang forward at once with a hoarse, high howl and, the other hand caught in its hackled ruff, Dog Boy went with it, grimly hanging on – Hal saw the blood on the dog's muzzle and marvelled at the boy's bravery and sharp eyes.

Mykel checked then, rounded on Dog Boy and he saw the maw of it, the reeking heat of the muzzle. Then the deerhound whined with concern and licked him, so that the stag blood smeared over Dog Boy's face. When Tod's Wattie came up with Hal and the others, he turned and grinned at Hal, nodding appreciatively because the boy, heedless of teeth and covered in blood and slaver, was examining Mykel's mouth to make sure all the blood belonged to the stag.

Tod's Wattie tied on a new leash, scowling at Gib. Hal leaned down towards Dog Boy and Sim Craw saw the concern.

'Yer a bit bloody, boy,' Hal said awkwardly and Dog Boy looked at him while the huge beast of a deerhound panted and fawned on him. He smiled beatifically. There was something huge and ecstatic in his chest and the raw power of it locked with this new lord and made them, it seemed, one.

'So is yourself, maister.'

Sim Craw's laugh was a horn bellow of its own and Hal, ruefully touching his cheek and forehead, looked at the blood on his gloved fingers, acknowledged the boy with a wave and went on after the hunt.

The pack was milling and snarling and dashing backwards and forwards, save for the powerful *alaunts*, who had caught up at last and charged in. One was locked to the stag's throat, another to one thin, proud leg and a third to the animal's groin, jerking it this way and that. The stag's dulling eyes were anguished and hopeless and, too weary now to fight, it suffered the agony in a silence broken only by the bellow rasp of its breathing, blowing a thin mist of blood from flaring nostrils.

White Tam, reeling precariously in his saddle, barked out orders and the hound and huntsmen moved in with whips and blades to leash the dogs and give the beast the grace of death.

'A fine stag,' he said to Hal, beaming. 'Though it is early in the year and there will be finer come July. What will you take for yon dugs?'

Hal merely looked at him, raised an eyebrow and smiled. White Tam slapped one hand on his knee and belched out a laugh.

'Just so, just so – I would not part with them neither.'

Dog Boy heard this as if from a distance, for his world had

folded to the anguish on Berner Philippe's face and the mournful dark eye of Sanspeur. The *rache* whined and tried to lick Dog Boy's hand and, for a moment, they knelt shoulder to shoulder, the Berner and Dog Boy.

'*Swef, swef, ma belle,*' Philippe said and saw that the leg was smashed beyond repair. There was a moment when he became aware of the boy and looked at him, the thought of what he had to do next a harsh misery in his eyes, and Dog Boy saw it. The Berner felt something sharp and sweet, a pang which drove the breath from him when he looked into the eyes of the dog he would have to kill. He loved this dog. The knife flashed like a dragonfly in sunlight.

'Fetch a mattock,' he grunted and, when nothing happened, jerked his head to the boy. Then he saw the look on Dog Boy's face as he stared at the filming eyes of the dying dog and the harsh words clogged in his throat. He found, suddenly, that he was ashamed of how hard he grown in the years between now and when he had been Dog Boy's age.

'If you please,' he added, yet still could not keep the slightest of sneers from it. Dog Boy blinked, nodded and fetched a mattock and a spade, while the dogs were hauled away and the stag butchered. Between them, they dug a hole under a tree, where the ground was mossy and still springy and put the dog in it, then covered it with mould, black leaves and earth.

Sanspeur, Philippe thought. Without fear. She had been without fear, too and that had been her undoing. It was better to be afraid, he thought to himself, and stay alive. The boy, Dog Boy, knew this − Philippe turned and found himself alone, saw the boy moving from him, back to the big deerhounds and the hard, armed men he now belonged to. He did not look afraid at all.

There was a flurry off to one side, a flash of berry red, and Isabel appeared, cheeks flushed, hood back and her fox-pelt hair wisping from under the elaborate green and gold padded headpiece, her face wrinkling distaste at the blood and guts and flies. Behind her came Bruce, riding easily, and after them Bangtail Hob and Thom Bell, all black scowls and slick with a sweat that was mead for midges.

'There's your wummin,' Sim said close to Hal's elbow. 'Safe enow. What was it ye called her – a hot-arsed . . . what?'

Then he chuckled and urged ahead before Hal could spit out for him to mind his business.

'Martens,' Isabel called out gaily and Bruce, laughing, came up with it almost at once – a richesse. Hal saw Buchan scowl and, fleetingly, wondered where Kirkpatrick was.

A tan, white-scutted shape burst out of the undergrowth, almost under the hooves of Bradacus, which made the great warhorse rear. Buchan, roaring and red-faced, sawed at the reins as he and the horse spun in a dancing half-circle, then lashed out with both rear hooves, catching Bruce's horse a glancing blow.

Bruce's rouncey, panicked beyond measure, squealed and bolted, the rider reeling with the surprise of it, while the dogs went mad and even the big deerhounds lurched forward, to be brought short by Dog Boy and Tod's Wattie's tongue.

Isabel threw back her head and laughed until she was almost helpless.

'Hares,' she called out to Bruce's wild, tilting back and Hal, despite himself, felt the flicker of his groin and shifted in the saddle. Then he realised the Berner was bellowing and half-turned to see the biggest brute of the *alaunts*, unused in the hunt and fighting fresh, rip its chains out of its handler's fists and speed off after Bruce, snarling.

There was a frozen moment when Hal looked at Sim and both glanced to where Malise, off his horse, stared after the fleeing hound with a look halfway between feral snarl and triumph. In a glance so fast Hal nearly missed it, he then turned and looked at the *alaunt* handler, who looked back at him.

The chill of it soured deep into Hal's belly. The hound had been deliberately released – and a trained warhorse frightened by a leaping hare?

'Sim . . .' he said, even as he kicked Griff, but the man had seen it for himself and spurred after Hal, bellowing for Tod's Wattie and Bangtail Hob. Buchan, bringing Bradacus miraculously back under control, watched them crash through the undergrowth in pursuit of Bruce and tried not to smile.

White Tam, hunched on the mare, ploughed on relentlessly while the hunt swirled and whirled around him, knowing the truth of matters – that he was too old and slow these days, so that he reached the hunt when it was all over bar the cutting up. White Tam knew the ritual of cutting up well now, talked more and more in a language gravy-rich with os and suet, argos and croteys, grease and fiants.

He was aware only of the vanishing of Bruce and the others as an annoyance by well-bred oafs who chased hares.

'Go after the Earl of Carrick,' he ordered those nearest. 'Mak' siccar he does not tumble on his high-born arse.'

Bruce, half-clinging on for dear life, finally got control of the rouncey and became aware, suddenly and with a catch of fear in his throat, that he was alone. He turned this way and that, hearing shouts but confused as to direction then, for fear his anxiety would cause the trembling horse to bolt again, he got off the animal and stroked it quiet, neck and muzzle.

The leveret was long gone and he shook his head at the shame of having let his mount bolt, even if it had been sorely provoked by a kicking *destrier*. Hares, he thought with a savage wryness. A husk of hares – he would take delight in telling her.

He looked round at the oak and hornbeam, the sun glaring cross-grained through branches, thinly prowling over his face like delicate, warm cat paws. The bracken was crushed here, there was a smell of broken grass and turned earth and the iron tang of blood, which made Bruce uneasy. The mystery of how a hare, which was not a forest animal at all, had been there at all nagged him a little and the worry of plots surfaced like sick.

Then he realised this was where the stag had been brought to bay by the deerhounds and relaxed a little, which in turn brought the rouncey to an even breathing. Even so, there was a musk that puzzled him, the more so because it came from the rouncey's sweat-foamed sides and the saddle; he had been smelling it all day.

The *alaunt* came out of the undergrowth like an uncurling black snake, a matted crow of snarls that skidded, paused and padded, slow and purposeful, the shoulders hunched and working, the slaver dripping from open jaws.

Bruce narrowed his eyes, then felt the first stirrings of fear – it was stalking him. Then, with a deep panic he had to grip himself to fight, he realised what the musk smell was and that hare scent, blood and glands, had been deliberately smeared on saddle and horse flank. A deal of hare scent, too, now transferred to himself.

There was a pause and Bruce fought to free the dagger at his belt, cursing, seeing the inevitable in the gathering tremble of the beast's haunches. Somewhere, he heard shouts and the blare of a hunting horn – too far, he thought wildly. Too far . . .

The black shape launched forward, low and fast, boring in to disembowel this strange, large, two-legged prey that smelled right and looked wrong. The rouncey squealed and reared and danced away, reins caught in the bracken, and the *alaunt*, confused by scent from two victims, paused, chose the smaller one and, snarling, tore forward.

There was a streak through the grass, a fast-moving brindle arrow, rough-haired and uncombed. It struck the flank of the *alaunt* in mid-leap and Bruce, one forearm up to protect his throat, reeling back and already feeling the weight and the teeth of the affair, saw an explosion of snarls and a ball of fur and fang rolling over and over until it separated, paused and then *alaunt* and Mykel surged back at each other like butting rams.

Their bodies whirled and curled, opened and shut. Fangs snapped and throats snarled; one of them squealed and bloody slaver flew. Bruce, shocked, could only watch while the rouncey danced and screamed on the end of its tether – then a second grey shape barrelled in and the ball of fighting hounds rolled and snarled and fought a little longer until the *alaunt*, outmatched even by one, broke from the pair of deerhounds and sped away.

Hal and Sim came up, trailing Tod's Wattie, the Dog Boy with a fistful of leashes and a cursing Bangtail Hob in his wake. They all arrived in time to see the *alaunt*, close hauled by the ghost-grey shapes, suddenly fall over its own front feet, roll over and over and then sprawl, loose and still. The deerhounds overran it and had to skid and backtrack, only to find their prey so dead they could only paw it, snarling and whining in a thwarted ecstasy of lost bloodlust, puzzled at the leather-fletched sapling which had sprouted from the hunting dog's neck.

From out of a nearby copse strolled Kirkpatrick, latchbow casually over one shoulder.

A fine shot, Sim noted with a detached part of his brain. What was he doin', sleekit in the trees with a latchbow? He could not find the voice for it – did not need to – as the Dog Boy ran to secure the hounds and Hal and Bruce exchanged looks.

'If you are allowed to search the saddle-bags of yon Malise,' Kirkpatrick said, in a voice as easy as if they were discussing horses at table, 'you will surely find it full of hare shite. Terrifying for a wee leveret, to be shut up in the bouncing dark until needed. You will find also that the *alaunt* handler has been spirited away, though I will wager he'll not long enjoy the payment he had for releasing yon monster on cue. You will not find him at all, I suspect.'

No-one spoke, until Bruce turned to the snorting, panting, wild-eyed rouncey and gathered up the reins, the trembling fear in him turning to anger at what had been revealed, at the cunning planning in it and, if truth be told, his own secret attempt against Buchan.

In his mind's eye, for a fleeting, bowel-wrenching flicker, he saw the dog's great jaws and the long, leaping shape of it – he wrenched to free the reins from the tangle, felt them give then catch again; irritated, he hauled with all his strength.

Death ripped up out of the earth and leered at him.

Douglas Castle
The next day

The hunt ended like a trail of damp smoke, filtering back in near-silence to the castle. Bruce, too bright and brittle to be true, flirted even more outrageously with the Countess, though her exchanges seemed strained and she was too aware of Buchan's glowering.

No-one could stop looking at the cart which held the body – though Hal had seen Kirkpatrick, riding silent and cat-hunched with a face as sightless and bland as a stone saint. Here was a man who had just seen his liege lord under attack and should be head-swinging alert – yet he stared ahead and saw nothing.

He should, Hal said to Sim later, be like a mouse sniffing moonlight for more owls.

'You would so think,' Sim agreed – but he was distracted, had come in from the dark night of the Ward to report that he'd seen the Countess, huckled like a bad apprentice across to the Earl of Buchan's tent by Malise and two men in leather jacks and foul grins. The noises that came from it then set everyone's teeth on edge.

In the comfort of the kitchen, old limbs wrapped to ease the ache, White Tam nodded approval; the Earl of Buchan had finally seen sense ower his wayward wummin.

'A woman, a dog and an old oak tree,' he intoned. 'The more you beat them, the better they be.'

'Why an oak tree, Master?' demanded one of the scullions and Tam told him — sometimes such a tree stopped producing valuable acorns for the pigs, so some stout men, including the Smith with his forge hammer, would walk round it, hitting it hard. It started the sap up again and saved the tree.

Dog Boy, fetching scraps for the hounds, listened to the sick sounds and thought of the Countess being hit by a forge hammer. He did not think her sap would rise.

There was worse to come, at least for Hal, as the morning crept closer — the Auld Templar shifted out of the shadows like a wraith and, with a pause for a single deep breath, like a man ducking underwater, said:

'I need to call on your aid.'

Hal felt the chill of it right there.

'I am, as ever, fealtied to Roslin,' he replied carefully and saw the old man's head jerk at that. Aha — so I am right, he thought. He summons me as a liege lord.

'Before my son came of age,' the Auld Templar said slowly, 'I was lord of Roslin. I taught the young Bruce how to fight.'

Hal said nothing, though that fact explained much about the Templar's presence with the Earl of Carrick.

'When my son was able, I handed him Roslin and gave my soul and arm to God,' the Templar went on. 'I have never regretted it — until now.'

He stared at Hal, pouch eyes flickered with torchlight.

'I cannot be seen to fight for one side or the other,' he went on. 'But Roslin must jump.'

'To the Bruce,' Hal said bleakly and had back a nod.

'The Sientcler Way,' Hal added, hearing the desperation in his own voice. The Sientcler Way was always to have a branch of the family on either side of a conflict. That way, triumph or loss, the Sientclers always survived.

The Auld Templar shook his head.

'This conflict is too large and the Sientclers are too thinned. This time, we must jump one way and pray to God.'

'You wish me to serve the Bruce, in your stead,' Hal declared flatly; the Templar nodded.

It was hardly a surprise. Roslin owed fealty to the Earl of March, Patrick of Dunbar – and so, therefore, did Herdmanston – but Earl Patrick was lockstepped with Longshanks and, with a son and grandson held by the English, the Auld Templar was inclined to those who opposed them.

'My father,' Hal began and the Auld Templar broke in.

'Is at home,' he said. 'He sent word that the Earl of March refuses to help return my boys to me. Just punishment for rebellion, he says. The Earl of Carrick has promised help with ransoms.'

Well, there it was – sold for the price for two men from Roslin. Hal felt his mouth dry up. Herdmanston was put at risk and his father with it – yet he knew the Auld Templar had weighed that in the pan and still found the price acceptable.

'Then we are bound – where?' Hal asked, sealing it as surely as fisting a ring into wax. For a moment the Auld Templar looked broken and Hal realised the weight crushing those bony shoulders, wanted to offer some reassurance. The lie choked him – and the Auld Templar's next words would have made mockery of it in any case.

'Irvine,' he said and forced a grin to split his snowy beard. 'The Bruce is off to treat with rebels.'

Hal stared at the space where the Auld Templar had been long after the dark had swallowed the man – until Sim found him and, frowning, asked him why he was boring holes in the dark. Hal told him and Sim blew out his cheeks.

'Rebels are we then?' he declared and shrugged. 'Bigod – that puts us at odds with the chiel who has also just asked for our aid. I would not mention it.'

The Earl of Buchan was in the undercroft, coldest hole in Douglas and the resting place of the mysterious body. In the soft, filtered light of early morning, you could see why the body had drained the blood from Bruce's face when he'd had it torn from the mulch almost into his face.

Kirkpatrick, too, had looked stricken – but, then, no-one was chirruping songs to May at the sight of the half-eaten, rotted affair, undeniably human and undeniably a man of quality from the remains of his clothing and the rings still on his half-skeletal fingers.

Not robbed then, for a thief would have had his rings and searched under armpits and bollocks, the place sensible men kept most of their heavy coin. The dead man had a purse with some little coin in it still snugged up in a scrip with what looked to be spare braies, but no weapon. No-one, at first, wanted to go near the corpse save Kirkpatrick and, when he left it, he closeted himself with Bruce.

Grimacing with distaste, Buchan had assumed the mantle of responsibility for it and now beckoned Hal and Sim Craw to where the reeking remains lay on the slabbed floor. He spoke in slow, perfect English so that Sim Craw, whose French was poor, could understand.

'White Tam has had a look but the most he can tell is that it is a year dead at least,' Buchan had declared. 'He says he is just a huntsman, but that yourself and Sim Craw are the very men for looking over bodies killed by violence. I am inclined to agree.'

Hal did not care for this unwelcomed skill handed to him by White Tam, nor did he want to be closeted with Buchan following the events of the hunt and the Auld Templar, but it appeared the earl was not put out at having his plans foiled by a wee lord from Lothian and a pair of splendid dogs.

Hal had to admire the blithe dismissal of what would have been red murder if he had been allowed to succeed – but he did not want to be cheek by jowl with this man, who held a writ from the distant thunder that was King Edward to hunt out rebels in the north.

He thought to refuse the earl, using the excuse of not wanting to go near the festering remains, but he had seen Kirkpatrick's face in the instant the effigy had been torn up by Bruce's reins and in the long ride back. Now such a refusal was a blatant lie his curiosity undermined. Swallowing, driven by the desire of knowing, Hal had looked at Sim Craw, who had shrugged his padded shoulders in return.

'A wise man wavers, a fool is fixed,' he growled meaningfully, then sighed when he saw it made no difference, following Hal to the side of the thing, trying to breathe through his mouth to keep the stink out of his nose.

'Christ be praised,' Buchan said, putting a hand over his lower face.

'For ever and ever,' the other two intoned.

Then Sim poked his gauntleted hand in the ruin of it, peeled back something which could have been cloth or rotted flesh and pointed to a small mark on a patch of mottled blue-black.

'Stabbed,' he declared. 'Upward. Thin-bladed dagger – look at the edges here. A wee fluted affair by the look. Straight to his heart and killit him dead.'

Hal and Sim looked at each other. It was an expert stroke from a particular weapon and only a man who killed with it regularly would keep a dagger like that about him. Wildly, Hal almost asked Buchan if he and Bruce had hunted in these woods before and had lost a henchman. He thought of the two deerhounds, slathered with balm and praises, and the dead *alaunt*, bitterly buried by the Berner.

'So,' Sim declared. 'A particular slaying – what make ye of this, Hal? When the slayer was throwin' him down, d'ye think?'

It was a cloth scrap, a few threads and patch no bigger than a fingernail, caught in the buckle of the dead man's scrip baldric. It could have been from the man's own cloak, or another part of his clothing for all the cloth was rotted and colour-drained, but Hal did not think so and said as much.

Sim thought and stroked the grizzle of his chin, disturbed a louse and chased it until he caught it in two fingers and flicked it casually away. He turned to Hal and Buchan, who was wishing he could leave the festering place but was determined, on his honour and duty as an earl of the realm, to stay as long as the others.

'This is the way of it, I am thinking,' Sim said. 'A man yon poor soul knows comes to him, so getting near enough to strike. They are in the dark, ken, and neb to neb, which is secretive to me. Then the chiel with the dagger strikes . . .'

He mimicked the blow, then grabbed Hal by the front of his clothes and heaved him, as if throwing him over on to the ground. He was strong and Hal was taken by surprise, stumbled and was held up by Sim, who smiled triumphantly and nodded down to where the pair of them were locked, buckle to buckle, Sim's leg between Hal's two.

Hal staggered upright as Sim let go, then explained what had just happened to the bewildered Buchan, who had understood one in six words of Sim's explanation in Lowland Lothian. Like wood popping in a fire, the earl thought.

'Aye,' Hal said at the end of it, 'that would do it, right enough – well worked, Sim Craw.'

'Which does not explain,' Buchan said, 'who this man is. He is no peasant with these clothes – Kirkpatrick said as much when he was here.'

'Did he so?' mused Sim, then looked closely at the dead man, half yellow bone, half black strips of rot, some cloth, some flesh. An insect scuttled from a sleeve, down over the knucklebones, slithering under a mottled leather pouch. Sim worried the pouch loose, trying to ignore the crack of the

71

small bones and the waft of new rot that came with him disturbing the body. He opened it, shook the contents on to the palm of his hand and they peered. Silver coins, a lump of metal with horsehair string attached, a medallion stamped with the Virgin and Child.

'No robbery, then,' Hal declared, then frowned and indicated the brown, skeletal hand.

'Yet a finger has been cut.'

'To get at a tight-fitting ring,' Sim said, with the air of man who was no stranger to it, and Buchan lifted an eyebrow at the revelation.

'Yet no other rings are taken,' he pointed out, and Hal sighed.

'A wee cat's cradle of clues, right enow,' he declared, looking at the contents of the purse. The medallion was a common enough token, a pardoner's stock in trade to ward off evil, but the teardrop metal lump and string was a puzzler.

'Fishing?' Buchan suggested hesitantly and Hal frowned; he did not know what it was but fishing seemed unlikely. Besides, it was knotted in regular progression and unravelled to at least the height of a man.

'It is a plumb line,' Sim said. 'A mason uses it to mark where he wants stone cut – see, you chalk the string, hold the free end and let the weight dangle, then pluck it like a harp string to leave a chalk line on the stone.'

'The knots?'

'Measurement,' Sim answered.

'A mason?' Buchan repeated, having picked that part out 'Is this certes?'

Hal looked at Sim, eyebrows raised quizzically.

'Am I certes? Is a wee dug bound by a blood puddin'?' Sim answered indignantly. 'I am Leadhoose born, up by the wee priory of St Machutus what the Tironensians live in. My father was lifted to work with the monks, who were God's gift for buildin'.'

'Tironensians. I know that order,' Buchan said, recognising that word in the welter of thick-accented braid Scots. 'They are strict Benedictines, finding glory in manual labour. They are skilled – did they not do the work at the abbeys in Selkirk, Arbroath and Kelso? You think this mason is a Benedictine from that place?'

'Mayhap, though he is not clothed like any monk I ken,' Sim declared. 'But my da was lifted from the cartin' to work with them at the quarrystanes and then came to Herdmanston to dig a well. Until I was of age to go off with young Hal here, I worked at the digging and the drystane. I ken a plumb line – the knots are measured in Roman feet.'

He closed his eyes, the better to remember.

'Saint Augustine says six is the perfect number because the sum and product of its factors – one, two, and three – are the same. Thus a thirty-six-foot square is the divine perfection, much favoured by masons who build for the church. Christ be praised.'

He opened his eyes into the astounded stares of Hal and the Earl of Buchan and then blinked with embarrassment as they stumbled over the rote response, almost dumbed by the revelation of a Sim with numbers.

'Aye, weel – tallyin' is not my strength, though I ken the cost of a night's drink. But my da dinned plumb lines into me, for ye can dig neither well nor build as much as a cruck hoose without it.'

'You think it was a mason from St Machutus?' the earl demanded, narrow eyed and cock-headed with trying to understand. Sim shook his head.

'It's a mason, certes. And a master, if his fine cloots are any guide.'

'Aye,' Hal said wryly. 'Since English Edward knocked about some fine fortresses last year, I daresay there are a wheen of master masons at work in Scotland.'

'Not our problem,' Buchan said suddenly, eager to be gone

from the place. He plucked weight, string, medallion and coins from Sim's palm and tossed them carelessly back into the mess on the table.

'Evidence,' he declared. 'We will wrap this up and deliver it to the English Justiciar at Scone. Let Ormsby deal with it. I have a rebellion to put down.'

Irvine
Feast of St Venantius of Camerino, May, 1297

The sconces made the shadows lurch and leer, transported a bishop to a beast. Not that Wishart looked much like the foremost prelate in Scotland, sitting like a great bear in his undershift, the grey hair curling up under the stained neck of it above which was a face like a mastiff hit with a spade.

'More of a hunt than you had bargained, eh, Rob?' he growled and Bruce managed a wan smile. 'Then to find a corpse . . . Do we ken who it is, then?'

The last was accompanied by a sharp look, but Bruce refused to meet it and shook his head dismissively.

'Buchan carted the remains off to Ormsby at Scone. I said to go to Sheriff Heselrig at Lanark, but he insisted on going to the Justiciar.'

He broke off and shot looks at the men crowded into the main hall of the Bourtreehill manor.

'Did he know? Did Buchan know that Heselrig was already dead and Lanark torched?' he hissed and Wishart flapped an impatient hand, as if waving away an annoying fly.

'Tish, tosh,' he said in his meaty voice. 'He did not. No-one knew until it was done.'

'Now all the realm knows,' growled a voice, and The Hardy stuck his slab of a face into the light, scowling at Bruce; Hal saw that he was a coarser, meatier version of Jamie. 'While you were taking over my home, Wallace here was ridding the country of an evil.'

'You and he were, if the truth be told, torching our lands around Turnberry,' Bruce countered in French, swift and vicious as a stooping hawk. 'That's why my father was charged to bring you to heel by sending me to Douglas – as well, my lord, that I had less belly for the work than you, else your wife and bairns would not be tucked up safe a short walk away.'

'You were seen as English,' The Hardy muttered, though he shifted uncomfortably as he spoke; they both knew that The Douglas had simply been taking the opportunity to plunder the Bruce lands.

'That was not the reason Buchan tried to have me killed,' Bruce spat back, and The Hardy shrugged.

'More to do with his wife, I should think,' he said meaningfully, and Bruce flushed at that. Hal had seen the Countess early the next day, mounted on a sensible sidesaddled palfrey and led by Malise out of Douglas, with four big men and the Earl of Buchan's warhorse in tow. Headed back to Balmullo, he had heard from Agnes, who had been her tirewoman while she stayed in Douglas. Ill-used to the point of bruises, she had added.

'He tried to have me killed,' Bruce persisted and Hal bit his lip on why Kirkpatrick had been loose in the woods with a crossbow, but the sick meaning of it all rose in him, cloyed with despair; the most powerful lords in Scotland savaged each other with plot and counterplot, while the Kingdom slid into chaos.

'Aye, indeed,' Wishart said, as if he had read Hal's mind, 'it's as well, then, that Wallace here put a stop to the Douglas raids on the Bruce, in favour of discomfort to the English in Lanark. A proper blow. A true rebellion.'

Douglas scowled at the implication, but the man in question shifted slightly, the light falling on his beard making it flare with sharp red flame. The side of his face was hacked out by the shadows and, even sitting, the power of the man was clear to Hal and everyone else. His eyes were hooded and dark, the nose a blade.

'Heselrig was a turd,' Wallace growled. 'A wee bachle of a mannie, better dead and his English fort burned. He was set to assize me and mine for a trifle and would have been savage at it.'

'Indeed, indeed,' Wishart said, as if soothing a truculent bairn. 'Now I will speak privily with the Earl of Carrick, who has come, it seems, to add his support to the community of the realm.'

'Has he just,' answered Wallace flatly and stood up, so that Hal saw the size of him – enough of a tower for him to take a step back. Wallace was clearly used to this and merely grinned, while The Hardy followed him as he ducked through the door, arguing about where to strike next.

Wishart looked expectantly at Kirkpatrick and Hal, but Bruce started to pace and glower at him.

'They are mine,' he said, as if that explained everything. Hal bit his lip on the matter, though he knew he should have walked away from the mess of it, before the wrapping chains of fealty to the Roslin Sientclers shackled him to a lost cause.

He glanced over at Kirkpatrick and saw the hooded stare he had back. Noble-born, Hal thought, and carries a sword, though he probably does not use it well. Not knighted, with no lands of his own – yet cunning and smart. An intelligencer for The Bruce, then, a wee ferret of secrets – and a man Bruce could send to red murder a rival.

'So – you and Buchan, plootering about in the woods like bairns, tryin' to red murder yin another?' Wishart scathed. 'Hardly politic. Scarcely *gentilhommes* of the community of the realm, let alone belted earls. Then there is this ither matter – ye never saw the body, then?'

Bruce rounded on him like a savaging dog, popping the French out like a badly sparking fire.

'Body? Never mind that – what in God's name are you up to now, Wishart? The man's a bloody-handed outlaw. Barely noble – community of the realm, my arse.'

Wishart sipped from a blue-glass goblet, a strangely delicate gesture from such a sausage-fingered man, Hal thought. The bishop stared up into Bruce's thrusting lip and sighed.

'Wallace,' he said heavily. 'The man's a noble, but barely as you say. The man's an outlaw, no argument there.'

'And this is your new choice for Scotland's king, is it?' Bruce demanded sneeringly. 'It is certainly an answer to the thorny problem of Bruce or Balliol, but not one, I think, that your "community of the realm" will welcome. A lesser son, a family barely raised above the level? Christ's Bones, was he not bound to be a canting priest, the last refuge of poor *nobiles?*'

'Aye, weel – some become bishops,' Wishart answered mildly, dabbing his lips with a napkin, though the stains down the front of his serk bore witness to previous carelessness and Bruce had the grace to flush and begin to protest about present company. Wishart waved him silent.

'Wallace is no priest,' he answered. 'No red spurs nor dubbing neither, but his father owns a rickle of land and his mother is a Crawfurd, dochter of a Sheriff of Ayr – so he is no chiel with hurdies flappin' out the back of his breeks. Besides, he is a bonnie fighter – as bonnie as any I have ever seen. As a solution to the thorny problem of Bruce or Balliol it takes preference over murder plots on a *chasse*, my lord.'

'Is that all it takes, then?' Bruce demanded thickly. 'You would throw over the Bruce claim for a "bonnie fighter"?'

'The Bruce claim is safe enough,' Wishart said, suddenly steely. 'Wallace is no candidate for a throne – besides, we have a king. John Balliol is king and Wallace is fighting in his name.'

'Balliol abdicated,' Bruce roared and Kirkpatrick laid a hand on his arm, which the earl shook off angrily, though he lowered his voice to a hoarse hiss, spraying Wishart's face.

'He abdicated. Christ and All His Saints – Edward stripped the regalia off him, so that he is Toom Tabard, Empty Cote, from now until Hell freezes over. There is no king in Scotland.'

'That,' replied Wishart, slowly wiping Bruce off his face and staring steadily back at the pop-eyed earl, 'is never what we admit. Ever. The kingdom must have a king, clear and indivisible from the English, and Balliol is the name we fight in. That name and the Wallace one gains us fighting men – enough, so far, to slay the sheriff of Lanark and burn his place round his ears. Now the south is in rebellion as well as the north and east.'

'Foolish,' Bruce ranted, pacing and waving. 'They are outlaws, cut-throats and raiders, not trained fighting men – they won't stand in the field and certainly not led by the likes of Wallace. Your desperation for a clear and indivisible king blinds you.'

He leaned forward and his voice grew softer, more menacing while the shadows did things to his eyes that Hal did not like.

'Only the *nobiles* can lead men to fight Edward,' he declared. 'Not small folk like Wallace. In the end, the *gentilhommes* – your precious "community of the realm" – is what will keep your Church free of interference from Edward, which is really what you finaigle for. Answerable only to the Pope, is that not it, Bishop?'

'Sir Andrew Moray is noble,' Wishart pointed out, bland as a nun's smile, and that made Bruce pause. Aha, Hal thought, the bold Bruce does not like the idea of Moray. Moray and Wallace as Guardians of the Realm would go a long way to appeasing nobles appalled at the idea of a Wallace alone.

Bruce would not then be at the centre of things – he had not been party to any of it so far, nor would he have been if he had not turned up on his own, dangling The Hardy's family as security of his intentions and looking for the approbation of the other finely born in Wishart's enterprise. Hal, dragged along in the Auld Templar's wake, had wondered, every step of the way, what had prompted Bruce to suddenly become so hot for rebellion and Sim had remarked that Bruce's da would not care for it much.

Bruce the son had not got much out of it. The Hardy had been grudgingly polite, the Stewart brothers and Sir Alexander Lindsay had been cool at best while Wallace himself, amiable, giant and seemingly bland, had looked the Earl of Carrick up and down shrewdly and wondered aloud why 'Bruce the Englishman' had decided to jump the fence. Now they were all glowering on the other side of the door, still wondering the same.

It was exactly what Wishart now asked.

'If you have set your face against this enterprise and my choice of captain,' Wishart grunted, slopping wine on his knuckles, 'why are you here when your da is in Carlisle, no doubt setting out his explanations to Percy and Clifford of why his son has gone over to Edward's enemies? I would have thought, my lord, that you would be bending your efforts against Buchan – and a body found in the woods.'

Hal leaned forward, for this was something he wanted to know as keenly – Bruce was young, his father's son in every way until now, and his family had been expelled from their Scottish lands by the dozen previous Guardians, only just returned to them by Edward's power. Why here? Why now?

Hal was sure the uncovered corpse had something to do with it, surer still that Wishart and Bruce shared the secret of it. He was also more certain than ever that he should not be here, mired in the midden of it all – how in the name of God and all His Saints had he become a rebel, sudden and easy as putting on a cloak?

He became aware of eyes, turned into the black, considered

gaze of Kirkpatrick and held it for a long while before breaking away.

Bruce frowned, the lip pouted and the chin thrust out, so that the shadows turned his broad-chinned face to a brief, flickering devil's mask – then he moved and the illusion shattered; he smiled.

'I am a Scot, when all said and done. And a *gentilhomme* of your community of the realm, bishop,' he answered smoothly, then plucked the prelate's glass from his fat, beringed fingers and drained it, a lopsided grin on his face.

'Besides – you have your fighting bear,' he answered. 'You need, perhaps, someone to point him in the right direction. To point you all in the right direction.'

Wishart closed one speculative eye, reached out and took the glass back from Bruce with an irritated gesture.

'And where would that be, young Carrick?'

'Scone,' Bruce declared. 'Kick England's Justiciar, Ormsby, up the arse, the same way we did Heselrig.'

Hal heard the 'we' and saw that Wishart had as well, but the bishop did not even try to correct Bruce. Instead he smiled and Hal was sure some subtle message passed between the pair.

'Aye,' Wishart said speculatively. 'Not a bad choice. To make sure of . . . matters. I will put it to the Wallace.'

He lifted the empty glass in a toast to Bruce, who acknowledged it with a nod, then smiled a shark-show of teeth at Hal.

CHAPTER THREE

Scone Priory
Feast of Saints Castus and Aemilius, martyrs – May, 1297

Dusk was hurrying on and dark clipping its heels, so that the heads and shoulders were stained black against the flames. Hal could hear the guttural snarls and spits of them, as fired as the sparks that flew; it had been a long time since he had heard such a large crowd of men all speaking Lowland and it brought back ugly memories of last year, when he and others had padded, cat-cautious and sick to their stomachs, in the fester that was Berwick after the English had gone.

The cooked-meat smells didn't help, for Hal knew the sweet, rich smell had nothing to do with food.

They came up through the huddle of wattle and daub that clustered round the priory like shellfish on a rock, crashing through the backland courts and the head riggs, splintering crude privy shelters, tossing torches, their own yelling drowned by the screams of the fleeing.

No looting or rape until the fighting is done, Wallace had said before they had set off, and Bruce, frowning at the impudence of the man, had been forced to agree, since the host was clearly his alone to command. At least there was no Buchan

81

salting the wound of it – he was gone into his own lands, ostensibly to prevent Moray from joining with Wallace and managing to look the other way at the crucial moment.

Hal strode alongside outlaw roughs from all over Ayrshire, kerns and caterans from north of The Mounth, all here for love of this giant called Wallace and what he could do. Hal saw him stride up the rutted track between the mean houses, blood-dyed with flames, surrounded by whirling sparks.

He had a long tunic and a belted surcoat over that, no helmet and bare legs and feet; he was hardly different from the wild men he led save that he was head and shoulders above the tallest and carried a hand-and-a-half, a sword most men would have clutched in two fists but which he carried in one.

Hal and Sim and the Herdmanston men were on foot for there was little point in trying to plooter through flames and back courts on horses, but Bruce and his Carrick men were mounted, trying to force through the mob up the main track to Scone priory. Hal heard him yelling 'A Bruce, a Bruce,' to try to keep his men from spilling off the road into the foundering tangle on either side.

'Christ save us,' Sim Craw panted, shouldering some dark shape away from him with a curse. 'What a mob. An army, bigod? A sorry rabble – the English will scatter this like chooks in a yard, first chance they get.'

It was true, but the English had no army here, only fleeing clerks, monks who wished they had never taken Edward's offer of Scottish prebenderies and a few soldiers. There were screams ahead and Hal saw Wallace's head come up, like a hound licking scent from the air. A snarling maurauder, wool cloak rolled up round his neck like a ruff, leaped a rickety fence, the woman he was chasing stumbling over her skirts and shrieking, he laughing with the mad joy of it.

Wallace never seemed to pause, but shot out his free hand and caught the man by the thick wool plaid, hauling him clean off his feet to dangle like a scruff-held cat, his toes scraping the road as Wallace walked steadily along.

'I warned ye,' Wallace growled into the man's face and, in the light of the flames, Hal could see the utter terror burned into the man's eyes. Then Wallace hurled him away like an apple core, striding on as if nothing had barred his way.

'He's feeling a wee bit black-bilious,' Sim Craw offered, but Hal never had a chance to reply, for the first serious resistance burst on them.

They roared out from the great dark bulk of the stone priory, a handful of desperately charging soldiers, the sometime-men hired to help collect taxes or bring in accused. They had padded jacks, heater shields, spears and all the skills of one-armed cripples. They were local men, who did not want to fight at all and were not English – save the one who led them, waving a sword and shouting; Hal couldn't hear what he said.

Surprise worked for them, all the same; they hit the leading straggle of Wallace men, who scattered away from them, too late. One, turning to run, was skewered and fell, screaming. The sword-armed leader hacked at another, who leaped away, cursing.

Wallace ploughed into them as if he was iron, the great sword whirring left and right, hardly pausing. He parried a spear thrust; his men rallied, sprang forward with hoarse shouts and daggers and spears of their own.

The soldiers scattered in their turn and a knot came stumbling towards Hal, who had blundered darkly into the midden of a back court, dragging his handful of men with him. Cursing, he saw Bangtail Hob and Ill Made Jock leaping as if in a dance with three men, while Sim Craw, spitting challenges and taunts, hurled himself at two more. Somewhere, he could here Maggie's Davey screaming.

Hal found a single dark shape in his way, saw the thrust of spear and batted it away with a yell, cut back, ducked, whirled and felt his second blow catch as if on cloth. There was a whimpering yelp and Hal saw the dark shape stagger away from him, run a few steps, then fall.

He followed, feeling the clotted black rot of the midden squelch under his boots. The shape mewed and clawed away from him, the fish heads and offal squeezing up between his fingers as he crawled.

Hal hit him on the back of the head, feeling the eggshell crunch of it, hearing the sharp cry. The shape went slack and still; Hal rolled him over, to make sure he was dead.

An unexceptional face, beardless and streaked with midden filth, a wish-mark clear on one cheek. A boy, no more.

Alive, but barely.

'Mither,' he said and Hal swallowed the bile rising in him, for he knew what his sword had done to the back of the boy's head and that he would never see his mother.

'Stop gawpin' at him like a raw speugh,' Sim growled in his ear. 'Finish it . . .'

He broke off when he saw how old the boy was and wiped his mouth with the back of one hand, looked at Hal's face and knew his head was full of wee Johnnie.

Sim knelt and whipped out his boot knife, slit the throat, swift and expert, closing the boy's eyes as he did so. Then he straightened, stepping in to break the shackle of Hal's stare on the boy's face.

'Done and done – lose the memory o' it,' he gruffed, and Hal, blinking, nodded back into the screams and the flames. Bangtail Hob and Jock came up, supporting a third man between them.

'Aye, we are braw rebels us, for we have gave this place freedom, certes,' Bangtail offered cheerfully and the sagging man in the middle cursed. Hal saw it was Maggie's Davey, then caught the reek of him and backed off a step.

'Aye,' declared Ill Made Jock bitterly, 'well may ye shy away – you do not have to lug him around.'

'I fell ower a privy,' Davey moaned. 'I have broke my neb, sure.'

'I wish to Christ I had broke mine,' Sim offered viciously, 'so that I could not smell your stink. That must have been the De'il's own jakes ye fell in.'

'Bide here,' Hal said to the three men, then jerked his head savagely at Sim Craw to follow him. He wanted away from the smell and the memory of the dead boy's wish-marked face.

Sim looked at the dead boy. Nothing like wee John, he thought bleakly, but every young lad stared back at Hal with his dead son's face, Sim knew. There will be more and more of wee dead boys when this rebellion takes hold, he added to himself, ducking under the eyes of the boy which, though closed, seemed to stare at him accusingly.

They came up through the screams and the flame-stains, crouching against lurid shadows that might have been friend or enemy – but, in the end, Hal and Sim realised there were no enemies left, only the madmen of Wallace's army, fired by blood and running prey.

Hal stepped over a corpse, visible only in the dark because of the grey hair – a dark-robed Augustinian monk, his scapular sodden with his own blood. Sim grimaced and looked round at the fire and shadows and shrieking. Like Hell he thought, as painted on the wall of any church he had ever been in.

'Priests yet,' Hal said and left the rest unsaid. Boys and priests, a fine start to resistance and made no better by the sight of Bruce, sitting on his arch-necked, prancing warhorse in the kitchen gardens, scattering herbs and beets while waving a sword, his jupon glowing in the light so that the chevron on it looked as if the dark had slashed it. Christ's Bones, he thought savagely – I will quit this madness, first chance I have . . .

'Look,' Sim said suddenly. 'It's yon Kirkpatrick.'

Hal saw the man, sliding off the back of a good horse and

throwing the reins to Bruce, an act which was singular in itself – an earl holding the mount of his servant? Hal and Sim looked at each other, then Sim followed after, into the splintering of wood and breaking glass that was now the priory. With only the slightest of uneasy pauses, Hal padded after him.

They turned warily, swords out and gleaming; a shape lurched past, arms full of brasswork, saw them and turned away so hastily that a bowl dropped and clanged on the flagstones. Somewhere, there was singing and Hal realised they had lost Kirkpatrick in the shadows.

They moved towards the sound, found the door, opened it as cautious as mice from holes and felt the shadowed shift of bodies as the monks inside saw their two meagre candles waver in the sudden breeze from the open door. Someone whimpered.

'A happy death is one of the greatest and the last blessings of God in this life,' said a sonorous voice and Hal saw the black-robed Prior step into the light of one candle, his arms raised as if in surrender, his face turned to the rafter shadows.

'We dedicate this Vigil to St Joseph, the Foster Father of our Judge and Saviour. His power is dreaded by the Devil. His death is the most singularly privileged and happiest death ever recorded as he died in the Presence and care of Jesus and the Blessed Mary. St Joseph will obtain for us that same privilege at our passage from this life to eternity.'

'There is cheery,' Sim muttered and someone came up close behind Hal and stuck his face over one shoulder, so that Hal saw the sweat-grease painted on it and smelled the man's onion breath. A cattle-lifting hoor's byblow, Hal thought viciously.

'Here is the English and riches, then,' the man spat out of the thicket of his beard and turned to call out to others.

Sim's sword hilt smashed the words to silence, broke nose

bones and sent the man to the flagstones as if he was a slaughtered ox.

'May St Bega of Kilbucho have mercy on me,' Sim declared, waving a cross-sign piously over the stunned man as he snored through the blood. Hal closed the door on the refuge of slow-chanting monks and looked at the felled cateran; he was sure his friends would come sooner rather than later and they had given the clerics a respite only.

'Kirkpatrick,' he said, shoving the fate of the monks to one side. Sim nodded. They went on.

'Who is St Bega and where the bliddy hell is Kilbucho?' demanded Hal as they crept along into the great, dark hall of the place, where only the shift of air allowed the impression of a lofty ceiling. Sim grinned.

'Up near Biggar,' Sim said mildly, peering left and right as they moved. 'Very big on St Bee there, they are. I thought we could do with her charms here, for her only miracle.'

'Oh aye? Good, was it?'

'If ye had seen it,' Sim said in a hissed whisper that did not move his lips, 'ye'd have begged a blessin'. Seems there was a noble who handed a monastery a wheen o'lands, but a lawsuit later developed about their extent.'

He moved in crouching half-circles, stepping carefully and speaking in a hoarse whisper, half to himself.

'The monks feared that they'd be ransacked. The day appointed for boundary-walk arrived – and there was a thick snowfall on all the surrounding lands but not a flake on the lands of the priory, so you could see where the boundary really was. The monks were smiling like biled haddies.'

'We could use some of her frost in here,' Hal answered, wiping his streaming face.

'Christ be praised,' Sim declared, chuckling.

'For ever and ever,' Hal responded piously, then held up a warning hand as they rounded a dark corner and came into an open area with an altar at one end and a series of fearsomely expensive painted glass windows staining the flagstones with coloured light from the fires that burned beyond. To the left was a door, slightly open, where light flickered and flared, falling luridly on the faded, peeling painting that graced one wall.

Daniel in the Lion's Den, Hal noted. Apt enough . . .

Sim thumped him on the shoulder and nodded to where, clear and blood-dyed by flames, Kirkpatrick shoved papers methodically into a fire he had started in the middle of the room. His shadow bobbed and stretched like a mad goblin.

Hal started to move when one of the glass windows above the altar shattered in an explosion of shards and lead which clattered and spattered over the altar and flagstones. There was a burst of laughter from beyond, then a series of angry shouts.

Hal glanced back into the room and cursed – Kirkpatrick was gone. He and Sim went in, their boots crunching on broken pottery and more glass; Sim circled while Hal stamped at the flames of the fire, which threatened to spread along the thin rushes over the flagstones. In the end Sim suddenly poured the contents of a pot on it and the fire went out, sizzling and reeking of more than char.

'What was in yon?' Hal demanded and Sim glanced at the pot and made a face.

'Ormsby pish, or I am no judge,' he answered, and Hal, looking round, realised this was the Justiciar's bedroom, with table, chair and straw-packed box bed; a wall hanging stirred in the night breeze through an open-shuttered window. Sim looked at the hanging, saw that it was a banner with a red shield of little crosses split diagonally by a gold bar.

Hal, making grunting noises of disgust, fished in the damp char for documents, squinting at them in the half-light and stuffing one or two inside his jack. There was a dovecote of similar rolls against one wall, the contents half-scattered on the straw, but Sim dragged down the fancy hanging, taken by the gilding work in it.

'Ormsby's arms,' growled a voice, making both men whirl round to where Wallace bulked out the staining light beyond the doorway. He had sword and dagger in each hand and a smear of blood on a face split by a huge grin. He nodded at the limp cloth clutched in Sim's fist.

'Ormsby's arms,' he repeated. 'We will add his head to them, by an' by and mak' a man of him.'

No-one spoke as Wallace stepped in, careful in bare feet, his head seeming to brush the roof.

'A good thought, comin' here, lads, but Ormsby has fled his bedroom. Out of yon unshuttered wind hole in his nightserk, so I am told. That must have been a sight – what have ye there?'

'Papers,' Hal declared, feeling the ones he had hidden burn his side as if still aflame. 'There was a fire.'

Wallace peered and nodded, then looked at the chambered library on the wall.

'State papers, nae doubt,' he declared, 'if the Justiciar of Scotland saw fit to try and burn them. So they might be of use – when I find a body that can read the Latin better than me.'

'It will be hard,' Hal said, not correcting Wallace on who had been doing the burning. 'Sim put the flames out with a pint of the great man's pish.'

'Did he so?' Wallace laughed and shook his head. 'Well, I will find a wee clever man with a poor nose to read them.'

Hal, who was also uncomfortably aware that he was not admitting his own reading skills, laughed uneasily and Wallace strode back to the door, then paused and turned.

'Mind you,' he said, innocent as a priests's underdrawers, 'I am wondering why yon chiel of The Bruce – Kirkpatrick is it?'

Hal nodded, feeling the burn of the eyes, while the sconce torch did bloody things to the Wallace face.

'Aye,' Wallace mused. 'Him. Now why would he birl his hurdies out that self-same unshuttered window not long since, as if the De'il was nipping his arse?'

He looked from Hal to Sim and back. Outside, something smashed and there were screams. Wallace shifted slightly.

'I had best at least try to bring them to order,' he said, his smile stained with fire, 'though it is much like herdin' cats. I will seek you later, lads.'

His departure left a hole in the room into which silence rushed. Then Sim let out his breath and Hal realised he had been holding his own.

'I do not ken about the English,' Sim said softly, 'but he scares the shite out of me.'

Nor is he as green as he is kail-looking, Hal thought and decided it was time the pair of them were elsewhere.

The quiet of the chapel refuge was fêted with a blaze of expensive waxen light and the soft hiss of babbled prayers, so that the flames flickered as the huddled canons gasped for air.

Cramped as it was, a clear space existed where Bruce knelt, though he did not bow his head. There was a fire in him, a strange, glowing flow that seemed to run through his whole body, so fierce at times that he trembled and jerked with it.

He looked at the painted walls of the chapel. In a cowshed, Mary nursed the newborn Child by her naked breast in a bed, while Joseph watched from a wooden chair to the right. They smiled at Bruce. In the foreground, the heads of an ox and an ass turned and regarded him with their bright, mournful eyes. An angel stood and regarded him coldly in the background and above, in Latin, the words *The Annunciation to the Shepherds* seemed to glow like the fire in his body.

Bruce bowed his head, unable to look at the face of the smiling Virgin, or the disapproval of the angel. The deed was done, the secret safe according to the gospel of Kirkpatrick, breathing hard from having had to run from burning the evidence.

More sin to heap on his stained soul. Bruce thought of the man he had killed, a perfect stroke as he cantered past the running figure; it was only afterwards he had seen it to be an old priest. Longshanks had replaced a lot of the livings here with prelates of his own and these were, Bruce knew, much hated and fair game for the lesser folk – but a priest, English or not, was a hard death on the soul of a noble, never mind an earl.

The Curse of Malachy – his hands trembled and the candle in it spilled wax down on to the black-haired back of it, cooling to perfect pearls.

The Curse of Malachy. His father had given the Clairveaux church where the saint was buried a grant of Annandale land in return for perpetual candles, and Bruce, for all he sneered at the spine his father seemed to have lost, knew that it was because of the Curse of Malachy. Every Bruce feared it as they feared nothing else.

The canons chanted and he tried to blot out the Curse and the thought that it had led him to slay one of their brothers on holy ground. Innocents, he thought. The innocents always die.

He saw the tiles in front of him, an expanse of cracked grey. Letters wavered, small and faint, in the top corner of one and felt a desperate need to see them clearly. Squinting, he read them: 'D i us Me Fecit'. The mark of the maker, Bruce thought. Alfredius? Godfridus?

Then it came to him. *Dominus Me Fecit*. God Made Me. He felt his hand tremble so violently that the candle went out and wax spilled on to his knuckles. The mark of the maker. God Made Me. I am what I am.

'My lord of Carrick.'

The voice brought him round and his sight wavered, blinded by staring at the candle and the tiles.

'God Made Me,' he muttered.

'As he did us all,' the voice answered, gruff and fruited with good living. Wishart, he recognised.

The chanting stopped as all the heads turned; the Prior stumbled forward and knelt while Wishart thrust out one hand to have his ring kissed. The ring was not visible under the armoured gauntlet and the Prior hesitated, then placed his lips on the cold, articulated iron segments.

Wishart hardly looked at him, watching Bruce get up. The Malachy Curse, no doubt, he thought to himself, seeing the grim face on the young lord of Carrick. It had hagged his father all his life, but Wishart had hoped it had passed this one by.

He knew the tale of it, vaguely – something about a previous Annandale Bruce promising a priest that he would release a condemned felon and then hanging him in secret. The said priest was angered and cursed the Bruces – which did not seem very saintly to Wishart, but God moves mysteriously and that is what Malachy eventually became. A saint.

The Bruces had been living under the shadow of it ever since and there was something, Wishart admitted to himself, in young Robert's assertion that it had unmanned his father completely. Hardly surprising, Wishart thought, when you find that a canting, irritating wee priest you have as a thwarted dinner guest later turns out to be Malachy, one of God's anointed, with the power of angels at his disposal. At the very least, you would have to question your luck. More seriously, every sick cow, murrained sheep and blighted crop was laid at the door of the Curse, so that the Bruces had sullen and growling commons to constantly appease.

'I was praying,' Bruce declared accusingly, and the Bishop blinked, looked down and waved the Prior to his feet.

'So you were,' he replied, as cheerfully as he could manage, 'and I will be joining you afore long, mark me. Prior, your robing room will be perfect for a quiet meeting.'

The Prior bobbed. He was not about to beg for what he

knew all the canons wanted – an end to the plunder and pillage and an assurance that no more robed prelates would be killed – for it did not seem the time for it, when the Bishop of Glasgow stood in maille coat and braies and coif. Ironically, the mace dangling from one armoured fist was the only reminder that he was a Bishop of the Church in Scotland and forbidden to use an edge on any man – though not, it seemed, forbidden to bludgeon one to death.

Bruce looked at the warrior Bishop, thinking the old man might expire of apoplexy wearing all that padding and metal in this heat. Thinking, also, that Wishart had the strained look of a man either unable to cope with a bad turd or bad news.

He followed the lumbering Bishop into the cramped, hot robing room and was surprised to find Wallace there, sitting on the only bench and leaning on his hand-and-a-half. He made no move to get up with due deference, which irritated Bruce, though he forgot it the instant Wishart spoke.

'The Lords Percy and Clifford have raised forces and are marching up through Dumfries,' Wishart said without preamble. 'Fifty thousand men, or so I am told.'

Wallace never blinked, but his fists closed tighter on the hilt of the sword and Bruce heard the point of it grind into the stone floor. He saw Wishart's stricken face and knew the truth of matters at once.

'You had counted on more time,' he accused and Wishart nodded grimly.

'Until next Spring,' he growled. 'Edward is far to the south with an army he wants to take to Flanders to fight the French and he and the likes of the Earls of Norfolk and Hereford are in a sulk ower baron rights and tolts on wool. I didnae think there would be a force got ready until too late in the season, so would wait out the winter and come in Spring. I had . . .'

'You had forgot the English Marcher lords,' Wallace interrupted, and his stare was cold on Wishart's red, sweat-sheened face. 'You had forgot the shadow of Longshanks is long,

93

Bishop, and growing ever closer. How is that from a man who is, folk tell me, a master of cunning?'

Wishart clanked as he flapped one dismissive hand.

'I did not expect Percy nor Clifford to raise forces,' he grunted. 'I thought they would not thole the cost of it, since they made such noises about the money for Edward's French affair. Besides – Percy is De Warenne's grandson and would not want to make the old Earl of Surrey look a fool for governing Scotland as Viceroy from his estates in England.'

Bruce laughed, nasty and harsh.

'Aye, well,' he said, shaking his head. 'There is you, scheming away and thumping every pulpit about how this is a kingdom, a realm separate from the English and with its own king – so much, it seems, that you have lost sight of what the English think.'

'Aye, ye would ken that well enow,' Wallace answered blackly, and Bruce's smile had no mirth in it that any of the other two could see.

'Percy and Clifford do not like Edward's foreign wars,' Bruce said bitterly. 'But this is not a foreign war. Edward treats these lands not as another realm but as part of his own – so Percy and Clifford cannot avoid raising forces to put down a home rebellion, no matter how it makes grandda De Warenne look. To do otherwise is treason. Besides – Edward is coming and none of his lords in the north will want to face him without having done something. Even the Earl of Surrey will have to lever himself off his De Warenne arse and play the soldier once more.'

Wishart looked miserably at the floor, then straightened, blew out of pursed, fleshy lips and nodded.

'Aye, right enough,' he said. 'It was a misjudgement. Now we have to deal with it.'

'Deal with it?' Bruce bellowed. 'How do manage that, d'ye think? Even allowing for your spies seeing triple, the English have too many men, it appears. A fifth of fifty thousand would be enough, for nothing I have seen persuades me that this rabble Wallace leads will stand in the open field against them.'

He broke off, breathing heavily, then nodded grimly at Wallace.

'No offence.'

'None ta'en,' Wallace replied, suddenly cheerful. 'You have the right of it, for sure – mine are men best fighting out of the hills and woods, my lords. So that is where we will go.'

Wishart looked as if he would protest and Bruce felt a sharp stab of anger at the presumption of Wallace, about to up and go without so much as a by-your-leave bow – but he swallowed the bile of it and nodded soberly.

'Aye, that will be the way of it – but you should go with what men you have and what will go with you who are free of obligation to myself and the other nobles.'

Wallace turned narrowed eyes and gazed at Bruce from under lowered brows.

'And yourself, lord of Carrick?'

'I will gather up the Douglas, the Bishop here and others and we will make what resistance we can from our fortresses. The English will have to deal with us and that will buy you time to cause havoc.'

Wallace stared at Bruce a long time, then slowly nodded.

'Longshanks is coming. This will cost you dear,' he said, looking from Wishart to Bruce and back.

'In the noble cause,' Wishart declared and Wallace clasped them both, wrist to wrist, then went out, silent as a wraith for all his bulk. It suddenly seemed to the others that the room had doubled in size. No-one spoke for a moment, then Wishart cleared his throat.

'And the truth?' he demanded. Bruce looked coldly at him.

'My purpose in joining this now-failed enterprise has already been achieved,' he said pointedly. 'The mason is buried anew.'

Wishart nodded weary agreement.

'So we will get ourselves to Irvine with what men we have

and prepare to negotiate,' Bruce added. Wishart's belly quivered under the armour as he dragged himself haughtily upright.

'Ye'd yield? Without a fight?'

Bruce's bottom lip stuck out like a shovel and Wishart, who knew the sign well, found some caution.

'The king himself will come north,' Bruce growled angrily. 'Like the black wind he is. Wallace will fight – he has to, for he has no lands to his own name and is an outlaw, no more. You lose nothing bar some dignity for having to kneel and kiss Edward's ring, for the Church lands are sacrosanct.'

He thrust his mace of a face into Wishart's own.

'But we,' he said, slapping the chevroned jupon, 'risk losing everything. We, the community of the realm you depend on to free it. Edward will come north with his scowl and his evil eye – I could lose Carrick and my father Annandale. God's Blood, Wishart, I place my rights to the crown in jeopardy here. Douglas will lose his Lanark lands – do you want us all fastened up in Berwick, or the Tower?'

More to the point of it, Wishart thought bitterly, is that Buchan and the rest of the Comyn, ostensibly supporting Edward but covertly allowing Moray's rebels free rein, would come out smelling as if they'd been dipped in crushed rose petals. They play this game of kings more skilfully than the young Bruce, he saw, who needed some cunning heads round him.

'Of course,' he said, bowing to the inevitable, 'negotiation is tricky business. Involved and sometimes lengthy. And what of Wallace?'

Bruce grunted sourly.

'Wallace owes nothing save allegiance to a deposed king who wishes nothing to do with his kingdom,' he growled. 'He owns no lands, suffers the worry of no tenant and looks down his sword at each man he meets, asking only if he is for The Wallace. If not, he is against him.'

'No bad thing in these days,' Wishart countered defiantly.

'Simplistic,' Bruce spat back over his shoulder as headed for the door. 'And probably brief. Whether negotiations are long or short, it will come out as it always does – with us on our knees.'

He paused and turned.

'Save for Wallace,' he added. 'He is of little account. Longshanks will never forgive him.'

I am of account, he was thinking as he spoke. God Made Me – and he made me to be a king.

The liberators of Scone toasted each other, their hero Wallace and even Bruce and the bishops. The alehouse was the only building not ransacked or burned, more sacred than any church to men with a thirst on them. Dark save for a few sconced torches gasping for breath in the cloy of the place, it heaved with bodies, stank of vomit and piss and stale sweat.

Sim, by main force, had found a corner and two scarred horn cups to blow the froth off, but Hal took time drinking his, squinting at the damp yellowed, blackened scraps he had pulled out from under his jack.

'What does it say, then?' the unlettered Sim demanded, loosening the ties of his own studded, padded jack and trying to struggle out of it in the roasting heat of the place.

'If there was light I would tell ye,' Hal muttered. It was too dark to see other than that the writing was cramped and in Latin. Still, he was fairly sure it concerned the death of the mason and was an investigation of his clothing, which had included a beaver hat tucked into his belt and cut in the Flemish style. Apart from that and a signature – Bartholomew Bisset – Hal could make out nothing more; he would have to wait for daylight.

'Kirkpatrick was burning this?' Sim muttered and paused as a loud jeering and catcalling erupted. A woman had come in.

'Aye, so it seems,' Hal said. The why of it escaped him, which he mentioned, sipping the beer and grimacing, for it was the temperature of broth. He felt the sweat sliding down him – the summer night was muggy and the rough walls of the place were leprous and dripping.

'Christ, I cannot think in here,' Hal said and started to rise, only to find the woman in front of him, so sudden that he recoiled.

'My son,' she said, her face twisted and worn with grief. 'Have ye seen him? A wee boy only. I have looked everywhere. Ye'll know him clear, for he has a wish-mark on his face.'

She paused and managed a wan smile, but it was clear the tears had not all been wrung out of her on a long, fruitless night of search.

'Strawberry,' she added. 'I ken well wishing for strawberries afore he was born. I had a wee passion for them . . .'

The boy's face, smeared with dung and midden filth, the strawberry stain bright in the flames . . .

'No,' Hal said desperately. 'No.'

The lies choked him and he dived headfirst into anger, the sudden face of his own dead son a knife-sharp image etched so bright he was blinded by it.

'Get away, wummin,' he blustered, ducking past her grief and hope, heading out of the linen-thick fug into the smoke-stained breath of the street. 'Am I the fount of knowledge? What do I ken of your son, mistress . . . ?'

He banged past her into the rutted street and stood, trembling like a whipped dog, sucking in air lashed with char and burned meat; after the inside of the alehouse, even that seemed nectarine. He gulped it and shook his head. Johnnie . . . the loss of him was an ache that only added to the misery of this night, this entire enterprise.

Christ's Bones – could matters get worse?

'Wallace sends for us,' said the growl of Sim's voice, and

his blackness bulked up at Hal's shoulder, his face pale and sheened, his stare pointed. Over his shoulder a man waited, dark and impatient, to take them to The Wallace.

'He wants to ask aboot a dead mason,' Sim added mournfully.

Wallace was in Ormsby's chambers, stirring the half-burned papers with the tip of a bollock dagger, while bare-legged kerns grinned savagely at a trembling canon. Outside, the rest of Wallace's army had muted itself to a roar.

'I have had a wee chance to consider matters,' Wallace said, slowly and in good English, Hal noted, so that the priest could follow it easily enough. Wallace jerked his head at the priest, but kept his eyes on Hal and Sim.

'This is Brother Gregor,' he said, while Hal stood, feeling like he was six and in trouble with his da. 'Brother Gregor has been . . . persuaded . . . to help. He reads Latin and had it dinned into him in Hexham Priory.'

He broke off and grinned at the shaking English monk.

'I well ken how that feels,' he said with some sympathy, 'though I never learned as much as I should, for my teachers were not inclined to belt me more than the once.'

Hal flicked a look at Brother Gregor, who stood with his eyes down and his hands trembling; he had an idea what sort of persuasion had been used − but why would you need to threaten a priest to read some documents? Why would a priest refuse in the first place?

'Brawlie,' Wallace said admiringly when Hal muttered this out. 'Your mind could cut yourself, it is that sharp − and so ye are the very man for what I have in mind.'

'Which is?' Hal ventured.

Wallace turned to the nearest kern and whatever he did with eyes and nods got Brother Gregor huckled out, leaving Wallace alone with Hal and Sim; the night wind sighed in through the unshuttered window, stirring the Ormsby wall hanging which Sim had replaced.

'I guddled about in the slorach of this,' Wallace said, indicating the charred, damp mess of papers that Hal had not dared take once Wallace had spotted them, 'and fished out some choice morsels – but the canons of this place refused to read them.'

He paused and looked at them.

'Only yin man could put the fear of God into them over this and that is the wee English Prior. Now where did he find courage for that?'

Bishop Wishart, Hal thought at once, and said so. Wallace nodded slowly.

'Aye. Promises made atween Christians, as it were. Well, I then sought Brother Gregor and almost had to hold his feet to the fire to persuade him to the work,' Wallace went on. 'In the end, he came up with a Scone mason red-murdered near Douglas and a report in a wee, crabbed hand by some scribbler called Bartholomew Bisset. That man is a notary to Ormsby. He has gone out the window as well but I will get him and put him to the question.'

He broke off and looked steadily at Hal until the eyes seemed to be burning holes; Hal fought not to look away and eventually Wallace nodded.

'Ye are joined to Bruce,' he said and then grinned and picked the polished table idly with his dagger point. 'But not willing. Nor favouring me neither.'

'I thought we were all on the same side,' Hal lied and then felt ashamed at the scornful stare he had back for his false naivety, admitting it with a shrug.

'Bruce and the Bishops and others are off to Irvine,' Wallace declared and cocked one eyebrow to show what he thought of that.

'Percy and Clifford are coming with an English army and Wishart has made a right slaister of matters, so Scotland's *gentilhommes* are waving their hands and sounding off like a kist of whistles. I am away to the hills and the trees and

100

most of the fighting men are with me – sorry, but a wheen of yer own are among them.'

Hal knew this already; the fealtied Herdmanston men, all five of them, were with him as well as one or two of the sokemen – free men holding lands under Herdmanston jurisdiction – but the bulk of Hal's March riders, out for plunder, had joined Wallace.

'Welcome men,' Wallace admitted, smiling. 'Nearest I have to heavy horse.'

'They will run at the sight of such,' Sim growled and Wallace nodded.

'As will I,' he answered vehemently and laughed along with Sim.

'Here's the bit,' he went on, losing the smile. 'Ye can come with me or go with Bruce. He says he an' the rest of the bold community of the realm are away to put their fortresses in order.'

He looked sideways, sly as a secret.

'That's as may be.'

Hal looked at him and saw the truth – felt the truth in the kick of his insides. They would truce their way out of it and the relief washed into his face.

Wallace saw that Hal had worked it out – saw, too, the reaction and nodded slowly.

'Aye,' he said with a wry smile. 'Ye have lands to lose, same as they. Not me, though. I do not think there will a kiss of peace for me, eh?'

Hal acknowledged it with a blank face and the shame-sickness that drove bile into his throat. Sim, realist that he was, merely grunted agreement; it was the safest way out of the mire they had plootered into – truced back into the King's peace and forgiven all their sins on a promise not to do it again.

'Well,' Wallace said. 'Go with Bruce then and go with God. Still – I wish I had yer help. I would like to root out why

Kirkpatrick tried to burn these papers, why Wishart bound these wee priests to keep their lips stitched – and what the bold Bruce interest is in it.'

'Ye want my help?' Hal asked. 'Even though I am in the Bruce camp?'

'In,' Wallace pointed out, 'but not of.'

'For a man who sees everyone not for him as against him, that's a quim hair of difference to put yer trust in,' Hal answered and Wallace grinned and raised the dagger, so that the torchlight stepped carefully along the razor edges.

'An edge as thin as this,' he admitted, 'which I have been entrusting my life to for a while now.'

'Still,' he added, standing suddenly and shoving the dagger back in its belt-sheath, 'ye are done with the business. Go with God, Sir Hal – though admit to me, afore ye do, that you are curious ower this matter.'

Hal did so with a grudging nod.

'I will not be a spy against Bruce,' he added firmly, 'nor for him against yourself.'

Wallace towered over him, placing one grimed ham-hand on his shoulder; just the weight of it felt like a maille hauberk.

'Aye, I jaloused that and would not ask. But mark me, Sir Hal – soon ye will needs decide what cote ye will wear. The longer ye take, the more badly it will fit.'

Hal and Sim had stumbled back into the chares and vennels of the priory garth, where light was spilling a sour stain on the horizon as dawn fought the dark over ownership of the hills.

He could scarcely believe that he had stumbled into rebellion so easily and offered a prayer of thanks to God that there was a way out of it; all he had to do was sit at Irvine with The Bruce and the others and make sure that the lesser lords such as himself were not overlooked in the negotiations.

Then it was back home, where he would closet himself with his auld da and they'd ride out this new dawn, he thought wildly, and Roslin be damned. Yet he wondered if even Herdmanston's thick walls would survive the harsh, cold hope of it. He said the bones of that to Sim, who shrugged, looked up, then hawked and spat his own pronouncement on matters.

'It will rain like pish from God,' he growled moodily, then paused, stiffening. Hal followed his gaze and they watched the boy's mother flit from kern to cateran, hard-faced roarer to grim growler, patient as stone and as relentless as a downhill roll.

'Have ye see ma boy? He has a wish-mark . . .'

CHAPTER FOUR

Douglas Castle
Feast of The Visitation of Our Lady with the Blessed Saint
Elizabeth, July 1297

The Dog Boy watched the slipper bounce with every jerk
of the foot it was barely attached to. The leg, bagged with
red hose, flexed and spasmed with every grunting thrust of
the unseen force pounding between it and the twin on the
side, beyond Dog Boy's vision.

Oh Goad, Agnes was saying. Ohgoadohgoadohgoad, a
litany that rose higher and more urgent with each passing
second.

Dog Boy had seen the dogs made blind and frantic by this,
so much so that he'd had to reach down and guide their
thrusting stiffness into the right hole when they were being
bred. He knew the mechanic of it, but the madness of it was
only just touching him, so that he only half understood what
he was feeling.

In the butter-yellow and shadowed dim, he sat and, prickled
with heat and half-ashamed, half-driven, kneaded his own
tight groin while he stared at the mournful brown eyes of
Mykel, head on paws and unconcerned that Agnes's knees

were locked behind the pillars of Tod's Wattie's arms. With every thrust Wattie grunted and Agnes squealed an answer; gradually the squeals grew higher in pitch.

Veldi snuffled hopefully, but Dog Boy had nothing for them to eat, nor looked to be getting anything until Tod's Wattie was done. So he sat in the strawed dim of the stable, right up against the back wall and almost under the huge iron-rimmed wheels of the wagon, with the ghost-coloured deerhounds waiting patiently on their leashes, heads on the huge, long-nailed paws.

He and Tod's Wattie and the hounds had been there two months, left behind by Sir Hal and the others, and he wondered why. Yet the idea of leaving Douglas was strange and frightening enough to catch his breath in his throat.

The castle at Douglas was all he had ever known and the people in it the only ones he had met, besides the odd peddlar or pardoner, until the arrival of Hal and all the other strangers. Now he was about to go off with this stranger, this Tod's Wattie.

The squeals grew louder and faster. Dog Boy, uncomfortably aware of his groin, traced the iron rim of the cartwheel with one grimy forefinger faster and faster, while unable to tear his gawp-mouthed gaze from her feet and the fancy slipper bobbing furiously. A window-slipper, Agnes had called it, because it had elegant cut-outs designed to show off the red hose that went with them, like the stained windows of a grand cathedral.

Agnes had been told this by the Countess of Buchan, who had given them to her when she had left, as a gift for her tirewoman help; Agnes had worn red hose and slippers ever since − until now, Dog Boy thought, for the hose garters lay like streaks of blood nearby and the slipper he watched had slipped from her bagged heel and wagged frantically on her toes. Her last shriek was almost so piercing as to be heard only by the dogs and she jerked and spasmed so furiously that the slipper flew off.

Tod's Wattie made a curious, childlike series of whimpers and slowed the mad pulse of him, then stopped entire. The straw stopped rustling like a rainstorm and Dog Boy shut his mouth with a click and heard their breathing, harsh and ragged.

'Aye,' said Agnes, in a thick, dreamy voice Dog Boy had never heard from her before. 'Ye've rattled me clean oot of my shoe.'

They laughed and then the straw rustled as they tidied themselves together. Tod's Wattie lumbered out, wisped with straw sticks, and looked over to where the dogs were, seeing Dog Boy and blinking.

'There ye are,' he said and Dog Boy knew he was wondering how long he had been sitting. In the end, he shrugged and passed a hand through his thick hair, combed out a straw and grinned.

'Go to the kitchen and see if you can find some scraps for the dugs,' he said and Dog Boy scampered off.

'I still have a shoe on the other foot,' said the throaty voice behind him and Tod's Wattie blinked a bit and shook his head. He knew he and Dog Boy and the deerhounds were at Douglas because Hal thought it safer to leave his expensive dogs away from the Scots camp at Annick, where Bruce and the others sat in wary conclave with Percy and Clifford and both armies tried hard not to break into pitched battle. Worse still was to try to travel alone on dangerous roads back to Lothian.

But, he added to himself, if Sir Hal delays longer in sending for us this hot-arsed wee besom will have me worn to a nub end.

The kitchen was a swelter. At the large table, Master Fergus the Cook and his helpers split a side of salt beef for the boiling pit, spitted geese, kneaded bread; Dog Boy saw that there was milled sawdust being mixed in with the rye, which meant grain was scarce.

A scullion elbowed his way past Dog Boy with drawn water,

piped cleverly from the stone cistern somewhere above; another lugged an armful of wood for the fire, which was bigger than the smith's furnace and hotter, too. Near it, the potboys withered, trying to stir without roasting themselves, huddled behind an old damped-down tiltyard shield. In the high summer some had been known to faint from the heat and only quick hands saved those from certain death; almost all of them had the glassy weals of old burns.

'Well, what do you want, boy?' demanded Fergus looking up. He was no advert for his craft, being a thin, pinch-faced man from Galloway, shaved bald on head and chin to better rid himself of vermin and stay cool.

'I beg the blissin' of ye sir,' Dog Boy said, 'Tod's Wattie asks if you can spare some meat and cleidin for his dogs.'

'Christ's Bones,' Fergus interrupted in his Gaelic-lilted English. 'Cleidin? Scraps for dogs, yet? Ask for a cone of sugar, why not? Everything is running low and little chance of it being replenished that I can see. Glad it is that almost all the visitors are after having gone, for another day would have seen us chewing our own boots.'

The implication was that some unwanted guests remained and it was a sudden, sharp pain to Dog Boy to realise that he was now one of them. In an eyeblink and a series of words from the mouth of the Lady, he had gone from the company of the castle to being a stranger.

'It will be for him, Master,' added one of his helpers with a grin as he worked at carefully stacking and tallying a pyramid of honeycakes without breaking them. 'He looks as if he would eat raw meat.'

'Perhaps if yon hunt weeks back had actually routed out something worthwhile,' Fergus grumbled, 'but hunted stag meat is tough and a brace of fine coneys make better eating and easier cooking. Now the game is scattered and wary and there will be no good hunting for weeks. All we had from it was a dead body and a mystery.'

107

He broke off and thrust a round pot at Dog Boy, bright and reeking with bloody pats, some of the blood and grease slathered on the outside.

'Here,' he said. 'Bring the pot back sharp, mind.'

Dog Boy grinned, nodded – then shot out one hand and grabbed a honeycake, fleeing from the new catcalls and the barrage of feral curses that brought. He was almost at the door when he slammed into something dark and a hard object that whacked him on the temple.

Dazed, he staggered, found himself held up by a strong hand clamped painfully round his thin arm and looked up, past the hilt of the dagger which had smacked him, into a smear of smile.

It was on a fox-sharp face, the eyes cold and dark, the nose speckled with old pox-marks. There was a chin but not much of one and it made the man's teeth stick out like a rat's from between wet lips limned by a wisped fringe of beard and moustache.

'A wee thief,' he said with suet-rich satisfaction and looked triumphantly at Fergus. 'It seems my arrival is timely.'

Fergus cleaned his hands on his apron and looked at the newcomer, whom he disliked on sight. He glanced pointedly at the blood-clamp fist that gripped Dog Boy's arm and the man raised an eyebrow and opened it with a sudden, deliberate gesture.

Dog Boy, pot in one hand, cake in the other, wanted to rub the affected bit but could only wriggle it, looking warily from the man to Fergus, who jerked his head silently at him to go. Heedless of the blood on his hands, Dog Boy crammed the honeycake in his mouth, then darted for the kennels, holding his puny biceps.

'You are?' Fergus said and the man lifted his head haughtily.

'Malise Bellejambe,' he declared. 'Sir Malise Bellejambe,' he added pointedly. 'And you will lose a kitchen full of honey-cakes if you keep that attitude with wee thieves.'

'Sir,' Fergus declared, in a tone that made it clear he did not believe the title for a moment. 'I remember you from before. You came with the Earl of Buchan. Now you are back. Whit why?'

Malise wanted to force the man to his properly deferential knees, but managed a shaky smile instead.

'The Countess has become strayed from his entourage,' he said. 'The Earl fears she may have gotten lost and is mounted on yon great beast of a warhorse, which is not one for a woman to ride. The roads are no place for a woman alone.'

He paused and smiled, as if a little ashamed of his lord's indulgences in letting his wife gallop around the country astraddle a warhorse, without escort or even chaperone. The memory of her escape burned him – Christ's Bones she was a cat-cunning imp of Satan. Stole away while they all slept and managed to take the damned warhorse with her; Malise had been in a panic since, for he knew Buchan would suspect that their sleep was fuelled by drink and that they had been less than watchful. It was the truth, but not what Malise wanted to have to tell his master.

'The Earl has sent me to guide her back. I thought she might have returned here.'

There was silence for a moment, for all remembered the noises of the Earl punishing his wife, and Fergus thought, vehemently, that it was scarce a surprise that the Countess had run off. Wisely, he did not voice it.

'Aye – as to that I could not say,' Fergus declared instead and rounded on the silent, still, open-mouthed scullions, raking them with his eyes until they became a sudden flurry of activity.

'No such lady is here,' he added. 'The Douglas Lord and Lady, bairns and all are gone elsewhere. Thomas the Sergeant is left as steward, so you would be wise to speak to him.'

Malise stroked his chin as if considering it.

'There was a quine,' he said. 'Agnes, I believe her name was. Acted as tirewoman to the Countess when she visited here. I would speak with her.'

His diffidence was a lie, for he knew the trull well enough to remember the sway of her hurdies and the lip-licking promise it gave. It was desperation to seek her out in the hope that she knew where the Countess had gone – but Malise was all rat-frantic now. Fergus raised an eyebrow.

'She will be here somewheres,' he said. 'As I say – best to talk to Thomas and let him ken you are nosin' around his charges like a spooring dog.'

The warning was sharp and Malise felt the sting of it burn him. He inclined his head, gracious, polite, innocent as a nun's serk.

'My thanks,' he said, fixing his eyes on Fergus's own. 'I will remember you for it.'

Stepping out from gloom to bright, he squinted against the light, then spotted the skinny runt of a thief, scuttling like a rat across the Ward towards the stable block. Aha, he thought, the little listening mouse hears much. If I were he, I would run to warn this Agnes, whom he no doubt kens . . .

Dog Boy half turned and saw the weasel-faced stranger look directly at him, then stride purposefully on. He gibbered in fear, the pain in his arm burning in stripes like the man's fingers.

He remembered that the hard blow on the side of his head had been made by the hilt of a dagger and the panic made him fumbling careless. He turned, half-stumbled, dropped the pot and went to pick it up, then realised how close the man was. He left it and ran. More convinced than ever of Dog Boy's intent, Malise followed after.

Agnes, pulling her shift straight and picking straw from her hair, was coming out of the stables, leaving first to try to put some face on the unavoidable gossip. She was dreamy and sticky, the sun seemed like honey on her skin and she started to adjust her cap when Dog Boy sped round the corner and skidded to a halt.

'Man,' he gulped.

'What troubles ye, my wee chook?' Agnes purred with a grin, which froze as Malise stepped round the corner. With a whimper, Dog Boy turned and sped away.

Malise smiled, which made Agnes's stomach lurch.

'You are Agnes,' he said and it was not a question. Agnes trembled, recovered and drew herself up a little.

'Aye. You are the Earl of Buchan's man. Malise. I mind you from before.'

She did, too, conscious then of his eyes griming over her and not liking it any better now.

'Indeed,' Malise replied and looked her up and down so that Agnes felt her skin ripple; she became aware, suddenly, of Tod's Wattie's stickiness on the inside of her thighs and prickled with a sudden shame that, just as suddenly turned to anger against this Malise for having driven away the fine moment of before.

'I thought you left with the Coontess,' Agnes declared haughtily and forced her legs to move, looking to get round and away from him. Malise stepped forward and blocked her.

'I did,' he replied and his eyes were like festering sheep droppings on her face. 'Fine slippers ye have, mistress.'

Agnes dropped her head to look and felt him grip her chin, his fingers like the hard, horned beak of a bird. She was so astounded at it that she could not move or make a sound.

'Too fine slippers for you,' Malise added, soft and vicious in her ear, his breath tickling the stray strands of her sweat-damp hair. 'They belong to the Coontess, if I am not mistaken.'

The fingers ground her jaw and, suddenly, let her go. She stumbled on weakened legs and would have fallen, but his hand shot out and held her under one arm, hauling her upright.

'You ken where she has gone,' Malise said and Agnes saw

his other hand, resting on the two-lobed pommel that gave the weapon at his belt its name – bollock dagger. She felt sick.

'She gave me the slippers,' she heard herself say. 'Afore she left . . .'

'She came back, did she not?' Malise persisted, his mouth close to her ear; his breath smelled like stale milk. 'Ran to here – who better to shelter the hot-arsed Bruce hoor than Douglas Castle's ain wee hot-arsed trollop, eh? Who was her tirewummin when she was first here.'

'Never,' Agnes said, feeling the fingers burn. Her head swam and she swore she heard the snake-slither of the dagger leaving the sheath. 'Came back.'

'Ye will tell me,' Malise started to say, then something clamped on the back of his neck and jerked him backwards. Loosed, Agnes crumpled in a heap.

At first Malise thought a horse had bit him and struggled, cursing, to get free. Then a second hand swam into view, a huge grimed affair with split nails which snaked out of the dazzle of sun and locked on his throat, instantly cutting off his breathing. Choking, kicking, Malise looked up into the big, round face of Tod's Wattie, boar-eyed with rage.

'Ye cantrips ye,' he bellowed. 'I'll maul the stanes with ye, ye bauchlin' wee bastard. I'll dunt ye some manners . . .'

Desperately, Malise half-fumbled out the dagger and Tod's Wattie spotted it and roared even louder. He shook Malise left and right like a terrier with a rat and Malise felt the world whirl and turn red at the edges. The dagger clattered from his fingers and his vision blackened and and started to narrow.

'Drag a dirk out on me, is it?' Tod's Wattie shouted and flung Malise away from him. 'I'll tear aff yer head and shite down yer neck, ye jurrocks.'

'Here, here – enough of that.'

The new voice brought Tod's Wattie round in a whirl, in

time to see one of the castle's garrison come panting up, sweating in his helmet and leather jack. He staggered to a halt and leaned on his spear, looking from one to the other.

'What's all this?'

Tod's Wattie had turned to help Agnes back on to shaky legs and he felt her hanging on him like a wrung-out dishcloth, which only made him angrier. He waved a free hand at Malise, who was on his hands and knees, retching and whooping in air.

'He was footerin' with Agnes here,' Tod's Wattie declared. He knew the guard, Androu, was sweet on Agnes, so he was not surprised at the narrow-eyed look the man gave Malise.

'Was he so?' Androu said, then looked at Agnes. 'Is this right?'

Agnes nodded and Androu shut one eye and glared grimly with the other, while Malise climbed, wavering, back to his feet.

'Right you,' Androu said, scooping up the dropped dagger. 'You and me will see what Tam . . . the Sergeant . . . thinks of this.'

'Mistake,' Malise managed to croak, appalled at the ruin of his voice. He has torn my throat, he thought wildly. I will be dumb.

'Aye,' said Tod's Wattie viciously. 'It was a mistake right enough. If ye make it again it will be your last.'

Androu soothed him, then prodded Malise with the spear butt, so that he was forced to weave off. Tod's Wattie, Agnes leaning on his arm, started to help her back to the kitchen.

'Dog Boy,' she said, but the Dog Boy was gone.

Dog Boy was not having the finest of days. He knew this when he ran in blind panic from the man, sure he could hear the boots scuffing after him. He went back across the Ward and found himself heading for the only safety he knew, the kennels.

He knew it was a mistake when he skidded round the

113

wattle-and-daub corner, into the raised, curious faces of the kennel lads, carrying the dirty straw out to the courtyard. Gib and The Worm stopped and straightened.

'Blood of Christ,' The Worm declared, snorting snot from his nose. 'It's yon hawk botherer who was too fine for the like of us.'

Dog Boy saw Gib's pig-faced pout. Almost everything irritated Gib and Dog Boy knew that included him – even more after the showing-up he'd had during the hunt and because Dog Boy had been plucked from the castle kennels to serve with the Lothian lord.

Now he wandered around with only two big dogs to see to, which was not work at all; Gib was convinced it should have been him chosen and that, somehow, Dog Boy had contrived his downfall.

'What are you seeking?' he demanded, slightly more curious than angry but still careful to sneer. He always sneered these days.

Dog Boy stumbled his tongue on an answer. The sight of them had been cold water on his panic and he realised, suddenly, that the man was nowhere to be seen and almost certainly not pursuing him. He felt confused and embarrassed.

'N-n-nothing,' he stammered eventually.

'N-n-nothing,' mimicked Gib in a piping voice, then chuckled nastily. 'Looking for hawks, probably.'

The Worm hooted at this, a few others joined in and Gib's sneering smile broadened with the audience. Dog Boy kept silent, for he knew Gib's moods well enough. He waited, leaden with inevitability, wanting to back away and unable to move.

'Well? Answer me, you dropping?'

Answer what? I gave you an answer. Dog Boy wanted to say this but stitched his mouth in a neat, tight hem and said nothing, sick with what he knew would come next.

114

'Whore turd,' Gib spat. He liked the sound of it and repeated it, rolling it off his tongue, savouring. The Worm laughed. Everybody laughed. Dog Boy tried one and Gib scowled at him and stepped closer.

'Think it funny, do you?' he snarled and cuffed Dog Boy hard. The blow stung, but Dog Boy made no sound and only half-ducked. Gib did it again, excited by the first one. It was an act worn by use, the steps in it as set as any dance, and Gib knew it well. He would strike a few more unresisted blows, then he would spring on Dog Boy, wrestle him down, punch him, then bounce on him until he had suitably shown his superiority among all the dog-boy barons. It was what always happened.

Except this time. Gib's second blow met air and his belly met a hard nut of fist that drove the air from him. Then Dog Boy's bare foot slammed into his cods and drove shrieking agony into him.

Dog Boy hardly knew he had done it. He wanted to leap on Gib and beat him to bloody paste, but his nerve broke as Gib, howling, fell to the filthy, dog-turd straw and writhed, curling and uncurling round his clutching hands. Dog Boy turned to run and the rest of the pack sprang on him and bore him down.

There was a confused welter of dust and flying fists, snarling faces and curses. Then came a series of sharp cracks and yelps and the bellow of a deeper voice until Dog Boy, curled into a ragged, bloody ball, found himself hauled up into Malk's scowl, while the others nursed the marks of the whip he had used on them.

Dog Boy wiped his bloody nose. It had been a bad day. He did not think he had ever had a worse one, or that this one could grow more rotten.

He thought to revise the opinion in the dim of the gatehouse arch, where the torch flickered red light on Berner Philippe's face. When he smeared the smile on it, he looked to Dog Boy

115

like one of the devils cavorting on the walls of the church in the nearby town. Gib moaned.

'Get in,' he ordered and Dog Boy swallowed. The black square gave off a faint stink of grave rot and led to the pit of the pivot bridge, a black maw where the weighted end hung and the great pivots waited to be greased.

Dog Boy felt Gib tremble and started to shake himself; they would climb into the pit with a pot of stinking grease and a torch and, in the tomb dark of it, they would labour, smearing grease on the pivots. It was Berner Phillipe's clever idea for punishment and Dog Boy never even dared point out that he was no longer the Berner's to command.

'The torch will burn for an hour,' Philippe said, the smile still a nasty streak. 'I will return in that time – give or take a minute or so. Take care of yon light, or you will be left in the dark.'

They stared into the pit, the dank, cold stink of it reaching out like coils of witch hair, the wood and knotted rope ladder dangling into the dark; Dog Boy sat on the edge, turned gingerly and slithered down. The grease pot was handed to him, then a shivering, weeping Gib thumped down beside him and the torch was flung in.

The trapdoor shut, cutting out the last of the dim, dappled sunlight under the gatehouse arch. With the final shunk, they were alone with torch and the flickering shadows and the huge roll of the bridge weight, locked in place by timber supports shoved through from the walls on either side.

'Jesu, Jesu, Jesu,' muttered Gib.

Dog Boy looked at his nemesis, at the pinch-face and the tear-streaked cheeks, then handed him one of the two flat sticks. Worldlessly, dry-eyed and shaking, he moved to the steps, climbed to one of the great pivots and began slapping grease on it. He could not believe he had been afraid of leaving Douglas and now could not wait to be quit of the place and all the folk in it.

* * *

Malise massaged his throat and fumed. Thomas the Sergeant had been no more than an old, scarred man-at-arms, no better in rank than Malise himself, yet he stood there like some belted earl and lectured, finally throwing Malise out of the castle.

Black scowled, Malise collected his horse and tried not to worry about bumping into Tod's Wattie, though he saw the dim grey shapes of the deerhounds in the depth of the stable. An idea came to him.

He went out and found what he sought – the discarded pot of offal, thrown away by that little rat-runt. The flies had found the contents, but nothing else had, and Malise scooped it back into the pot wearing his gauntlets, then fumbled out a small glass bottle, unstoppered it and poured half the contents in, tossing the whole to mix it.

He went back to the stable and gingerly came close to the dogs, making kissing sounds. He laid the pot down, backed away and watched as the nearest hound sniffed, rose up, stretched front, then back and ambled towards the delicious smell, click-clicking across the flags. The other followed. Malise smiled and collected his horse.

Thomas the Sergeant, from the window nook high above, watched Buchan's creature slither towards the gatehouse with his horse. Good riddance, he thought to himself and then shook his head. How had he gotten in? Androu, half-shamed, had thought it was probably because Crozier the Keep had recognised him from before as the Earl of Buchan's man and saw no reason to keep him out.

'Christ's Wounds,' Thomas declared, watching Malise leave. 'You would think the year was all good crops and peace. Our lord is at odds with the English again and his enemies are everywhere.'

It had been a moment of crushing despair for Thomas when the Lady had admitted a Bruce into the sacred centre of The Hardy's Douglas, but nothing more than he expected from the woman, who did not have much inkling of what that meant. Nor cared, he thought.

Mind you, he had expected better from the hard-eyed Sientcler lord from Lothian with his blessing of good men – but then another Sientcler, a Templar no less, had stood on the Bruce side and, of course, that high and mighty family had no thought for Douglas then, only themselves.

As if to make a mockery of it all, the Earl of Buchan had arrived at the gates not long after to find Bruce on the stone gatehouse battlements, making sure his red chevronned surcoat was clearly visible. That had been worse still, for the Comyn and Bruce hated each other and none of them, as far as Thomas knew, supported the cause of his master, Sir William.

He had stood beside the Earl of Carrick and the Herdmanston lord, Sir Hal, looking out on the patient riders on mud-spattered horses, armed and righteous and wanting entry. Bruce, Thomas recalled, looked young and petted – more two than twenty-two – and he'd felt a momentary spasm of concern about how the Earl of Carrick would handle this affair.

There had been two others on the wooden battlements – Bruce's sinister wee shadow, the man called Kirkpatrick, who had nodded to the giant called Sim. That yin had needed nothing more than the nod to foot one worn boot into the stirrup of his great crossbow and, scorning the bellyhook, drag the thick string up by brute force and click it into place. Thomas had been impressed by the feat, yet mortally afraid of what might result.

He recalled the riders' pale faces looking up, framed in arming cap bascinets and maille coifs, their great slitted helms tucked under one arm and shields pointedly brought forward.

'Open in the name of the King,' one had shouted, urging his mud-spattered horse forward a little. Davey Siward, Thomas remembered, with John of Inchmartin behind him – a clutch of Inchmartins had been there, in fact.

'Which King is that, then?' Bruce had asked. 'John Balliol,

in whose name you attacked me and my father in Carlisle last year? Or Edward of England, whose army you are supposed to be with? I should point out that I am here because Sir William Douglas has also absconded from that army and King Edward is less than pleased.'

Which was as sure a seal on the fate of Douglas as any Thomas had heard and he burned with indignation. Before he could say anything at all in his master's defence, a light, easy voice rolled sonorously up like perfumed smoke.

'Is that a shivering cross I see? Could that be young Hal Sientcler from Herdmanston?' the Earl of Buchan had asked. Thomas remembered the way the Lothian lord had unconsciously touched that engrailed blue cross on his chest. It was an arrogance, that symbol, signifying a Templar connection and allusions to the Holy Grail, as if only the Sientclers held the secret of it beyond Jesus himself.

'Sir William of Roslin is also here,' the Lothian lord had replied and Thomas knew he had done it deliberately, hoping a mention of the Auld Templar might unlatch the situation a little. Buchan had sighed a little and shook his head, so that the sweat-damp hair stirred in the bold wind.

'Well, there it is,' Buchan answered. 'God's Own Chosen, the Sientclers, together with the Young Himself of Carrick, all descended here to punish a wee woman and her wee sons. Such we have been driven down to, Bruce.'

There had been a clipped, frosted exchange after that, Thomas recalled, but more to score points than for any serious questioning of intent. Buchan presented his Writ from King Edward, permitting him to go home and contain the rebels of Sir Andrew Moray. Bruce had taken his time to study it, letting Buchan savour the fact that he had no more than sixty riders, too few to tackle a castle like this, stuffed to the merlons with Carrick men.

Some had grown impatient and Sim had spotted it, for which Thomas had been grateful and furious with himself for having been so lax.

'Is that you there, Jinnet's Davey?' Sim had called out in a friendly voice, and the man with a crossbow in one hand and the reins of a horse in the other looked guiltily up.

'Yer da back in Biggar will be black affronted to see you in sich company,' Sim chided, 'and about to shoot from the cover of other men's back. If ye try I will pin your luggs to either side of your face and slide ye aff that stot ye are riding.'

Thomas remembered that more for what he overheard, whispered by Bruce to the Lothian lord.

'I have only a little idea what he said, but the sentiment seems fine.'

Thomas marvelled at it anew. The great Earl of Carrick, heir to the Bruces of Annandale, speaks court French, southern English and the Gaelic – thanks to his mother – but he has poor command of English as spoken by a good Scot.

Yet the gates of Douglas had opened and Thomas, feeling the slow burn of resentment at having had his charge swept from under him as if he was of no account, had been forced to watch as the Ward bustled, rang with shouts and horse-snorts and neighs. Bruce had stepped forward, the red chevron on his surcoat like a bright splash of blood, his arms expansively wide as he and the stiffly dismounted Buchan embraced like old friends well met.

Well, now they were all gone and the Lady and her bairns with Bruce, Thomas thought. Poor sowls – God ensure that they go where Bruce promised, to The Hardy at Irvine. No matter if they did, or ended up in Bruce's power, or whether the Earl joined with patriots or the English, or whether Sir William The Hardy won or lost – Thomas swore that the fortress of Douglas would not fall as easily again.

He rounded on Androu and pointed an accusing finger.

'From this moment Douglas is in a state of war, man,' he declared. 'I want yon Lothian man and his dugs gone from here in short order – I do not care if it puts them into danger. I do not trust any of that Lothian lord's chiels and do not want any Lothians inside looking out for Sientclers coming back here, having wormed their way into the English peace at Irvine and looking to advantage themselves.'

Androu had not thought of the Sientclers turning their cote and wanted to defend them, to point out how they had come originally, at considerable risk, to defend the place. He opened and closed his mouth like a landed fish, but the words would not marshal themselves in any order.

Thomas frowned down at the retreating back of Malise Bellejambe, then rounded on Androu like an unleashed terrier.

'And as soon as that ill-favoured swine is on the far side of the ditch, that yett is closed and the bridge raised, to be lowered only on my say.'

He turned away to stare out the slit window, high in the great square bulk of keep.

'When The Hardy comes back,' he said, half-muttering to himself, 'he will find his castle ready for war.'

Androu, who could see Tam's mind was made up, scurried to obey.

When the bridge trembled, Dog Boy paused, then looked at the guttering torch. Gib whimpered and it was only then that Dog Boy understood what the tremble meant. They both heard the rasping thump, felt rather than saw the supports being windlassed back. Then the massive counterweight shifted and Gib gave a moan, dropped his pot and went for the rope ladder, elbowing Dog Boy to the clotted floor of the pit.

At the top, Gib shoved at the unresisting trapdoor, then started beating on it, screaming. The counterweight, a great long roll like a giant's stowed sleeping blanket, started a slow, downward swing, dragging the outthrust, unseen beams attached by chains to the moatbridge, hauling it up.

Gib shrieked and dropped off the ladder, his hands bloody from beating the wood.

'Flat,' Dog Boy yelled. 'Get yourself flat.'

The smoothed granite went over Dog Boy, a huge, round crush of weight, moving ponderously, yet more swiftly than before with its new grease. Dog Boy felt the touch of it, the plucking fingers of it along his back like some giant's fist.

Gib was caught by it. Dog Boy saw his wild face, the staring eyes, the red maw of his mouth, twisting with shock as he realised that he was too big, that the skinny runt he had always despised for his size could get under the rolling weight, but not him.

It scooped Gib up and carried him back, back to the far wall, and Dog Boy, head buried in his arms, heard the cracking splinter of bones and a last, despairing shriek in the cold dark.

Temple Bridge, Annick Water
Division of the Apostles Across The Earth – July, 1297

The rain lisped down, dripping from the bell hanging over their heads on the arch of the glistening wet timber bridge. Hal knew the bell was called Gloria because Bangtail Hob had told everyone so, squinting into the falling mirr to read the name etched on it and proud of his ability to recognise the letters, however long he had taken to spell them out.

The bell could be rung by tugging on a white rope, pearled with sliding water drops now, to warn the Poor Knights of the Temple Ton that travellers were coming to them in peace, seeking succour or sanctuary. Hal fervently wished he was in the small Temple out of a rain as fine as querned flour, soaking the men who were huddled on the bridge, waiting and watching the men on horseback on the far side.

His own men had taken off their quilted gambesons, trading the protection for the agility; the rain had soaked the garments heavy as armour. They had tied their right shoe into their belt or round their necks, for the right was the bracing foot, rutted into the churned earth and needing all the grip it could get.

The left, shoved forward, required a measure of protection and, though it would not divert a cut or a stab or the crush of a hoof, the leather of a shoe was still a comfort.

Hal did not expect hooves. His men were bunched and dripping, a hedge of spears and blades and wicked hooks, and Hal expected that the English horse – decently armoured *serjeants* – would climb off and tramp on foot the length of the bridge to attack.

He wished they would not, that they would try to ride them down and suffer ruin for it. More than that, he wished they would just go away, thinking like sensible men, and that, any day – any moment – they would all be friends, with the Scots back in the King's peace and no harm done.

More than that, he wished that John the Lamb, wherever he was, had seen sense and was not trying to bring the reived cattle out of the dripping trees and across the bridge to join them. That would be all the provocation the English needed.

The last hope was driven from him by the distant bawl of a miserable cow. Sim slid up beside him, rusted rain running off the brim of his iron hat and his crossbow swathed in his cloak to try to keep the string from getting wet and slack.

'John the Lamb,' he said and Hal nodded. He saw the head of the English captain come up, cocked to hear the same mournful lowing and knew, with certainty, that both were now caught in the whirling dance of it, borne along to the inevitability of blood and slaughter by honour, duty, chivalry and desperation. And all over a handful of rieved coos for a hungry army waiting for their betters to set seal to their deals.

He looked at the man's shield, the six little legless birds on it, three on top of a diagonal stroke, three beneath. *Argent, a bend between six martlet, gules*, he thought automatically to himself and smiled. All those days of bruised knuckles and scowls as his father dinned Heraldry into him – no, no, ye daftie, a bird which is facing you is full aspect, any other beast similarly displayed is affronty. Repeat, affronty.

No practical use at all, for he still had no idea who the man opposite him was, or even if he was English. The only thing he did know was that the martlet marked him as a fourth son and that, in a moment, they would be trying to cleave sharp bars of iron into each other.

Furneval sat as haughtily as he could while rain slithered off his bascinet and down under the maille; his padded, quilted gambeson was sodden and weighed four times as much as normal and so would those of the rest of his men – they would feel the dragging weight when they had to dismount and fight in them, as well as the maille, the heavy shields and the lances, too long to make comfortable spears.

For now, he was watching the sudden antheap stir of the little group under the bridge-bell arch. Behind, his men shifted in their ranks, hunching down so that their rimmed iron helmets were all that could be seen above the long shields. That and the lances.

Behind that, Furneval knew, was William de Ridre, up in the trees with even more men and watching closely what happened here. Furneval felt the surge in him, a fire of pride and joy, for he had been chosen to demonstrate the power of the Percy and had his own lord, de Ridre, watching him do it.

They had chased these foragers a long way over the fields and Furneval had some sympathy for their desperate plundering – small though it was, the Scots force at Annick still needed fodder and meat – and some admiration of their skill.

Fast riders, skilled at herding the small, black cattle, he had been thinking to himself, so no strangers to such thieving, and it was right and proper that, even though a truce pertained here, such raiders were not permitted to plunder as they chose. They were, until announcements were made to the contrary, rebels after all and just a rabble of brigands.

Now that Furneval had seen them for himself he was sure of the second part and suspicious of the first.

They were waiting at the far end of a narrow bridge across a steep-banked, undergrowth choked stream called the Annick Water, knowing that this was their best chance of defence. It was clever and determined, the weapons they had were like polearms only worse, so that Furneval felt a flicker of doubt, a sharp little dart that flew into his heart like a sliver of ice.

A sensible man would have let them go, with their sumpter cart of stolen rye and wheat and their handful of cattle, but de Ridre was not about to go back to Percy and admit that a raggedy bunch of Scots foot had forced back sixty mounted *serjeants*.

A sensible man would not try to ride down a hedge of spears, but dismount and march on them, and Furneval would do that, at least; he had seen what spear-bristling foot could do at Dunbar. He wished for some crossbows, for they had split the spear rings of the Scots apart at Dunbar. He wished for de Ridre to send him a message telling him to pull off and leave it. He knew neither wish was possible, yet he waited in the lisping rain, ever hopeful.

Then the first cow stumbled out of the woods with others at its back and men behind, running their weary, stumbling horses like shambling bears and sealing the fate of them all.

Hal watched as the rider reached up and dropped the great sugarloaf helm over the bascinet, becoming a faceless metal creature in an instant. Furneval adjusted his grip on the shield with the birds, blew out to make sure the cruciform breathing holes were clear and wished his nose was not so big, since it squashed against the full-face helm.

Hal watched him tap the helm a little to settle it, then draw out his long sword; he barked something and the men behind him climbed off their horses.

'Ah, ye thrawn, bloody limmer,' Hal heard himself say wearily.

Too much to hope they would be stupid and try to ride them down.

'Drop the kine, ye bliddy fools!' hissed Sim to no-one in particular, but even if he had bellowed it, neither John the Lamb nor Dand would have heard. Even if they had heard, they would not have obeyed, for they had harried and herded this meagre handful of black cows for miles and every time they looked at the green-streaked arse of one they saw roasted beef, dripping and savoury.

Yet it was death to them and everyone knew it. The rider with the six red martlets swept his sword up like a bar of light – then brought it down and a roar went up from the horde of throats behind him as they surged past on to the bridge.

'Stand fast, lads,' bawled Sim, switching back the cloak and sticking one foot in the crossbow stirrup. He hauled it up without using the belt-hook, stuck in a four-sided bolt and brought it up to his chest.

'*Dirige, Domine, Deus meus in conspecto tuo viam meam.*'

Hal stared at Bangtail Hob as the man crossed himself. Direct my path, Lord my God, in your sight – he had not known that the likes of Hob knew the English, never mind the Latin. Life was full of surprises, even now.

'Christ be praised,' roared Sim.

'For ever and ever,' the men roared back.

'Mither of God,' whined Will Elliott, and Hal watched the bobbing wall of shields and spears and helms crush itself down the length of wooden bridge, while John the Lamb and Dand veered off, heading for the bank and throwing themselves off their horses; cattle scattered, bawling mournfully.

He saw, too, in a fixed instant that seared itself on his mind, the horseman in his great helm and shield of birds turn away from the bridge and the backs of his men, watched the bunched flank muscles of the powerful beast as he spurred it towards John and Dand.

'Sim,' he yelled and pointed. Cursing, Sim levelled the bow and shot; the bolt hissed past the hindquarters of the horse and Sim howled with frustration, frantically spanning the weapon again.

Furneval caught up with the fleeing Dand as he plootered and plunged through the tangling bushes and undergrowth, hearing the wet thunder behind him closing in and the whimper in him rising to a scream.

'Jump, Dand, jump.'

He heard it, saw, out of the corner of his eye, John the Lamb spring up like the beast he was named for and spin in the air, a whirl of already sodden arms and legs that hit the black ripple of the water and exploded it to spray.

He was a step away. One step and a leap and his lungs burning . . .

Furneval gave the sword a little wrist flick, brought it back and then forward and up. The last third of blade caught Dand on the back of his head, exploding it into black blood and shards. His body stumbled on two, three steps, then fell, tumbled over and over, then slid in a tangle down the bank and slithered softly into the water.

Furneval reined round, knowing it had been a perfect stroke and hoping de Ridre had been watching. He reached up and hauled off the full-face helm, feeling the cool blast of damp wind on his sweating face, then half turned in the saddle, stiff-necked with maille, to see what his men were doing.

He heard a bellowing, as if there had been a bull among the cows – then the second bolt from the roaring fury that was Sim took him in the centre of his bascinet-framed face, a sudden huge hissing black approach that drove life from him in an instant and shot him sideways off the horse in a great whirl of pearl sky and wet bracken that dropped him into darkness.

Sim's great bellow of triumph was swallowed in the crashing tide of men, four wide and infinitely deep, it seemed, who

127

rolled up to the hedge of Jeddart staffs and clashed into it, so that it rocked and slid a little before bracing on all those bared right feet. Mindless as some beast, the ranks piled on, those in front unable to move or do much more than waggle their too-long lances.

Bangtail Hob and Hal stabbed and cut. Will Elliot and Red Cloak Thom slashed and hooked, while Sim spanned his bow and shot between their heads into the packed ranks, where he could not miss. Men screamed; curses went up and the front four men, the sense crushed out of them, lost the use of their limbs and suddenly vanished as if sucked under a bog. Four more were crushed forward; the wooden archway splintered and rocked.

Red Cloak Thom's staff snapped and he threw it away with a curse and whipped out his bollock dagger. He parried a thrust that would have skewered him, missed another and took it in the throat, went over gurgling and drowning in his own blood. Hal leaped, shrieking, to Thom's slumped, twisting, gasping corpse, heedless of the blindly stabbing lance points. A huge figure moved forward, as if wading into a hip-deep stream, and a man went backwards with the bolt of a crossbow in the face.

Hal felt a hand grip and pull him free, then he was staring up into Sim's scowl.

'No more of that, ye sou's arse,' he growled. 'Yer father would take ill of it if I was to let ye be killed dead here.'

'Never fash yourself,' Hal managed and then grinned, ashamed at his stupidity and knowing Red Cloak was dead from the moment his throat had been opened.

'I am a lad of parts, me' he added. 'Such bravery is auld cloots and gruel to the likes of me.'

The archway lurched and the bell clanged. Cries and grunts and shrieks splintered their conversation and Sim dropped the crossbow and dragged out his sword, the blade of it dark with old stains and notched as a wolf's jaw, the end honed to a point thin enough to get between the slits of a barrelled heaume.

'A Sientcler,' he bellowed and leaped in long enough to stab and slash before losing his balance in the slither of it all and stumbling out again

'The bell,' said Hal, hearing it clang as the arch swayed. The English weight shoved the Scots back, their bared feet scoring ruts in the mud; they were almost at the sumpter cart now, almost pushed away from the narrow part of the bridge. Once that happened, the English would spill out right and left and numbers would do it.

The English sensed victory and the men in the rear ranks pushed relentlessly and started to sing, while the ones in front, crushed even of breath, lost consciousness and slid under the feet of the next rank.

Hal was aware of the sea of helmets and snarls, the great bristle of spears, as if some massive, maddened hedgepig was trying to crush itself under the arch – then he felt a hot burn in his calf, slipped to one knee and felt himself falling backwards, slashed wildly with the spear. Lying on the wet, smelling the fresh-turned earth like ploughland round Herdmanston, he saw the forest of straining legs and feet and the last splinters of wood uncurl slowly as the arch buckled.

Then the bell fell, smashing the front ranks of the battering English spearmen. The great, hollow boom of it drowned their screams.

There was a pause then, while thoughts and rain whirled with the dying echoes of the tolling bell. Hal, deafened and stunned like everyone else, felt himself hauled out and up, stared, mouth open, trying to make sense of the screaming and the dying, while the ranks of men washed away from where the bell had fallen.

Gloria, Hal saw and laughed like a grim wolf, for he knew what Bangtail Hob had seen – Gloria In Excelsis Deo, lovingly engraved along the slowly rocking bell's rim, now fluted with rivulets of blood and crushed bone.

'*Deus lo vult!*'

They all heard it and turned, fearing the worst. Up behind them came a rider, mailled top to toe, the pointed Templar cross blood-bright on a billowing white *camilis*, streaming behind him like a snow wind, another gracing the linen purity of the horse barding. Behind him came a handful of men on foot, grim in black tunics and hose and porridge-coloured, rust-streaked gambesons. Their rimmed iron hats were painted black, with white on the crown and the black cross of Christ on the front.

'*Deus lo vult!*' the knight bellowed, the words crushed and muffled inside the great, flat-topped barrel heaume. He thundered up past Hal and his pillar of Sim, while men scattered away from him. He circled his wrist with quick flick, so that the hammer in his armoured gauntlet, an elegance of gleaming steel with a fluted head and a pick on the other side, glittered like ice.

The great warhorse hardly balked at the splintered wreckage and the bell, leaping delicately over the first and round the second; a wounded man screamed as an iron hoof cracked his shins, others tried to scramble from underneath the delicately stepping beast.

The ranks on the bridge broke like a dropped mirror. They turned and ran and the knight rode them down, while the handful of men he brought charged, red mouths open, faces twisted in savage triumph. Bodies flew over the parapet of the bridge and crashed into the stream, others were bounced into the splintered planks and mashed with iron hooves, and, all the time, the arcing gleam of hammer swung right to left and back again; with every swing a head cracked like an egg.

Deus lo vult. God wills it, the cry from the time Jerusalem fell, a potage of vulgar Latin and French and Italian, the *lingua franca* everyone used to make themselves understood on crusade.

'Sir William,' Hal said dazedly.

'Blessed be his curly auld Templar pow,' Sim muttered and they looked at each other, heads down, hands on knees. Will Elliot was throwing up and Thom was dead; in the river, Dand turned and floated like a bloated sheep, while John the Lamb hauled himself, dripping, out of the other side. A cow bawled plaintively.

'Aye til the fore, then,' Sim said and Hal could only nod. Still alive. God had willed it. They almost laughed, but the great white knight reappeared, his horse high-prancing delicately over the debris and blood, the great helm tucked under his shielded arm, offering them a salute with the gore-clotted silver hammer.

His snowy robes and the horse's barding were spattered red, so that even the small cross over his heart seemed like a splash of gore; his face, framed by maille coif and the steel of a bascinet, was as blood-bright as the cross and sheened with sweat.

'I am thinking,' he said, as if remarking on the rain, 'that if ye shift, ye can gather up some of they kine and drive them across the bridge. I am thinking that the Templars of the Ton deserve a whole coo to themselves.'

Then he grinned out of the scarlet, streaming, grey-bearded face

'Best no stand like a set mill,' Sir William Sientcler added, 'for it is my opinion that this brig can no longer be held.'

'I am standing beside you there, Sir Will,' Sim declared and went off to fetch the sumpter horse. Hal stood on wobbling legs and looked up at the Templar knight.

'Timely,' he declared, then sagged. 'More than timely . . .'

'Ach,' Sir William said, his voice clearly alarmed that Hal was about to unman himself. 'I had a fancy to some beef.'

Beef, Hal thought, watching men sort out the mess, picking

their way back over the litter of corpses and blood-stained timbers, guddling in viscous muck for what they could plunder. All this was just for something to eat. He said as much aloud.

'*Ave Maria, gratia plena,*' Sim declared cheerfully, backing the horse between the cartshafts. 'And may the Lord God help us when all this starts to get serious.'

They left the bloody-wrapped body of Red Cloak Thom to be buried at Temple Ton, whose quiet, grim-faced warrior monks went about the gentle business of piously collecting, washing and burying the English they had so recently fought. Everyone, especially John the Lamb, was painfully aware that Dand had drifted far down the Annick, but took some comfort from the assurances that he would be found and decently buried.

'You will be in a peck of trouble for riding the Temple against King Edward,' Hal said to Sir William and the Master, a man in a black robe and the soft hat of a monk, with the hard eyes beneath hinting at how he had been a wet-mouthed, spear-wielding screamer not long before.

'We defended our Temple,' the Master declared. 'Crossing the bridge placed you on Commanderie ground and in our hospitality, so they have no-one to blame but themselves for attacking those under the protection of the Order.'

The soft-voiced Master, iron-grey beard like wool, bowed his neck to Sir William.

'It was fortunate that the Gonfanonier was present,' he said, and Hal heard the respect in his voice for the presence of one of the Order's Standard-Bearers.

'I will send money for the relief of Thom's soul,' Hal said awkwardly, but the Master shook his head.

'No need. We are entitled to the escheat of the slain, though we will restrict this to weapons and equipment, so that the personal items of these poor souls can be returned. Likewise the body of their leader – Sir John Furneval, was it? He shall be returned with all possessions, save for the warhorse.'

132

The Master smiled, a complex rearrangment of reluctant muscles; it never quite made it to his eyes.

'For two Poor Knights to ride,' he added and Hal thought it a jest and almost laughed; then he saw Sir William's sober, long-moustached face and swallowed the chuckle.

'*Ave Maria, gratia plena*,' Sir William said.

'Christ be praised,' answered the Master and blessed them both as they intoned, 'For ever and ever.'

'Anyway,' Sir William declared when he and Hal were moving out into the mirr again, 'all this is moot – I was coming to find ye, to let ye know that terms have been agreed.'

'Terms?' Hal muttered, only half-listening. He had seen the body of the English knight being lugged in, four men sweating with the weight of the man in his sodden clothing and armour. The face was a fretwork of shattered bone and flesh, fine as clergy lace.

'Aye,' Sir William went on cheerfully. 'Bruce and the rest are welcomed back into the community of the realm, lands intact – though Bruce is charged to appear at Berwick and Wishart stands surety for him. Douglas is taken into custody so that his wife and weans are not taken as hostage, though Bruce is still debating as to whether he will allow his wee daughter, Marjorie, to be held at the king's pleasure and surety for his future behaviour.'

He frowned and shook his head. 'As well he might. Wee mite is awfy young to be so caught up in this, so you can see the point of his arguing against it.'

Hal blinked. Terms.

'When?' he asked.

'Three . . . nay, I lie, four days since,' Sir William said, scowling at the bloodstains on his white robes.

Three or four days ago. This bloody mess had been pointless; the war was over.

'Aye, well,' Sir William said when Hal spat this out, bitter as bile, 'not quite, young Hal. Wallace is not included and is warmin' the ears of English from Brechin to Dundee and beyond. Bands of riders skite from the hills and woods, two or three long hundreds a time. They climb off their nags and proceed to the *herschip* with a will.'

The *herschip* Hal knew well enough – he had taken part in his share of those swift, burning raids for plunder and profit – but it seemed now that the army of the noble cause was inflicting it on the very people it was supposed to defend.

'This is true war,' Sir William said, pulling Hal round by the arm to stare into his face with watery-blue eyes, his grey-white beard twitching like a squirrel tail. 'Red war, Hal. Forget yer notions of chivalry – Wallace does what we did in the Holy Land against the heathen; ye scorch them, Hal. Ye leave them nothin' and then, when they are gaspin' with their tongues lollin' like hot wolves, their belts notched to the backbone, ye ride out and smack them into the dust.'

'You lost,' Hal answered savagely and Sir William blinked.

'To our shame and everlastin' stain, aye. Outremer's finest were too high and chivalric by hauf and the Saracen were fuller of guile,' he answered morosely. 'There will be another crusade, though, mark me.'

Until then there is here and there is Wallace – Hal said it aloud and Sir William shot him a look from under the snowed lintel of his brows.

'I am a Templar,' he replied piously, with a lopsided, hypocritical grin, 'and so cannot be involved.'

God help us if it gets serious, Sim had said. Hal shook his head. It was already past that and, despite having been negotiated back to land and grace, he could not feel sure that the stones of it were settled firmly.

Annick Water
Feast of St Swithun, July 1297

The fires were small, but a welcome warmth to the long hundreds of Scots huddled under rough shelters listening to the rain drift. In the dying light of a summer's day which had never been graced by much sun, the shadows brought chill and the men huddled, enduring and mournful, waiting for the moment when they could all go home, trailing after the lords who had finally agreed on a peace.

Bangtail Hob was more furious than mournful, for the bodies he had plundered the day before had turned out to have cheated him.

'Bloody hoor's by-blows, the lot,' he muttered again, a litany which those nearest now endured with an extra sink of the shoulders, as if hunching into more rain.

'Bloody crockards. Pollards.'

Hal and Sim exchanged looks and wry smiles. Soon Sim would have to have words with Bangtail before he rasped everyone raw, but there was a deal of sympathy for man stuck with crockards and pollards, debased foreign coinage now flooding the country thanks to English reforms a decade since. Silver light, they looked like sterling English money until you brought them close.

It was yet another layer of misery to spread on the death of Dand and Red Cloak Thom the day before and the gratitude of hungry men for beef only went a little way as salve. The army, if you could call it that, was now all Carrick men, for the other nobles had taken their forces and gone their separate ways, having promised to turn up at this or that English-held place and bring their sons, daughters or wives as surety for their future good conduct.

Douglas men were trailing homeward, fretted and furious at having seen The Hardy taken off. That was bad enough, Hal thought, but he had been told by those who witnessed it that Percy had insisted on chains and The Hardy had been bound in them, kicking and snarling; it had not been a pleasant sight.

Even Wishart had gone, leaving Bruce to argue out the last hard-wrung details with Percy, who had already sent triumphal messages south to King Edward and his grandfather, De Warenne, that the rebellion had been dealt with. Yet Clifford's forces were fumbling northwards, trying to bring Wallace to bay and having no luck.

Hal would leave, too, he had decided. Tomorrow, he said to himself. I have had enough of the community of the realm – let them kick spurs at each other like cocks battling for a dung-hill . . .

'Forty bloody days,' Bangtail announced bitterly, which was different enough to bring some heads up.

'Forty days?' John the Lamb repeated. 'Is that how long yon crockards and pollards last before turnin' into powrie mist?'

Men groaned; they had hoped to hear no more about the contents of Bangtail's dull-clinking purse.

'Rain,' Bangtail spat back scathingly.

'St Swithun's day if thou dost rain; for forty days it will remain,' he intoned.

'Christ's Bones,' said Red Rowan, scrubbing his autumn bracken head, 'you are a bowl of soor grue, man.'

'Aye, weel,' Bangtail muttered back sourly. 'I was thinkin' of Tod's Wattie, warm and fed and dry an' rattlin' the hot arse off that wee Agnes. I had some hopes for that quim, save that we were untimely torn apert.'

'Man, man,' said Will Elliot admiringly, 'Untimely . . . it is just like yon tale of the Knight and the Faerie. Ye ken – the yin where the Knight . . .'

'O God, who adorned the precious death of our most holy Father, Saint Benedict, with so many and so great privileges,' declared a sonorous voice in good English; it brought all heads round to where the silver-grey figure moved.

136

'Grant, we beseech You, that at our departure hence, we may be defended from the snares of the enemy by the blessed presence of him whose memory we celebrate. Through Christ our Lord. Amen.'

'Amen,' men muttered, crossing themselves.

'Christ be praised,' Sim offered.

'For ever and ever,' they all repeated.

The monk squatted by the fire and took his hands from the sleeves of the rough, grey-white habit. His cadaverous face, flooded with firelight, became a death's head of shadows.

'We have some meat,' Hal offered and the monk showed some teeth in a bearded smile.

'This is a meatless day, my son. I came to offer both blessing and advice.'

'The blessing is welcome,' Hal answered warily, expecting a sermon on the defilement of a meatless day; the rich smell of the roasting beef wafted betrayingly. The monk laughed softly from the depths of his cowl.

'The advice is this – the picket guard is one Fergus the Beetle,' the monk said. 'He is not one of God's sharpest tools, but honest and diligent. I fear, though, he is out of his depth with the visitors who have arrived at his post. He can understand only that your name was mentioned.'

He put his hands back in his sleeves and moved off, seeming to drift between the men, who crossed themselves humbly as he passed and tried to hide marrow bones. Sighing, Hal got up, looked at Sim and the pair of them went to find Fergus, the picket guard.

Fergus watched the company ahead of him closely, especially the rider with a face like a fat moon and the air of someone too close to the crotch of another's ancient hose. Fergus was from the north and, like all those men, disliked anyone from south of The Mounth ridge, who dressed peculiarly and spoke in ways hard for an honest man to understand. Further south than that, he knew, were men who scarcely warranted the

137

name, soft perfumed folk who curled their hair and spoke in strange ways.

Hal and Sim, coming up behind the guards, saw the huddle of kerns and the short, dark little man, made darker by the black wolf cap and pelt he wore over bits and pieces of maille and leather filched from dead enemies. The black, hardened leather jack he wore made him look like some beetle, newly surfaced from the forest mulch, but no-one would voice that; they all knew the killing reputation of Fergus and his men who came from north of The Mounth with all the strangeness that implied.

'Atweill than,' Fergus declared to the haughty rider, 'this wul dae brawlie. Gin ye haed spoke The Tongue at the verra stert, ye wad hae spared the baith o us aw this hatter. Tak tent ti whit Ah hae ti say an lippen ti me weill – ye maun bide ther until I lowse ye.'

The rider, mailled and coiffed, flung up his hands, so that wet drops flew up from his green-gloved fingers, and cursed pungently in French.

'I am Sir Gervaise de la Mare. Do you understand no language at all?'

'Ah prigg the blissin o the blue heivins on ye,' Fergus scowled back. 'There are ower mony skirrivaigin awhaurs, so bide doucelyke or, b'Goad's ane Wounds, Ah wul . . .'

'Fergus,' Hal said and the dark man fell back and turned, his black-browed face breaking into a wary grin.

'Yersel,' he greeted with about as much deference as he ever gave and then jerked his head contemptuously at the rider.

'This yin an' his muckle freends came sklimming the heich brae, aw grand an' skerlet and purpie. Luikin to spier you somewhiles.'

'You can understand this oaf?' demanded the rider. 'Thanks be to God – I seek one Hal of Herdmanston and would be obliged if you . . . him . . . anyone, would find him.'

'I am Sir Henry Sientcler of Herdmanston,' Hal declared

138

and Gervaise blinked once or twice from under his hooded riding cloak.

'You . . .' he began, then a rider moved from the shadows and laid a hand on his arm to silence him. Hal looked at this newcomer, sensible in brown and green though the cloth was quality. He had a long face made longer by the great droop of a wet moustache from his top lip and the washerwoman look of his arming cap, while his eyes were large and seal-soft.

'I am Sir Marmaduke Thweng,' he announced and Hal felt his eyebrows raise. The man did not, he said to himself, look like one of the foremost knights in Christendom. A walrus in mourning, perhaps, but not Sir Galahad.

'I have two folk to deliver safely,' Sir Marmaduke went on and offered a wan smile, the rain sliding off the length of his moustaches.

'Sir Gervaise is proud of his skills with foreign tongues,' he added, 'but seems to have met his match here.'

'Ye have not the Scots leid, then,' Sim scoffed, which was rich coming from him, since even he barely understood what Fergus was saying and Hal frequently lost track of it altogether.

Gervaise, wet and ruffled, drew himself up and tilted his nose even higher to look down it at Sim, who was not about to give the noble his due, with a 'my lord' and deferential bow.

'I speak Spanish to my wife, Latin to my God, French to my king, English to my mistress and German to my horse,' Gervaise declared, then leaned forward a little and smeared an ugly little smile across his face.

'I speak Scots only when I bark back at my dog.'

'Deliver your visitors, Sir Marmaduke,' Hal interrupted, feeling Sim start to struggle forward and barely held by an arm and Hal's command.

'Bigod,' Sim bellowed. 'Let me loose on him the bauchlin' wee . . .'

139

'Steady,' Hal interrupted harshly and Sim subsided, breathing like a mating bull. Hal turned to Thweng, whose mourn of a face had never altered.

'Take this wee papingo away before his feathers are plucked.'

'Only one visitor is for you,' Sir Marmaduke replied mildly and waved a hand. This brought up a palfrey and a small man on its back, hunched and dripping.

'This is one Bartholomew Bisset,' Sir Marmaduke said. 'He arrived without warning or writ in the English lines, saying he was bound for you and no other. Not even the Earl of Carrick, he says, to whom my other charge is due.'

Bisset? Hal knew the name but could not place it, and the wee fat man sat on the horse, drenched in rain and misery and silence. Then, out of the shadows, came a huge beast of a stallion that Hal knew well enough and his heart skipped. Sir Marmaduke's other charge.

Sitting on Balius, swathed in a dark cloak, Isabel, Countess of Buchan offered Hal a weary smile.

Bruce was with Kirkpatrick in his panoply, a sodden flap of red and white sail canvas reeking of old mildew, wet wool and stale sweat. It was scattered with a discard of hose, boots, maille *chausse,* and a squire worked furiously at ridding good leather boots of water stains.

'The Comyn is out,' Bruce had said to Kirkpatrick and did not need to add anything. The Lord of Badenoch, kin to Buchan, had clearly been sent back north from Edward's Flanders-borne army to help bring Moray's rebellion to heel. Though all of that branch were known as Red Comyns because of their shield colours, the Lord of Badenoch was called John the Black as a grim joke on both his demeanour and his implacablity.

His return to Scotland meant that all the disgraced and dispossessed enemies of the Bruces had been restored to their rights and Kirkpatrick could almost hear Bruce's teeth grind on it. It was as well, he thought, that we were all bound for Lochmaben and some comfort, else The Bruce's bottom lip would trip him every time he stepped.

There was a noise from outside and a guard stuck his wet head inside.

'A knight, my lord. Sir Marmaduke Thweng . . .'

Bruce was on his feet even before the man stepped through the flap on to the wooden boards.

'Sir Emm,' he bellowed.

'Sir R,' Thweng replied, grinning. It came out as 'sirra', which was the jest in the piece, and they both growled like delighted dancing bears as they hugged and slapped.

'Bigod, it is fine to see you,' Bruce exclaimed. 'When was the last time we met?'

'Feast of Epinette,' Thweng replied. 'The tourney at Lille four years ago. You did that trick of facing a fully armed knight on a palfrey and daring him to hit you. Fine feat of horsemanship — but you were young then and reckless. Besides, they were all full of the French Method at Lille that year.'

'Ha,' Bruce roared back. 'The German Method will always defeat it.'

Kirkpatrick sat quietly and if he thought anything of being ignored it never showed in his face. In fact, he was so used to being overlooked that he was actually trying to recall what the French and German Methods were — and smiled when he remembered. A tourney style of fighting, the French Method involved training a warhorse to run full tilt and bring an opponent down by sheer momentum of horse and rider. The German was to use the dexterity of a much lighter horse to avoid such a rush, wheel round and reach the opponent before he could re-engage.

Thweng accepted the wine a squire brought him and sat, shoving aside a puddle of clothing. He looked pointedly at the smiling Kirkpatrick and Bruce waved one hand.

'My man, Kirpatrick of Closeburn,' he announced. 'Kirkpatrick, this is Sir Marmaduke Thweng of Kilton. He is kin — a cousin by marriage, is it? More than that, a friend from the tourney circuit.'

'My lord,' Kirkpatrick replied softly, with a short bow. 'Your reputation goes before you.'

Thweng nodded and sipped, while Kirkpatrick showed nothing on his face at all. More than a mere landless Bachelor knight of the household, Thweng thought as he studied the man. Less than a friend.

'What brings you forth from Yorkshire, Sir Emm?' asked Bruce.

'I bring greetings from your father in Carlisle,' Sir Marmaduke said and watched Bruce's face grow cold, though he managed a stiff nod of acknowledgement and thanks. Thweng drank and said nothing more on the subject, though there was a lot more he could say — Bruce the Father had spat and snarled like a wet cat and the pith of it was not what his son had done but that he had dared to do it at all. This was the first time young Bruce had acted for himself in matters of the Kingdom and it would not, Thweng knew, be the last.

'I am off to Berwick from here,' Thweng said and looked sideways up at Bruce. 'Edward is no fool. He in no wise believes Percy's assurances that the north is safe, but has held it up to the others so he can get the army off to Flanders to fight the French. However, he has kicked the Earl of Surrey off his estates to come up with another army to finish this Wallace off. I daresay the Scots are unimpressed by an old man who complains of the cold in his bones when he comes north — but come he now must and Treasurer Cressingham waits impatiently in Roxburgh. Ormsby is in Berwick, telling all who will listen about how he fought like a lion to escape the clutches of the infamous Wallace at Scone.'

'A tale of marvels, for sure,' Kirkpatrick offered wryly, and Sir Marmaduke smiled.

'I hear he ran out of a window,' he said and had it confirmed by a nod. Thweng laughed, shaking his long head.

'The wolves gather, then,' Bruce said moodily. None more ravening than Edward himself, the Faerie mist of him drifting steadily, mercilessly northward like a pall. Longshanks, Bruce thought, will not be pleased at having this Scots boil erupt on his kingdom's neck and still remain unlanced. His interests are in France – further still, if truth be told, in the Holy Land.

Yet he was old and such temper was not good for an old man . . .

'How is the English Justinian these days? Choleric as ever?'

Sir Marmaduke smiled at the new name given to King Edward, only half in scathing jest, as he rampaged through the laws of the land creating and remaking them to suit himself as he went. It was not, Thweng was sure, anything approaching the legendary codifying of the Roman emperor.

'Liverish,' he replied diplomatically. 'The wool business has caused him problems as you might imagine, while he will not debase the sterling coinage against all the crockards and pollards from abroad. That decision, at least, is a good one.'

Bruce stroked his beard – in need of trim, Thweng noted – and pouted, thinking. The wool business – seizing the entire country's output on the promise to pay for it later – had caused most of the dissent in Scotland, mainly because it was Cressingham as Treasurer who had ordered the Scots to conform to it and no-one believed his promises of future payment, never mind Edward's. The profit from it had been eaten by armies for all the wars King Edward seemed to embroil England in and his own barons were growing tired of it. Wishart's timing had not been out by much, Bruce realised.

'The Jew money will have run out,' he mused and Thweng nodded. The Jews of England had been summarily thrown

143

out of the country not long since and all their assets taken for the Crown – again, eaten by armies.

'At least you are returned to the loving grace of the English Justinian,' Thweng declared, 'so proving that you are not so reckless as the youth I traded lances with at Lille.'

'Just so,' Bruce replied and Kirkpatrick saw his eyes narrow a little, for he could sense a chill wind blowing from Sir Marmaduke. When it came, it was pure frost.

'I also came bringing a visitor,' Thweng went on, savouring the wine. 'One who asked for you particularly. Before I deliver your guest, let me once again congratulate you on maturing into a man and leaving the furious, reckless boy behind.'

Now the hairs on Kirkpatrick's arms were bristled and you could stand a cup on the thrust of Bruce's bottom lip.

'You will do right by this guest,' Thweng declared, leaning forward and lowering his voice. 'The sensible course. You will know what it is.'

He rose, idly tossed the empty cup to a frantically scrabbling squire, then stuck his head out of the tent flap. When he drew back, Isabel entered.

Bruce saw her, the hood of her cloak drawn back to reveal the copper tangle of her hair, the damp twisting it tighter still, the eyes bright and round, blue as sky and feverish – he thought – with longing.

He was, as ever, wrong. The wet had soaked her to the bone and the long ride on Balius had made her weary to the marrow, yet none of that had dented the hope she felt, the hope that blazed from her eyes.

His face shattered it.

She saw him blink and, in the instant before he spread a great, welcoming smile on it, saw the flickers of annoyance and irritation chase each other like hawk and heron across it. It had been forlorn hope, of course and she had known it in the core of her. Love was not anything deep between them but she had hoped for a better affection than what she saw.

He would not take her into the safety of his arms, his castle and away from Buchan, and the weight of that descended on her.

She had taken her chance on the road back to Buchan, knowing that her refuge at Balmullo was probably gone from her, that she would be cloistered in some lonely Keep until such time as arrangement were made to cloister her somewhere more holy and uncomfortable. The aching memory of the bruises and angry lust Buchan had inflicted added urgency to her escape; getting away from the oiled skin-crawl of Malise only sauced the affair.

Yet it was all for nothing – Bruce would not help. Even as it crushed her, she cursed herself for having given in to the foolishness of it. There had been similar in her life – an older knight and, after him, the ostler boy, neither of whose names she could remember. All she recalled was the delicious anguish, the laborious subterfuge to be in that part of the world at the same time as they were. The smile to be treasured, the fingertip touch that thrilled, the sticky paste in a pot that was valued simply because his fingers had touched it.

She had, she remembered, thought such tender secrets were her own, hugged them to herself because of that fact alone – with a murdered father and all her other kin seemingly uncaring, it was a slim path picked through thorns to the vague promise of a distant garden.

Only her old nurse had noted it all and the truth of it came out later – too late, when Trottie lay, dying slowly and gasping out her last secrets. Then there was shared laughter over the wonder and worry of a nurse confused by her charge's seemingly bad fetlocks that needed such a pot of evil-smelling ointment.

The self-inflicted pain of it, married to the pleasure, had been a game. You need suffer only as much as you need and the promise of something real a finger-length away was an awareness that grew less innocent the closer you approached to it.

When it came to losing that innocence, she knew what to do with it and put away, she thought, the foolishness of love.

Until Bruce. Until she dared hope for the distant promise of that garden.

Even as she stepped into the sun of that smile, she felt the hope shred away, like a mist before a cold wind, and it made her sag against the length of him so that, for him, it felt like a flirting.

Over her head, Bruce looked at Thweng's long mourn of a face and knew now what the knight had meant – Isabel had to be returned, quietly and without fuss, to her husband.

There had been a time when she helped salve the loss of his wife, Marjorie's mother, and the thrill of bedding her and cuckolding his enemy had been heady. Now the first was palling and the second was, as Thweng had hinted, too much of a risk in awkward times.

He nodded and Thweng returned it. Isabel felt his chin move on the top of her head and almost wept.

'It was her right enow, eh?' Sim growled, hunched up with a corner of cloak over his head and the drips sliding along it like bright pearls. Beside him, the exhausted Bartholomew Bisset snored and they could do nothing with him until he woke, that was clear.

Hal and Sim now knew who he was, for he had managed to get that out, voice slurred with fatigue – Ormsby's scrivener and notary, the one Wallace had sworn to find and the signature on the documents pertaining to the mason's death.

Hal had almost forgotten about the entire affair and the arrival of Bisset was an amazement in more than one way – he been sent on his way under a writ from Wallace that promised, in return for his life, that he put his tale at the disposal of Sir Henry Sientcler of Herdmanston. When the said Sir Henry was satisfied and quit him of his obligation, Notary Bisset was free to go.

146

'I am told to speak to you and no-one else, not even The Bruce,' the fat little man had said, swaying with weariness and drenched to the bone. 'I beg you – let me sleep before you put me to the question.'

Sim had been astounded, but Hal had more than a touch of admiration, both for Wallace's unshakeable trust in certain folk and the fact that the little scrivener, who could simply have run off, seemed to have more chivalric honour in his butter-barrel body than any of the nobles who had spent weeks here haggling like horse-copers.

'It was her, for sure,' Sim repeated, dragging Hal away from studying the sleeping Bisset.

Hal said nothing. It had been her. Run away yet again and come straight to The Bruce. He felt a sharpness in him at that thought and quelled it viciously. Stupid, he thought, to go rutting after an earl's leman. It was only what old Barnabus, the local priest, had said would happen – time had healed over the scars of his wife and woken his loins.

Any lass with her clothes inside out, as the law demanded of whores, would do, he thought viciously, while the nag of Isabel, Countess of Buchan, fern-tendrilled hair dripping like wet autumn bracken, blue eyes weary, her smile still warm on his face, all made the dreich of this place even harder to bear.

That and Bisset, who snored softly, each one a tearing nag at Hal's heart, for he sounded like wee John when he slept. Well, his son slept now and made no sound at all. Slept forever . . .

Christ, Hal thought savagely, can matters get worse?

'Sir Hal. Sir Hal.'

The voice brought their heads round and they stared in wonder at the pair, lurching out of the dark, propelled by the stiff, haughty Sir Gervaise.

'More little barking dogs,' the knight said and pulled the head of his mount round and away. Hal stared at Tod's Wattie, the Dog Boy a shadowed skelf close behind, hugging himself against the rain.

'Christ's Bones,' Tod's Wattie bellowed, 'am ah glad to see ye. Ye will nivver ken whit has happened.'

CHAPTER FIVE

Roxburgh Castle
Feast of the Transfiguration of Christ, August 1297

A groan; the coverlet stirred. Ralph de Odingesseles waited warily with tunic, judging tenor and temper before stepping forward to the half-asleep figure who rolled over in a rustle of straw and feather mattress to sit upright, blinking, on the edge of the canopied box bed.

Ralph moved to a covered pitcher of heated water, which he poured into a basin and brought forward. He discreetly handed his master a gilded pot and watched it vanish beneath his night-shirt; water splashed and Ralph stood patiently holding the basin, a towel and a clean tunic draped over either forearm; his master grunted, groaned and cocked one buttock to let out a squeaky fart.

Yawning, Hugh Cressingham handed the chamberpot back to Ralph, dabbed water from the basin on his face and his close-cropped head, then dried his meaty jowls on the presented towel. Slowly, he woke up and blinked into a new day.

Ralph de Odingesseles watched him, dispassionate but cautious – Cressingham was not tall, running to fat, had eyes

149

that bulged like a fish and his cheeks were stubbled because a skin complaint made it painful to pumice off a beard and irritating to grow one. Nor did he keep his hair fashionably neck length and curled, as Ralph did – Cressingham paid lip service to his prebendery stipends by affecting the look of a monk, though untonsured, and that left him with a hairstyle like an upturned bird's nest.

He seemed, in his crumpled white nightserk, as bland as plain frumenty, but Ralph de Odingesseles knew the temper that smouldered in the man, stoked by pride and envy.

By the time Cressingham was in tunic, hose and a cote embroidered with the – as yet unregistered – swans he claimed as his Arms, the whole sorry mess of life had descended on him afresh and Ralph de Odingesseles, coming forward with the *gardecorps*, was more cautious still. Experience had taught him that the storms forming on Cressingham's brow usually resulted in a sore ear, which was the lot of a squire, he had discovered.

Sufferance, on the other hand, was better than the alternative for the son of a poor noble. Ralph de Odingesseles's only claim to fame was that he was related to an archdeacon and his grandfather had been a well-known knight on the Tourney circuit, who had once been beaten into dented metal by the then king's French half-brother, Sir William de Valence.

Eventually, Ralph would be made a knight and take no blows he would not return. The thought made him forget himself and smile.

Cressingham looked sourly at the smirking squire holding the *gardecorps*. The garment was elegant and in the new shade of blue which was so admired by the French king that he had adopted it as his colour. Not diplomatic, Cressingham thought, and made a mental note never to wear it in the presence of Longshanks.

He did not much want to wear it at all and, in truth, hated

the garment, for the same reason he was forced to wear it – he was fat and it hid the truth of it. It was, he knew, not his own fault, for he was more of an administrator than a warrior, but you did not get knighted for tallying and accounts, he thought bitterly, for all the king's admiration and love of folk who knew the business.

As always, there was the moment of savage triumph at what he had become, despite not being one of those mindless thugs with spurs – Treasurer of Scotland, even though it was a Gods-cursed pisshole of a country, was not only a powerful position, but an extremely lucrative one.

As ever, this exultant moment was followed by a leap of utter terror that the king should ever discover just how lucrative; Cressingham closed his eyes at the memory of the huge tower that was Edward Plantagenet, the drooping eyelid that gave him a sinister leer, the soft lisping voice and the great, long arms. He shuddered. Like the grotesque babery carved high up under cathedral eaves and just as unpredictably vicious as those real apes.

He slapped Ralph de Odingesseles for it, for the smirk, for Edward's drooping eye and this Pit-damned brigand Wallace and for having to wait in this pestilential place for the arrival of De Warenne, the Earl of Surrey.

He slapped the other ear for the actual arrival of De Warenne, the hobbling old goat complaining of the cold and his aches and the fact that he had been trying to retire to his estates, being too old for campaigning now.

Cressingham had no argument with this last and slapped Ralph again because De Warenne had not had the decency to die on his way north with the army, thus leaving Cressingham the best room in Roxburgh, with its fire and clerestory.

Worst of all, of course, was the mess all this would leave – and the cost. Gods, the cost . . . Edward would balk at the figures, he knew, would want his own inky-fingered clerks

151

poring over the rolls. There was no telling what they might unveil and the thought of what the king would do then almost made Cressingham's bowels loosen.

Ralph de Odingesseles, trying not to rub his ears, went to the kist in the corner and fetched out a belt with dagger, purse and Keys, the latter the mark of Cressingham's position as Treasurer, designed to elicit instant respect.

Like most such observances, the truth was veiled, like statues of the Lady on her Feast Days; everyone knew the Scots called Cressingham the 'Tracherer' and you did not need to know much of the barbaric tongue to know it meant 'Treacherer' and was a play on his title.

Yet he was also the most powerful in Scotland, simply because he held the strings of the purse Ralph now handed him.

He helped fasten on the belt, then adjusted his master's arms in the sleeves of the long, loose *gardecorps*; Cressingham consoled himself with the fact that at least his *gardecorps* was refined. No riotous colours here, no gold dagging along the hem, or long slits up the sides, or three-foot tippets. Plain black, with russet *vair* round the sleeves and neck, as befitted someone of probity and dignity.

'I will break fast now,' Cressingham said and Ralph de Odingesseles nodded, took a step back and bowed.

'The Seneschal is here. Brother Jacobus also.'

Cressingham frowned and swallowed a curse – couldn't they at least let him wake up and eat a little? He waved his page away to fetch food and told him to let the Seneschal in, then went to brood at the shuttered window, peering through the cracks rather than open it to the breeze – even in August it was cold. Outside, the river flowed, gleaming as quicksilver and he took comfort from the Teviot on one side and the Tweed on the other, so that the castle seemed to sail on a sea, a boat-shaped confection in stone.

Roxburgh was a massive, thick-walled fortress with four towers and a church within the walls. Cressingham's room was on a corner of the main Keep overlooking the Inner Bailey and, because of that, had a proper window of leaded glass rather than the shuttered arrow slits that faced the outside. The other sides of his room bordered on a corridor, so there were no windows at all, which made it dim and dark. Not for the first time, Cressingham thought of the light-flooded solar tower and its magnificent floor tiles, where De Warenne had installed himself.

A polite cough turned him and the Seneschal, Frixco de Fiennes, stood, waiting patiently in his sober browns and greens.

'Christ be praised,' Frixco de Fiennes said and Cressingham grunted.

'For ever and ever,' he responded automatically. 'What problems have surfaced this early in the day?'

Frixco had been up for several hours and all the lesser folk of the castle hours before that. Half the day was gone as far as Frixco was concerned and he had already dealt with most of the castle's problems – the cook needing the day's salt and spices, the Bottler warning that immediate ale stocks were low and small beer lower still.

The other problems he had no answer for were worse – supplies for the 10,000 men currently filtering through Berwick and heading this way, the timber to the workmen scaffolding the Teviot wall in order for minor repairs to be done, men to make spears and quarrels and bows. Where grain for bread was to come from, or fodder for animals, or bedding for horse and hound.

'The world turns, Treasurer,' he replied. He should properly have addressed Cressingham as Lord but that was a step too far for the fine-bred Frixco de Fiennes, who was brother to the Warden here. Frixco, however, was not brave, or clever. He should have gone to the Church but liked women too much even to suffer the slight restriction priesthood would place on his whoring – the thought of the splendid Mattie down at the Murdoch's Tavern in the town tightened his groin so much he almost bent over, convinced it could be seen.

Seneschal here was perfect, for it let him use his skills in tallying and reading and writing in English, French and Latin while leaving him free to plough whatever furrows he could find.

He laid out the problems as Ralph de Odingesseles returned with bread and dishes of mutton, pork and fish. The squire poured watered wine and Frixco stood while Cressingham chewed and swallowed, toying absently with the bread as he walked to the shuttered window and, finally, opened it to the day. Behind him, sly as a mouse, Ralph filched slices of meat and fish, popping it in his mouth at once and ignoring the frowning Frixco.

There was Stirling, one of the main fortresses still held by England. Frixco meticulously listed the castle stores there – 400 barrels of beer, four of honey, 300 of fat, 200 sides of beef, pork and tongue, a single barrel of butter, 10 each of pickled meat and herring, seven of cod, 24 strings of sausages, two barrels of salt and 4,000 cheeses.

'Enough for six to eight months,' Frixco de Fiennes ended, 'given that the garrison is not large. I have assumed that the townsfolk will seek sanctuary within.'

'If we do not succour the town?' Cressingham asked and the Seneschal looked astonished at the very idea of not taking in Stirling's desperate. That was the purpose of the castle, one of the three such purposes fortresses were designed for. One was as a base for the destruction of enemies, the second was the succour of guests and pilgrims and people in their charge and the third was to stamp the authority of the king on the area.

Frixco de Fiennes said nothing, all the same, for he knew that Stirling should have had stores for two years, but complacency and greed had corroded that. In the end, Cressingham gave up expecting a reply.

'The townspeople of Stirling must work if they wish the

protection of the fortress,' Cressingham declared. 'Make it clear to them that rations will be given to those who volunteer for service.'

Frixco duly made a note, tongue between his teeth, juggling parchment and quill and the ink pot hung round his neck, though he knew Cressingham only did this because the commander at Stirling was Fitzwarin, a relative of the Earl of Surrey.

Frixco had already delivered lists to Cressingham regarding Roxburgh itself, which should have made it clear to the man how unlikely it was that any castle in Scotland could fully equip enough townspeople – Roxburgh had 100 iron helmets, 17 maille tunics cut for riding, seven pairs of metal gauntlets, two sets of vambrace and a single cuisse. What use a solitary thigh guard? Frixco wondered. And if one was found – what use a one-legged knight?

'My lord.'

Ralph was back, announcing that the Earl of Surrey and Sir Mamaduke Thweng were in the main hall, awaiting Cressingham's pleasure. Brother Jacobus had joined them.

The scathe of it lashed Cressingham, so that he scowled. My pleasure, indeed. He was tempted to let them wait – two tottering old warhorses, he thought viciously, though he had to temper that in Sir Marmaduke's case, since he was younger than De Warenne by a decade or more and still held a formidable reputation as a chivalric knight. Muttering, he swept from his room.

The three sat at the high table benches in the huge hall, misted with faint blue smoke from badly lit fires and empty but for De Warenne, Sir Marmaduke and Brother Jacobus, Cressingham's chaplain from the Ordo Praedicatorum.

Before Cressingham had even slippered his way across the flagged floor, Frixco scuttling behind him, he could hear De Warenne's complaints, saw that Thweng stared ahead, forearms on the table, and with the air of a man shouldering through a snowstorm while Brother Jacobus, piously telling his rosary, listened without seeming to listen.

'Plaguey country,' the Earl of Surrey was saying, then broke off and looked up at Cressingham with watery, violet-rimmed eyes.

'Here you are at last, Treasurer,' he snapped. 'Did you plan to sleep all day?'

'I have been busy,' Cressingham fired back, stung by his tone. 'Trying to sort out the feeding and equipping of this rabble you have brought, claiming it to be an army.'

'Rabble, sirra? Rabble . . .'

De Warenne bristled. His trimmed white beard was shaped into a curve and pointed; with his round arming cap he looked like some old Saracen, Cressingham thought.

'Good *nobiles*,' chided Brother Jacobus and the soft voice stilled everything. De Warenne muttered, Sir Marmaduke went back to staring at nothing and Cressingham almost smiled, though he resisted the triumph of it, for fear the priest would notice. *Domini canes* – God's Dogs – folk called the Order of Preachers, but not to their face, since they had been given the papal permission to preach the Word and root out heresy, a wide and sinister writ.

Now this bland-faced little man sat in his frosting of habit and jet *cappa*, the over-robe that gave them yet another name, Black Friars. He let the polished rosewood beads slip, sibilant as whispers, through his fingers.

Shaven and washed so clean his face seemed to shine like a white rose, Jacobus was, Cressingham knew, using the rosary as a pointed reminder to everyone that this was the Thursday of the Transfiguration of Christ, one of the days of Luminous Mystery. He also knew those beads were just as easily used to tally and list in the service of the Treasurer; if Jacobus was a hound of God, Cressingham thought, then he is kennelled at my command – though it would be prudent to check his chain now and then.

The beads, click-clicking through the friar's smooth fingers, brought tallying surging back to Cressingham.

'Gascons,' he declared viciously, startling De Warenne out of a slump so suddenly he could not form a response; the air hissed out of the Earl and he gobbled like a chicken.

'Three hundred crossbows from Gascony,' Cressingham went on accusingly. 'Now more than half have no crossbows.'

'Ah,' said De Warenne. 'The carts. Missing. Lost. Strayed.'

'It was the Earl of Surrey's quite proper military decision,' Sir Marmaduke said suddenly, his voice a slice across them both, 'to relieve the march burden on the Gascons by loading their equipment on wagons. After all, they were not to need it until Berwick, at least – unless your reports were misleading about the extent of the rebel problem and it was possible to have encountered this huge ogre Wallace somewhere around York.'

Cressingham opened and closed his mouth. De Warenne barked a short laugh.

'Ogre,' he repeated. 'I am told he is as large as Longshanks – what say you to that, eh, Cressingham? As big as the king?'

Cressingham did not take his eyes from the long-faced Thweng. Like a mile of bad road in England – or two miles of good in Scotland, he thought.

'What I say, my lord Earl,' he said, biting the words off as if they had been dipped in aloes, 'is that you claim some eight hundred horse and ten thousand foot on the rolls. If they are all as good as your Gascons, we may as well quit this land now.'

'Equip them with new,' De Warenne snapped back, waving one hand. 'Make 'em if you have none in stores.'

'We have sixty crossbows only here,' Frixco murmured.

'Make 'em bowmen then – one is as good as the other.'

'We have some fifteen thousand arrows, my lord,' Frixco declared humbly, 'but only one hundred bows.'

'Then make the damned crossbows,' bellowed De Warenne.

157

'Ye have wood and string, d'ye not? Folk who know the way of it?.

Cressingham's jowls quivered, but he closed his mouth with a click as Jacobus cleared his throat.

'If it please you, Lord Earl,' the friar said, 'we are short on sturgeon heads, flax threads and elk bones.'

De Warenne blinked. He knew flax was used in the making of the bowstrings, but had no idea why a crossbow needed elk bones or, God's Wounds, sturgeon heads. All he knew of crossbows was that the lower orders could use them without much training. He roared this out, to the satisfaction of the smirking Cressingham.

'One is for the sockets,' Brother Jacobus explained quietly to the Earl. 'The sturgeon heads supply a certain elasticity not found from any substitute.'

De Warenne waved a scornful, dismissive hand.

'What do you know, priest? Other than one of your old Councils banned the thing.'

'Canon 29 of the Second Lateran,' Cressingham offered haughtily.

'I understood,' Sir Marmaduke said, his lips curled in what might have been a wry smile or a sneer. 'that it was a ban only on foolish marksmanship. Shooting apples from heads and such. A ban on that seems sensible enough.'

Brother Jacobus nodded unctiously.

'Even if it had been an entire ban,' he replied, 'such would not apply to use against unbelievers – Moor and Saracen and the like. Happily, English bishops have declared the Scots rebels excommunicate, which means we may use these anathema weapons freely.'

'Unhappily,' Thweng replied dryly, 'I believe Scotch bishops have excommunicated us, which means the rebels can point them our way, too. The Pope is silent on the matter.'

Jacobus looked at Thweng. It was a look that had seldom failed to make folk quail, combining, as it did, displeasure and pious pity. Sir Marmaduke merely stared back at him, eyes blank and glassed as the black friar's beads.

Sturgeon bones, De Warenne thought wildly. God's Wounds, this whole enterprise could fall because we don't have enough fish heads.

Men and food, the endless problem since armies had started marching. De Warenne felt the crushing weariness of it all – the whole business of this pestilential country was a clear message that Longshanks had displeased God and He had turned His Wrath on them. More to the point, De Warenne thought sourly, Longshanks has displeased the likes of me and, one day soon, I will turn my wrath on him, together with all the other lords fretting under the divine right.

Yet the king was not the throne and De Warenne, Earl of Surrey would defend that to the death. His grandfather had been uncle to the Lionheart himself, his father had been Warden of the Cinque Ports and every De Warenne had been a bulwark against the foes of God, for whoever attacked the throne of England assaulted God Himself. John De Warenne, Earl of Surrey, Warden of Scotland, would hold His Fortress against all the rebel scum of the earth.

The thought drew him up a little, even as a cold wind curled the length of the hall, stirring the smoke into swirls and eddies.

Strike north. Find this Wallace and cut him down shorter than Longshanks, so that the king would be pleased with his earl at that. The thought made De Warenne bark out a laugh.

'Then there are the Welsh,' Cressingham declared and De Warenne looked at him with a curled lip. Like a fly, he thought, buzz-buzzing in the ear. One good slap . . .

'What of the Welsh?' Sir Marmaduke asked and watched as Cressingham fussily arranged his blue robe – bad choice of colour for a pasty man, Thweng thought – and imperiously waved at some distant servant. An instant later a man slouched through the far door from the kitchen and across the floor to be eyed up and down. He studied them back from a face dark as an underground dwarf, black-eyed and challenging.

A fist of a face, the beard on it cropped to stubble, but with a great gristle of moustache, as if some giant black caterpillar had crawled under his nose. Cheekbones like knobs and a single scowl of eyebrow — typical Welsh, Sir Marmadule thought, from the south, where the archers are, for the north are mainly spearmen. He said so and De Warenne nodded. Cressingham pouted and scowled.

'Look at him,' he said, quivering. 'Look at what he is wearing.'

Not much, Sir Marmaduke thought — a ragged linen tunic in a distant memory of red, a great shock of dark hair like a sprout of bush on a rock. Nothing on his legs but his bare feet, though there were shoes hung round his neck. He had a leather bracer on one arm, a bow the same size as himself in a bag of some strange-looking leather and a soft bag of the same hanging from one side of a belt, a long, wicked-looking sheathed knife from the other.

In the bag at his hip were arrows, though they were all neatly separated by leather to keep the fletchings from fouling, and the way the bag swung told Sir Marmaduke that it had damp clay shaped to the bottom of it, to prevent the points bursting through.

Across the powerful shoulders, one humped slightly as if he was deformed, hung a long roll and fall of rough wool fabric which had been russet-brown once and was now just dark.

'A Welsh archer,' Sir Marmaduke said, 'with bow, a dozen good arrows and a knife. The thing round his shoulders is a called a *brychan* if I am not mistaken. Serves as cloak and bed both.'

'Well, you would know that, certes,' Cressingham declared with a sneer, 'since you have spent a deal of your life fighting such. No help in present cirumstances, mark me.'

160

'Is there a point to this, Treasurer?' De Warenne sighed. Cressingham made a show of plucking a paper from Frixco's fingers.

'Item,' he said. 'Welsh archer, *cap-a-pied*, with a warbow of yew, one dozen goose-fletched arrows, a sword and a dagger.'

He thrust the paper back at Frixco.

'This is what is being paid for from the Exchequer,' he declared triumphantly. 'And this is what I expect for the price. *Cap-a-pied*. Which means one hat of iron, one coat of war, either maille or a leather jack, studded for preference. One sword. One yew bow and a dozen finest shafts. That is what is being paid for and that is what we do not have. This man is a ragged-arsed peasant with stick and string, no more.'

Addaf had followed a deal of it, despite their being English, for that tongue was now heard more and more in Wales and it was a sensible man who learned it and spoke it well. Then, he thought, they turn round and speak an even stranger tongue, the French, which wasn't even their own but belonged to the people they were fighting. Among others.

He had listened quietly, too, for it was also a sensible man who realised that fighting against these folk was now old and done, though the defeat in it was still a raw wound no more than a handful of years gone. Yet taking their money to fight with them was almost as good a revenge for Builth and the loss of Llewellyn and better than starving in the ruin war had made of the valleys.

Yet peasant was too hard for a man of those same valleys to bear.

'I am Addaf ap Dafydd ap Math y Mab Lloit Irbengam,' he growled in English, 'and no peasant with an arse of rags.'

He saw the look on them, the same as the look on folk's faces when they had seen the two-headed calf at the fair the year he had left. The fat one looked bemused.

'Do. You. Speak. English?' this one demanded, leaning

forward and talking as if Addaf was a child. The tall one with the long face, the one pointed out as having fought Welsh once, twitched the mourn of his moustaches into a brief smile.

'You are annoying a Welshman, Treasurer,' he said, 'for English is what he is already speaking.'

Addaf saw the fat one bristle like an old boar sow.

'His name,' Sir Marmaduke explained, speaking English, both clear and slow, Addaf noted, so that everyone would understand, 'means Addaf son of David, son of Madog, though the last part confuses me a little – The Brown Lad With The Wrong Head?'

He knew the Welsh – Addaf took to this Sir Marmaduke at once, for he had once been a bold adversary and he knew the Welsh a little and the English as spoken by True People; Addaf heaved a sigh of relief.

'Dark and stubborn, I am after believing it is in your own tongue,' he said and added 'Lord,' because it did no harm to mark the trail of matters politely.

'I am from the *gwely* of Cilybebyll,' he explained earnestly, so that these folk would know with whom they dealt. 'I have a cow and enough grazing land to feed eight goats for a year. I am a free man of the True People, by the grace of God, sharing an ox, a goad, a halter and a ploughshare with three others in common. I am not a serf with ragged arse.'

'Did you understand any of that?' Cressingham demanded waspishly. Sir Marmaduke turned slowly to him.

'You have offended him, it appears. In my experience, Cressingham, it does no good to offend a Welshman. Particularly bowmen – see you the shoulder? That hump is pulling muscle, Treasurer. Addaf here has some twenty-odd summers on him and I'll warrant at least seventeen of them have been used to train with that bow until he can pull the string on one taller than a well-made man and thick as a boy's wrist, all the way back to his ear. The arrows, I will avow, are an ell at least and are fletched, not with goose, but with peacock, which means they are his finest. This man can put such a shaft through an oak church door at a hundred paces and then another ten or so of its cousins within the minute. If he does his job aright, he will not need iron hat or studded jack or maille – all his enemies will be dead in front of him.'

He broke off and stared fixedly at Cressingham, who did not like the look of him nor of the scowling black-faced Welshman.

'Christ be praised,' murmured Brother Jacobus and crossed himself into the twist of Addaf's smile.

'For ever and ever,' they intoned – Addaf louder than the rest, just so the crow of a priest would get the point.

'I would take our Welshman as is, Treasurer,' Sir Marmaduke added gently, 'and be glad of it.'

'Just so,' De Warenne added and thumped the table. 'Now, Treasurer, you can carry on doing what you do best – scribbling and tallying up how to get my army, well fed and in good humour, to where I can meet this Wallace Ogre and defeat him.'

Sir Marmaduke watched Addaf the Welshman slap barefoot back across the flags, dismissed with barely controlled fury by Cressingham, who now closed his head with the Black Friar and his ink-fingered clerk. De Warenne, hugging himself in his cloak, fell back on complaint.

It was bad enough, Sir Marmaduke thought wearily, that the pair of them were in charge of this *battue* without there being a Wallace at the other end of it.

Blind Tam's tavern, near Bothwell
Feast of the Transfiguration of Christ, August 1297

He came down on the road on a tired horse, hood up and cloak swaddling him. The horse was being nagged on and did not like it much, balking now and then, tugging Malise's arm and stumbling. It was no wise thing to be out on the roads alone at the best of times and certainly not now.

Even so, Malise was half-asleep and daydreaming of himself on one of the Buchan's great warhorses, or a captured stallion of The Bruce, all fire and rearing, a stiff prick with iron hooves. He was riding down fleeing men and closing in on a woman, who ran screaming, until he got close and found himself, suddenly, off the powerful horse and staring at her. She lay helpless, bosom heaving after the running – but gave him a knowing smile and a look, then put one finger between her impossibly red lips and sucked it. She was Isabel and he had his hands on her thighs . . .

The sudden clatter startled him and he jerked awake, in time to see a man duck out of a sacking-covered doorway, unlacing his front and cursing as he stumbled over a discarded bucket. He gave Malise the merest bleary glance, then directed a stream of steaming relief on the dungheap, farted noisily and stared with unfocused eyes at the wattle-and-daub wall of what Malise realised was not a stable for the tavern, but the man's home.

Malise blinked once or twice and forced the tired mount down the length of road where buildings straggled, separated by drunken fencing and strips of bare, turned-earth plots. Ahead lay the great ramshackle arrangement of an inn, two storeys high and timber-framed on stone; the smell of food flooded Malise.

A woman appeared from one of the houses, driving a cow to be staked on a small patch of communal grass. It dropped dung with a splatter and, without breaking stride, she scooped it up in a basket and went on, looking briefly at Malise, who glared back from under his hood until she dropped her eyes.

She might well have been pretty once – her dress had the memory of bright colour in it somewhere – but she was long severed from cleanliness or good manners, with a face roughened by wind and weather, yet pasty and pinched under the windchape. Malise slithered off the horse at the tether pole, hearing movement inside the inn and a burst of laughter; the horse sagged, hipshot and relieved.

The inn was dim inside and the moment of stepping from light to dark left Malise disorientated, so that he panicked and fumbled for the hilt of his dagger. Then the stink hit him – thick air, old food, spilled drink, farts, shit, vomit and, with a thrill that made him grunt, the thin, acrid stink of old sex. The place was also a brothel.

When his eyes adjusted, he was in a large room with a beaten earth floor and roughcast walls laced with timber. There were rushes strewn on the floor between the tables and benches, but it was clear they had not been changed in some time. Two great metal lanterns with horn panels hung on chains from the main rafters, together with tray-pulleys, for hauling drink and food to the gallery that went all round the square of the place. Up there, Malise reckoned, were sleeping rooms and the stair to them was behind the earthen oven and the slab of wood that served as a worktop. It was altogether a fine inn.

A girl was wearily slopping water on the slab of wood and raking it back and forth with a cloth; she looked up as he stood blinking, his hood still up. She was dirty, the ingrained dirt of a long time of neglect and her eyes were dull, her hair lank, lusterless – yet it was tawny somewhere in the depths of it and those dead eyes had sparkled blue as water once.

'We are not open,' she said and, when he did not respond, looked up and said it again.

'Please yourself,' she added with a shrug when he stood there with his mouth open. He almost started towards her with a fist clenched, then remembered what he was after and stopped, smiling. Honey rather than Hell.

'What have we here, then?' demanded a loud voice and a shape bulked out a door at the far end of the room. Naked

165

from the waist, the man was a huge-bellied apparition, hairy as a boar, with the remnants of a moustache straggling greasily through many chins, though the hair on his head was cropped to iron-grey stubble. He was lacing up braies under the flop of the belly and beaming in what he fondly imagined was genial goodwill.

Malise was appalled and repelled. The man looked like a great troll, yet the swinging cross on his chest belied that. 'Tam,' he announced.

'You don't look blind to me,' Malise managed and the man chuckled throatily.

'My auld granda,' he declared proudly, 'dead and dead these score of years. A father-to-son wee business this.'

'Sit,' he said, then slapped the dull-eyed girl on the arm. 'Stir yourself − start the fire.'

Malise sat.

'Come from far?' Tam rumbled, scratching the hairs on his belly. 'Not many travel up this road since the Troubles.'

'Douglas,' Malise lied, for he had actually travelled in from Edinburgh, where he had spent a fruitless time searching out the Countess after the events at Douglas. He had missed her there, tracked her to Irvine and knew she was headed for The Bruce, the hot wee hoor. But he had missed her there, too, and the money the earl had given him was all but run out; soon, he would have to return north and admit his failure. He did not relish the idea of admitting failure to the Earl of Buchan, even less admitting that the bloody wee hoor of a Countess had not only outwitted him by escaping, but continued to do so.

'A long journey,' Tam said jovially. 'You'll bide here the night.'

Then his brows closed into a single lintel over the embers of his eyes and he added, 'You'll have siller, sure, and will not mind showin' the colour of it.'

Malise fished out coin enough to satisfy him, then had to

seethe silently as it was inspected carefully. Finally, Tam grinned a gap of brown and gum, got up and fetched a flask and two wooden cups.

'Fine wine for a fine gentle,' he declared expansively, splashing it into the cups. 'So the road is safe? Folk are travelling on it?'

He would be interested in the trade, of course. Malise shrugged.

'What is safe?' he replied mournfully, graciously accepting the cup of wine. 'A man must make a living.'

Tam nodded, then called out to the girl to fetch him a shirt, which she did, dusting her hands of ash. Malise drank, though he did not like the thin, bitter taste.

'What is your business?' Tam demanded, licking his lips.

'I negotiate contracts,' Malise said, 'for the Earl of Buchan.'

Tam's eyebrows went up at that.

'Contracts, is it? For what?'

Malise shrugged diffidently.

'Grain, timber, wool,' he answered, then glanced sideways at the man, watching the chins of him wobble as he calculated how much he could dun and how much profit there was to be had out of this meeting. Malise handed him an opportunity.

'I also look out for his wife,' he said carefully. 'When she is travellin' up and doon the roads, like, on the business of Buchan.'

Tam said nothing.

'I was thinking, perchance, ye had heard if she'd passed this way,' Malise persisted. 'A Coontess. Ye would know her in an instant – she rides a warhorse.'

Tam turned the cheap red earthenware round and round, pretending to think and studying Malise. A weasel, he decided, with a tait of terrier there. No contract scribbler this – a rache, huntin' the scent of some poor soul. A Coontess, he added to himself, my arse. Alone? On a warhorse? My arse.

167

Malise grew tired of the silence eventually and spread his hands, choosing his words carefully.

'If the road keeps clear and the garrison at Bothwell chases away its enemies, ye might get a customer or two.'

'God preserve the king,' Tam said, almost by rote and leaving Malise to wonder which king he was speaking of. Malise was about to start placing coins on the table when a frightening apparition appeared at the head of the staircase.

The face had once been pretty, but was puffed and reddened by late nights and too much drink. Malise saw a body made shapeless by a loose shift, but a breast lolled free, darkened by a bruise.

'What a stramash,' she whined, combing straggles of hair from her face. 'Can a quine not get sleep here?'

She saw Malise and made an attempt at a winning smile, then gave up and stumbled down to slump on a bench.

'Where's your light o' love?' demanded Tam sarcastically.

'Snoring his filthy head off – Tam, a cup?'

Tam grunted and poured.

'Just the single Lizzie, my sweet. I want you at the work the day.'

'What for is wrong with that bitch upstairs?' Lizzie whined and Tam grinned, lopsided and lewd.

'You ken the way of it. It is your affair if you stick yer legs in the air when you should be sleepin', but this is your day for the work.'

Lizzie's teeth clacked on the cup and she drank, coughed, wiped her mouth, then drank again.

'Ye have to have rules,' Tam said imperiously to Malise, 'to run a business in these times. This place will be stappit with sojers the night, seeking out a wee cock of the finger an' a bit of fine quim.'

He nudged Lizzie, who forced a winsome smile, then looked at Malise, sparked to curiosity now that wine was flooding her.

'What are you selling – face paints and oils?' she asked hopefully.

'Seeking, not selling,' Malise answered and the whore pouted and lost interest.

'So,' said Tam expansively, sliding into the shirt which had been brought to him at last. 'Ye were sayin'. About a Coontess.'

'The road is clear,' Malise answered. 'though few travel. Too many sojers of the English, who are just as bad as Wallace's rebels.'

'Never speak of him,' Tam spat, thinking moodily of wagon drivers bringing stone for the completion of the castle, their thirsty helpers, the woolmen and drovers and pardoners and tinkers, all the trade he was not getting.

'The road would be clear save for they bastits, God strike them,' he added. 'They'll not come here, though, so close to the castle.'

'I heard it was not completed,' Malise mused.

'The walls are big enough,' Tam retorted, wondering if this stranger was a spy and regretting what he had said about Wallace. Then the stranger wondered out loud if the Countess had gone there.

'Coontess?' Lizzie declared before Tam could speak. 'No Coontess has rested here. No decent wummin since the Flood.'

She shot Tam a miserable look and he parried it with a glare, seeing his chance at money vanish. If he had planned to inflict more on her, it was lost in a clatter and a curse from upstairs.

'So he's up,' muttered the whore, glancing upwards. 'A malison on his prick.'

'To speak the De'il's name is to summon him,' chuckled Tam as a second figure appeared at the top of the stairs, took two steps, stumbled and slithered down another four, then managed to make it to the table, whey-faced and with a beard losing its neat trim. He had a fleshily handsome face, dark hair fading to smoke and spilling in greasy curls to his ears,

169

a stocky body and wore shirt, boots and not much else – but Malise saw the bone knife-handle peep from the boot top.

He did not see the face until the man spilled down the steps and into the sour, dappled light dancing wearily through the shutters.

His heart juddered in him; he knew the man. Hob, or Rob – one of the men from Douglas who had been with the Sientcler from Lothian. His mouth went dry; if he was here, then the other one might also be, the one called Tod's Wattie, and he had fingers at his throat, massaging the memory of the gripping iron hand before he realised it and stopped.

'Lizzie, my wee queen,' Bangtail Hob said thickly, 'pour me some of that.'

'If you can pay, there is another flask,' Tam declared and the man nodded wobblingly, then fished a purse from under his armpit and counted out coins. Malise fought to control his shaking, to stop glancing behind him, as if to find Tod's Wattie there.

'Ah, God take my pain,' Bangtail said, holding his head. The wine arrived, the man poured, swallowed, puffed, blew and shuddered, then drank again. Finally, he looked at Malise.

'I ken you, do I not?' he asked and Malise could not speak at all, but wondered, wildly, if he could get to the dagger through the tangle of his clothes and under the table.

Bangtail drank deeply again and wiped his mouth with the back of one hand as his brain caught up with his mouth and he regretted admitting he knew this man. In Bangtail's experience, almost all the half-remembered men he knew were husbands or sweethearts of the quim he was stealing from them; he did not not want to press this in case memory returned for both of them.

'See men?' he asked, swallowing more wine. 'Carts. Horses. Men on the road ye came up?'

Malise swallowed, found words and croaked them out, nodding.

'Took the turn for Elderslie,' he lied and saw Bangtail jerk his head up.

'Ach, no. Away. Ye are jestin', certes.'

Malise shook his head and then had to fight to stop shaking it. Bangtail Hob cursed and slammed away from the table, heading for the stairs.

'You told me they would be here the day,' Tam yelled truculently to the vanishing back of Hob. 'A wheen of sojers an' a knight, you said, needin' lodgin. I have been sair put out to accommodate them.'

'Away,' scoffed Lizzie, slack smiled and bathing in warm pools with the drink. 'Ye have had no visitors at all, ken.'

Tam's hand smacked her in the mouth, just as the cup was rising towards it. The cup and the wine went one way, Lizzie went the other and she lay for a moment, dazed. Then, slowly, she climbed back to her knees and then feet.

'Any further lip from you, my lass . . .' Tam added warningly.

Malise sat still as rock. He could not have moved if he had wanted to and all the time he ached to turn round and yet did not dare, for fear of seeing Tod's Wattie and the face on him for what had been done to the dogs. Not pleasant, Malise admitted. Henbane, realgar and hermadotalis, better known as Snake's Head iris, was a vicious poison on man or beast and they did not die peacefully.

Hob clattered back down the stairs, this time dressed in boots and braies and shirt, with a studded leather jack, a long knife and a sword at his waist and a round-rimmed iron helmet in one hand. He shouted for his horse to be got ready and Tam jerked a sullen head at Lizzie to tell the ostler.

Hob paused at the table and snatched up the flask he had paid for, grinning from his broad-chinned face.

'Elderslie, ye say,' he said, then frowned and shook his head. 'Bastits. They were to come this way. No man tells me a thing.'

171

Malise smiled nervously back at him and the man swept out. There was a pause, then the sound of hooves, speeding away. Malise forced himself on to unsteady legs and, as soon as he was up and moving, he was almost in a panic to be gone. The tavern keeper looked moodily at him.

'God speed,' he said sourly, 'for it appears ye are no decent luck for business.'

Malise would have slit him for his attitude on another day. This day, though, he only wanted distance between him and the Sientclers from Lothian and was so gripped and blinded by it that he never saw the flitting figures in the trees as he whipped the staggeringly exhausted horse out on to the muddy road.

He did not know that they had let him by as too small a prize when there was an inn to be plundered.

Bangtail Hob was not a happy man, as he kept telling everybody out of the sour scowl of his face. It did not help that it had rained on his ride from a warm, comfortable inn and that he had left his cloak behind.

'When I find yon arse who swore he had come up this road and saw ye turn for Elderslie,' he growled for the umpteenth time, 'I will hand him a lick such as to dunt his head from his neck.'

'She was a rare piece, then, this quine ye climbed off?' demanded Will Elliott, who was licking his lips in anticipation of the delights of the inn Bangtail Hob had described.

'She was,' Hob enthused, then blackened his face with a new scowl. 'Now we will be lucky to get a whiff, when these lads reach it. Elderslie road – the serpent-tongued hoor-slip.'

'Enow, ye midden,' Sim growled and nodded towards the palfrey, approaching at a posting trot, the Countess riding as easily as was possible on a sidesaddle. Hal and Sim Craw looked at each other, though there was only mild amusement

172

in it for the entire affair was, as Sim put it when they'd set out, a guddle of nae good.

'Master Hob,' the Countess called and Bangtail turned obediently, smiling his most winsome.

'You are certain of the description of this man? That it was Malise Bellejambe?'

'I am, Lady,' Bangtail replied firmly. 'I kent his face, but he flustered me with his falsehoods and it was only when I reached here that I minded him. Malise, for sure. It is not a face I will forget again, mark me.'

'He seeks me,' she said and Hal heard the catch in her voice.

'You're safe with us,' he said firmly and she shook herself, as if a goose had walked over her grave.

'I am in no danger from him,' she replied. 'He would have the skin taken off his back by my husband if he as much as bruised me. That privilege belongs to Buchan.'

Hal blinked at the bleakness of the last words and Isabel came out of the dark place she had gone, blinked and forced a new smile.

'But he is not . . . pleasant,' she said. 'And he may do harm to others.'

'I would worry about Tod's Wattie if I were he, lady,' piped a new voice and they looked at the Dog Boy, hovering round Isabel's stirrup. 'Tod's Wattie loved they baists and yon man killed them with evil potions.'

Sim studied the Dog Boy, seeing the pinch of his face, the bruised eyes. Seeing what Hal saw, that wavering faint image of wee dead Johnnie. God alone knew what had gone through this lad's mind while he had been in the moatbridge pit but it had only been the grace of Our Lady that it had not been the moat weight itself. Yet the lad had had to listen to it crush Gib to bloody fragments and the Lord alone knew what that had done to him.

The Dog Boy felt the eyes on him and grinned at Sim before

turning back into Isabel's fond stare. He was not sure what it was he felt for this high-born woman but he wanted, at one and the same time, to put his head on her breast and have his forehead stroked – and his hands on those same breasts. The combined raggle of these feelings frequently left him flustered, tight in chest and groin.

Hal caught Bangtail's eye and sent him off down the column. Twenty riders and four wagons had set off from Annick Water three days ago, following the arrival of Tod's Wattie just as peace broke out and everyone went their way. Hal and his small *mesnie* were headed north, first to Stirling, then on into Buchan lands. Delivering, Hal thought, like a mercantile carter.

Not all the men at Annick had traipsed homeward and the roads were shadowed with folk gone back to brigandry, either in the name of Wallace, or King John – or just themselves. Now there were at least a dozen carts and wagons, upwards of seventy folk, all trailing after for the protection of the armed men and despite Hal's protests, cajoling and even threats.

Travellers all, they were latched on for safety and with their own reasons for getting down this road; one even hirpled along on a crutch refusing all invites to be taken into a cart, since he had sworn to walk to the Priory of Scone, in penance and surety of a miraculous cure. Each day they left him behind, each evening, he hobbled painfully in to the nearest fire and Hal wondered if the Priory had recovered enough from the scouring of no more than a few weeks ago to offer him succour.

Then there was the Countess. Hal sighed. Bruce had been almost wheedling, but it was Sir William who had finally persuaded Hal to escort the Countess back to her husband.

'It has to be done and it were best done by someone unlike to be seen grinning at the husband's cuckoldin',' the Auld Templar had said, then handed Hal a folded white square of fine linen with a thick black bar across the top.

'That is a Templar *gonfanon*,' he said. 'Though you are not strictly a Poor Knight, ye are being asked to serve yin, namely masel', so such a banner will keep ye safe frae both sides. Naebody with sense will want to irritate the Templars, even an earl havin' his wayward wife returned by them.'

Hal could not find a good reason for refusing the man who had come to their rescue at the bridge and, besides, Hal had had another request that sent him in the same direction and the irony of where that had come from did not pass him by. It seemed Sir William knew something of it, too, since he asked, polite and innocent, about the fat wee man, Bisset, who had arrived looking for Henry Sientcler and no-one else.

'A wee relic from Douglas, Sir William,' Hal declared, shrugging lightly. 'Wallace promised to hunt the man – he was scrivener or somesuch to Ormsby at Scone and it was thought he might ken something about the murder of yon mason.'

Sir William stroked his grizzled chin and nodded, only half listening.

'Oh aye? And does he?'

Hal shrugged.

'Nothin' helpful,' he said and wondered then why he lied. Sir William grunted and patted Hal on the shoulder, a gesture that brought a memory of his father so sharp it nearly made Hal grunt. He wanted to get back to Herdmanston, to put the confusion of Bruce and Wallace and Buchan and Englishmen far away from him, and said as much.

'Aye, well,' Sir William said thoughtfully. 'Deliver the Coontess and yer done with Bruce – though I would seriously consider where yer future lies. Wallace is off to Dunkeld, I hear. Or to besiege Dundee. Or Stirling. Ye see the way of it – his rabble flit like wee midgies and clegs here and there and everywhere. He is not the man to tak' on the English in the field, no matter what Wishart thinks.'

He patted Hal again.

'Anyhow – not your problem. Let that flea stick to the wall,' he said. 'Tak' yon wayward wummin home and be done with matters until Bruce or myself send word. Send that wee scribbler Bisset away as well and forget about dead masons – Christ's Bones, Hal, there are corpses enow in every ditch from here to Berwick.'

It was sound advice and Hal was determined to follow it and praise God for having slid out from under the threat of Longshanks so easily. Yet the nag of the mystery stuck him like a stone in his shoe every now and then – when 'yon wayward wummin' gave it a chance.

The Countess of Buchan, Hal thought miserably, was both an irritation and a delight. She was wearing her only dress, a fitted green affair whose sleeves flapped loose because she had no tirewoman to sew her into them. She wore the same battered riding boots Hal had seen at Douglas. Yet now she affected a barbette under her chin and a neat wee hat to go with it, a smile that never reached her eyes and a sidesaddle on a palfrey – handing Hal the bold Balius.

'It is,' she had declared winsomely, 'not seemly for me to be returned astraddle a warhorse, according to the Earl of Carrick and Sir William Sientcler and every other one of the community of the realm who passes and seems to have an opinion on it.'

She clicked her teeth closed, biting off more and widening the smile.

'So, as a knight, you had better take the beast home to the Earl of Buchan's stables.'

Hal had stammered some platitude about treating the beast like silk and gold, but the truth was he felt a long way from the ground after Griff and felt the raw power of it in every step.

He should not even have been riding the beast at all – no sensible knight used a warhorse except for battle and, besides, it was not his. As Isabel winsomely pointed out, cheerful as

176

a singing wren, she had probably already ruined the beast by using it like a common palfrey and, because it had been stalled at Balmullo, which was hers in her own right, she could give permission and did so.

Hal viewed this last with a jaundiced eye, but could not resist the chance of it.

For all her cheer, the lady herself seemed clenched as a curled fern, full of brittle laughter and too-bright eyes, which only softened when she laid them on the Dog Boy – and there was a fondness they shared.

More than ever he reminded Hal of his dead son – yet each time, the memory of it seemed less of an ache just because the Dog Boy was there. Hal marvelled at the change in the lad in so short a time and could only speculate on what had tempered the steel in him, down in that dark hole, listening to Gib's bones crunch. Hardly a friend, Gib, but even hearing a mortal enemy screaming his way out of the world would change you forever.

'That and the dugs,' Tod's Wattie had said, in the grim firelit tale he had told the night he had arrived. 'They died hard and sair, the dugs, and the only blessin' of the lad being in the pit was that he was dragged from it senseless an' so never saw them.'

Hal knew, from the unfocused eyes and the hard set of him, that Tod's Wattie had watched them die and that had altered him, too. The mere mention of Malise Bellejambe sent him coldly murderous and Hal saw him now, hunched aboard his garron, his face a dark brooding of furrow and brow.

It was a sorry cavalcade, he thought. He had sent Bangtail ahead, to secure the inn and warn them that a cavalcade was coming down the road, because Bangtail had some sense about him and could handle an encounter with suspicious English from the Bothwell garrison. Not that Hal thought many of them would venture out so far from the safety of the half-finished castle, but it was was better to be prudent; besides,

Bangtail swore he spoke French, though Hal was sure it was just enough to order another ale or get his face slapped by any well-spoken woman.

Then there was Bisset. The man jounced on a cart like a half-filled sack of grain, since the insides of his thighs had been rubbed raw on the journey to Annick and he could no longer ride. He was going as far as Linlithgow and would then go south to Edinburgh, while Hal went north.

Fussy, precise and complaining, Bisset was also, Hal realised, brave and a man of his word. He had promised Wallace to deliver information and he did. He had promised to deliver Wallace's request to pursue the matter and he did that, too, though Hal wished he had laced his lip on that part.

'The dead man was Gozelo de Grood,' Bisset had told Hal and Sim, quiet and head to head. 'Almost certes. He disappeared from Scone in the summer of last year. Stabbed the once and a killing stroke, very expertly done. Not robbed.'

'Apart from his name,' Sim growled, 'we are no better informed.'

Bisset offered a sharp-toothed mouse of a smile.

'Ah, but he had a close friend who is also missing,' he declared, and that raised eyebrows, much to the secretary's delight. He liked the possession of secrets, did Bartholomew – liked better revealing them to those who would marvel.

'Manon de Faucigny,' Bisset declared, like a mountebank producing coloured squares from his sleeve. 'A Savoyard and a stone carver. A good one, too, brought over by Gozelo to do the intricate work.'

'Where is he?' demanded Hal and Bisset nodded, smiling.

'Just what Master Wallace asked,' he declared and pouted. 'He went either south or north, two weeks after Gozelo de Grood left Scone.'

'Helpful,' Sim growled and Bisset, ignoring him, leaned into the tallow light.

'It is my surmising,' he said softly, 'that this Manon fled when it became apparent that Gozelo was not returning when he had said he would. Gozelo left, telling the Savoyard it was for a week and no more, then did not return because he was killed, we know. This Manon fled – I know this because he took only his easily portable tools and no craftsman would leave the others except under extreme duress. He told folk he was going to Edinburgh, to meet Gozelo, but it is my belief that this was mummery . . .'

'And he was trying to send someone in the opposite direction from the one he travelled,' Hal finished. 'Who?'

'Wallace's second question,' Bisset declared delightedly. 'He said your wits were sharp, Sir Hal. I give you the answer I gave him – I do not know. But Manon de Faucigny expected person or persons to be searching for him and expected also no good to come of it. So he fled. To Stirling, or Dundee. He will, I am sure, be thinking of hiding and trying not to do the obvious – run to the Flemish Red Hall in Berwick and be got away to safety.'

The Red Hall, Hal knew, was the Flemish guild hall in Berwick and he doubted it would be of any use, since the Flemings had defended it to the last man when the English sacked the town last year and around thirty had been burned alive in it. Now it was no more than charred timbers – though the Flemings were still in Berwick.

'Why would person or persons want the man dead?' demanded Sim.

'For the same reason they wanted the mason killed,' Bisset replied primly. 'To stop his mouth. They both hold a secret, good sirs, but now only de Faucigny can tell it – and Master Wallace offers you this as promised. He said to say you would know what to do with it.'

Forget it. That was the sensible choice, but even as he turned the coin of that over in his mind, he knew it had never been a possibility. A pollard, he thought wryly. Just

179

as refusing Bruce was a crockard. He had been summoned into the service of Bruce and, suddenly, had become part of the kingdom's cause. Now, just as suddenly, he was part of the forces dedicated to crushing that cause – and, he realised, bound now to oppose Wallace if he encountered him. Yet he had regard for Wallace, the man still fighting when everyone else had scrambled to bow the knee. Because he has nothing to lose, Hal thought, unlike myself and others.

Hal felt trapped – like yon Trojan crushed by the coils of sea-serpent, he thought and wished he had spent more time actually listening to the *dominie* his father had hired to 'put some poalish oan the boy'.

The men with him were the last of the loyal – all the others had gone off with Wallace, for the plunder in it. Sim, Bangtail, Tod's Wattie and Will Elliott were Herdmanston men – Red Cloak had been the fifth and his death lay heavy on them all. The rest, some fifteen, were local Marchers some of whom trusted Hal more than anyone and knew a cousin, or some kin who had ridden with him before and profited from it. A few – and even this number astonished Hal – came for the belief in the realm and imagined Hal would know the right path to take when the time came.

'Farthing for them.'

The voice licked round him like the Trojan's snake and led him back to the present, the wet road, the August drizzle licking under his collar. He thought of the stone cross at Herdmanston, the woman and bairn buried underneath it – and how far away it seemed.

He turned into her smiling face. Hair had straggled free from under her hat and barbette; there was nothing, it seemed to Hal, that could keep the wild freedom in the woman contained for long.

'Not worth that much,' he responded. 'You'll have clippings back, even from a mite like a bonnie new siller fairthing.'

'You are not half as country witless as you aspire to, Sir

Henry,' she said, the lilt of her robbing it of sting, 'so I wish you would not speak as if you followed the plough.'

He looked at her. They had been together long enough for him to already know her moods by the way she held herself – anger stiffened her body, which actually enticed Hal, even if he knew the lash that would accompany it.

'I have followed the plough,' he said, remembering the days when, as a boy, he had trotted after the brace of oxen driven by Ox Davey, walking in that straddle-legged way ploughman do, one foot on weed, one foot on soil and a valley, deep as a hand, between. Davey had been Red Cloak's da, he remembered suddenly.

Sim himself – older and stronger, as it seemed he had been all through Hal's life – had showed him what to do with the worms. They would carefully pick the wrigglers, exposed by the scart of the plough, heel a hole in the soil, drop the worm in and say, like a ritual, 'There ye be, ya bugger. Work'

Isabel was not surprised by the statement; it came to her that nothing this man did would surprise her.

'You have not followed the plough for a while,' she replied, smiling, and he looked at her, stern as an old priest, which did not suit him and almost made her laugh.

'When I became a man, I put aside childish things,' he said and, because he was perched on the back of Balius, was able to look down his nose at her.

'And took up the pompous, it appears,' she answered tartly. 'I take the hint that I should also put away the childish, but have no fears – I imagine my husband has a lesson or two prepared, while the De'il, as anyone will tell you, has a special room made ready for my imminent arrival.'

She reined the palfrey hard, so that it protested as its head was wrenched.

'It is hard to decide which is worse,' she called out as she turned away from him, 'though the De'il, I am thinking, will be less vicious than the Earl of Buchan – and less tedious than a ploughman from Herdmanston.'

Cursing, Hal half turned, looking for words of apology and racking himself for his stupidity – what in the name of God had made him sound like some crabbed auld beldame?

The great warhorse grunted and leaned on the reins, testing the limits of the rider. Hal, though he was still getting used to the distance from the ground, had ridden a warhorse like this before – Great Leckie, his father's *destrier* – to learn the ways of fighting with lance and sword. Leckie had been a lesser radiance than this Balius, though just as expensive to keep.

Hal saw Pecks, the ostler released by Bruce to make sure Balius reached Buchan in pristine condition, sitting sullenly on the cart solely committed to the oats, peas and beans for the beast's fodder. It was moot, Hal thought moodily, whether Bruce was more concerned about returning a glossy Balius or a glossy wife to the Earl of Buchan.

He slewed back round to face front – and stiffened. Black, greasy, sullen as raven feathers, the smoke trails drifted wearily into the leaden sky and he reined in Balius, feeling the gathered power of the beast, which always seemed on the point of exploding. Pecks, lurching with the bounce of the cart in the ruts, stood up a little and craned to see.

'Are we biding yonder?' he asked cheerfully. 'I see they have the fires stoked. Hot commons and warm beddin' the night, is it yer honour?'

Hal growled and spat and Pecks, who was used to working for better than his master's discarded leman and a supposed knight with the ways of a dog, looked at Hal with some disgust; these Lothians were filthy as pigs, with manners to match and the finest thing about their leader, this so-called Sir from Herdmanston, was the horse that was not his own and which he should not be riding.

The blow on his chest reeled him backwards and he gawped

at the arrow. Then the world sped towards him, big and black, and he jerked instinctively, but something seemed to hit him in the face. Alarmed, he then felt a crashing blow on his shoulder and the side of his head and, at last, realised that they were attacked and tried to get off the bed of the cart.

Around the time he found out the crash on shoulder and head had been his falling off the cart to the road, the arrow that had gone through his eye and into his brain finally killed him.

Hal saw the ostler hit, saw the brief astonished look, then the second arrow took the man in the eye and he went down. An arrow whacked into Hal's chest – but he was wearing an arming jack and a coat of plates and a cloak, all sodden, so the shaft bounced, caught and hung pathetically, snagged to the cloth of his coat. The hard blow of it, even cushioned by padding, rocked him backwards and rattled his back teeth.

Then Hal saw the men pelting out of the trees and the entrance to the inn, yipping with little bird-like cries. Behind, he heard more high-pitched screeches and the screams of the attacked.

Screwing round in the saddle, he yelled for Sim Craw, then bellowed out one word.

'Coontess.'

Sim spurred forward and grabbed the waist of the bewildered woman, hauling her out of her sidesaddle and half-throwing her into a sumpter wagon, as running figures, the unlucky followers, tried to crash away from the flicking arrows and tangled themselves up with Hal's horsemen. Swearing and yelling, the riders lashed out with the butts of Jeddart staffs and Ill Made Jock, turning into the path of a stampeding pack horse, was thrown to the ground with a harsh cry.

Cursing, Hal faced front again. Horsemen had appeared, spear-armed and wearing leather – three of them, yelling instructions to the men milling and circling, clearly blocking the head of the column, while the ones behind prevented it from retreating. God-fucking kerns and caterans from north of The Mounth, hooching and wheeching like mad imps – yet as classic an ambush as any you would read in Vegetius, he noted, with that part of his mind not involved in wildly trying to work out what to do now.

Balius solved it.

His father had given Hal the garron, Griff, claiming it as a by-blow of Great Leckie, and had added, 'Gryphon will see you through well enough if you dinna do anythin' fancy.' If he had been on Griff, Hal would not even have considered doing anything fancy – certainly not what Balius clearly thought was inevitable.

This was what the big warhorse had been bred and trained for and now he stamped his iron-shod trencher hooves and bunched the great muscles of his flanks. Hal felt it, swallowed a little and drew his sword, then settled his bascinet tighter on his head with a tap of the wheel pommel and slung his shield from his back down to his left arm with a twitch. He had never liked the combination of maille coif, metal bascinet and the full-face great helm – like many others, he preferred to do without the latter and tourney knights sported scars like badges from Grand Melee fights. Now, as arrows wheeped and hissed, he was pricklingly aware of his exposed face.

Balius felt the bang of the shield on Hal's leg and the change of tension on the rein and started to bait, huge hooves stamping as he trotted on the spot; twin plumes shot hot and misted grey from his flared nostrils. Hal took a breath, let the rein loose and then spun the sword up, forward and back with a flick of his wrist.

The bright flash of the blade appearing on one side of him was all the signal the warhorse needed; he gave a snorting squeal, then plunged forward, his great feet kicking up the mud and wet of the road in fountains. The knot of yelling horsemen, waving their spears, grew closer and an arrow buzzed past Hal's ear like a mad wasp.

A little late, the riders realised this huge beast was not about to stop or turn sideways. Balius plunged into the core of them, snapping right and left with his big yellow teeth. Hal, trailing his swordhand down almost on the horse's flank, brought it up in a whirling cut that caused a rider to shriek, but there was only a slight tug and Hal kept going, bringing the sword up alongside the beast's head, then up and over to the far side. Then he back-cut the other way and someone else screamed.

The *destrier*, the bright blade-flashes at the corner of his eye urging him on, slammed into one of the enemy ponies and it bounced away, all four legs off the ground. Crashing heavily and squealing with terror, it threw the rider into the mud and then rolled on him, flailing wild hooves.

Then they were through the pack and Balius, who knew the business as well as Hal – better, Hal decided – was skidding on his haunches, iron hooves scoring ruts as he scrabbled to brake, spinning round even as he did so.

As suddenly as they had come, they were thundering back and Hal had time enough to see three men in the mud and a horse flailing on its back before he was plunged into the swirl of them once more, his breath rasping and his arm coming up, the maille-backed gauntlet full of bloody blade.

Balius shunted into a pony, which went backwards, but the huge horse lost momentum and was balked, so he reared and struck out, the fearsome hooves cracking the pony's shoulder and a man's knee.

Another rider had hauled out a wicked sword and was flogging an unhappy mount to get alongside and land a blow. On Hal's other side, one rider flung an axe as he sped off, almost turned completely backwards on the running hobby; the weapon clattered off Hal's shield.

Hal took the battering sword cut on the metal-bar vambrace on his right forearm, a homemade bar-iron cage from wrist to elbow, then found himself face to face with his attacker, a scarlet-mouthed screamer with a leather helmet, a mad beard the colour of old bone and angry slits for eyes.

He popped the fat wheel pommel of his sword between the slits and then cut viciously backwards as Balius took a mighty leap and shot out of the pack. He felt the blade tug, but did not know what he had hit.

Then they were back at the lead wagon and turning again, Balius blowing and snorting and stamping. Up in the sumpter wagon, Sim Craw levelled his crossbow and shot, but Hal did not see what he hit.

Then the riders were gone. There was a flurry of confusion and shouts from the cavalcade and the women would not stop screaming, but the attackers suddenly vanished as swiftly as they had appeared. Ahead, a horse limped off, trailing reins. Three bodies lay like bundles of old clothes.

Sim dropped from the wagon and walked to where Ill Made Jock sat, his arse wet and his arm wrenched.

'A sair dunt, but not broken,' he remarked to the ugly wee fighter. 'All that's damaged is your pride, for birlin' off yer cuddy on to your arse.'

'Moudiewart arse of a sway-backed stot,' Jock agreed sourly, massaging his arm.

Sim clapped him the shoulder, which brought a wince from Jock and a laugh from Sim. A man crawled out from under the wagon, offered Sim a wan, bob-headed smile and scurried off like a wet rat looking for a hole, clutching a leather bag tight to him.

Hal had dismounted and was stroking Balius's soft muzzle, the stiff hairs sparkling with the diamonds of his own hot breath; Hal led him, Sim on the other side, down to the bodies.

'Imps from Satan's nethers, right enough – what are they, d'ye think?' Sim asked, stirring one with his foot. They were grim, filthy corpses, all yellow-brown snarls and hung about with bits and pieces of filched armour.

'Unfriendly,' Hal replied shortly and Sim agreed. In the end, both were decided that these had been some of Wallace's raiders, out on the *herschip* and seeing what looked like an easy and profitable target.

There had been four killed – three women and Pecks the ostler. One of the women had been Ill Made Jock's, so he was having a right bad day, as his friends were not slow to point out. Someone else asked about the man with the crutch, but no-one expected to see him again.

Hal rode to Isabel, who fought her wet skirts back over the wagon to where the Dog Boy, her devoted slave, waited to leg her up on to her horse again.

'Are you well?' Hal asked, suddenly anxious at her limp. Isabel turned, a poisonous spit of a reply already wetting her lips, when she saw the concern on his face and swallowed the bile, which left her flustered, as did the sudden leap inside her, a kick like she had always imagined would come from a child in the womb.

'Bruised,' she replied, 'but only from riding, Sir Hal. Who were they?'

Hal was admiring of her acceptance of events and almost envied the Dog Boy his closeness to her when she got back into the sidesaddle.

'Wallace men,' Hal said, 'the worst of them, if they are still Wallace men at all and not just trail baston, club men and brigands off on their own. There will be a deal of that from now on.'

'As well The Bruce thought of sending me with yourself,' Isabel replied. 'You seem to have acquainted yourself well enough with a warhorse for a ploughman.'

Hal acknowledged the compliment and the implied truce, then carefully inspected Balius, relieved to find not a mark. He handed it to the care of Will Elliot and mounted Griff, then found the garron suddenly too low and too slow and wished he had never ridden the big warhorse at all.

They collected themselves, loaded the dead ostler on to a

wagon, got Jock back on his horse, then slithered cautiously down the muddy road to the inn.

It was, as Hal had feared, burning, though the sodden timbers and thatch of it had conspired to reduce it from a conflagration to a slow-embered, sullen smoulder. There was a fat man at the entrance with his throat cut. A woman lay a little way away, stuck with arrows so deliberately that it was clear she had been used as sport.

'Ach, that's shite,' declared Bangtail Hob, hauling off his leather arming cap and scrubbing his head with disgust.

'What?' demanded Will Elliott, but Hob simply turned away, unable even to speak at the loss of Lizzie. He had been rattling her silly only a few hours before and it did not seem right to be standing there seeing her like a hedgepig with arrows and the rain making tears in her open, sightless eyes.

Out on the road, Hal was of the same mind.

'Well,' he said grimly, 'there is no shelter here, for sure. We will push on across the bridge to the town and politely inform the English commander here that he has Scots raiders on the road.'

Sim nodded and stood for a while, watching the caravan of wagons and horses and frightened people rushing past the inn and down the road after Hal and the unfurled Templar banner, the Beau Seant, held high by Tod's Wattie in one massive fist.

Despite 'baws'nt', that fancy flag, Sim was sure they were sticking their heads in a noose the further north they stravaiged. He just wondered how tight the kinch of it would be.

CHAPTER SIX

Edinburgh
Feast of St Giles – August 1297

The church of St Giles was muggy, blazing with candles and the fervour of the faithful. Hot breath drifted unseen into the incense-thick air, so that even the sound of bell and chant seemed muted, as if heard underwater. The wailing desperate of Edinburgh crowded in for their patron's Mass, so that the lights fluttered, a heartbeat from dying, with their breathy prayers for interces-sion, for help, for hope. There were even some English from the garrison, though the castle had its own chapel.

The cloaked man slipped in from the market place, slithering between bodies, using an elbow now and then. In the nave, the ceiling so high and arched that it lost itself in the dark, the gasping tallow flickered great shadows on stone that had never seen sunlight since it had been laid and the unlit spaces seemed blacker than ever.

In the shade of them, folk gave lip-service to God and did deals in the dark, sharp-faced as foxes, while others, hot as salted wolves, sought out the whores willing to spread skinny shanks for a little coin and risk their souls by sweating, desperate and silent, in the blackest nooks.

189

'O Lord,' boomed the sonorous, sure voice, echoing in dying bounces, 'we beseech you to let us find grace through the intercession of your blessed confessor St Giles.'

The incense swirled blue-grey as the robed priests moved, the silvered censers leprous in the heat. The cloaked man saw Bisset ahead.

'May that what we cannot obtain through our merits be given us through his intercession. Through Christ our Lord. Amen. St Giles, pray for us. Christ be praised.'

'For ever and ever.'

The murmur, like bees, rolled round the stones. The cloaked man saw Bisset cross himself and start to push through the crowd – not waiting for the pyx and the blessings, then. No matter . . . the cloaked man moved after him, for it had taken a deal of ferreting to get this close and he did not want to lose him now. All he needed to know from the fat wee man was what he knew and whom he had told.

Bartholomew was no fool. He knew he was being followed, had known it for some time, like an itch on the back of his neck that he could not scratch. Probably, he thought miserably, from the time he had left Hal Sientcler and the others at Linlithgow long days ago.

'Take care, Master Bisset,' Hal had said and Bisset had noted the warning even as he dismissed it; what was Bartholomew Bisset, after all, in the great scheme of things?

He would travel to his sister's house in Edinburgh, then to Berwick, where he heard the Justiciar had taken up residence. He was sure Ormsby, smoothing the feathers that had been so ruffled at Scone, would welcome back a man of his talents. He was sure, also, that someone had tallied this up and then considered what Bartholomew Bisset might tell Ormsby, though he found it hard to believe Sir Hal of Herdmanston had a hand in it – else why let him go in the first place?

Yet here he was, pushing into the crowded faithful of St Giles like a running fox in woodland, which was why he had turned into Edinburgh's High Street and headed for the Kirk, seeking out the thickening crowds to hide in. He did not know who his pursuer was, but the thought that there was one at all filled him with dread and the sickening knowledge that he was part of some plot where professing to know nothing would not be armour enough.

He elbowed past a couple arguing about which of them was lying more, then saw a clearing in the press, headed towards it, struck off sideways suddenly and doubled back, offering a prayer to the Saint.

Patron Saint of woodland, of lepers, beggars, cripples and those struck by some sudden misery, of the mentally ill, those suffering falling sickness, nocturnal terrors and of those desirous of making a good Confession – surely, Bisset thought wildly, there was something in that wide brief of St Giles that covered escaping from a pursuer.

The cloaked man cursed. One moment he had the fat little turd in his sight, the next – vanished. He scanned the crowd furiously, thought he spotted the man and set off.

Bartholomew Bisset headed up the High Street towards the Castle, half-stumbling on the cobbles and beginning to breathe heavy and sweat with the uphill shove of it. The street was busy; the English had imposed a curfew, but lifted it for this special night, the Feast of St Giles, so the whole of Edinburgh, it seemed, was taking advantage.

In the half-dark, red-blossomed with flickering torches, people careered and laughed – a beggar took advantage of a whore in the stocks, cupping her grimed naked breasts and grinning at her curses.

Bisset moved swiftly, head down and peching like a mating bull – Christ's Wounds, but he had too much beef on him these days – half-turned and paused. He was sure he saw the flitting figure, steady and relentless as a rolling boulder; he half-stumbled over a snarling dog tugging at the remains of a bloated cat and kicked out at it in a frenzy of fear.

191

That and the sheer tenacity of the pursuer panicked Bisset and he swept sideways into Lachlan's Tavern, a fug and riot of raucous bellowing laughter and argument. He pushed politely into the throng, to where a knot of drovers, fresh down from the north, were starting in to singing songs off key. Big men, they smelled of sweat and earth and wet kine.

The cloaked man ducked in, blinking at the transfer from dark to dim light, the sconce smoke and the reek of the place attacking his nose and eyes – sweat, ale, farts and vomit, in equal measure. He could not see the fat little man, but was sure he had come in here – sure also that the fat man now knew he was being followed, which made matters awkward.

Bisset saw the man, a shadow with a hood still raised, no more than two good armlengths away. He whimpered and shoved the nearest drover, who lurched forward, careering into a clothier's assistant, spilling ale all down his fine perse tunic and knocking the man off-balance into a half-drunk journeyman engraver, who swung angrily, missed his target and smacked another of the drovers on one shoulder.

The cloaked man saw the mayhem spread like pond ripples from a flung stone. He cursed roundly as a big man, a great greasy shine of joy on his fleshy face, lurched towards him swinging. He ducked, hit the man in the cods, backed away, was smashed from behind by what seemed the world and fell to his knees.

Bisset was already in the backland, stumbling past the privy, hearing the shouts and splintering crashes from inside Lachlan's. The Watch would arrive soon and he hurried off until he was sure he was safe, then he stopped, hands on thighs and half-retching, half-laughing.

He reached the safety of his sister's house moments later, found the door unlatched and fixed it carefully behind him, leaning against it and trying to stop the thundering of his heart – yet he was smiling at what he had left behind. That will teach the swine, he thought with savage joy.

He was still laughing quietly to himself when the hand snaked out of the dark and took him by the throat, so hard and sudden that he had no time even to cry out, even as he realised he had not been as clever as he had thought. An unlatched door. On a silversmith's house – he should have known better . . .

'Happy, are we?' said a voice, so close to his ear he could smell the rank breath. From the side of one eye, he caught the gleam of steel and almost lost the use of his legs.

'Good,' the voice went on, soft and friendly and more frightening because of it. 'A wee happy man is more likely to give me what I need.'

The shadowed man came in through the back court, limping slightly and almost choked by the smell from the garderobe pit. The windows here were wood shutters over waxed paper and no match for the thin, fluted blade of his dagger, but there were bars beyond that, installed by a careful man, with wealth to protect. He moved to the backcourt door, which was stout timbers, nail-studded to thwart savage axes – yet it was unlatched, so that he was in the dark, still room in a few seconds.

He stood for a moment, listening, straining against the thunder of his heart blood in his ears, feeling the matching throb of his cheek and the knuckles of one hand; the drover who had done the first and received the second had the bones of his face broken, but it was small comfort for the cloaked man.

He had come here because it was Bisset's sister's house and the place where he had picked up the Edinburgh trail of the fat wee man who had – he was forced to admit – cunningly contrived to thwart him at the tavern.

Now he listened and peered into the grey-black, took a step, then another and stopped when he crunched something under one foot. Glass or pottery, he thought. Smashed. He heard soft scuttling and froze, then heard it again and felt slowly into his belt, fishing out fire-starter and a nub end of candle. He took a deep breath and struck.

The sparks were dazzling in the dark, even through the veil of his closed eyes and, after the first strike, he waited, alert and ready. No-one came; something scuttled at floor level. He struck sparks until the treated charcoal caught, then he fed the wick to the embers and blew until it caught, flaring like a poppy.

He held it up, saw the overturned chair, the smashed crockery, the spilled meal and the mice scattering away from it. He fetched up a fallen candlestick holder, found the fat tallow that had been in it, replaced it and fed that from his nub end.

Better light, held high, flooded yellow-butter around him, glowing sullenly off the rock crystal board and the spill of chess pieces. He turned slowly; gryphon and pegasus stared unmoving back at him, their winking silver bouncing light that turned the tarn of blood to a dark pool. A woman – the sister, he imagined – white face bloody, eyes wide and one of the straw rushes stuck to her cheek with her own blood. Naked and bruised. Knifed, too, the cloaked man saw, with as expert a stroke as he had ever seen – or done himself.

She had let her murderer in herself, quiet in the dark and had not, the cloaked man decided, died easy. Not a lover, then, he decided, but a clever man who knew how to imitate the voice of the woman's brother. Let me in, hurry in the name of God – he heard it as if he had been there himself, hoarse and urgent in the dark.

She had let him and the stark purple finger marks round her face showed she had been silenced, forced to strip off her flimsy nightdress. Used, he thought, then killed, all without her having said a word.

Yet not silent, all the same. The next body was not far off, a man in his nightshirt – the sister's husband, armed with a fire iron and fresh from bed, following the whimpers and scuffles of a savage man and a terrified woman. A journeyman silversmith, thinking his gryphon and pegasus were under threat from a wee nyaff of a thief, finding his wife violated, probably already dead, for the red curve along the silversmith's throat showed he had been taken by surprise. Fixed by the horror of seeing his wife, dead and naked, the cloaked man thought, easy prey for a murderer as ruthless as this one appeared.

He was dry-mouthed and sweating, moved cautiously, rolling along the length of his feet, although he was sure the murderer was long gone, and cursed the brawl in the tavern. He had been lucky to get away from that when the English soldiers from the garrison waded in, cracking heads and shouting. A good trick, Bartholomew Bisset, he thought . . . you delayed me a long time.

He found the fat man near the door, so near it that he knew Bisset had barely stepped inside before he had been attacked. He had been stripped and lay with his hands above his head and still tied by the blue-black thumbs; looking up, the cloaked man saw the lantern hook and the length of line from it.

Strung up and ill used, he thought grimly, by someone who not only knew the work but liked it and had the leisure to indulge himself, because he knew everyone else in the house was dead.

If Bisset, the poor doomed sowl, had not contrived to delay me with fighting drovers and determined guards chasing me ower the backcourts, I might have been here in time to save him, the cloaked man thought.

He peered more closely, saw the single wound, a lipless mouth that led straight up and into the heart, killing the little fat man so completely and suddenly that he had barely bled. A death stroke, then, from a man with a flat, sharp-edged dirk who had learned as much as he would get, enjoyed as much as he dared and had no more use for Bartholomew Bisset.

The cloaked man heard noises in the street, people passing and calling out to each other, guttural as crows; he blew out the candle and stood, thinking. Nothing here, then. Back to the Lothian man, Hal Sientcler, though the cloaked man was sure that lordling had nothing to do with this.

As he wraithed back out past the choke of the garderobe pit, the cloaked man wondered who did.

The Abbey Craig, Stirling
Feast of Saint Lawrence – August 10, 1297

For two nights the Earl of Surrey's host had been watching the dull red glow that marked the Scots campfires, across the valley and up to the piously named crag beyond. Like the breath of a dragon, Kevenard had said, which made the rest of the men laugh, the thought of a good Welsh dragon being a comfort to the archers.

Addaf did not think about dragons when he marked it; he thought about Hell and that the Devil himself might be up there for once, when the wind had changed, they all heard the mad skirl and yell of them, like imps dancing.

'Hell is not up there, look you,' Heydin Captain had growled, sucking broth off the end of his moustache. 'Hell will be in the valley, where it is cut about with ponds and marsh and streams. It is there we will have to stand and shoot these folk down and when we start in to it, they will not be singing, mark me.'

In the Keep of Stirling, Sir Marmaduke Thweng watched the ember glow and thought about all the other times he had seen it – too many times, standing in one mass of men about to try to hack another mass of men to ruin.

If he had known Heydin Captain at all, he would have

been able to nod agreement to the Welsh file commander; the carse, that low-lying meadow beyond Stirling Bridge cut about by waterways the locals called 'pows', was just the place the archers would stand to shoot ruin into the rebel foot.

'They have no horse at all,' De Warenne had been told, and the lords who revealed it, shooting uneasy looks at Cressingham and Thweng and Fitzwarin as they did so, would be the ones to know. James the Steward and the Earl of Lennox, fresh from negotiating their way back into Edward's good graces, now offered to try the same with Sir Andrew Moray and Wallace.

'I doubt it will do much good,' De Warenne declared, 'since Moray might grovel his way back to his lands and titles, but Wallace will not be granted anything, my good lords. Not even a quick death.'

'For all that,' Lennox said morosely, 'it would be worth the try and you lose nothing by it – you are waiting for Clifford.'

'Ha,' snorted Cressingham and De Warenne shot him an ugly glare. Thweng said nothing, but he could see the two Scots lords look round them all, then to each other. No-one offered an explanation, but Thweng knew, as they left, that they would find out soon enough – Robert De Clifford, Lord Warden of the English March and the man who had been assiduously gathering troops for the Earl of Surrey's host, had been sent packing by Cressingham. He had been turned back as 'not needed', Cressingham ranting about the cost of defraying Clifford's expenses when the army was already large enough to deal with a rabble under a mere brigand.

That had been before they set out, of course and between Roxburgh and Stirling, the great army had melted like rendering grease and the countryside for miles around, in a broad band along the road, was filled with plundering deserters and stragglers.

197

Now they needed Clifford and that outraged lord would not come even to piss on a burning Cressingham.

Thweng left De Warenne and Cressingham arguing about dispositions and went out into the wind-soughed night, high on the battlements of the castle where sentries marked steady progress between flickering torches. He wondered if he would have to fight anyone he knew tomorrow.

Out on the road to Cambuskenneth's Abbey, far enough from Craig for the fires there to be pale flowers in the dark, Bangtail Hob wrapped himself tighter in his cloak and brooded, half-dreaming of Jeannie the miller's daughter, who could get you cross-eyed with just hands and lips. It was a fair trod to get to her at Whitekirk, but worth the shoeleather . . . he heard the hooves on the road and raised his head above the tussocks he hid behind.

The wind sighed, damp off the carse, and the loop of wide river was a black shining ribbon in the last light. The rider, hunched on the back of a plodding mount, was a silhouette heading down to the great *campanile* tower which marked where the abbey stood.

Since the only road led down from under the Abbey Craig, it meant the visitor had come either from the Scots camp, or across the brig, up the causeway and along under the Abbey Craig. There had been a few desperate refugees earlier, all handcarts and hurry, but none for some time.

Bangtail watched the rider vanish towards it, then settled back into his half-dream. Stop folk getting out of the Abbey, he had been told – so anyone coming in was not a problem. He glanced up to the distant balefire lights of Stirling's hourds, then across the stretch of dark to the flowered blossom of fires on the hill and wondered what it might be like to be there, waiting on the morrow.

He was certain Sir Hal knew what he was about, trying to avoid the great scourge of soldiery coming up on Stirling, full of vengeance against all matters Scots. Heading for the rebel camp was dancing along a thin edge, all the same – on the one hand, Hal would be seen as a Bruce man and so on the English side. On the other, he had the Countess of Buchan with him and she was the wife of the Earl who, if not actively supporting Wallace and Moray, had contrived to turn a blind eye to their doings, permitting them to unite here.

There were other reasons, Bangtal Hob was sure – or else why would he be sitting here, making sure no wee stone carver crept out of Cambuskenneth in the dark? Yet he did not fully understand them – nor needed to. He had been told what to do and he settled to it, huddling into his cloak against the chill.

Up on the crag, Dog Boy sat in the lee of the striped tent, watching the nearby fires and, beyond that, the little red eyes, like weasels in a wood, that marked where the English walked the walls of Stirling Castle.

He sat listening to the nearby men chaffering each other, arguing about this and that, fixing leather straps, honing the points of the great long spears. He had been watching the spearmen, fascinated, for days; they were being drilled in how to work together, hundreds and more in a block. Level pikes. Ground pikes. Support pikes. Butt pikes. Charge pikes. The Dog Boy had watched them stagger round, clashing into each other, cursing and spitting and tangling up.

Some, he saw, were more advanced than others – the men of Moray's army – and these were a joy, moving and turning like a clever toy. Wallace's kerns did not like the work, but were whipped to it by the lash of his great booming voice and the expert eye of Moray's commanders.

Hal sat nearby and watched the Dog Boy watching the flames of cookfires flatten and flicker in the wind up on Abbey Craig. He was waiting to speak to Wallace and curiosity – Christ, now *there* was a curse on him – had driven him within earshot of the tent, where he could hear the arrived lords try to persuade Wallace and Moray to give in.

'So you stand with the English,' Wallace said and Hal heard Lennox and John the Steward splutter their denials through the canvas.

'So you stand with us.'

This time there as silence and then Moray's bland, calming voice broke a silence so uncomfortable Hal could feel it from where he sat.

'You have our thanks, my lords,' he said in French. 'Take to Surrey our fervent wish that he withdraws from here and the realm.'

'Surrey is not the power here,' John the Steward answered, 'Cressingham will lead the army in the morning.'

Wallace's laugh was a bitter bark.

'He is no leader of men. He is a scrievin' wee scribbler, who would skin a louse for the profit of the hide,' he growled. 'Tell him that, if ye like – but mark me, *nobiles*, there will be no repeat of Irvine here.'

'Those negotiations held the English there. Bought you the time for all this,' Lennox answered sullenly in French, and Hal heard Wallace clear his throat, could almost see the scowl as he made it plain he wanted no more French here, which he could understand much less than English. Quietly, Moray translated.

'You bought your lands back,' Wallace answered bluntly. 'With a liar's kiss and betrayals. Soon, my lords, you will have to choose – tak' tent with this; those come last to the feast get the trencher only.'

'We will not fight with ye, Wallace,' the Steward said defiantly, preferring to irgnore the insults. 'It is the belief of the community of the realm that a peaceful settlement is by far the best, no matter the considerations.'

'That will never be from my hand,' Wallace answered, bland as mushed meal and speaking in carefully modulated English.

'I wish you well of your own capitulation. May your chains sit lightly on you, my lords, as you kneel to lick the hand. And may posterity forget you once claimed our kinship.'

There was silence, thick as gruel, then a voice thicker still with anger; the Steward, Hal recognised, barely leashed.

'You have nothin' to lose, Wallace, so casting the dice is hardly risk from your cup.'

'And from mine?' Moray asked lightly. There was silence.

'We will not stand against ye,' Lennox persisted.

'So declared another of your brood, Sir Richard Lundie, afore he leaped the fence to the English,' Wallace answered, his voice bitter. 'He now thinks Edward is the braw lad to put this realm in order and has joined them to fight us. That is what came of your antics at Irvine. If you fine folk persist in grovelling, there will be a wheen more like him.'

'By God, I'll not be lectured by the likes of you,' the Steward thundered. 'You're a come-lately man, a landless jurrocks with a strong arm and no idea of what to do with it until your betters tell ye . . .'

'Enough.'

Moray's voice was a harsh blade and the silence fell so suddenly that Hal could hear the ragged bull-breathing through the canvas.

'Go back and tell the Earl of Surrey, Cressingham and all the rest that we await their pleasure, my lords,' Moray added, gentle and grim. 'If he wishes us gone from here, let him extend himself and make it so.'

Movement and rustle told Hal that Lennox and the Steward had gone. There was silence, then Wallace rumbled the rheum out of his throat.

'Ye see how it is?' he declared bitterly. 'Apart from yourself, the community of the realm spits on me. We can never mak' Wishart's plans work if there is only us pushin the plough of it.'

'Never fash,' Moray said. 'For all they think it, it is not the community of the realm who fight here the morn. It is

201

the commonality of the realm and you are their man. Besides – the *nobiles* of this kingdom follow us because neither the Bruce nor the Comyn can walk in the same plough trace. In the end all we have is a king, for Longshanks has broken Scotland's Seal, stolen the Rood and purloined the very Stone of kings. There is no-one else to dig the furrow, so we must.'

The Dog Boy had only half-heard this, understanding little, watching the feet come and go. He was an expert on feet, since it was usually what he saw first from the rabbit crouch he always adopted, halfway between flight and covert.

He saw the horn-nailed bare feet of men from north of The Mounth, who scorned shoes for the most part save for clogs or pattens in the deep winter. These were the wild-haired men with wicked knifes and round shields and long-handled axes, who spoke either a language the Dog Boy did not understand at all, or one which he recognised only vaguely. They sibilated in soft, sing-song tones and made wild music to dance to.

There were turnshoes and half-boots, ragged and flapping some of them, belonging to men from Kyle and Fife and the March. These were the burghers and free men, ones who could afford iron hats and fat-padded jacks with studs, the ones who carried the long spear, the pike, in the marching formations which so fascinated the Dog Boy. *Schiltron*. It was a new word, to everyone else as much as the Dog Boy; he rolled it round his mouth like a pebble against thirst.

The men from Ayrshire and those from Fife contrived to sneer at each other for their strange way of speaking – and both walked soft around the men from the north. Yet they were here, all facing the same direction, and the Dog Boy was aware, as if he had lain back in grass and started to look clearly at clouds, of the vastness of that revelation.

They were here because, for all they might dislike each other and the men from north of The Mounth look on the likes of Bruce and Moray and Comyn as incomers, the one thing they hated more was the idea of being ruled by invaders from the English south.

The Dog Boy had also seen the fine leather boots, or the maille *chausse* with leather sole that marked a knight or man-at-arms, but there were precious few of those iron leggings. He had thought of Jamie Douglas then and had asked round the campfires until he had found men from Lanark, one of whom knew the tale of it.

'Away to France,' he told the Dog Boy in the guttering red light. 'Away to safety with Bishop Lamberton, since his da is taken off in chains.'

The man who told the Dog Boy looked at the boy's pinched, sunken-eyed face as he added that Jamie's da was unlikely to be seen again, carried off to the Tower from his cell in Berwick, where he raved, ranted and finally annoyed his gaolers once too often. Beatings, he had heard, and worse. The Hardy would not be back in a hurry, his woman and Jamie's siblings were living with her relations, the Ferrers, somewhere in England – and Douglas was now an English castle.

The Dog Boy had wandered in a daze back to the lee of the striped tent where Hal found him. Douglas held by the Invaders. Jamie in France. The Dog Boy only had a vague idea that France was somewhere south of England, which was south of Berwick; it seemed a long way off, even if the high and mighty spoke the language of the place to one another and there was actually a man from France here, on Abbey Craig.

In the middle of the flickering fires, like roses in the dark, the men huddled close and the Dog Boy felt utterly alone, felt the great, black brooding of the surrounding trees, sighing and creaking in the dark.

Jamie, Douglas Castle – everything he had known was gone, even the Lothian lord's fine dogs. Now most the few men he knew – Tod's Wattie and Bangtail and the others – were far across the night and the swooping loops of the river, down where the faint pricking lights marked Cambuskenneth Abbey. He was glad that Sim and the Lord Hal were close.

'Get yourself to Sim,' Hal said to the huddled Dog Boy, the tail-down hunch of him wrenching his heart. 'He is by a fire with something in a pot.'

The Dog Boy went into the night. Hal heard the tent rustle again as Moray left it and then Wallace's bass rumble slipped through the canvas.

'Ye can stop skulking at the eaves, Hal Sientcler, and come and tell me about a stonecarver.'

Wearily, Hal levered himself up and went in to where the air reeked of stale sweat and wet wool. Wallace lay slumped in a curule chair, the hand-and-a-half no more than a forearm length from his right hand. He listened as Hal told him about the Savoyard stonecarver.

'Forty days, is it? We never have forty days, Hal. We have the night and the morn and, God willing, if battle be joined as we wish it, the morn's morn.'

Hal shifted slightly and inwardly cursed the great giant lolled opposite. He wore better clothes these days – even hose and shoes, as befitting one of the saviours of the realm – but it was still the same brigand Wallace.

'I can hardly assault Cambuskenneth,' Hal declared. 'The man has sanctuary for forty days. He has thirty-seven of them left. He cannot get out without being seen, for I have posted men to watch every way away from the place.'

Wallace heaved a sigh and shook his shaggy head.

'The army had been here a week waiting for the English to relieve out threat against Stirling. I cannot believe the man was under my nose for that time,' he said and then grinned ruefully. 'Ye did good in tracking him, more praise to ye for that.'

Hal did not feel comforted; it had not exactly been difficult to work out that Manon de Faucigny would head for the abbey at Stirling – Cambuskenneth was perfect for a man of some quality, with skills and tools specific to kirk stonecarving and the history of having worked at Scone.

Since he was a Savoyard, it was not hard to find out that he was in residence – but the questioning had revealed their presence and the abbot, initially smiling and helpful, returned grim-faced to tell Hal that the man they sought was now in sanctuary. In forty days, he would have to leave, until then he was inviolate. He did not want to see or be seen by Hal or anyone else.

'Well,' Wallace answered. 'After the morn, all matters will be resolved, win or lose. The abbey included.'

Hal did not doubt it; here was a man who had sacked Scone, who had burned Bishop Wishart's house – in a fit of temper some said, after hearing that his mentor had given in at Irvine. The likes of an abbey was no trouble to the conscience of a man like that, yet Hal did not like the idea of sacking it and said so.

'A wee bit too much brigand for ye, Sir Hal?' said Wallace, his sneer bitter and curled.

'Did clerics do ye harm afore?' Hal countered, stung to daring. 'When ye were up for the priesthood?'

Wallace stirred from his scowling and grinned, slack with weariness.

'No, no – I was a bad cleric always – though a good man, John Blair, tried to put me on the path. But my wayward young nature had mair affinity with Mattie.'

He glanced up and smiled wryly.

'Son of my uncle, who was a priest,' he added. 'Like all such, he was neither sheep nor wolf and suffered because of it. Wanting no part of priesthood and yet stepping into the robes, like myself. What dutiful sons we were – I am sometimes sure that bairns weep at birth because they know the estate they are born into.'

Hal recalled the few priests sons he had known, pinch-faced boys living in a nether world where they were unacknowledged and yet given the advantages of rank as if they had been. Even Bishop Wishart had sons, though no-one called them anything other than 'nephews'.

'Mattie,' Wallace went on, dreamy-voiced with remembering, 'showed me the way of survival as an outlaw, mind you, so the life clerical was not all wasted time.'

Hal had heard vague tales of the wayward Wallace, of the robbing of a woman in Perth. He mentioned it, quivering on the edge of fleeing at the first sight of black on the Wallace brow.

'She was a hoor,' Wallace admitted ruefully. 'She robbed us – but it did not look good, a fully fledged cleric regular and a wee initiate boy visiting her in the first place. So we took what we could and ran. Not fast enow, mind – but since Mattie was a priest and I was so young, they let us off.'

'Is that why ye gave Heselrig a dunt, then?' Hal asked. 'I had heard it was because of a wummin.'

'I have heard this,' Wallace answered slowly. 'No wummin and no petty revenge for an assize that freed us. I went after Heselrig because he went after me – I had a stushie with a lad who fancied I had no right to wear a dagger and made his mind up to remove it.'

He paused and shook his head – in genuine sorrow, Hal saw.

'I was a rantin' lad then, a hoorin' brawler in clericals and aware that the cloots did not fit me. I did not want the Church, Sir Hal, nor did it care much for me – but there was little other course open for a wee least son of a wee least landholder.'

He paused, frowning and pained.

'I did no honour to my father with such behaviour and am not proud o' it.'

'What happened?' Hal asked. 'With the lad ye argued with?'

Wallace glanced up from under lowered brows, then stared back at the scarred planks of the floor.

'He was a squire to some *serjeant* in Heselrigg's *mesnie*, who contrived the quarrel in order to put down a wee strutting cock of a Scottish lay priest.'

He stirred at the memories of it, hunched into himself like a great bear.

'It should have been a matter for knuckles and boots, no more,' he went on bleakly. 'Yet there was a dirk involved in the quarrel and, in the end, I gave it to him – though it did him little good, since it was buried in his paunch. He did not deserve such a fate and the Sheriff of Lanark agreed. No matter my guilt – aye and shame over the affair – I was not about to stand around like a set mill and be assized for it. So matters took their course.'

He was silent for a time, then shook his head and stirred.

'Such tales do not endear me to the *nobiles*,' he noted grimly. 'They have no use for a wee outlaw, a landless apostate clerical of the Wallaces.'

'Hardly wee,' Hal returned wryly. 'Betimes – ye have a wealth of brothers and cousins, it appears.'

'Peculiarly,' Wallace said bitterly, 'this is timely with my elevation to the status of Roland and Achilles. I could not beg a meal at Riccarton, Tarbolton or any other Wallace house afore now. Only Tam Halliday in Corehead ever gave me room and board and he was kin only by being married on to my sister.'

He yawned and his eyes half-closed, so that Hal saw the weariness slide into the etched face of the man. Tomorrow, this giant would take the weight of the kingdom on his broad shoulders and lead Scotland's army against their enemy.

Tomorrow, I will be gone from here, Hal thought. I can leave the Countess here and say I delivered her as far as safety allowed – which was no lie, he tried to convince himself. If I had taken her to the English in Stirling, only to find her husband was now actively a rebel, I would have delivered her into the hands of his enemies. Taking her to the rebels

207

on Abbey Craig, on the other hand, placed her in hands which, at least, would not use her as ransom. Yet.

Not for the first time, Hal cursed the whole uncertain business, as he had done, silent and pungent under his breath, all through the town, under the brooding scowl of the English-held castle and out over the brig to Abbey Craig.

Yet he remembered the long days up to Stirling as ones marked by glory. As Sim said when they were rumbling up Bow Street, you would not think the world was about to plunge into blood and dying.

'You will be wishing yourself back behind the plough, Lord Hal,' Isabel said to him, gentle and smiling. He was glad of the smile, since it had been fading the closer they got to the northland of Buchan.

Back at Herdmanston, Hal said, it would be the barley harvest, the big one of the year. With luck, he told her, there would be no scab on sheep, or foot-rot, or cracked udders on cattle, or staggers or overlaid pigs. Even as he spoke, he felt the crushing weight of knowing that there were too many men away from home and not enough to get the harvest in, a tragedy repeated across every homestead in Scotland.

Every day the sky was faded blue, streaked with thin, cheese-muslin clouds. The barley and rye was ripening, waiting to be reaped, tied and winnowed without blight or burning, just enough rain had fallen to turn the millwheels and fill the rain-butts. Yet the land was empty, for everyone was with the army.

Yet the memory of Herdmanston bleared him as he spoke. You will, he told her, feel the first breath of autumn, cool, but not cold. It would be a place of precious metals, the sun shining through a soft silver, lying green-gold on the harvest fields. In a sea of haze, great iron bull's head clouds would float up from the west and the breeze, he added, has a trick of rising suddenly, running through the trees.

She listened, marvelling at the change in him when he spoke of the place, finding that same strange leap deep in her.

There would be sunsets, he began to tell her – then stopped, remembering the last one he had seen, etching the stone cross stark against the dying blaze of day.

She knew of the dead wife and son from others.

'What killed them?' she asked and the concern in her voice robbed it of sting.

'Ague,' Hal answered dully. 'Quartan fever – she died of the same disease as Queen Eleanor, my boy a week after his mother. I had the idea for the stone cross from all the ones the king put up for her.'

'Longshanks loved her,' Isabel said, 'hard man though he is.'

'Aye,' Hal said and shook himself from the memories. 'We share that pain, if little else.'

'One other thing you share,' Isabel said impishly, 'is a horse. The king's favourite horse is Bayard and the Balius you ride is from the same stock.'

Bayard, Hal knew, was the name of a magical bay from children's stories, a redhead with a heart of gold and the mind of a fox and would have been a good name for Isabel herself. He said as much and she threw back her head and laughed aloud, a marvellous construct of white throat and rill that left Hal grinning, slack and foolish.

'I heard he rode Bayard at Berwick,' Sim growled, coming up in time to hear this last, crashing into it like a bull through a bad gate. 'Leaped the wood and earth rampart and led his men in for the slaughter, so it is said. We are nearly at St Mary's Wynd – do we cross the brig and join the rebels up on Abbey Craig?'

'Join the rebels,' she had said and laughed.

Hal shook himself from his revery, back to the present. Easy for you to laugh, Lady, he thought bitterly, who are never done rebelling, one way or another. Yet I have been charged to see you safe and so it must be . . .

Wallace had nodded off and Hal felt a sharp sympathy

with the sleeping giant, hair spilling over his face, one grimed fist a finger-length from the hilt of the hand-and-a-half. Keeping all these men together was a hard enough task, never mind trying to turn them from fighters into soldiers, trying to outthink the enemy, trying to plan how to win a battle against the finest cavalry in the world.

Join the rebels. By God, not again, Hal thought. Bringing the Countess here was the safest course for her, Hal thought, since her husband was a Comyn and so more kin to the rebels than English Edward. Now that it was done . . .

He stepped out into the night air, hearing the strange, wild sound of sythole and viel and folk wheeching and hooching in a dance, as if tomorrow was just another day, with time enough to work off a bad head. The world was racing towards dawn and Hal felt a leap of panic to be away from here before light . . .

'Let us hope they dance as well the morn,' said a voice and Hal spun to where Moray stepped from the shadows. He was young, thick-necked and barrel-trunked and would go to fat like his da, Hal thought, when he got older. For now, though, he was a solid, formidable shape in fine wool tunic and a surcoat with a blue shield and three stars bright on it, even in the dark. Behind him came the foreign knight who spoke French but was Flemish with some outlandish name Hal scourged himself to remember.

'He's asleep,' Hal said jerking his head back into the tent. Moray nodded and shrugged.

'No matter, the ring is arranged and all that remains is for us to take our partners and jig.' Moray said, breaking into French for the benefit of his companion, then paused, a smile, half-affection, half bitter rue on his face.

'I came to make sure The Wallace followed the steps,' he added. 'He has a habit of dancing away to his own tune.'

'Will you join us tomorrow, Lord Henry?' the foreign knight asked and Hal blinked, then realised the knight – Berowald, he remembered suddenly, Berowald de Moravia, the Flemish kin of the Morays – was inviting him to be part of the hundred or so horse, all that the Scots army possessed and almost none of it heavy warhorsed knights and *serjeants*.

He shook his head so vehemently he thought it might fall off. Balius belonged to Buchan and could not be risked in a battle like this, he babbled, while Griff was too light to be of much use. Andrew Moray nodded when this was laid out.

'Aye, well, it will be a painful dunt of a day,' he declared grimly, then nodded to Berowald as he spoke to Hal.

'The winning of it,' he added in French, 'will depend on the foot and not the horse, for all my kinsman here wishes it otherwise.'

Berowald said nothing, but the scowl spoke of his distrust at relying on ragged-arsed foot soldiers who were wildly dancing away the night before they had to stand and face the English horse. A thousand lances, Hal had heard, and he shivered. A thousand lances would do it – Christ, half that would plough them under, he thought.

He thought of Isabel and what would happen to the camp and the women and bairns in it if the battle was lost and panicked at that – the pull of her was iron to a lodestone.

She was in with the Grey Monks, the Tironensians from Selkirk, who had made a good shelter from tree branches and tent cloth, consecrating it into both a chapel and a spital for the sick and, soon, the dying. Hal found her arguing with a frowning cowl about how best to treat belly disease.

'Chew the laurel leaves, swallow the juice and place the mulch on the navel,' she said wearily. '*He* chews the leaves and swallows, not you. I would not stray far from the jakes now if I were you.'

The monk, pale faced in the shadows under the cowl, nodded and reeled away; Isabel turned to Hal, raising eyes and brows to the dark. She jerked her head and he followed her to a curtained-off chamber, where, once inside, she hauled off her

211

headcovering and scrubbed the spill of dark unbraided red-auburn hair which fell to her shoulders, like a dog scratching fleas and with every sign of enjoyment.

'God's Wounds, that feels good,' she exclaimed. 'All I need now is a chance to wash it.'

She became aware of Hal's stare and met it, the headcovering dangling in one hand like a limp, white snakeskin. Under his frank, astonished stare she felt herself blush and became defiant.

'So?'

'My . . . I am sorry . . . you took me by surprise,' Hal stammered and turned his back. She snorted and then laughed.

'There is not much you do not know of me now, Hal. Whore of Babylon is the least of it. Unhappy wife, certes. Unhappy and spurned lover. Showing my unbound hair to man not my husband or kin is the least of it.'

She sank on a long bench. 'No worse than having to be restrained by outraged monks from actually putting a mulch of leaves on a sick man's navel.'

'I was not expecting the hair,' Hal said.

'I admit it needs a comb and a wash,' she answered, 'but surely it is not as ravaging as a basilisk to the eye?'

'No . . . no,' began Hal, then saw her wry little smile. 'No. I was not expecting so much of it – I only saw it once down and in the . . .'

He stopped, realising the mire he had blundered into and the widening of her eyes.

'When was this?'

He felt himself prickle and flush.

'Douglas,' he admitted. 'I saw you and The Bruce . . . young Jamie's shield and gauntlet . . .'

It was her turn to redden.

'You were spying on me,' she accused and he denied it, spluttering, then realised she was laughing at him and stopped, scrubbing his own head ruefully.

'Aye,' she said, seeing this, 'the pair of us will have to shave like clerics to rid ourselves of all that is living in it.'

'Like your spital,' Hal answered, straight-faced, 'it seems to have offered space to all the poor souls who can cram in.'

Now it was her turn to smile and the sight warmed Hal. Outside, someone started to scream and Isabel's head came up.

'Maggie of Kilwinning,' she said, frowning. 'Her man is with Moray's *mesnie*. She was brought in raving about tigers of flame tearing her body. Four other pregnant women were brought in, spontaneously aborting. Three of them will probably die.'

Her shoulders slumped and he found his hand on her head before he knew he had even done it. She straightened and looked at him, halfway between flight and astonishment. He took it away and then she stirred and smiled.

'I would wash that if I were you,' she said.

'There are those who will say it is possession by demons,' Hal offered cautiously. 'A punishment for the sin of rebellion. A sign, perhaps, that God has forsaken us.'

'Bollocks,' said Isabel savagely and Hal jerked. Their eyes met and both smiled.

'So,' Hal said finally. 'A sickness. Of the mind, perhaps? The madness of the doomed?'

It was shrewd and Isabel acknowledged it with a nod of approbation into those cool, grey eyes. Then she shook her head.

'There are herbs that do that, though not so violently as this.'

'Poison, then?' Hal suggested and they looked at one another. She knew he was thinking of his dogs and Malise; for a moment she shivered, then shook it off.

'No,' she answered, 'nothing so murderous – St Anthony's Fire.'

Hal had heard of it though he did not know what it was.

213

'The curse of a saint,' she said. 'Which is never dismissed lightly. Ask the Earl of Carrick.'

She sighed and rubbed her tired eyes.

'One day we will find how the saint does it and why it is always the poorest of the sma' folk who suffer. I have no proof of it, but I suspect the bread. Or the herbage they put in potage. The poor do not have the luxury of refusing even the stuff that looks worst.'

'You know a deal on medical matters,' Hal said and she looked sideways at him.

'For a Countess, you mean? Or for a woman?'

'Both.'

She sighed.

'Well, remember I was once the daughter of MacDuff. My father was murdered, by his own kinsmen. The true lord of Fife is a a wee boy and a prisoner in England. I had no great expectations, even of a good marriage and, certes, not one by choice of my own hand.'

'Unlike Bruce's mother,' Hal said tentatively and saw the flicker of her lips at the memorable tale of how the Countess of Carrick had kidnapped the young man, Bruce's father, come all the way from the Holy Land to tell her that her first husband, Adam de Kilconcath, had died.

'Aye – maybe I should have followed her and locked up the son until he agreed to carry me off,' Isabel sighed. 'Then, he is not his father and holds that kidnapping up as yet another indication of how little spine his father has, to be so overcome by a woman.'

'Would it have been worth it, such a kidnap?' Hal asked cautiously.

'No, for certes,' she answered with a frankness that stunned him. She saw his face and managed a grim little smile.

'Once I thought there was love in it, but I always thought the Earl of Carrick was as good a refuge from the Earl of Buchan as I would find,' she said and her face darkened as

214

she spoke of Buchan. 'That one behaves as if I was a dunghill hen to his rooster – the day he realises I cannot give him the egg he wants will be the one that dooms me to a convent, I am thinking. As you can see, lord Hal, I am not suited to a cleric life.'

'You cannot have childer?' he blurted and the concern in it was balm enough for her to reply without anger.

'It would seem not,' she answered. 'I am young yet, but women with those years on them have a brood and more.'

The bitterness in it was a wormwood Hal could almost taste himself, so he sought to dilute it.

'Or are dead in the birthing,' he pointed out, then saw the bleak that scorched her eyes grey as ash.

'Better that,' she said softly and he saw the lip tremble, just the once.

'So – this is why you study the medical?' he asked hastily, levering matters back on track.

'At first,' she answered flatly, 'but that was not for a daughter, let alone one of Fife. I contrived a deal of it on my own, though books and treatises are hard to come by – and none of it was any help. Strangely, as the Countess of Buchan I had better freedom to indulge it and my own house at Balmullo.'

She stopped and he saw the beautiful eyes of her pool with tears, which she shook away with an impatient gesture.

'I have books there and kept Balius stabled at it,' she went on. 'My husband will want to burn it to the ground after this unless I prevent him.'

Hal did not want to know how she would prevent him. He did not want to know that she was returning to Buchan at all, or that he was the jailer taking her. Yet the thought of what might happen if the English stormed into this camp, all vengeance and victory, made him take her by the hand, so suddenly that it was moot who was more surprised by it.

'We could leave,' he declared. 'Tonight – afore the battle . . .'

She blinked once or twice, disbelieving – then the great warm rush of it hit her like a wave and it did not matter if they stayed or left, only that he had offered. She took her hand back, gently.

'You have done enough, Lord Hal,' she said and meant it. 'Go home. As I must.'

There was silence, long and aching.

'I even contrived to have a master from Bologna visit once,' she declared, suddenly brittle bright. 'The Earl was pleased, since it would keep me from shaming him at home.'

'Bologna?'

'Buchan no doubt hoped I would find humility, but I was gulling him. I said he was a priest from Rome.'

She broke off, sighed and shook her head.

'I have treated Buchan poorly and have sympathy for the man,' she added bleakly, 'but only to the point when he goes red in the face and punishes me, one way or another. Yet I have treated him as ill, in my way.'

'Does this excuse beatings?' Hal growled. 'A knight is supposed to protect a lady.'

Isabel smiled sadly.

'Ah, would it not be nice if the world was Camelot,' she answered. 'It is not, of course, so I cheated him to get this Master Schiatti from Bologna, for the best medical teachers are there at the University. What in the name of God and all His Saints I thought to do with what he taught I do not know – but I learned, among other matters, that even the most recalcitrant can be persuaded, for a price, to teach some of their art to a woman. Some of it was valuable, other aspects less so. I was good with the astrology, but mediocre with pigs at best.'

'Pigs?' asked Hal. Talking to this woman was like learning to skate on thin ice.

'Nearest to humans in anatomy and skin and bone,' Isabel replied. 'In Bologna, real corpses are kept for examinations and most everyday work is done on pigs. Strangled, burned,

216

poisoned and buried for a day, a week, longer. Bologna is a dangerous place to be a pig, Sir Hal.'

'If I ever take Sim Craw to the Italies, I will bear it in mind,' Hal said laconically, 'since his manners clearly endanger him with dissection. Mark you – it seems Balmullo is no place to root for acorns either.'

She looked at him sideways a little.

'You are not fond of physickers?'

Hal started to deny it, unwilling to annoy this woman, but the truth choked him. The ague was a pest which began as innocent as a shiver on a warm day, as if some sudden unseen breeze had caressed the spine. In three days or less, the shiverers were rattling their teeth on a rack of sweat-soaked bedding, the air in their chest wheezing like leaky forge bellows. They complained of the cold and burned away to a greasy husk before your eyes.

Others got it, too – from the vapours of the fetid, warm marshes according to the physickers and lazar priests – and some of them died swiftly, while others were abandoned even by their fearful priests and died of neglect.

One, the lovely young Mary of the Saltoun Mill, crawled from her sickbed and slipped into the river, drawing the cool water over her like a balming coverlet. After they found her, the same Saltoun priests who had abandoned her refused her consecrated burial, since she had taken her own life.

Not that they were any use when they found the courage to remain with their charges. Rosemary and onions, wormwood and cloves, vinegar and lemons, all mixed with henshit like some bad pudding or capon stuffing and smeared on the forehead and under the arms.

A live toad, fastened to the head. A live pullet, cut in two and held, bleeding and squawking, to anything that looked like a sore – though sores were no part of the ague that took Hal's wife and son, only a shaking sickness that boiled them away to wasted sweat, to where death was a merciful release.

She listened to him in silence, feeling the bile, the venom pus of it. When he had finished, she laid a hand on his arm and he felt strange and light-headed.

Another scream echoed and he saw her leap up, then waver uncertainly before recovering.

'Have you eaten?' he asked and she stared at him for a moment, then shook her head.

'Well, if you provide the wine, I will provide some oatcakes and a little cheese,' he said with forced cheer.

She didn't argue, so that they sat in a makeshift House of God and ate.

'Cygnets' Hal said, rinsing the cling of oatcake from the roof of his mouth.

'What?'

'Cygnets,' Hal repeated. 'A teem of cygnets. The game you like to play.'

He saw her face flame and her head lower. The oatcake turned to ash in his mouth.

'Pardon,' he stuttered. 'I thought . . .'

It tailed off into silence and he sat, mouth thick with oats he could neither spit nor swallow.

'It was a silly game for lovers,' Isabel said at last and raised her head defiantly, staring him in the face. 'To see who would be horse and who the rider.'

Hal forced the lump down his throat, remembering as he gagged, the high table at Douglas and her triumphant shout as she beat Bruce with her blush of boys. Ha, she had declared. I come out on top.

He found her hand thrust at him and a cup in it.

'You will choke,' she said and he forced a smile.

'Water,' said Hal with certainty, 'has fish dung in it.'

Then raised the cup in salute and drank.

'Which is as good a reason as any to avoid it and keep to wine.'

'That is Communion wine,' Isabel said wryly and Hal

spluttered, then put the cup down carefully, as if would bite him. Isabel chuckled.

'You have already swallowed enough to be allowed to sit at the feet of Christ Himself,' she said and Hal found himself grinning. They could both be ducked, or even burned at the stake for what they did here, drinking Holy wine and laughing blasphemously, her unchaperoned.

'Shrews,' she said suddenly and Hal blinked. The silence stretched and then she raised her head and looked into his grey eyes.

'A rebel of shrews,' she declared and added softly, 'I win.'

The thunder of blood in his ears drowned the sudden arrival, so that only the blast of air snapped the lock of their gaze. Like the opening of a chill larder door, the man crashed in on them.

'Ah might have weel kent ye would find the cosiest nook,' growled the voice. 'Wine and weemin – I taught ye well, it appears.'

Hal whirled, as if caught fondling himself in the stable, stared up into the fierce, grey-bearded hatchet face.

'Father,' he said weakly.

The Abbey Craig, Stirling
Ninth Sunday after Pentecost, Solemnity of the Most Holy
Trinity – August 11, 1297

They came to him just before dawn, as the sky lightened in a sour-milk smear, two earnest men already accoutred for war and clacking as they walked. Thweng watched them, seeing the grim eagerness in their hard young eyes, flicking over the blazons that let him know who they were. In the midst of their differing heraldry, a little badge in common – St Michael with flaming sword.

'The Wise Angels request a boon,' one of them said, bowing,

and Thweng sighed, trying not to let it out of him in a weary puff. Mummery. Chivalric posturing from folk gripped by Arthur and the Round Table – yet, beneath it, the very real courage and skill that might win the day. So he forced himself.

'Speak, Angel.'

'The Wise Angels request to be your boon companions in the Van this day, lord.'

'How many angels ride at my shoulder?'

'Twenty, lord. Sworn under Christ.'

'Welcome, Angels.'

He watched the men clack happily away. The Wise Angels were one of many little companies of knights who swore oaths to do great deeds of bravery on the eve of battle, although Thweng knew these were one of the better ones, composed of tournament-hardened knights. They had come to him, one of the foremost fighters on the circuit – and commander of the Van horse.

They had taken their name after Christ's rebuke to Paul when men arrived to arrest them and Paul wished to fight. 'Do you not think,' Christ had said, 'that, if I had asked, my Father in Heaven would not send me a legion of wise angels, against whom no man will stand?'

Today, a legion of twenty Wise Angels, against whom no man will stand, would ride at Thweng's shoulder, swelling the numbers of barded horse under his command. The Fore-Battle, the Van, would be led by Cressingham, around two thousand foot and Thweng's one hundred and fifty heavy horse designed to plant themselves firmly on the far side of the long brig and allow the Main and Rear battles, another two hundred knights and sergeants and four and a half thousand spearmen and archers, to form up under Barons Latimer and Huntercombe.

After that, it would simply be a matter of shooting the Scots to ruin and then riding the remnants into the dust.

It would have been simpler still if half the army had not melted away on the road up from Roxburgh and most of the rest sent home by the Treasurer on grounds of cost. Now the forces arrayed opposite each other were roughly equal, though Thweng knew the heavy barded horse and their lances would be the deciding factor. All the same, there were far fewer than he would have liked and Cressingham bore the blame for that.

Thweng heard the low, beast-grumbling groan of the army surfacing into the day, saw the spark of hasty fires in an attempt by some to get warmth in their bellies. Somewhere across the slow, ponderous loops of the river, he heard bells pealing. It is the Sabbath, he remembered suddenly.

Across the looped river Scots knelt while the wind ruffled through them as if in a forest. The Abbot from Cambuskenneth and his coterie of solemn priests walked the length of the humble horde, the pike blocks kneeling in ranks a hundred wide, six deep to be blessed. Men who had been cursing and wheeching carelessly in the night, hunting out the oblivion of women and drink in the baggage camp, now faced the cold silver of the day, shivering and crossing themselves as they begged forgiveness, knowing there was no time for everyone to take the abbot's pyx.

The wee Abbot would be less even-handed with the wafer, Hal thought, if he knew that Wallace would burn him out in an eyeblink to get at his sanctuary sparrow once this bloody affair was concluded satisfactorily. A Wallace, buoyed by such a victory, would want to get at the truth of why a master mason was murdered – and whether a Bruce or a Comyn had done it. That knowledge would be a weapon of considerable sharpness.

The last censer swung away in a trail of dissipating smoke and Hal got to his feet and faced his father.

'You should not be here,' he said accusingly, raking the coals of the argument that had heated them both the previous night. 'I left you safe, harvesting in Herdmanston.'

His father squinted a glare back at him, his iron-grey hair wisping in the breeze. Sir John Sientcler – The Auld Sire of Herdmanston, they called him, and he had been the capstone of that place for longer than the world itself, or so it seemed to Hal.

'We ploughed that rigg last night,' he growled back. 'For my part, I thought you would be back long since. I sent ye to Douglas a terce of months ago an' now find ye gallivantin' about with rebels and another man's wife.'

'Ye . . . I . . .'

His father chuckled and laid a steel hand on Hal's forearm.

'Do not gawp like a raw orb,' he chided gently. 'We have shouted at yin another and there is an end to it, for this cannot now be undone.'

Which was a truth Hal did not care for, since it wrapped himself, his father and his men in the coils of that Trojan serpent. The Auld Templar, back at Roslin to see to his great-grandweans, had told Hal's father what his son was about. Worse than that and unable to thole not being a part of any strike against the English, he had sent Roslin men to join Wallace – and stayed at home himself.

That last scorched Hal with a banked fire of fury. Stayed in Roslin and sent his steward – and the Auld Sire of Herdmanston. Who was no younger, Hal thought savagely, but a sight more honourable, so that he would not wriggle his way out of it with pleadings of old age, or that he was the only one to look to Herdmanston's safety.

'I have no fine warhorse and so cannot ride like a *nobile* this day,' his father declared suddenly, bland as a wimple.

'Balius is not mine. He is the Earl of Buchan's and I am charged with taking him back, hale and hearty,' Hal retorted, seeing the sly look the old man shot him. His father stroked his ragged beard and nodded.

'Aye, aye, so I heard. Stallion and mare both back to the Comyn – the young Bruce is feeling generous. Pity, though,

222

for I would have liked to have ridden as a knight proper in a great battle, just the yin time.'

'It is a young man's sport,' Hal said, ignoring the wistful longing. Concern made him brutal. 'That will be why the Auld Templar bided at home and sent his steward in his place. Sense would tell ye that is where you should be. You will note also the absence of a single chiel belonging to the Earl of Buchan, who still sits on his fence – or to Bruce, who is supposed to be on the English side. Save for us, who are in the wrong God-damned place.'

'Weesht,' he father chided softly. 'The Auld Templar bides in Roslin because he cannot be seen involvin' the Order in this stushie. And yourself is free to go – only I am sent to fight in this affair.'

He glanced at the outraged face of his son, already gasping out protest about how he was unable to leave his own da to certain death.

'Certain death, is it?' answered his father, cocking an eyebrow. 'Bigod, ye set little store by my abilities these days. Besides – there was never a thought about yer auld faither when you were clatterin' about with a coontess and a mystery. Ye have contrived to tangle yerself in the doings of Bruce, the Balliol and Comyn an' this Wallace chiel. As if there was nothing left for you at home but a wee bit stane cross.'

Then his father relaxed and paced a little.

'I ken why ye do it, boy,' he said more softly and shook his head. 'I miss them too. Grief is right and proper but what you are doing is . . . unhealthy.'

He stopped. Hal had nothing he could say that would not bring argument and anger, so he stayed silent – in the core of him he felt shame at what he had abandoned for grief and a sense that, like some chill cloud, it was lifting off him. His father waved a metal hand into his silence.

'There's sense in silence. No point in blowing away like a steamy pot,' he said. 'I have got myself dressed in all this iron at the behest of our liege lord, who seems determined to put Sientclers in harm's way, God bless the silly auld fool. So I have come here to this field to dance, not hold a rush light on the side. I do not have a warhorse, but I will have a wee wheen of Roslin pike to order so it is not all bad. What we should be discussing is this mystery of the Savoyard and who you should be unravellin' it to.'

'Wallace . . .' Hal said uncertainly and his father nodded, pursing lips so that his moustache ends stuck out like icicles.

'He has asked you to look at it, certes. But a Bruce or a Comyn is involved in it, for sure . . . so trust nobody.'

He looked at his son steadily, his eyes firm in the middle of their pouched flesh.

'Tak' tent – trust no man. Not even the Auld Templar.'

'What does that mean?' Hal demanded and his father rolled his eyes and flung his hands up.

'Christ's Balls – may God forgive me – do ye listen or not? Trust no man – Sir William asks me a deal about this affair for a casual aside. A man has been red murdered already and whoever did it is no chivalrous knight. I ken Sir William is our kin in Roslin, but he is sleekit in this, so – trust no man.'

He looked at his son, a hard look filled with a desperation that stitched Hal's arguments behind his lips.

'Whoever did such a kill will come at you sideways, like a cock fighting on a dungheap,' his father went on bleakly. 'Even from the dark.'

He clasped his son by both forearms and drew him into a sudden, swift embrace, the maille of his shoulder cold, the aillette with its shivering cross rasping on Hal's cheek. Then, just as suddenly, he stepped back, almost thrusting Hal away from him.

'There,' he declared huskily. 'I will see you on the far side of this affair.'

Hal stared, wanting to speak, dumbed and numbed. He

watched the armoured figure stump away into the throng, felt a presence on his shoulder and turned into Sim's big squint.

'Is Sir John fechtin' then?' he demanded and Hal could only nod. Sim shook his head.

'Silly auld fool,' he declared, then added hastily. 'No slight intended.'

'None ta'en,' Hal answered, finding his voice. Then, more firmly, he added, 'He will be fine, for we will be guarding his back. Seek young John Fenton, the steward of Roslin – that's where father is, and so we will be.'

'Good enough,' Sim declared, glad to have some sort of plan for the day. Then he jerked a grimy thumb at lurking figures behind him; Hal realised, slowly, that they were Tod's Wattie, Bangtail Hob and the rest, their faces shifty and eyes lowered. His heart sank.

'Ye let the Savoyard get away,' he said softly.

'Aye and no,' Tod's Wattie began and Bangtail shushed him, stepping forward.

'The Abbot came this morn,' he said, 'to tell us that a man arrived in the night and put the fear of God and the De'il both into the Savoyard. This stranger never got near our man, the Abbot says, but the Savoyard took fright and went out the infirmary drain.'

'The what?'

Tod's Wattie nodded, his eyes bright with the terror of it.

'Aye. Show's how desperate the chiel was. The spital drain, man . . .'

He left the rest unsaid and everyone regarded the horror for a silent moment. The infirmary drain was where every plague, every foulness from the sick lurked. For a man to risk himself to that, plootering like a humfy-backit rat through a slurry of ague, plague and worse . . .

'Who arrived in the night?' Hal demanded, suddenly remembering Bangtail's words. Bangtail twisted his hands and cursed.

'I saw him,' he declared in a pained voice. 'But ye said to

keep folk from leaving, not to stop them getting in. If I had known who it was . . .'

'Malise,' Tod's Wattie said, his voice like two turning querns. 'Malise Bellejambe, who pizened the dugs. He is in there now, claimin' the same sanctuary from us that the Savoyard did, for he kens what will happen whin I get my fists on him.'

'I have sent men to find which way the Savoyard went,' Sim added and Hal nodded slowly. Malise was on the trail of the Savoyard, which meant Buchan and the Comyn were involved.

Nothing more to be done with it on this, of all days. On the other side of it, God willing, he could start thinking matters through again.

Cressingham was a ranting, red-faced roarer, which did no good to his dignity with the troops he was supposed to be leading, Addaf thought. Mind you, the man is after having some reason.

The reason trailed behind him, coming back over the brig they had just crossed, led by the fat man bouncing badly on the back of his prancer of a horse so that the swans on his belly jumped.

'I am thinking folk do not know their own minds, mark you,' Heydin Captain declared, able to be loud and sour in Welsh, as they crowded back across the brig and sorted themselves out. Addaf saw the long-faced lord, Thweng, turn his mournful hound gaze back to where the Fore Battle straggled.

Cressingham scrambled off his horse and, already stiff and sore, stumped furiously up to the knot of men surrounding the magnificently accoutred Earl of Surrey, who stood deep in conversation with two men. One was the Scots lord, Lundie, the other was Brother Jacobus, his face quivering with outrage and white against his black robes.

'He dismissed us, my lord. As if we were children. Said he

had not come here to submit and would prove as much in our beards.'

Men growled and Lundie waved a dismissive hand.

'Aye, Wallace has a way of speaking, has he not?' he said, mockingly. 'But Moray's is the voice to listen to, my lords, and he will have some plan to take advantage of having to cross this narrow brig, my lord. You have seen how it is – two riders side by side can scarce find room to move. There is a ford further up. Give me some men and I will flank him – it will take me the best part of this day and you can cross in perfect safety tomorrow.'

'Tomorrow,' bellowed Cressingham, forcing everyone to turn and look at him. The Earl of Surrey saw the red pig-faced scowl of him and sighed.

'Treasurer,' he said mildly. 'You have something to add?'

'Add? Add?' Cressingham spluttered and his mouth worked, loose and wet for a moment. Then he sucked in breath.

'Aye, I have something to add,' he growled and pointed a shaking, gauntleted hand at De Warenne. 'Why in the name of God and all his Saints am I marching back and forth across this bloody bridge? Answer me that, eh?'

The Earl of Surrey felt men stir at the insulting way Cressingham was speaking, but quelled his own anger; besides, he felt tired and his belly griped. *Deus juva me*, he thought as the pain lanced him, even the crowfoot powder no longer works.

'Because, Treasurer,' he answered slowly, 'I did not order any movement.'

Cressingham blinked and his face turned an unhealthy colour of purple. He will explode like a quince in a metal fist, De Warenne thought.

'I ordered it,' the Treasurer exclaimed, his voice so high it was nearly a squeak. 'I ordered it.'

'Do you command here?' De Warenne responded mildly.

'I do when you are still asleep and half the day of battle

wasted,' roared Cressingham and folk started make little protesting noises now.

'Have a care,' someone muttered.

'Indeed,' De Warenne agreed sternly. 'I will have my due from you, Treasurer. Remember your place.'

Cressingham thrust his great broad face into the Earl of Surrey's indignantly quivering beard. Sweat sheened the Treasurer's cheeks and trembled in drips along jowls the colour of plums.

'My place,' he snarled, 'is to make sure you do the king's bidding. My place is to get this army, gathered at great expense, to do the job it is supposed to and destroy this rabble of Scots rebels. My place is to explain to the king why the Earl of Surrey seems determined not to do this without spending the entire Exchequer. If you wish to stand in my place before the king himself, my lord earl, please feel free.'

He stopped, breathing like a mating bull; the coterie waited, watching the Earl of Surrey, who closed his eyes briefly against the hot wind of Cressingham's breathing.

He wanted to slap this fat upstart down with a cutting phrase, but he knew the Treasurer was correct; the king wanted this business done as quickly and cheaply as possible and the last thing De Warenne wanted was to have to face the towering menace of Edward Plantagenet with a monstrous bill in one hand and failure in the other. He gathered the shreds of himself and turned to the Scot.

'As you see, Sir Richard,' he declared, mild as milk, 'the ink-fingered clerks will not permit delay. I am afraid your war-winning strategy will have to be foregone in favour of Cressingham's crushing delivery.'

Then he turned to Cressingham, his poached-egg eyes wide, white brows raising, as if surprised that the scowling Treasurer was still present. He waved a languid hand.

'You may proceed across the river.'

* * *

228

Hal stood to the left of the little pike square, the front ranks heavy with padded, studded gambesons and iron-rimmed hats, the back ones filled with bare heads and bare feet, trembling, grim men in brown and grey.

A hundred paces in front of him was a long, thin scattering of bowmen, right along the front to right and left and for all Hal knew there were some four hundred of them, it looked like a long thread of nothing at all.

There were shouts; a horseman thundered past and sprayed up clods so that everyone cursed him. He waved gaily and shouted back, but it was whipped away by the wind and he disappeared, waving his sword.

'Bull-horned, belli-hoolin' arse,' Sim growled, but the rider was simply the herald for Wallace and Moray. Hal saw the cavalcade, the blue, white-crossed banners and then the great red and gold lion rampant, with Moray's white stars on blue flapping beside it. Wallace, Hal saw, wore a knight's harness and a jupon, red with a white lion on it. He also rode a warhorse that Hal knew well and he gaped; Sim let out a burst of laughter.

'Holy Christ in Heaven, the Coontess has lent Wallace your big stot.'

It was Balius, sheened and arch-necked, curveting and cantering along the line of roaring squares as Wallace yelled at them. When he came level, Hal heard what he said clearly, a shifting note as the powerful figure, sword raised aloft, rode along the line, followed by a grinning Moray and the scattered band of banner-carriers.

Tailed dogs.

As a rousing speech, Hal thought, it probably fell far short of what the chroniclers wanted and they would lie about it later. Six thousand waited to be lifted and not more than a hundred would hear some rousing speech on liberty, with no time to repeat it, *ad infinitum*.

'Tailed dogs' repeated all the way along the long line did

it this time: the ragged, ill-armoured horde, half of them shivering with fear and fevers, most of them bare-legged and bare-arsed because disease poured their insides down their thighs, flung their arms in the air and roared back at him.

'Tailed dogs,' they bellowed back with delight, the accepted way to insult an Englishman and popularly believed as God's just punishment on that race for their part in the murder of Saint Thomas a-Becket; the Scots taunt never failed to arouse the English to red-necked rage.

Hal leaned out to look down the bristle of cheering pikes to where his father stood, leaning hip-shot on a Jeddart staff which had the engrailed blue cross fluttering from a pennon. He had his old battered shield slung half on his back, the cock rampant of the Sientclers faded and scarred on it – that device was older even than the shivering cross.

Beside him stood Tod's Wattie, offered up as standard-bearer in a cunning ploy by Hal to get him close enough, so that he now struggled with both hands to control the great wind-whipped square of blue slashed with the white cross of St Andrew. He had that task and the surreptitious protection of the Auld Sire to handle and he did not know which one was the more troublesome.

The great cross reminded Hal of the one he wore and he looked at the two white strips, hastily tacked over his heart in the X of St Andrew. A woman with red cheeks and worn fingers had done it when he had taken Will Elliot to Isabel in the baggage camp, finding her with the woman and the Dog Boy, moving among those already sick.

'This is Red Jeannie,' Isabel declared and the bare-legged woman had bobbed briefly and then frowned.

'Ye have no favour,' she said and proceeded to tack the strips on Hal's gambeson while he told Isabel that Will Elliot was here to guard her and the Dog Boy should the day go against them.

230

'He will keep ye safe,' he added. 'Mind also you have that Templar flag, so wave that if it comes to the bit.'

She nodded, unable to speak, aware of the woman, tongue between her teeth, stitching with quick, expert movements while Hal looked over her head into Isabel's eyes. She wanted to tell him how sorry she was, that it was all her fault that he was here, trapped in a battle he did not want, but the words would not come.

'I . . .' he said and a horn blared.

'You had best away,' Isabel said awkwardly and Red Jeannie finished, stuck the needle in the collar of her dress and beamed her windchaped face up into Hal's own.

'There, done and done,' she said. 'If ye see a big red-haired Selkirk man with a bow, his name is Erchie of Logy and ye mun give him this.'

She took Hal's beard and pulled him down to her lips so hard their teeth clicked. He tasted onion and then she released him as fiercely as she had grabbed him.

'God keep him safe,' she added and started to cry. 'Christ be praised.'

'For ever and ever,' Hal answered numbly, then felt Isabel close to him, smelled the sweat-musk of her, a scent that ripped lust and longing through him, so that he reeled with it.

'Go with God, Hal of Herdmanston,' she said and kissed him, full and soft on the lips. Then she stepped back and put her arm round the weeping Jeannie, leading her into the carts and sumpter wagons and the wail of women.

The kiss was with him now, so that he touched his gauntlet to his mouth.

'Here they come again,' Sim declared and Hal looked down the long, slope, sliced by the causeway that led to the brig. On it, small figures moved slowly, jostling forward, spilling out like water from a pipe and filtering up.

'Same as afore,' Sim said. 'It seems they are awfy fond with walking back and forth across the brig.'

231

'Good of them to show us the way of matters afore they did it for true,' said a voice and they turned into the round red face of John Fenton, steward to the Auld Templar. He was nicknamed The Son Of Roslin by Hal and Sim and the others who had all gone rabbiting or hare coursing together, long days ago.

A good joke for young boys, since John's cheeks were always fiery as the sun at summer noon; now they flared in the constriction of the bascinet helm, his dark-brown beard sticking over the lip of his maille coif like horsehair from a burst saddle.

The sight of it brought back smiling memories for Hal, of himself and John Fenton, young Henry Sientcler and his wee brother William, who had gone to the Church in England. The Sientclers, all Henrys, Johns and Williams, had rattled around the lands of Roslin and Herdmanston in company with the older Sim Craw and other lesser lights, sons of herdsman, ploughman and miller, causing mischief and being young. Hal grinned at the memory.

'How's your sister?' Sim asked and John nodded his thanks for the inquiry.

'Bearing up,' he said. 'The children keep her busy – Margaret is a handful.'

Fenton's sister, Alice, was married to the imprisoned Henry Sientcler. She would be sitting close to tears in Roslin, Hal knew, trying to find soothing explanations for a toddling girl and two boys – John and William. Christ's Wounds, Hal thought – John, William and Henry, do we have nae better names to pick for Sientclers? What was the collective for Sientclers, he wondered? A gaggle? A clutch? A brooding?

John Fenton looked up at the sky, squinting, then smiled.

'Nice weather for it,' he said. 'A wee bit rain earlier to add damp and make it hard going for men on heavy horse, dry enough for foot to skip when it comes to it.'

'Are we skippin' then, young John Fenton?' Sim asked laconically.

'In a whiley, Sim Craw,' John Fenton answered mildly. 'You'll hear a horn blaw when my Lord Moray decides enough English have been served up for breakfast. Then we will fall on them, like the wolf on the fold.'

'Christ betimes,' Sim declared with a lopsided grin, 'ye have become a fair battler since the days when Fat Davey used to wrestle ye into the mud.'

There was a moment of shared memories, of the reeve's great bully of a son, bigger even than Sim, who had terrorised them for years until, under Hal and Henry Sientcler, the other lads had joined forces and jumped him. They had tied him to a tree in the bull's field, with a long red streamer of cloth whipping in the wind and, when his furious father had finally released him, Fat Davey the Reeve's Boy was a wiser shadow of himself.

John Fenton took a breath or two, slapped the bascinet harder on his head and looked from Hal to Sim and back.

'Fat Davey,' he said with a grin, 'is a score of paces from ye, grippin' a bull's horn and waiting on me to tell him when to blaw.'

Then was gone from them, shouting.

CHAPTER SEVEN

Cambuskenneth Brig, Stirling
Ninth Sunday after Pentecost, Solemnity of the Most Holy
Trinity – August 11, 1297

This was no place for a bowman, and Addaf, jostled and elbowed, was not the only one to think it. As he cradled the bow-bag to his front, protecting the fletches and shafts from the crush as if it was a babbie, he heard other voices curse in Welsh.

'Make room for us,' Heydin Captain bawled, red-faced. 'Make room.'

There was no room; the horse had crossed and the foot after that, but the line of enemy was a distant raggle of spearpoints – about ten times our killing range, Addaf thought, measuring it with one closed eye as they staggered in the press.

The horse was closer, waiting impatiently for the crush of foot to sort themselves out from a mass of iron-rimmed hats and skull caps, spears, round shields, bucklers – not one of them, Addaf thought to himself, is armed the same as the next. Only the Welsh, he corrected, as a knot of them panted past in padded jacks, their spears and shields ready and the trailing red and green braid round their kettle helmets marking who they were.

He saw the last of them run off the bridge, lumbering like upright bears.

Far away, a horn blared.

Malise came up the causeway from Cambuskenneth at a fast lick on the horse, fearful that the Lothian men were hunkered and hidden, even though he had risked this throw of the dice by betting on all of them not wanting to miss the fight.

It had come as a shock to find the Abbey surrounded by hidden men – the thought that he had ridden so close to the likes of Tod's Wattie made his hole pucker enough to shift him in the saddle.

Having arrived, he found himself no closer to the Savoyard Bisset had told him of – the stone carver had panicked at having an enemy so close and had sneaked off. How he had got out was a mystery to Malise but, he thought savagely, it left me the one seeking sanctuary.

On his right, the Abbey Craig loomed like a hunchback's shoulder. Malise glanced to his left, seeing the banners and pennons waving, the fat white flags with red crosses snapping in the breeze, the St Andrew's cross flags whipped steadily in answer. No sign of hunting men . . .

Let them fight, Malise sneered to himself. If things contrived out the way he had planned it, he would skirt the left of Wallace's rebels and come up into the camp. There he would find the Countess – at last – and remove her. There, too, he might find the Savoyard, or a clue as to why the Lothian lord Hal hunted him and, more importantly, for whom he did so; there was Bruce in it, Malise was sure of it and he wanted to take the certainty of it to his master, the Earl of Buchan.

The horse skidded on the muddy road almost pitching him

off and he cursed, steadied and slowed a little – no sense in panicking now. Careful and steady . . .

Far away, a horn blared.

Almost in his ear, it seemed, a horn blared. Here we go, God save us. Hal heard someone yell it and then the whole line of hedgepig squares surged forward, like stones dropping from a castle wall. As if he was tethered like a goat, Hal felt himself move too, half stumbling over the tussocked, boggy ground, while the great murmuring beast-growl began, low and rising, to hackle his neck.

'They are coming,' shouted a voice, high and thin with disbelief and Thweng turned to where the man was pointing. Dear God preserve us, he thought bleakly, Moray has gulled us after all.

'Whoever heard of foot attacking horse?' demanded a voice and Thweng turned into the astonished gaze of the Wise Angel who had craved to be at his side. The dark little imps of the Welsh for one, he wanted to say, and those Englishmen who had been in those wars would know that – but few of them were here.

He said nothing, for it made no difference – if the Scots kept going they would roll down and trap the Fore Battle in the loop of the river. Water on three sides, no room to form anything coherent, no way back save across the brig, two at a time. Only one way out and that was ahead, into the shrike's nest of points.

'Cressingham,' he bawled and the fat Treasurer saw it, his mouth opening and closing soundlessly, the growl and roar and wind whipping the words away.

'. . . charge them, my lord. Charge.'

Thweng saw the Treasurer's sword come up and the Van knights stirred like a pack on the scent. The sword came down and the horse moved out at a walk, growing faster with each pace.

There was no other way to buy time for the foot, especially the archers, Thweng saw. All of them Welsh – the irony was not lost on him and he wondered, briefly, if the likes of Addaf would stand and fight.

He slipped into the great cave of his helmet and adjusted his shield, then moved out after Cressingham, hearing the sudden rise of song, high and firm. Young Angel voices, their sweetness not yet muffled by the steel of their great helms.

Foolish men, buried in evil, listen.
The Almighty shines all His power of joyous faith into
your hearts,
May not the serpent drive you back to former perdition.
Our best and true Redeemer will restore you to His
kingdom
And his wise angels will conquer by the sign of the Cross.

They were singing. Hal could hear it faintly as he loped past the archers, who were lobbing high, ragged shots into the mass of men crushed between the shining snake coils of the river. The Selkirk men were snatching up what shafts remained in front of them, for they heard the singing too, saw the movement of horse towards them and wanted away from it, back to safety behind the relentless boulder-grind of pike squares.

The slow, rolling roar of those squares drowned out the voices of angels. It swelled, red and angry, bloated with fear and fury, almost in pace with the approaching horses, now into a flogged trot, until it vomited out in a great, throat-ripping scream as the pikes stopped raggedly and braced.

The front ranks dropped their chests on to the left knee, supporting the pike, right leg trailing. The men behind raised their long pike spears over their heads and heeled the butt of the front man's pike into the soft ground with the stamp of a left foot, then leaned their weight to keep it fixed. The men behind them thrust long shafts between heads, resting them

237

on shoulders in front of them when the weight became top heavy, butting the shafts into their own cloak-padded shoulders against the expected impact.

Breathing hard, sweating like bulls, roaring like wet-mouthed beasts, they stood in their own stink and fear, close as lovers, waiting for the curling wave of spurred horse to fall on them.

Time flowed, thick and golden as honey. Sheltered in the rear of his father's pike square, Hal saw the horses, each barded, snorting, mad-eyed beast, the waving lances, the bouncing shields – white swans, red boars, chequered, ermined. The breath crawled in and out his nose, his palms itched and his groin felt drawn in, tight and hard; he wanted to run, to piss, to scream. It did not seem possible to resist . . .

They struck, with a crashing splinter like falling trees, and time howled back. Horses shrieked and flailed and reared, yellow teeth gnashing, necks snaking this way and that. Men screamed and stabbed, fell into the grinding, mud-splattering whirl of hooves and metal to be chewed and pounded.

Hal heard someone yelling meaningless sounds, discovered it was his own voice and started to move, crabbing into the maelstrom whirl that had the hedged knot of pikes at the centre of it, looking for the fallen and the dazed. A figure crawled, shoving and pushing out from under the dead weight of his horse, barded in thick padding and leather studded with bronze rings. He wore maille and a surcoat of the same leather and bronze, emblazoned with a blue lion on a yellow shield. He saw Hal and staggered weakly upright, holding out his hands to yield.

Knights did not die in tourney melee. Knights lost, were unhorsed and taken as ransom. Even in battles, only the ill-armed scum died. The slash of Hal's sword brought reality slicing in on the knight, a cut that spilled the fine wool padding from his cuisses and the blood from the thigh beneath it. He had time to feel the pain and shock of it, then the point of Hal's sword, growing as large as the whole world, came in through the slit of his helmet and stole his life.

No quarter here. Not with Berwick a raw wound on the body of the Kingdom – community and commonality were as one in the pain of that and no ransoms would be accepted by Scots this day. No-one had said so – but every Scot had determined it.

Hal felt something smack the back of his armoured head, the glancing blow staggering him, deafening as a bell. He whirled as the rider, twisting in the saddle as the warhorse skidded and turned, tried to face front and find a better blow from the axe he swung. A pike swung sideways, caught in the horse's legs and it went down with a high, angry scream, scabbing clods up with flailing hooves.

A figure covered in mud and streaks of blood lurched out of the press, swinging a sword in one hand and tearing off the domed full-face helm with the other, which he flung at Hal, roaring after it with his sword in both hands. The helmet clattered off Hal's shield, knocking him sideways, and he barely wobbled a parry with his sword as the second blow cut low at his legs.

Then Sim was at the knight's elbow, the crossbow slung and his long, thin dirk in one hand, the other snaking round the knight's neck, dragging him backwards with a crash. The sliver of blade gleamed like a silver snake tongue, flickered at the corner of the knight's eye and he shrieked and thrashed even before Sim lanced it into his skull.

The knight with the axe had crashed down, flailing in the mud. He scrambled away from the licking spear points of the hedgepig square while his horse kicked and shrieked, then he rolled over, sprang up, tearing off the great helm, as most knights did when it came to the heat of battle, eager for the air and the vision, leaving maille coif and open-faced bascinet to protect head and neck.

He stumbled towards Sim, ring-metalled feet sucking out of the mud, only to to take Hal's sword on the side of his bascinet helm, a bell-clang that drove the metal in on his cheek and knocked him sideways. He fell down, blood leaking from his eyes in red tears.

Hal and Sim gripped each other upright.

'Aye til the fore,' Sim said, his face streaked with sweat and someone else's blood.

Still alive, Hal thought.

Cressingham had balked at the final charge, but the maddened warhorse had the bit and did it anyway, somewhere in the maddened brain of it remembering all the training. Rearing and flailing, it struck out with huge metalled hooves and the fat Treasurer, a bad horseman at best, lost his seat and fell off into the mud, with a great crash that whirled stars into him.

Something huge and heavy stepped on his thigh – his own horse – and he heard the bone break. A great blow smacked him in the back as he struggled to rise and pitched him face first into the soft ground and he struggled like a pinned beetle, tasting the musky fresh earthworm of it, choking and blind because it had clogged up breathing holes and eyeslit.

He scrabbled frantically at the helmet ties, lost in the dark and airless cave of the bucket helm; finally, he tore it off in a mad, frenzied shriek and whooped in a breath, his vision no more than a blur. He saw the man come at him and lifted his good hand, free of weapons, out in front, sobbing with relief and pain. Ransomed.

Fat Davey saw a man fatter by far than himself these days, a man weeping with fear and holding his hand out, pleading for mercy. He had no idea who he was, only what he was.

Nae quarter the day wee mannie, he snarled to himself and drove the pike deep into the three swans on the man's swollen belly, put his horny, crusted. bare foot on the astonished terror of the man's iron-framed face and levered the weapon free again.

'Remember Berwick,' he growled and moved on.

*　*　*

No quarter today, thought Addaf, seeing the horses crashing and falling. Which made this no place for us. He turned to Heydin Captain and saw the grim set of his face.

'Away lads,' he heard Heydin say. 'Away as you value your lives.'

Addaf looked at the bow and the nocked arrow. He had not shot once, he thought with disgust, drew back to his ear in a sudden, swift movement and released the shaft blindly into the air, heard it screech away from him as the air hissed through a maker's flaw in the head.

He threw the bow-bag to one side and slung the weapon across his back still strung, wincing at what that would do to the tiller. He headed after the others, throwing away the entangling shoes from around his neck, the iron-rimmed hat, unlacing the gambeson as he went.

Down at the river, with the howling at his naked heels, he threw off the precious, expensive gambeson and wondered if he could dog-paddle well enough with a bow in one hand, for he would not give that up save at the very last.

They were broken and Thweng was not surprised. The French Method, he thought bleakly, which means ruin when inflicted on a wall of points. His own horse fretted and mewed from the pain of the great bloody scar down one shoulder, where a pike had torn through the thick padding, spilling out the wool in pink-stained skeins.

The Angels circled and milled, no more than a dozen of them now, balked by spearpoints, reduced to hurling insults and their lances and maces and even their great slitted helmets; he heard one chanting, as if he knelt in the cool still of a chapel – *blessed be the Lord my strength, who teaches my hands to war and my fingers to fight.*

Around him, Thweng saw the foot waver, take a step back, away from the wet-mouthed snarls behind the thicket of

241

steadily approaching spearpoints. A blade was thrown down; a shield was dropped.

Then they were off like a flock of chickens before the fox.

'The bridge,' Thweng yelled and pointed. The Angels swung their mounts.

The bridge. The only way left to safety and plugged by a ragged square of points, like a caltrop in the neck of a bottle.

The arrow came out of nowhere, spinning and wobbling, the weight of the bodkin point dragging it down like a stooping hawk and shrieking as the wind howled through a small maker's flaw.

Moray, who was trying to send the Selkirk bowmen to the right, down the river to dissuade the other two English Battles from crossing, had just turned to Berowald, smiling.

'*Et fuga verterunt angli,*' he had called out and Berowald, who knew the last words embroidered on the cloth story consecrated to Norman victory in Bayeux, waved one hand. *And the English fled* – he was chuckling at it still when he saw Moray look up at the sound of the thin whistling, his domed, crested helm under one arm so that he could call out clearly. He was smiling, because he knew they had won.

The arrow hit him below the right eye, drove downward, smashed the teeth on his right jaw, came out under the lip of the bascinet, speared through the coif and into the join between neck and shoulder, finding the thin treachery of space between flesh and the protection of padding, iron and maille.

Not long after, a rider churned his way over the litter of bodies and blood and bits that had been men until he found the panting, gasping figure he sought. Clotted with gore to the elbows, his wild hair stiff with it, Wallace snarled like a mad dog, dancing his own bloody jig in the raving centre of a knot of axemen. His new lion-blazoned jupon was shredded and he had long since hurled himself from the unfamiliar horse to fight on foot.

The rider was almost attacked, but someone spotted that he was the Flemish knight, the kin of Moray. Wallace heard the man's news and the axemen, panting and straining impatiently at the leash to be led back into the mad slaughter, were rocked back on their heels at the great, rolling, dog-howl of pain and anguish that came from the flung-back throat of their hero.

Hal saw the knot of riders split from the mass. The pikes were being flung to one side now, the squares melting away into vengeful packs of men dragging out long daggers, swords and falchions. The kerns and caterans, whooping now, unshouldered the long axes looped on their backs and plunged, like joyful leaping lambs, into the slaughter.

But a knot of riders headed for the brig, led by a man whose silver shield had a red slash and some birds on it. *Argent, a fesse gules between three papingoes, vert,* Hal translated and grinned to himself, wondering where the Auld Sire was at this moment. The arms of Sir Marmaduke Thweng, he remembered suddenly, the knight who had delivered Isabel and Bisset to the camp at Irvine.

Headed, he saw with a sudden lurch of utter terror, for the ragged knot of wavering spears blocking the escape route, already beset by fleeing hordes of the desperate, where a familiar figure stood in the midst of a misshapen copse of shafts like a rock in a flood.

His father.

'Sim,' he bawled and started running, whether Sim followed or not. A figure cannoned into him, realised he was an enemy and spilled away, weaponless and panicked. Another came at him, swinging a sword; Hal took it on the shield, cut left, then right and lurched through the blood the man spewed down his front as he died.

His horse was flagging and, later, Thweng realised it had probably saved him, for it let Angels overtake him and smash into the pikes in front of him, a terrible rending, ripping sound of metal and splintering wood. The French Method, he thought again, seeing a warhorse leap entirely off the ground, as if trying to clear a fence. It smashed down and died almost at once, but the carnage it created broke the hedge of points apart.

Thweng hit the remnants, striking left and right, trotting through almost unopposed, a handful of knights trailing after him. The helmetless, white-haired man weaved out of the press, almost in front of him; behind him came a snarling, stocky figure in a torn, studded coat, who swung the tangle of a blue, white-crossed banner at the legs of Sir Marmaduke's staggering horse and brought it down.

It was the tourney that saved him, the much-used roll from the saddle of a falling horse that had kept him in the fray many times before. He hit the scarred planks of the bridge and felt the pain lance into his shoulder – dislocated, he thought, perhaps even broken. Then he was up and on his feet, facing the white-haired man, who came at him, shield up, sword ready, his mouth open and gasping from weariness. Behind him, the man with the banner struggled to bring it upright in one hand and fend off the Angels clattering past.

A Sientcler, Thweng saw as his sword spanged off the cock rampant on the shield. Not the Auld Templar of Roslin, though – he took the weak return blow, stepped, half spun, smashed his shield forward despite the pain that stabbed him with and saw the old man go down, the sword spilling from his grasp.

'My lord . . .'

An Angel had flung himself from his horse, his earnest bascinet-framed face flushed and concerned. He handed the reins to Thweng in a clear indication and Thweng felt a pang at the youthful, careless courage that put chivalry beyond life. He wondered where along the way he had lost it in himself – then the old man at his feet coughed and stirred.

'Up,' he said, dragging the man to his feet. 'Sir Marmaduke Thweng.'

'Sir John,' gasped the man. 'Herdmanston.'

'Do you yield?'

'My lord . . .' the Angel said warningly, seeing men spill up the bridge to them. He cast the horse reins at Sir Marmaduke and moved to meet them, shield and sword up.

'I yield,' the old man declared.

'Just as well,' Thweng answered, dropping his sword and putting a supporting arm round him. He threw the reins away and, supporting the old man, hobbled after the ambling horse.

'The pair of us are done up.'

Hal saw his father go down and roared. He hit the crush of men around the brig entrance, was caught and held by it like a fly in amber, struggled and cursed and raved to be free. He used his elbows and knees, snarling his way through them, stumbled and fell, found himself staring into the dead, blood-streaked face of John Fenton.

He forced himself up, there was a blow on his back that shot him forward, out of the press and on to his hands and knees again, then Tod's Wattie was hauling him upright with one hand, the other still clutching the tangle of banner.

'Yer da,' he yelled in anguish and Hal followed his gaze, numbed.

Sir Marmaduke Thweng had hauled his father up and the pair of them were lurching away, like drunk friends from an alehouse. Hal screamed with frustration, for he knew his father had yielded.

The knight got in the way. He was off his horse, which wandered absently behind him and a brace of his friends stopped in the middle of the brig, uncertain as to whether to go to his aid, or continue protecting the back of Sir Marmaduke and his prisoner.

Hal knew, with a sinking lurch, that he was too late to free his father – then saw the knight in front of him, yellow surcoat stained and torn, the battered shield scarred, but up and set. *Or, three chevrons gules, avec a fleur-de-lis* – Hal had no idea who it was, only what it was.

'Sim, Wattie – tak' him alive. Alive, ye hear? Ransom.'

Sim heard and knew at once. Ransom this knight in exchange for the Auld Sire – he swung wide and Tod's Wattie, cursing the flapping tangle of blue banner, went the other. Hal closed in, yelling, 'Mine.'

Sim swore. If this chivalry matter was to be done right, it had to be Hal who did it, for he was a knight and Sim a commoner to whom no knight would properly yield.

They closed and the knight fell into a crouch, crabbing sideways; arrows wheeped and plunked round them – short dropshots, Hal realised, from the English bowmen on the far side, shooting overhead at their Scots counterparts.

He was fast and skilled, the knight. A tourney knight, Hal thought, used to rough and tumble, but not what was happening out in the pows and burns, where the kerns and caterans were butchering with no thought of ransoms, screaming 'Berwick' as a watchword.

Hal snarled and swung a sideways scythe that struck the knight's sword and made the man yelp, the clang of it belling out. He fell back, hefted the shield and launched himself at Hal.

A point flashed, Hal twisted sideways, gasping as the cold slither of it rasped past his cheek, skidding along the maille coif, dangerously close to his eyes. He felt the skin-crawling lack of a helmet of any kind, turned fear to anger and swung; he felt the blow, heard the clang and then was away.

A cut left, then right; the knight whirled the sword in a fancy display of wrist and strength, closed in again, slammed his shield into Hal's and staggered him, hooked it to one side, stabbed viciously so that his blade again glissaded along the maille on one side with a snake hiss.

The knight knew how to use sword and shield and Hal buckled under his attacks, while Sim growled, watching the men on the far side, trying to keep an eye on Hal, so that he could leap in if things went badly wrong.

The next blow tore wood and leather from Hal's shield, bounced up and spanged off his helmet. Sweat stung his eyes and he could barely see, his breath loud and rasping in his ears. His limbs were made of melting wax and the sword seemed to have gained three times its old weight.

He knew he was done and the next blow ripped the sword from his grasp. He heard the knight cry out in triumph, thought of his father and gave a roar, hurling himself at the man like a battering ram. His head caught the man's metal framed cheek and stars burst in his head; yet he heard the knight yell, high and thin with shock.

They went over in a crashing tangle of metal and grunts, Hal flailing his way past the knight's shield, battering his bare face with quick, ugly stabs of his forehead, pounding the man with huge two-handed blows of his own shield.

He crashed the sharp end of it just below the man's breastbone and heard the air drive out of the knight like a sick cow dying. He heard himself scream; his mouth was full of the salted metal taint of his own blood and his head throbbed with the thundering of his heart. He lost the shield, grabbed the knight's bloody head and slammed it again and again into the timbers of the bridge, so that the bascinet turned slick with gore.

Then, suddenly, Hal was upright, weaving and staggering. The knight lay gasping, bloody, half-blind, dazed, astonished. This was not Tourney. Not even the worst of Melee was like this . . .

'Sir Henry Sientcler,' Hal yelled in French. 'Do you yield?'

The fallen knight acknowledged it with a weak flap of one gauntlet.

'Sir Richard Fitzralph,' he replied in a weak voice, thick blood and mushed with the loss of teeth. 'I am an Angel.'

'If you do not yield,' Hal bellowed, all courtly French lost, 'ye will be singing with them, certes.'

'I yield.'

Thank Christ, Hal thought and slumped, panting, to the slick planks of the brig.

'My lord, where is Cressingham?'

Thweng turned as the rider came up, his face stiff with shock and bewilderment. The Main and Rear battles waited in serried ranks to cross, but fully a third of the army was gone and Thweng looked wearily up at him, then back across at the carnage.

'Almost certainly dead,' he said and the knight's face paled, throwing his neatly clipped black beard into sharper focus

'Taken, surely, my lord.'

Thweng turned to look at the maggot boil across the bridge, the howling, shrieking slaughter of it, then turned back into the knight's shocked gaze and said nothing at all, which spoke loudly enough to turn the knight's face paler still.

'What should I do?' the knight said uncertainly and Thweng pointed a weary flap of hand back to the eyrie perch of Stirling Castle, where he knew De Warenne watched.

'Who are you?' he asked and the knight, for all his shock, drew himself up a little. Proud, this one, Thweng thought wearily, to be so vainglorious in the face of all this.

'Sir Robert Malenfaunt,' the knight answered, his saturnine face sheened with sweat and so pale now that Thweng thought the man might faint at any moment. One of Lord Ughtred of Scarborough's men, he recalled, and part of the retinue from Bamburgh.

'Gather oil and anything that will burn,' he said. 'In a little while, a messenger will arrive and tell you to torch the bridge and retire.'

Malenfaunt nodded dumbly and Thweng could see the relief in him, that there had been a plan for this moment. There had

not, Thweng knew, but it is what he would have done. In the
end, it was what must be done – though God save us all when
Longshanks hears of this.

There had been a moment when Malise felt the fire of it
course in his blood, when he saw the blocked shapes crash
on one another and heard the distant rumbling roar, the
strange eldritch shriek of dying horses brought by a stray
tendril of wind.

By Gods Wounds, he exulted, we are winning this. Scots
are winning this. Then sense flooded back and doused any
flames of triumphant passion. Rebels were winning this and
so the Buchan and Comyn cause was not served by it, no
matter how huggingly gleeful the thought of such a victory
might be.

He hunched himself back on the horse and urged it on up
the slope of Abbey Craig. This was none of his business, he
reasoned. His business was with the Countess and a Savoyard
mystery.

It took him until the sun was sinking to get to the baggage
camp, which swarmed like crows on a ploughed field, and
Malise was barely challenged, for the only men he saw were
the ones hauling themselves in, or being helped by friends.
Blood skeins slicked back and forth, giant slimed snail-trails
marking the wounded and dying brought out of the fighting;
no-one here knew who was winning.

He found himself numbed, almost fixed by the screaming,
groaning, dying horror of it, managed to snag a passing
brown-robed figure.

'Countess of Buchan,' he growled and the priest, his eyes
haunted and the hem of his robe sodden with blood, blinked
once or twice, then pointed to a bower with a drunken cross
leaning sideways outside.

'Hold him,' he heard as he came closer. 'Hold him – Jeannie,
cut there. There – that's it. Now stitch that bit back together.'

She turned as he came in and her eyes widened a little, then went flat and cold. She was bloody to the elbow, her green dress stained, her cheeks streaked. Hair fluttered from under the creased ruin of her wimple.

'Come to help? Well done, Malise . . . take the legs of this one.'

Dumbly, Malise realised he had done it only when he was lifting the man. On the other side, the Dog Boy held the shoulders and tried not to look Malise in the eye.

'Over there,' Isabel said and was amazed when Malise obeyed like a packhorse to the rein. It was only when he realised that the man he carried was dead and he was stacking him with a host of others, like cut logs, that Malise stopped, then stared at the Dog Boy.

'I know you,' he declared, then curled his mouth in a sneer and dropped the legs. 'The wee thief from Douglas.'

The weight of the released dead man dragged the shoulders from the Dog Boy's grip and the man lolled, his head bouncing.

'No thief now,' the Dog Boy spat back, though his heart was a frantic bird in the cage of his chest. 'Ye have drapped him short. Do ye pick him up, or leave me to struggle?'

Malise took a step, his mouth working and his face blackening, but found the Dog Boy crouching like a snarling terrier, not about to back away. It astounded him as much as it did the Dog Boy, but Isabel's voice cut through the moment.

'Christ, Malise − can ye not even do a simple thing like lift a dead man to his final place?'

Malise rounded on her.

'Ye are to come with me,' he said firmly and Isabel laughed and rubbed another streak across the wimple and her forehead.

'I am busy, as you can see,' she said and turned back to the next man being brought in, holding the side of his face together with both hands and screaming bubbles through the blood.

'Now, lady,' Malise roared, driven past the reasonable now.

He grabbed her by the muscle of her arm, squeezing viciously as he did so, and she yelped, turning into the twisted mask of his face close to her own. The men who had brought their screaming friend in bellowed at him.

'Enough of this, ye wee hoor,' he hissed. 'Yer man, the earl, sent me to bring ye home and, by God wummin, you come willing or tied, but you'll come.'

The blow sent him sprawling into the mud and blood and entrails, face first so that he came up out of it soaked and spitting, to see the Dog Boy, triumphant eyes blazing at having shoved him in the mire.

He had no words, only a shrieking incoherent rage of noise as he whipped out the long dagger and headed for the Dog Boy, who looked wildly around. Isabel saw the red murder in Malise's eyes and tried to step between him and his prey, but he slapped her sideways with his free hand.

The blow took her hard on the side of her head, burst stars and red into her and, for the first time, a real fear. Malise had never dared touch her before . . .

Men growled at that, Malise rushed at the boy, slipped and slithered, regained his balance – then the world came flying out of the corner of one eye and exploded with a clang in his face.

Men cheered as Red Jeannie lowered the skillet and spat on the crawling, choking man on his knees, his nose flattened and his breathing snoring blood in and out. He lurched to his feet, the dagger still locked in his white fist and the world reeling; Red Jeannie stood with the skillet held like a Lochaber axe, while other faces, pale, ugly blobs swimming in and out of Malise's focus, snarled and spat.

They watched him back away, the dagger wavering in one fist. The Dog Boy looked wildly round for the Countess, but she was gone.

Malise found himself leaning against a tree and did not know how he had reached the place. The bark was rough and damp, the moss on on it cool on the crushing agony that was his face. He knew that he had been struck by something and was afraid of it, afraid to touch what had been done to him. He spat out two teeth, wondered how many more he had lost and hirpled away, to where a flicker of fires offered some comfort; he realised it was twilight and that, somewhere, he had lost an hour or two.

He had a horse somewhere, but he did not expect to find it anytime soon. Eaten, he suspected, by these animals from the far north. He sank down, away from the fire, starting to shiver with all that had happened to him, cursing the pain, the earl, the countess and God, who had all forsaken him.

Then he discovered that the Devil, at least, held true. The fire he half-crawled to, wary as a fox round a kennel, had two men at it, one lying in a shelter, one tending something in a pot.

'Not be long, your lordship,' the fire tender declared cheerfully. 'Good kail brose and a wee tait of black bread will return the life back in ye, eh?'

'My thanks,' answered the man wearily and Malise saw the torn yellow surcoat, the arms on the front. A prisoner, he thought, and then saw the face of the fire-tender, red-stained with flame as he leaned forward to taste the brose on a horn spoon.

Tod's Wattie. The belly clench of it almost made him whimper and he bit his lip, bringing more pain to his face. He started to back away, then stopped. The Lothian has taken a lord for ransom; the thought of such riches for the likes of Hal of Herdmanston and his crew burned fear and pain out of Malise in an instant. And Tod's Wattie had his back to him . . .

'Could use some meat, mark ye,' Tod said. 'But, parole or not, my lord, I dare not leave ye.'

The slumped figure moaned slightly and Tod leaned down

252

to rake through the contents of a pack, hoping the lord Hal had captured would not die; he felt the burn of shame for having failed to protect the Auld Sire of Herdmanston, paused as if frozen, his mind locked back to the madness of pikes and screaming, the bloody dying and that cursed, tangling blue banner.

John Fenton had died, falling under the iron-shod hooves of those English knights escaping across the brig, and Tod's Wattie still found it hard to believe the steward of Roslin was gone. He had known John Fenton all his life and now he was gone, as if he had never walked and breathed at all.

He shook himself; there was, he was certain, a peck of oats which might thicken the broth, shove some life into the English lord who would be exchanged for the Auld Sire . . .

The blow was hard and low on one side of his back, hard enough to make him grunt and pitch forward on to his knees. Furious, bewildered, he staggered upright and turned to see Malise standing there, his face bloody and misshapen.

'Ye gobshite,' he snarled and started toward the man, only to find himself falling. He thought he had tripped and tried to spring up, aware that the blow on his back had started to burn.

'Not so cantie now, houndsman,' Malise hissed, wincing at the pain it caused him, and now Tod saw the dull winking steel in his hand, knew he was knifed and that it was a bad wound. He couldn't seem to get up, though he kept trying, watching Malise's booted feet move to the slumped, groaning figure of the knight.

Malise found the pulse of the moaning man's neck with his fingers. The knight stirred, half-opened his eyes, wet and miserable in their pits of bruising.

'Who is there?' he asked in French and Malise cut the throat and the life from him in a swift, easy gesture of point and ripping edge.

He turned back to Tod's Wattie, gasping and clawing up the

mulch with one hand, the other trying to reach round to the pain in his back. Malise's grin was feral and bright.

Slick as lamp oil, viscous with fluids, thick with dead like studs on a leather jack, the causeway to the brig was Hell brought to the surface of the earth and Isabel staggered along it, half-blind with fear and tears, falling as often as she walked and with no clear idea of where she was, or where she was going. Away. Just away from the unleashed monster that was Malise.

Figures moved in the twilight of the dying day, flitting like crouching demons, spitting out incoherent curses whenever they encountered another of their kind as they crow-fought over the dead.

The smell was rank and there was a noise, a low hum like the wind through a badly fitting door, as those still alive moaned out the last of their lives, calling on God, their mothers, anyone. They had lain here all through the day, dying hard and slow and untended save for the birds and the pillagers.

Isabel stumbled, fell, got up and staggered on, the silent terror behind her pushing her forward like a hand in her back. He had never hit her before. Never. The leash on him was off and Isabel knew Malise only too well, knew what he was capable of.

She weaved like the shadow of a drunk, found herself staring, slack-mouthed, at a knot of half-crouched figures, growling beast-shapes, half-silhouettes against the last greying light of the day, half gilded by the yellow light of a guttering horn lantern. One turned and she saw the knife, blood-sticky in a clotted hand. His other fist held a long, raw, wet strip of flesh and his eyes a crawling madness; the others never looked up, simply went on cutting and growling, as if butchering a fresh-killed sheep.

'Get away from here, wummin,' the man said and watched

her lurch away before bending to his work again. It was only later, when the stories began to circle like a black wind, that Isabel realised that they had been flaying the English Treasurer, Cressingham.

Not then, though. She realised nothing but shapes and terror. A shadow fell on her as she collapsed, finally, to her knees and she whimpered; Malise had caught her. She looked up, squinting into the twilight and, with that part of her brain not screaming, she realised there was a splinter in her knee and that she was halfway across the brig.

'You hag,' said a voice out of the great black shape, a snorting Beelzebub whose cloven hooves stamped on the splintered planks. 'There is no plunder on this side of the bridge, only death.'

Behind him, she saw the flames of hell leap up. Not Malise at all, but the Devil . . .

'Mercy,' she sobbed. 'Have mercy on a poor sinner.'

She said it in French and the black shape paused, then leaned down. A strong arm grasped her own, hauling her upright. A face, sharp, black-bearded and weighing, thrust itself into her blurred vision, studied her for a long, curious moment, then turned his horse, so that she was hauled after him in a grip of iron.

'Move if you want to live,' the demon answered and she careered after him, shackled to his hand while the flames gibbered and danced, only vaguely wondering, in that small peach pit of sense left to her, why the Devil spoke French.

CHAPTER EIGHT

Balantrodoch, Templar Commanderie
Feast of St Andrew Protoclet, November 1297

Death came soft and gentle, yet harsh as haar, on the snow's back. The news of it filtered down like the sifting flakes and crushed everyone with the chill of it.

The Hardy was dead in the Tower. The Auld Templar's son was dead in the Tower. It was clear that the English Justinian, even though he was now in Flanders, had a long and petulant reach.

Worse still, the Auld Sire of Herdmanston was dead in Hexham Priory. Of his wounds, the messenger from Roslin said, but Hal knew better – his father, he was sure, had died of having been taken for ransom, at the realisation that he had fought bravely but with little skill and no strength, for age had robbed him of both.

He died from the knowledge that he had ruined Herdmanston, too, for the ransom would beggar the place and that, more than anything, Hal knew, had broken the life from the Auld Sire, like marrow from a snapped bone. The last thing Sir John could do to rescue the situation and all those who depended on him was to die.

And all because he had jumped off the fence, straight into the mire of a war where no-one was sure of his own neighbour. At the behest of the Auld Templar, too, which was worse still, for Hal was twice robbed of folk he held in high regard.

Now Herdmanston was threatened, because Hal had stayed and fought with his father, become a rebel for the Kingdom. The only saving grace in it was that the high wind of victory had stirred all the others off the fence. Bruce and Buchan, Badenoch and all the others – even the Scots lords who had argued the bit with Wallace and Moray the night before the battle – were all now committed to the Kingdom.

At least Wallace and Bruce and myself are all facing the same direction and foe, Hal thought.

The Dog Boy saw the misery etch itself into the face of Sir Hal, so that even the joy of the yapping, squirming terriers of Herdmanston's kennels was driven from him by the sight.

'Christ's Bones,' he heard Sim growl when he thought no-one could hear. 'God and all his angels are asleep in this kingdom.'

The kingdom itself seemed asleep, as if so stunned by the victory at Stirling Brig that no-one could quite believe it. Yet the *nobiles* of the realm shifted and planned while the world draped itself in a mourn of frost.

Hal rode out from Herdmanston in a black trail to recover the body of his father. It had been brought by the Auld Templar to the Templar Commanderie at Balantrodoch in a lead-lined kist from Hexham and under a Templar writ which no sane man, Scot or English, would challenge.

The dour cavalcade from Herdmanston held Hal, Sim, Bangtail Hob, Ill Made Jock, Will Elliott and Lang Tam Loudon, all the men bar two from the square fortalice. The Dog Boy drove the jouncing, two-wheeled cart which would take the kist back to Herdmanston, tagging along like a terrier at Hal's heels.

Sim knew that, for all Hal affected indifference, he was

257

constantly aware of the boy and it was made clear when Sim saw him manage a wan smile at the sight of the Dog Boy's face when they rode up to the Commanderie at Balantrodoch.

It was the first time the Dog Boy had been to the Templar headquarters in Scotland and it dropped the mouth open on him. Even the spital was a wonder. The roof was shaped like the hull of a ship turned upside down, to symbolise charity sailing about the world as a boat does on the sea. From the flagstoned floor to the apex of the roof was as tall as six men standing on each other's shoulders and coloured glass windows spilled stained light everywhere. Even Hal was impressed, for it was the first time he had been inside the spital with enough light to see it clearly.

It was as wide as three men laid end to end, with king posts carved with gargoyles and the beams brightly painted and marked at regular intervals with the Beau Seant, the white banner with its black-barred top that marked the presence of the Order. Over each doorway was etched *Non nobis, Domine, non nobis sed nomini tuo da gloriam,* the beginning of the first verse of Psalm 115, 'Not unto us, O Lord, not unto us, but unto Thy name give glory.'

Each bedspace, motifed in dark red and gold, was an alcove with drawn curtains for privacy and a table with its own pewter bowl, goblet and copper vessel. Across one end was a small but beautifully appointed chapel, so arranged that, when the door was opened and the rood screens drawn back, patients could attend Mass and follow the service without moving from their beds.

It was, Hal thought, a good place to be ill-healthed, was the Commanderie Hospital of Balantrodoch. There were six people trained to heal those Poor Knights wounded or fallen sick in the charge of the Chaplain – but they were not for the shivering mass outside the garth.

Like an accusing stare, they were huddled and ragged, the sick and well cheek by jowl and no way of really telling which was which. Hands and eyes pleaded for food, or water, or hope and the voices were a long, low hum of desperation – but these were the Knights Templar, not the Knights of the Hospital; charity was not their reason for being and the fine spital was for care of the Templars' own. Yet the Hospitallers' own headquarters at Torphichen was swamped and the ones around Balantrodoch were the truly desperate and abandoned.

Outside, the garth of the Commanderie was a silent, still wasteland of rime, a world shrouded in a winter mist that turned the sun to a silver coin. The worst poor, first victims of the unreaped, burned-out harvests and the early winter, had come here looking for hope and the plunder the army had wrenched from the English March – but there was little enough for fighting men, let alone bairns and women and the old. They had already started dying.

The sensible stayed in their homes and battened them; even then there were bodies found, frozen dead, with desperate hands bloody from scrabbling in the iron ground of kitchen gardens for the last remnants.

The world was gaunt and hungry, a dark rune of women and bairns and men, all half-starved, ragged and dirty with the carts they had trundled this far stuffed with the uselessness of their old lives – wooden stools, tin pots, ploughshares, tools for smithing, for farming, for carpentry. Mostly, the carts were full of misery and draped with makeshift shelters, the people in them clotting the lands round the Temple with their rubbish, their pleading, the smell of their sullen threat and fear.

There were fires and folk fought to defend the wood of their old tables, their carts and chairs. There were no horses or ponies – if there ever had been for some of them – and the meat was either carefully hidden, or bartered for other foods and fuel.

This was the price of red war, on both sides – the victorious

259

Scots starved because the harvests rotted unreaped in the fields. The defeated English starved because the Scots harried them in the *herschip*, vicious raids for the plunder of food as much as riches, raids that ravaged Northumberland from Cockermouth to Newcastle.

They ravaged the lands under the sheltering bulk of Barnard Castle and, if any noted that this was Balliol's English fortress, they stayed their lip and kept to a slaughter made bloodier still by the vengeful battle cry of 'Berwick'.

All this barely kept the army alive, though there was little of it left; men were taking what they could and going home in the hope of feeding their own kin through the winter.

The desperate came after the army like crows round a plough, risking the danger in it for the chance of a meal. Hal watched well-armed men arrive with a cart and start doling out maslin bread, the flour mixed with sawdust, saw the snatching hands and darting feet of those clutching the prize and wary of others lurking on the fringes to take it from them.

Hal, Sim and the others from Herdmanston had been stunned to find themselves riding into the midst of the slowly disintegrating Scots army and the desperate hopeful who trailed after it like gulls following a fishing boat. It was the Dog Boy who pointed out the lack of children, which made everyone realise it and look the harder, finding none; like their parents, the children were too cold, too tired from lack of food and there was no play, only forage.

A child found gnawing the stone of the chapel at Balantrodoch was taken to the Chaplain himself, Walter de Clifton, and, before the girl died, she claimed that the walls were made of gingerbread and that she was in the Land of Cockaigne, where fences were made from sausages and grilled geese flew directly on to your tongue.

She said this, smiling through a mouth of blood, and even the stern Sir Walter felt beaten by the hopelessness of it all – though the Templar Master of Scotland himself was unmoved

260

and more concerned about the interruption to the Order's routine. He called himself Brother John of Sawtrey and, for all his pious devotionals, Clifton thought, was a haughty void of Christian charity.

'Christ's Bones, Hal, this is a poor sight,' Sim growled, shaking his head. 'Winter has not even bitten hard yet.'

Hal had half expected something like this and was not so surprised by it, though the bleakness wasted his heart.

He and the other Herdmanston men had quit the *herschip* in mid-October and gone home. Wallace had permitted it, Hal knew, because he had seen the sickness in Hal's soul over the capture of his father, the death of Tod's Wattie and the knight, Fitzralph – and the loss of Isabel, who had simply disappeared from view. Not even Wallace knew if she lived or died – but offered the consolation that she had last been seen in the company of a knight fleeing Stirling, which meant ransom sooner or later. No-one would pass up the cost of a Countess.

The army had wandered, seemingly aimless, with little discipline and only one purpose – to winter itself on the English. After a few weeks of mindless burning and harrying had scorched the anger out of him, Hal wanted away and Wallace agreed, his own gaunt face blazoned with eyes as haunted as a midnight graveyard.

Hal and the others had ridden home with their share of plunder, to the cold comfort and tears of those left to care for the solid square tower and barmkin of Herdmanston. Tod's Wattie, wrapped and kisted up, had been delivered weeks before and decently buried at Saltoun, so the Herdmanston men trooped out to pay their respects and then shouldered their bags and burdens, nodded to one another and went home to their pinch-faced weans and wattle-and-daub hovels.

The Auld Templar, wasted by cold and effort to a husk of himself, rode over from Roslin because he knew the burning

261

concern folded into Hal's soul – knew also that the young lord blamed him for the capture of his father.

He tried to make some amends, with news he knew Hal would want and, if the truth was told, had called in favours with Templars everywhere to find it out, driven by his own sense of guilt that Hal was right, that he had asked too much of others in pursuit of his own devisings. Pride, anger and worse, he thought, while he knelt in the cold of Herdmanston's wee church, aware of the garishly painted tree, each branch holding one depiction of the Seven Deadly Sins.

God save me, he prayed, but there was no comfort in it and less in Hal's face when, eventually, they met in Herdmanston's hall.

'Taken south, I hear,' he said into the flat, cold stare of Hal's welcome. 'Her and yer father both. We have Stirling Castle under siege and, with a tait of luck, it will fall sooner rather than later, which will give us Sir Marmaduke Thweng, Fitzwarin and a wheen of lesser lights to trade.'

When Hal said nothing at all, the Auld Templar bowed his head.

'We will get the Auld Sire back, never fear, and mayhap the Countess Buchan as well – whoever holds her will demand ransom soon enough.'

Then he raised it up, for nothing could keep him staring at the floor for long.

'Though I doubt ye will find much happiness returning her to her husband.'

Then came the litany of deaths that left Hal in the great grey emptiness that was now Herdmanston and sent the Auld Templar south on his pilgrimage to fetch the body, scourged by guilt. He stopped at Herdmanston to tell Hal what he planned and spoke only to Sim, riding away with two servants and a cart, no more than dark figures on a rimed landscape.

On that same day, of hissing wind and snow swirling into

262

the half-frozen mud, Hal stood by the grey stone cross and watched a robin sing lustily, flaming breast puffed out as if it was spring.

Nearby, the small, half-built stone chapel that his father had petitioned the Franciscans at Saltoun to build was a rime of ice, no more than a cold catacomb for his mother's bones and a mortuary jar with her heart. Now her husband would lie beside her and Will Elliott patiently, painstakingly, carved out the marks that Father Thomas, the Franciscan from Saltoun who had been part of the price for the chapel, had scratched as a guide on the kist.

Hic est sepultus Sir John de Sientcler, miles militis.

In time, the bones of Hal's wife and son would be translated into the chapel. In time, he was to enlarge it for the glory of the Sientclers of Herdmanston and, in time, he would lie in it himself. Yet, for all the black dog of it, Hal could not think fully on that chill place, or the cross itself, for thinking of where Isabel was and how she fared.

Sim had no-one waiting for him, save a brace or two of women who would welcome him, and no other home but the tower at Herdmanston. He found, to his surprise, that he and the others were greeted as lions and heroes, that anyone who had fought with Wallace at Cambuskenneth was entitled to respect and a fete.

The Dog Boy found the delight of a straw mattress by a fire and two hot meals a day, mean though they were. Yet he missed Tod's Wattie, like the nag of something valuable mislaid.

When they clacked into Balantrodoch, they found the Auld Templar standing over the kisted up remains of Hal's father, the lid off to show his swaddled body, bared face stiff with rime, sunken and blue . . . it was so cold there had been little need of the lead lining for the box, but the Auld Templar had done it anyway and rumour had it he had stripped it from the gutters and roof of Hexham Priory.

His own face shocked all who saw it, for the death of his son, following hard on the loss of John Fenton, chewed on him, harsh as a dog's jaw. His pale cheeks were sunk, the eyes violet rimmed and, to those who had always thought the Auld Templar indestructible, the stoop of his bony shoulders frightened them. Hal remembered him, scant few months before, charging over the bridge with his hammer swinging left and right and, for a moment, felt some of the old love he'd had for this man.

It came to Hal that, if he thought grief hugged Herdmanston, then it must be throttling Roslin, where a woman wept now for her dead brother, her missing husband and the husband's dead father, while her weans stood, bewildered. The Auld Templar, Hal thought, was the mortar that kept Roslin from dissolving into tears and for all I find him guilty of driving my da to his doom, I cannot hate him entirely.

And all this to the victors.

The Auld Templar greeted Hal with a nod, was surprised at the brief, shared moment of warmth that was no longer than the beat of a bird's wing.

'Christ be praised,' the Auld Templar managed to husk out.

'For ever and ever,' came the litanied response and men crossed themselves.

There was precious little else to be shared round at Balantrodoch – when they came out of the crowded entrance to the Temple precincts, a sullen crowd, half begging, half resentful, watched them and their horses hungrily.

'Stay here,' Hal said to the Bangtail Hob, looking round. 'Sim and I will find out if there is a possibility of quarters here. If we leave our mounts they will be eaten by the time we get back.'

Bangtail nodded, looking at Ill Made Jock, the Dog Boy, Will Elliott and the handful of others who made up the party; he wished they had come properly armed.

Inside, his breath smoking in the chill stone of the place,

264

Hal came to a halt in mid-step, so that Sim had to dance to one side to avoid walking up his heels. He glared, then saw what had stopped Hal in his tracks.

'Herdmanston,' said Bruce, nodding in a grim way. He looked groomed and trimmed, healthy and young in his swaddling, fur-collared cloak, his shadow Kirkpatrick behind him. There were grim, spade-bearded knights behind him, crow-black save for the white cross that marked the Order of St John and that made Hal pause.

'You made good time, my lord,' Hal managed, 'seeing as how my father is not more than a five-day dead.'

Bruce grunted, his lip pensive, thought about the lie of it, then decided Hal needed better.

'I did not come for your father,' he declared, 'though it is a sore loss, all the same. A good man lost – though the cause he fought for was fine.'

He cocked his head sideways a little and smiled.

'Ye fought in it, I hear,' he added. 'A born rebel Scot, it appears, Sir Hal – ye even contrived to rebel against me at the time.'

'A happy anticipation,' Hal answered flatly, which made Bruce lose his smile.

'As well ye won, then,' he countered, 'otherwise you would not be back in the fold of my care.'

Hal said nothing, aware that he was still shackled to Bruce thanks to his fealty to Roslin. For all his passion to oppose the captors of his kin, the Auld Templar was not fool enough to attach himself to Wallace, victor or not. After what had transpired, Hal thought bitterly, it is good, if a little late, that the Lord of Roslin reins in his nature.

Bruce mistook Hal's silence for passive acquiesence to his censure, which mollified him. He smiled at Hal, nodding his head to where a familiar figure, bulked in wool, rolled through the clamouring press of begging hands, ignoring them all with a bland, fixed smile.

265

'I came down from the parliament at Torphichen with John the Steward there,' Bruce said, his face like an ice wall, 'to tell Wallace that Moray died. Since it seems he is too busy to attend it in person.'

'Died on St Malachy's day,' the Steward boomed, coming into the tail end of this; Hal saw Bruce wince and wondered at it, but only briefly. Another death – but he was now so numbed by them that the loss of Sir Andrew Moray, who had been hovering at the edge of it since the battle at Cambuskenneth, was muted.

'It was a curse for him, if no-one else,' the Steward said pointedly and Bruce managed a wan smile, while inwardly heaping another curse of his own on the pile dedicated to all those who offered continual, harping references to St Malachy.

'A curse for everyone,' Kirkpatrick muttered, 'since it leaves Wallace as the realm's sole hero and commander of the army.'

The Steward shot him a glower, then drew his cloak round him, shivering.

'Just so. Now we will confirm him a sole Guardian, as we agreed at Torphichen.'

'In the name of King John Balliol,' Bruce added, his voice slathered with bitterness.

'Indeed,' the Steward replied blandly. 'Bishop Wishart would say the same were he not fastened up in Roxburgh, prisoner of the English – which is a sore loss to the Kingdom.'

He smiled into the storm of Bruce's face.

'At least all the *nobiles* of the Kingdom are together at last. You and the Earl of Buchan, the Comyn of Badenoch and all the rest of us *gentilhommes* will stand side by side as we did at Torphichen's parliament, smile and agree to it. God's Wounds, if I can thole it, then you can as well.'

They would, since the alternative, Hal saw, was either the Red Comyn of Badenoch or The Bruce as Guardian, and neither faction would agree on that. Small wonder that the parliament had been held at Torphichen, with its preceptory to the Knights of St John a long-known sanctuary unlikely to be breached by murder. He wondered what Wallace had to say and wished he had not come here at all, plootering back into the mire of it all. At least Herdmanston had been a relief from that.

He made enough small talk to be polite then left, conscious of the gimlet eyes of Kirkpatrick following him, making the small of his back itch. Hal did not care for Kirkpatrick, thought him no better than Buchan's man, Malise. The death of Fitzralph and Tod's Wattie both burned and haunted him, for he knew who had done it – Christ's Wounds, they all knew who had done it – but had no proof to offer that would bring the man to justice.

It was a day for the black dog to howl, a dreich, frozen world of misery, from the hungry suffering of the living, to the cowled loss of the dead. Loading his father on to a cart was almost an afterthought in the swirl of events, for the real business of Balentrodoch was for the great and good to agree that Wallace be made sole Guardian now that Moray had died.

It was not an easy business for anyone, especially Hal and the Herdmanston men, for the Earl of Buchan stood no more than a score of paces away with his kinsman, the little stiff-faced Red John Comyn standing in for his father, the sick Black John, Lord of Badenoch.

For all Buchan was an Earl, it was the vain little strut of Red John who mattered, since he was, after Balliol himself, invested with the main claim to the Scots throne in opposition to the Bruces.

The Buchans and Comyn glowered at Bruce and Hal alternately, while Hal and the others had to stand, ruffed as guard dogs and barely leashed, watching Buchan and the skulker at his back – Malise Bellejambe. It gave them no pleasure to see his battered, broken-nosed face, though he had the sense to stay quiet and keep it out of the line of sight of men he knew trembled on the brink of springing at him with blades.

267

They had come to append seals to previous agreements, now written up in crabbed writing by a slew of inky-fingered clerks. There were few surprises in the entire affair save one and it was clear that it was not a surprise to the Steward or the Bruce entourage, though it stunned everyone else, even Wallace. Numbed with a genuine grief over the death of Moray, he walked like a man underwater, saying little while argument, mostly for the sake of it and to score points one off the other, rolled over his head between Bruce and the Comyn.

In the end it came down to a half-hearted excuse by the Comyn that Wallace was not a knight, so could hardly be elected sole Guardian, commanding the *gentilhommes* of the community of the realm.

'A fair point,' the Steward admitted, stroking his neat beard, his shaved-fresh cheeks like spoiled mutton in the cold of the Temple chapel. Buchan looked at Red Comyn and they both scowled suspiciously back at the noble; they had not been expecting agreement.

'Time he was made a knight, then,' the Steward decreed and Bruce, on cue, stepped forward grinning, to be handed a naked sword unsheathed by Kirkpatrick in a slither of noise that made everyone give ground a little and clap hand to hilt.

'Kneel, William Wallace,' Bruce commanded and the man did so, like some stunned ox about to be slaughtered. Hal saw the Comyn faces blazing with anger at having been so outflanked and upstaged – and having to swallow it until they choked.

The ceremony was over in an eyeblink. No vigil, or final blow either – even Bruce could not find it in himself to strike Wallace. Someone should, Hal thought, if only to wake the man up; he turned away, ruffled as a windblown cat by the whole affair.

He had planned on finding lodging for the night at the Temple, but that seemed unlikely and it was now late; it would be a long night's ride back to the nearest shelter, a farmstead with a decent – and starving-empty – cruck barn on the road back to Herdmanston.

Hal was giving orders for it when the Chaplain came up, white robes bright in the twilight.

'Sir William requested lodging for you and your party,' he said. 'He would deem it a considerable favour if you would stay and attend him later. Of mutual benefit, he says.'

For a moment, Hal was confused, then realised the 'Sir William' was Wallace. The title did not sit well even with the man himself, who was with three others in a cramped room of the guest quarters. One was Bruce, the second was the brooding Kirkpatrick and the third, Hal saw with some surprise, was the grim hack face of the Auld Templar.

'Well,' Wallace was saying as Hal was ushered in by a hard-faced kern, 'ye have had your wee bit fun – now ye will have to live with it.'

Bruce flapped a dismissive hand.

'That was Buchan and Badenoch,' he answered curtly. 'They will say black if I say white. I would not put much stress on what they think of your knighting.'

'Sheep dressed as lamb,' Wallace spat back. 'At best. Gild it how ye will, tie what bright ribbons ye care on it – I am still the brigand Wallace, landless chiel of no account.'

He paused then and offered a lopsided grin out of the haggard of his face.

'Save that I am king in the name and rights of John Balliol,' he added softly. 'And the commonality of this realm esteem me, even if the community does not.'

Hal saw Bruce's eyes narrow at that; the idea of Wallace being king, in any name, was not something he liked to dwell on even if he saw that Wallace was being provocative.

The Auld Templar saw it too and tried to balm the wounded air.

'Ye would have a hard time at a crowning, Sir Will,' he

said lightly. 'No Rood, no Crowner – and no Stone of Scone.'

Wallace, taking the hint, offered a wan smile of his own.

'That last is an especial loss to the Kingdom,' he said. 'Though it guarantees the surety of any Guardian – without the Stone there can never be a new king, only the one we have already.'

Hal braced himself for a snarling storm from Bruce, always jealous of his claims to Balliol's crown, and was rocked back on his heels when the Earl smiled sweetly instead.

'Indeed,' he said, then turned to the Auld Templar. 'As you say, Sir William – such a loss cripples kingship.'

'Just so,' the Auld Templar muttered, his face strange enough to make Hal look more closely, before the old man's next words drove curiosity out of him.

'Young Hal,' he said with a bow, which Hal gave back. 'I am right sore about your father. I hear he fought bravely.'

'He is . . . was . . . an an auld man,' Hal answered brusquely, which was as far as could go in forgiveness. The Auld Templar acknowledged it with a nod and a wry smile, though his eyes were still and steady on Hal's face.

'It was an ill day.'

'For some more than others,' Hal replied, sullen with the memory of Tod's Wattie and John Fenton.

'Fitzralph was also a hard loss to bear,' the Auld Templar replied pointedly and saw Hal bristle; he cursed inwardly, for he did not want an enemy of this young man.

'Come, come,' Bruce clucked. 'There was blood let on both sides and no blame accrues to you for the death of Fitzralph.'

'We all ken who killed Fitzralph,' Hal spat back. 'And Tod's Wattie. And my dogs at Douglas.'

'Aye, aye, just so,' Bruce interrupted. 'And yon wee scribbler Bisset in Edinburgh, I have learned. And his sister and her man. And others, no doubt.'

He paused and turned his fist of a gaze fully into Hal's

face, which was cold and flattened by the news of Bisset. Another stone to the cairn, he thought bitterly. He had liked wee Bisset.

'Unless ye have proof, or witnesses, ye might as well add the crucifixion of St Andrew, the betrayal of Our Lord and the forging of every crockard in the country at the man's door,' Wallace was saying. 'None of it will stick to him.'

Hal winked on the brim of it for a moment, then the reality pricked him and he sagged. Bruce saw it and patted his shoulder, patronisingly soothing.

'Aye, the loss of Fitzralph was sad,' he said jovially, 'but I am here to put some of that right – we have taken Stirling and can offer Fitzwarin as ransom for Henry Sientcler of Roslin.'

That was news – the fall of Stirling had been imminent for some time, but the sudden capitulation was a shock, all the same. And, thought Hal wryly, Bruce announces it and so links himself with the glory.

No-one spoke for a moment, then the Auld Templar shifted.

'He had a mother living, and brothers,' he said. Bruce looked bemused and the Auld Templar turned his long-moustached wail of a face on him, like black light.

'Fitzralph,' Hal added and Bruce, seeing he was being corrected, thrust out his bottom lip; he had been expecting beams of approval and effusive thanks and been rapped across the knuckles instead, but he managed a smiling face on matters.

'You are over-solicitous of a wee knight's death,' he countered, 'brave though it might have been. There is more at stake than this – your own grandson.'

'God is gracious and merciful,' the Auld Templar growled. 'He is also watching.'

Bruce acknowledged the fact with a display of crossing himself, though his face was a stone.

'The exchange will be conducted at Hexham. I will take Carrick men and Fitzwarin,' Bruce went on, 'once we have

271

all the writs we need to traverse the country peacefully. Sir Hal – it would be good of you to join us . . . I am sure the young Henry will be glad to see a kinsman.'

Hal looked at the impassive Kirkpatrick, then to the Auld Templar and finally to Bruce. It was clear the Auld Templar was not up to the travel and that Bruce knew it. Proposing Hal into his retinue for the affair was a considerable honour, though one Hal could have done without.

He managed to stumble out enough thanks to draw the Carrick lip in and Bruce gathered his dignity round him like a cloak then left, trailing Kirkpatrick in his wake.

There was a long pause while the Auld Templar looked mournfully at Hal and seemed about to speak. After working his mouth like a fish for a moment or two, he suddenly clamped it shut, nodded brusque thanks and left.

There was silence afterwards, then Wallace sighed and rubbed his beard.

'Young Bruce means well,' he said, shooting a sideways look at Hal, 'though he cannot help but seek some advantage from it.'

'Which is?' Hal asked, still brooding about Malise Bellejambe and how unassailable he seemed to be.

'Leverage with yourself,' Wallace replied and Hal blinked at that. For what end?

Wallace shrugged when it was put to him.

'You will ken by and by. He will not be backward in coming forward on it. He will find something in exchange for him using Fitzwarin to ransom yer kinsman. Besides – he is stinging over his own father, who was removed from command of Carlisle because of his son's antics. Not to be trusted now, it seems. So Bruce The Elder has gone off with his face trippin' him and the young Bruce is facing the prospect of his Comyn rivals triumphant and does not care for it.'

He stopped and shook his head in weary, wry admiration.

'Christ's Bones,' he added, 'the Bruces have a mountain of prideful huff at their disposal, have they not?'

'I thought Fitzwarin was yours to dispose,' Hal responded. 'Since it is yourself who is Guardian. Him and Sir Marmaduke Thweng both belong to the Kingdom and so to you.'

Wallace chuckled grimly, a rumble of sound Hal swore he could feel through his feet.

'Bruce takes pleasure in removing Sir Marmaduke to spend the Christ's Mass with himself; keeps me in my place, ye ken. Reminds me that I am, for all the new dubbing, not anythin' like a *nobile*, no *gentilhomme* with lands north and south. Like Sir Marmaduke, who is Bruce kin by marriage. So I am constrained to give him to the care of the Bruce, which infuriates the Comyn.'

He broke off and worried his beard with one hand, almost thinking aloud rather than speaking directly to Hal.

'In turn, mark ye, I have ordered that Sir Marmaduke will be ransomed for Comyn's cousin, Sir John de Mowbray, instead of being set ransom-free as Bruce wishes – and that is only to put the Earl of Carrick in his place, for I have a strong regard for yon Sir Marmaduke.'

He twisted his beard and matched it with a wry smile.

'Ye see the glaur I have to step through? So Fitzwarin's exchange is fine by me, even if the bold Bruce takes credit for it.'

'Ye are Guardian of Scotland,' Hal answered, astonished and Wallace's smile was bitter.

'Aye. As I was pointing out when ye came in – few of the *nobiles* like the idea. Christ's Wounds, the Steward is the ox pulling this along and you heard him at Cambuskenneth, the night afore that melee? How did it go? "A landless jurrocks with a strong arm and no idea of what to do with it until yer betters tell ye" if I recall. Spat from a face like a bag of blood.'

He stopped and sighed.

'I need Bruce and I need Comyn both. It was fine when Moray stood at my shoulder. Sir Andrew was their first choice and, by Christ's Wounds I wish he had lived, for I would rather it were him here and me in the grave.'

His vehemence and clear pain at Moray's loss stunned Hal to silence and it stretched like a shadow at sunset, to the point of painful. Then Wallace broke it with a growl that cleared his throat.

'Go to Hexham, get yer kin hame and then forget this business entire,' he said in a sudden, savage hiss.

'The Savoyard . . .' Hal began.

'He is dead or fled abroad, it seems to me. Yet wee Bisset, God rest his soul, was red murdered and put to some hard questioning first. If it was Malise Bellejambe, as we all suspect, then Buchan is on the track of matters.'

'So – all this footering after the Savoyard has gone for nothing,' Hal pointed out bitterly.

'It may be no more than another red murder for profit, by trailbaston long vanished. Or it may be Bruce's men. Or Red John, or the Earl of Buchan, or even Sir William The Hardy afore he was carted away to the Tower,' Wallace answered moodily.

'The community of the realm is a snakepit of plots, as I am findin' – and even Bishops are not abune poking their nebs in. My money is on Bruce, though the why of it eludes me yet – and probably will forever now. Best ye keep away from it, like me.'

He stopped and stared into the middle distance.

'Anyway – Longshanks is coming and, win or lose, everything will be birled in the air by that.'

The name itself seemed to chill the air. Longshanks was coming and when he reached the north, he would, for certes, raise the Dragon Banner and declare no quarter. Everything, as Wallace said, would be birled in the air. Including the Countess.

'Isabel,' Hal murmured and suddenly found the great grave-shroud face of Wallace close to his own.

'That especial you should forget,' the Guardian declared firmly. 'Bad enough ye should be trailing after another man's wife like a wee terrier humpin' a leg – but that it should be the Earl of Buchan's wife is a writ for ruin. Nor does he need Malise Bellejambe to commit his next red murder on you, for there are laws and rights that will break you just as readily.'

'There is him, too,' Hal said, recovering himself and feeling a cold slide into him, as if steel had been thrust into his belly. 'If I was to tak' tent with everything else ye say, I would not forget the business of Malise Bellejambe.'

Wallace sighed and waved a dismissive hand.

'Weel, I have done my duty,' he said, 'and warned you, both as the Law of the Kingdom and as a friend.'

'The Law?' Hal repeated and glanced sideways, to the great sheathed sword beside Wallace's chair. Wallace flushed; the tale of Cressingham's flaying had whirled like a spark, become an ember, then a fire that said Wallace now used a strip of the dead Treasurer's flesh as a baldric – other strips had been dispensed all over Scotland. The fact that Wallace never denied it told a deal about how the Kingdom was changing him, even as he changed the kingdom.

He paused and then grimed a weary, slack smile across his bearded face.

'Get ye gone. Do what ye must and I will likewise. It is better that ye forget the business of the Savoyard, but I jalouse that your neb is longer than your sense. So, if ye find the wee Savoyard and the secret he holds, I trust ye will let me ken it. Mark me – if this places a rope on yer neck for breaking the law of the land, I will kinch it tight myself.'

Hal saw the gaunt pain behind his eyes at that and nodded, then managed a smile as he turned to leave.

'Fine turn, this,' he said, grinning bleakly over his shoulder, 'when a brigand like yourself becomes the Kingdom's Sheriff.'

Spital of St Bartholomew, Berwick
Feast of St Athernaise the Mute of Fife, December 1297

The wind battered on the walls like a sullen child on a locked door, the chill haar-breath of it guttering the candles so that shadows swung wildly. The two men stood by the pallet bed and listened to the man thrash and groan.

'Stone,' he said. 'Stone.'

'He has been saying that since you brought him in,' the priest said, almost accusingly. He had a square face with a truculent, stubbled chin and eyes that seemed as black and deep as catacombs.

The wool merchant did not like to meet those eyes, but he did it anyway, with as blue-eyed and smiling a stare as he could manage, for he needed this priest, this place.

'He is a carver of stones,' the merchant answered blandly, 'for the church at Scone. An artist. Scarce a surprise that it should be in his fevered mind a little.'

'A little? He has been repeating it more thoroughly than any catechism.'

'A facet of his illness,' the merchant soothed, then frowned. 'What exactly is wrong with him?'

The priest sighed, lifted the crusie higher, so that the flame danced wildly.

'Best ask what is not,' he replied, then looked squarely at the merchant.

'I do not ask how you came by him, Master Symoen. I ken you brought him here because of the nature of his condition, but there are worse matters than leprosy and I have to ask you to remove him.'

Symoen stroked his neat beard, trying to cover his alarm. The arrival of a half-babbling Manon de Faucigny, smelling like a dog's arse and clearly diseased, had been shock enough, but this was . . . disturbing.

'Worse than leprosy?' he said and the priest laughed to himself as he saw the merchant put a hand to his mouth and step back a pace. He had seen it all in his years serving the Spital of St Bartholomew, which even the ravaging English had avoided – the lipless, noseless, rotting, foul souls who pitched up at the leper hospital were old clothes and porridge to the likes of Brother John.

Yet this Savoyard had everything. His blood was viscous, hot, greasy and tasted of too much salt. He had lacerations, ulcerations, abscesses, skin affections, partial paralysis, at least four festering bites from vermin and, almost certainly, a fever from one or more agues, each capable of killing him on its own.

'And intestical worms,' Brother John finished, seeing the wool merchant's eyes widen until his brows were in his hairline.

'Worms,' Symoen repeated, hearing the dull clank of the word in his head, like a cracked bell. 'Intestical.'

Manon was his nephew . . . he'd had hopes for the boy.

'I can do little,' Brother John said. 'All I do here is mop brows and pick up the bits that drop off.'

Symoen stared at the priest, who broadened his lips in a smile.

'A jest,' he said pointedly, but saw that Master Symoen was not laughing. Still, the man was a considerable patron of St Bartholomew's, so Brother John did what he knew he must. He offered every help.

'I will do what I can,' he said slowly. 'But it is as if he opened the gates of Hell and guddled inside it. Every sin has been visited on him.'

The wool merchant nodded, licking his lips and breathing

through his fingers, while the gaunt, sheened face of Manon swung wildly on the yellowed pillow.

'Oh Dayspring, Radiance of the Light eternal and Sun of Justice; come and enlighten those who sit in darkness and the shadow of death,' Brother John intoned, and Master Symoen, in a daze, descended to his knees and clasped his hands, grateful not to be looking at the tortured face of his nephew.

'Oh King of the Kingdoms and their Desire; the Cornerstone who makest both one: Come and save mankind, whom thou formedst of clay. Come, Oh Emmanuel, our King and Lawgiver, the Desire of all kingdomss and their Salvation: Come and save us, Oh Lord our God.'

'Stone,' babbled Manon. 'Stone.'

Nunnery of Saint Leonard, Berwick
Vigil of the Nativity, December 24, 1297

The woman with the cross sat at the head of the table, where the head man would usually sit; many other women, in similar grey clothes, sat around her. Isabel had seen brides of Christ before, though not in their setting and was shocked at the removal of headcovers, the shrieking laughter, the splashes of wine.

The woman who had brought her in saw her face and laughed as the woman with the cross got up and came to Isabel, dragging her from the room by an elbow. The door was closed on the gull-chatter.

'You were instructed to take her to my quarters,' the woman with the cross snapped at Isabel's guardian, who gave back a sullen pout. The sharp crack of palm on cheek made Isabel leap and her grey guardian reeled back and fell, her headcover awry; she cowered on the flagstones, whimpering and holding her face.

'Obey,' the woman with the cross said, soft and sibilant,

278

then turned to Isabel. If she strikes me, Isabel thought, I will rip the face from her.

The woman saw the fire in those eyes and smiled at it. Not for long, lady, she thought viciously.

'I am Anna, Prioress of Saint Leonard's,' she said. 'You will be taken to my quarters and made comfortable.'

The other nun climbed to her feet, nursing her face with one hand.

'This way, mistress,' she said numbly and Anna's voice was a lash.

'Countess. She is a countess, you dolt.'

The nun cringed and bobbed apologies, then scuttled off so fast that Isabel had to walk swiftly to keep up, through a bewilder of barely lit stone corridors sparkling with cold rime.

The nun led her through a door into an astonishment. Isabel stared at the fine hangings, the clean rushes, the benches, chairs and chests, the fine bed – and the fire. This was the warm room of a great lady, not a nun, even a Prioress.

'Countess,' the nun said in a dead voice and Isabel felt some pity then.

'That was a hard blow,' she said and the nun looked bitter as a thwarted rat, then to the left, then right. Finally, she moved to the wall, holding the light high and, satisfied, turned back to Isabel.

'This place,' she said in a whisper so soft Isabel could barely hear it, 'is cursed.'

The light made mad shadows dance on her face as she indicated the wall she had just peered at.

'There is a hidden way to watch,' the nun said. 'He likes it. All the women here are his.'

Isabel felt a sudden deadening sickness, for she knew the 'he' the nun spoke of, had endured the company of him since he had plucked her from the burning bridge at Stirling. A demon she had seen him as then and though sense and better

279

light had revealed him to be a dark, saturnine man, that first impression was not far from the truth.

'Sir Robert Malenfaunt,' she said and saw the nun shiver, so that tallow from the candle spilled down on to the back of her hand; she never flinched.

'All the women are for his pleasure,' she declared suddenly and half-sobbed. 'They are brought here and never allowed to leave.'

Isabel remembered the griming eyes of Malenfaunt, surveying her in better light. They had lit like balefires when he learned who she was and she had disliked him from that point, even though he had given her no cause and treated her with scrupulous politeness.

She watched the nun scurry out into the dark and sat on a bench while the tallow sputtered. She tried not to be beaten by the crush of loneliness, the realisation that she would go from here but only back to Buchan. She tried not to think of Bruce and failed, so that the added weight of that sagged her head limply on her neck. She tried not to cry and failed.

Then, to her own surprise, she thought of Hal of Herdmanston.

In a chamber off the main refectory of the nunnery, the Prioress listened to her charges laugh in wild shrieks, flamed by the wine brought by their benefactor, who stood half in shadow, half in the blood of the sconce light.

'Keep her fed, wined and secure,' Sir Robert Malenfaunt declared. 'And away from those harpies.'

'Special, is she?' sneered the Prioress and Malenfaunt smiled.

'A Countess. From Scotland, admittedly, but an important one. From a powerful family in her own right and married into another.'

He leaned forward, so that his sharp, shadowed blade of a face cut close to her own.

'Special, as you say. Worth her weight in shilling, so keep her fattened and untouched.'

He took her chin in cruel fingers then.

'Untouched,' he repeated. 'I want none of your charges to put their grimy fingers near that quim.'

She pulled away from him, though her heart thundered, even as he peeled off her headcover and ran his hands over her stubbled scalp; it excited him, that style, so she kept it close-cropped for that reason. Fear and lust made her breath shorten to gasps and she knew he would bend her over the only chair in the room, throw her grey habit up and over her head and take her, grunting and panting like a dog. He did it each Christ's Mass, to as many of the nuns as his strength and fortified wine would allow.

She was at once repelled and frantic for it.

Herdmanston, East Lothian
Ash Wednesday, March 1298

Hal watched the plough from the roof of the square block of Herdmanston, feeling the smear of ash on his forehead itch. He watched it with a warmth that had only partly to do with the sun, was as happy as any man can be on the first day of Lent, seeing his fields being turned back like bedcovers.

The ploughman was Will Elliot's da, his two brothers darting in and out to heel exposed worms back into the ground, or watching for the twitch of an ox tail that showed dung was coming, so the brace could be brought to a halt, to dump their precious cargo into the furrow.

The earth was new bread. The frost had cracked it, the thaw and rain had watered it, a week of late February sun had warmed it and it crumbled, heaving with furiously busy earthworms, little ploughs shifting the earth into a bed for oats and barley.

Gulls screamed, the coulter-knife scooped up clod against

the mouldboard, a great wave of new-turned earth rearing up, curving over and falling into a furrow. Below Hal, the Dog Boy was trying to teach the yapping terriers, all mad wriggle and fawning tails, some obedience and, from the laughter of those watching, was not having the best of it.

There was laughter, too, from the stone chapel where Father Thomas exercised his skills with a brush to construct a glowing Saint Michael, patron of the church in Saltoun, on the internal plastered walls – and emerged covered in ochre-red and looking like a man who had fallen in a slaughterhouse pit.

It was easy, on a day like this, to forget the winter, the war, the deaths. Isabel. Yet the world would not be kept back and its herald was Sim lumbering up the last steps, panting with climbing the winding stair to the roof.

'Rider coming,' he grunted. 'It will be the messenger from Bruce about the ransom for Sir Henry. At bloody last – God curse all notaries and inky-fingered clerks.'

An uneasy truce had been agreed with the English, but raids continued – more from the Scots side than the English – and only the winter weather had halted them. Getting agreement on ransom, then writs of safe conduct to travel south had taken a long time and the weather had closed in the north until no more than a few weeks ago. The Auld Templar will be fretting at the delay, thought Hal. Not to mention Sir Henry's wife and bairns, spending the Christ's Mass without husband and father.

He watched the horse and man come up over the great expanse of open ground, studded with copses, that surrounded Herdmanston, a rise and fall that hid the rider for a time. It was only when he got closer that Hal started to feel anxious; the horse was lathered and had been ridden harder than a mere message about an exchange warranted.

The rider was from Roslin, a broad-faced man Hal knew slightly, a labourer rather than a soldier, whose right thumb,

Hal noticed incongruously, was cracked open by cold and work. That must hurt, he thought . . .

It was a message from Fat Davey, who had taken over John Fenton's duties at Roslin.

The Auld Templar had turned his face to the wall.

Cloaked in misery, they rode over to Roslin, where the Lady stood with her bairns gathered into her skirts and her lip trembling at the edge.

'I am sorry for your loss, mistress,' Hal told her, hearing the dull pewter clunk of the inadequate words.

'Aye,' added Sim and then tried to brighten matters. 'We will ride south and bring your man home, mind you, so have comfort in that.'

It was a comfort, too, Hal saw, but only a little one. He met Fat Davey in the main hall of the stone keep that was perched on an outcrop of rock and surrounded by the timber and ditch of the old motte and bailey. They had started rebuilding Roslin in stone, but work had ceased when the Sientclers were captured, the money hoarded for expected ransom. At least they can start anew on that, Hal thought bleakly. Two dead, one to be freed and no money paid out at all.

Fat Davey was grateful for Hal's offer to take the Auld Templar to Balantrodoch, as was proper. Him and his clothes, his maille, his equipage and his warhorse all belonged to the Temple in common; another knight would have it.

But not everything, it seemed. Hal found Fat Davey's face staring into his own like a bleak moorland that sucked the life from any muttered commiserations.

'It was too much for him, the loss of John Fenton and then his son,' Fat Davey said, shaking his head. 'He just took to his bed and stared at the wall.'

He paused, fought for control and wrenched it into himself.

'Save for the once,' he added, fished in his pouch and brought out a small linen bag, handing it to Hal.

'He said, just before the last, that you should have this,'

he said, his cheeks a shadow of the squirrel satchels that had once bulged there. 'For varying reasons, he said. Not least of them being ye are the only grown Sientcler free and in the world.'

Hal thought of the Auld Templar's son, dead in the Tower and almost certainly bowstring murdered, or starved like The Hardy. Grandson Henry, father to the three bairns still at Roslin, was held in one of Edward's own castles, Briavel in Gloucester and, with luck, would be home soon – if Edward continued to think Fitzwarin more of a gain than the loss of a Sientcler prisoner. Or was not simply feeling waspish over the Scots affair.

His shadow was long, dark and unpredictable, Hal thought and soon Edward Plantagenet would be back, when matters would rush like a flood. There would be no exchanges then, when Longshanks turned all his energy to the Scots; Hal had a moment of panic to be on the move, to have Henry Sientcler back with his wife and weans before the raging storm of a vengeful king broke on the world.

Hal realised that Davey was right – with his own father dead and the Auld Templar himself stiff in the neighbouring chamber, Hal was the only adult Sientcler left out in the world; the linen bag suddenly started to burn the palm of his hand.

He tipped it out, saw that it was a ring and heard the thunder in his ears for the seconds it took him to realise it was not the seal of Roslin.

'Aye,' Davey said with a grin, 'I admit I was a wee bit facered when I first saw it. I thought the Auld Templar was offerin' ye the keys of Roslin. He was awfy quiet and prayerful when he heard John Fenton had died at Cambuskenneth and the news of his son's death cracked his heart open.'

'Christ's mercy on us all,' Hal declared, astonished. 'Roslin belongs to his grandson, Henry, whom we will bring back safe. And after him are his sons.'

He studied the ring. Sim peered at it over his shoulder.

'Silver, chalcedony,' he declared loftily, then looked blandly into the stares of the others. 'What? It is a wise man who kens the look of baubles. Saves ye guddlin' in a dead man's armpit for the cess when ye can lift the real shine.'

'What's the markings, then?' Hal challenged and Sim squinted, then shrugged.

'A wee fishie,' he said and Davey shrugged when Hal questioned him with silent eyes.

'No wisdom from me,' he said. 'The Auld Templar just gave it me and told me to deliver it to yourself. His only words on the matter were that it was an auld sin.'

Hal studied it carefully. A series of lines drawn into a fish shape. The old Christ symbol from Roman times, he recalled vaguely, though he could not bring the Latin of it to mind. He tried it on, but his knuckles were too big.

An auld sin. Hal shivered.

CHAPTER NINE

Northumberland, on the road to Hexham Priory
Vigil of Saint Ebbe the Younger, April, 1298

The oaks unfurled new leaves and the world was raptured by
rainbows. The writs came and Hal rode out with his men to
join the Bruce cavalcade; on the ride south, they saw cows
wrap their tongues round fresh green and rip it up, chewing
contently; sheep nibbling in hurdled areas, brown land turned
under the plough.

'I thought Wallace had harried this place thoroughly,' Bruce
said, with a half-sneer, half-wry laugh. He sounded disappointed
to see this evidence of life, even if folk hurried off, running
out of their pattens to get away from the cavalcade.

'Folks ken where to hide a brace of kine so that even the
herschip misses it,' Sim grunted back with his usual lack of
deference. Hal said nothing, though he marvelled at the folk
they passed, ploughing and husbanding, hoping to squeeze in
a desperate harvest before war came in the summer and
knowing there was a fair chance all that effort would go to
waste. Yet they would burn fields and slaughter livestock
themselves rather than see it fall into the hands of invaders
– as the Scots would in their turn.

Like Saint Ebbe, he thought, who took a blade to her nose and face so that the invading Danes would think her too ugly to rape. The ones who suffer most are the innocent.

Some folk never made it as far as the dreaming summer and they came on the evidence of it a day later, moving through lush valleys and low woodlands, the sweat itching them, the insects humming and pinging. The smoke brought half dreaming heads up and the scouts – Hal's men on their sturdy garrons – came galloping back with the news that a steading burned on the far side of the ridge.

'I would see,' Bruce declared and was off before anyone could tell him differently. With a muffled curse, Kirkpatrick followed after, looking wildly round and waving to Hal. Wearily, Hal kicked the sleepwalking garron into surprised life, heard Sim bawling for Bangtail and Lang Tam to move.

It was an outwork of Hexham's holding; probably, Hal thought, the peasant who worked it thought that the further he was from the influence of the priory reeves, the happier his life would be. Well, he had paid a high price for the freedom to cut firewood rather than collect it, or poach for the pot and miss a few plough days for the lordship.

He and his family lay on the sheep pasture near the softly muttering stream, not far from the blackened bones of their home; the wattle had burned, but the daub had hardened and cracked, so that the roof had fallen in and the walls stood like the shell of a rotted tooth.

The dead were all close together, Hal saw, and the women – a mother and a daughter becoming a woman, he thought – were still clothed. Led from the house and murdered, with no chance to flee and no attempt at rape.

'Baistards,' Sim growled and waved a hand at the churned earth. 'Took what they needed in a hot trod and did red murder for the sake of it.'

'How many, d'ye think?' Bruce demanded, circling his horse.

'Twenty,' Kirkpatrick declared after a pause to study the hoof chewed ground and Sim nodded agreement.

'Why would they kill them?'

The question was piped clear from the Dog Boy's bewildered voice and Hal saw his face – puzzled, but not so shocked as it should have been for a young lad of a dozen years or so, coming on death on a warm April afternoon. He was growing fast, Hal thought. And hard.

'For the sport in it,' Sim declared bitterly.

'For the terror in it,' Bruce corrected. 'So that others will see this and fear the ones who did it.'

'Scots, then, you think?'

'Aye,' Bruce answered, 'though belonging to no army. Left behind and on the *herschip* for the profit.'

'We should rejoin the main force,' Kirkpatrick offered nervously, as Bruce stepped his horse delicately round the strewn bodies.

The mother looked old and death had not been kind to her, yet she was no older than his own wife when she had died, Hal thought. No older than Isabel . . .

'A mercy the child was slain,' Bruce said, his voice a cat's tongue of harsh rasp, and Hal blinked, then realised Bruce was thinking of his own dead wife and Marjorie, the daughter left to his care.

'A father is no nurse. A young girl needs a mother,' Bruce went on softly, speaking almost to himself. He remembered his own daughter then, dark eyes, little full lips parting in a smile, the image of her mother; he closed his eyes against the memory of the chubby-faced mommet he had so neglected. The best he ever did for her was keep her from being taken as a thumb-sucking hostage after Irvine – which was as well, since he had broken all his oaths since.

'Riders,' Bangtail called out sharply.

There were three, padded and mailled, mounted on good horses, with latchbows bouncing at the saddle. They all had

288

little round shields and rimmed iron helmets and one carried a banner, yellow with a red cross on it. Behind were more; around thirty, Hal tallied swiftly.

'Norfolk's arms,' Kirkpatrick murmured to Bruce and he nodded. Roger Bigod, earl of Norfolk was, with his peers Hereford and Arundel, providing most of the army controlled by De Warenne for the defence of England. These riders, Bruce thought probably amounted to about half of the mounted crossbows in that army – his spies had told him there were scarcely 1,500 foot and 100 horse left to De Warenne.

The lead rider was tall, with a wisp of black beard and a dagger of cold stare which he switched between Bruce and Hal, taking in the jupons and surcoats, the heraldry there. On his own part, Hal saw a white shield with three little green birds on it, their wings folded across their backs. *Argent, three alaudae, vert, addorsed*, he registered and smiled; the Auld Sire would always be with him, in every coat of arms he looked at.

'I thought you might be from the Priory,' the rider said, his voice an accented French burr. 'But I see you have come further than that – Carrick men, is it? I do not know the engrailed blue cross, mark you.'

'We are passing through,' Bruce replied easily. 'To the Priory. We are Carrick men with a writ of *utbordh* from De Warenne – you know this term?'

'I know it,' the man said stiffly, then managed a smile. 'Safe passage. I am Fulk d'Alouet.'

'Oh, very good,' Hal said before he could stop himself, and the cold stare settled on him.

'Lark,' he added limply, waving at the man's shield with its three larks. 'Your device.'

'You are?'

Wishing I had kept my lip fastened, Hal thought, but forced a smile.

'Sir Henry Sientcler of Herdmanston.'

There was no answering smile from Fulk.

'I thought you were the ones who had done this,' he declared, encompassing the tragedy with a spread of one arm. 'They were Scots, of course.'

'We had no hand in this,' Bruce replied. 'Though you are correct that they were Scots. Possibly some English there as well. Mayhap a Gascon or two.'

The smile broadened and Bruce knew he was right – D'Alouet and the riders coming up behind him were all Gascon mercenaries, last remnants of the ones who had ridden away from Stirling.

'Yes. Brigands, then,' Fulk d'Alouet replied, then sighed wearily. 'I knew these folk well enough. We came to water our horses several times.'

'Feel free to water them now,' Bruce answered and the Gascon's face darkened.

'I am already free to water them,' he snapped. The rider with the banner, dark-eyed, dark-bearded, dark-mannered, gave a little grunt and a gesture across his throat.

'See to the horses,' Fulk said to him and climbed heavily out of his saddle. Hal watched Bruce do the same and, with a glance to Kirkpatrick, levered over the rump of the animal and dropped to the ground, legs stiff as old logs.

There was a show of stretching and grunting while a Gascon led off the horses, leaving Fulk and the young man, on foot now and swaddled by the limp banner. Fulk unlaced the bascinet and pulled it off, then hauled off the maille coif and the padded arming cap, rubbing one hand through the sweat-streaked crop of his hair. Without it, he seemed younger, though the corners of his eyes were hardened with lines.

'What is your business this far south?'

'An exchange,' Bruce answered, though he had been tempted, with a flash of anger, to tell this minor that it was none of his business.

'My lord,' Kirkpatrick said, 'we should be rejoining the others.'

It was timely and calculated, letting this Fulk know that Bruce was someone of quality and that he had more men at his back. Yet Fulk's head came up like a hound on scent.

'You are the younger Bruce,' he said slowly, the realisation closing on him. 'The rebel Earl of Carrick.'

'I have the honour,' Bruce replied. 'Though rebel is harsh.'

Hal saw that Kirkpatrick was watching the dark man with the banner and the line of dismounted men leading their horses to the stream, with little flicks of his eyes, one to the other. He turned to watch Bruce and the Gascon, who suddenly grinned broadly and dropped the helmet to his feet.

'*Bon chance* to you, my lord earl,' he said and thrust out a hand, which Bruce automatically took, found the Gascon's grip on his wrist hard and realised, in a sudden, shocking flash, that Fulk had dropped his helmet to free up his left hand – which was now behind his back.

In that moment, he was fourteen and back with the Auld Templar on the tiltyard at Lochmaben – and the knight had seemed old even then – being taught how to fight and, for the first time, given a real sword instead of a blunted one. Because of it, he had not tried to strike the Auld Templar once in the fight and, eventually the knight stopped and looked at him.

'What,' he said heavily, 'd'ye think ye are at here, boy?'

'Defending myself,' Bruce answered sullenly, more question in it than certainty.

'No,' the Auld Templar replied, 'for the best way to achieve that is . . . ?'

'Attack?'

'So set to, laddie.'

Bruce swallowed.

'You are unarmoured, sir,' he pointed out stiffly. 'Whereas I have helmet and maille and padding.'

He said this bitterly, for the weight was crushing him and

the Auld Templar insisted he wore it from the moment he stepped on the yard to the moment he left it.

'Are ye feared, laddie?'

The soft voice stung Bruce and the Auld Templar saw the lip come out.

'I might hurt you, sir.'

'You may dream of it,' the Auld Templar chuckled, then his face grew set and dark. 'I will come at ye, sirra, in the count of three. There will be blood on this yard and if ye don't fight me as if ye meant it, it will be yer own, I swear. Mak' a warrior of ye, yer da declares, even if it kills ye. So set to.'

Bruce felt the prickle of anger and fear.

'Three,' said the Auld Templar suddenly and came at him, so that Bruce yelped, barely managing to deflect the overarm broadsword stroke in a bell-clang shock that stunned his whole arm. What followed was the most intense three or four minutes of his life to that point, a whirr of blades scything like light and, at the end of it, the Auld Templar cursed and hurled himself away, sucking the back of his hand, where Bruce's blade had nicked him.

Bruce, panting and wild-eyed, watched him suck and spit, then chuckle, his grey beard splitting in a smile.

'Now ye ken what it is like when some enemy aims to kill ye. Now here is what ye do to thwart him.'

He remembered it all in the time it took Fulk to flick out the dagger from the small of his back and bring it round in a wicked snake-strike aimed at Bruce's throat.

Kirkpatrick called out, sharp and high, but Bruce did not shy away from the stroke; the Auld Templar's lessons were strong in him and he stepped forward into the attack as smooth as dancing and slammed his armoured forehead into Fulk's face. The Gascon dagger ground off the rim of Bruce's bascinet helmet and hissed harmlessly over the maille aventail.

The Gascon, with no maille or helmet, went reeling away, spitting blood and pungent curses. The man with the banner started forward only to stop short, as if leashed by Sim's great bellow. He paused, half-crouched and scowling, looking at the great, spanned crossbow pointed at him.

'At this range, chiel, it will rip ye a new hole in your arse,' Sim declared, smiling amiably, even though he knew it was unlikely the man understood him.

Fulk struggled like a beetle, finally righted himself and sat up; his men were milling, seeing their leader go down and shouting out, collecting weapons.

'That was well done,' Fulk said, climbing to his feet, a lopsided bloody smile on his face. He spread his arms in apology. 'I had to try. You are a fair ransom and we are mercenaries, when all said and done. I would not have lasted long as leader if I had passed up this chance. Now, of course, matters are worse for me.'

'You are a fool,' Bruce said and Hal saw that rage had switched him to French. 'I have a writ from the lord who pays you – if you had succeeded, he would have hanged you. There was no reason for blood to be spilled here. There still is not – walk away.'

Kirkpatrick had reined round and was galloping off, but Bruce did not turn at the sound, though Fulk did, knowing the man was going to fetch more men. It had been a bad day, dumped on his nethers like a child in front of his hard men. There was only one way back from that . . .

He drew his sword and Bruce sighed.

'My lord . . .' Hal said, concerned that an earl was putting his life at risk in a brawl. Sim kept the crossbow levelled at the banner-carrier, while the Dog Boy sat his mount, eyes wide, mouth open.

Fulk came forward, all at a rush, so that Bruce barely had time to clear his scabbard and parry the brief flurry of strokes. That had been the mercenary's best chance, though he did

293

not know it at the time. What followed, Hal saw, was a lesson in fighting.

Fulk was powerful and skilled, fought like a mercenary, without finesse and out to finish matters as swiftly as possible. He cut left, right, feinted, slashed at the legs, and Bruce, stepping backwards, weight on the back foot, met each one; blades clanged, sparks flew.

The Gascon paused then, breathing heavily, realising he faced a different temper of opponent than usual. Yet the man was an earl, a Tourney fighter, unused to the real world . . .

He started on a new series of cuts and slashes, found himself, shockingly, face to face with Bruce, who had stepped inside the arc of the sword. A hand took his wrist; Bruce spat in his eyes and stabbed downward with his own weapon, so that the fine-honed point went into the instep of Fulk's left foot.

Blinded, the agony a shriek that went all the way to the groin and belly of him, Fulk staggered away, flailing wildly though he could not do much since his swordhand was gripped in what seemed like a forge vice. Bruce followed, jerked savagely and tore the sword from the Gascon's grip as the man dragged screaming pain across his face, raking his own nose and forehead with his maille-backed gauntlet in an attempt to get Bruce's spit out of his eyes.

He cleared them, but had time only to see Bruce's sword go up and shied away from it. His own, in Bruce's left hand, came up in a whirling stroke, wet and ugly, that took him under the armpit, cut the arm, half the chest and all life bloodily away.

The Gascons growled and started forward – then stopped. Kirkpatrick came pounding up with a score of riders behind him, Bangtail and others to the fore with their wicked Jeddart staffs waving.

'We are leaving,' Bruce said to the banner bearer. 'You may have this offal when we are gone.'

He wiped Fulk's blade clean on the man's own jupon, smearing a red slick through the three green larks. Then he drove it into the ground, sheathed his own, mounted and rode off, his back to the Gascons in as pointed a gesture of scorn as anyone had seen.

'By Christ, he can fight, though,' Sim said admiringly as they caught up with each other, trailing in his wake and surrounded by the warm, safe, leather and horse stink of their own men. Bruce heard it and half turned, smiling wryly.

'The German Method,' he said and saw their bemused looks. Then he laughed and spurred ahead, so that only Kirkpatrick saw the tremble in the hands that held the reins so lightly, for he knew The Bruce as he knew his own hands, knew the fears in him were the same as other men and that the greatest one was not the Curse of Malachy, but failing to be anything less than best.

Kirkpatrick also knew that Bruce, for all he treated his henchman like a loyal dog, had long since relied on the skill, discretion and care Kirkpatrick lavished. Bruce thought he knew why the Closeburn noble did this and would have been surprised to find that Kirkpatrick, though he had once thought the same, was no longer as sure that it was only for advancement.

That night, with the fires sprouted like red flowers in the dark, Bruce came down to where Hal sat with the rest of the Herdmanston men. That itself was strange, for he had a panoply to shelter in, a great affair of blue and white with ropes as complex as ship rigging and a whole bed frame in it – he was a belted earl of the realm and used to the style of it.

Yet he arrived into the middle of the Herdmanston clutter, so that the chat died like a smothered candle.

'I would share fire and a cup, if you have it,' he said in careful English and with a lopsided smile, then waved a leather bottle in one hand so that it sloshed. 'In case the cup is empty, I brought something to fill it.'

'Welcome and doubled,' Hal answered, realising Bruce was drunk. Since there was little else to do but be polite, he smiled and offered the earl his own seat by the fire. Yet Bangtail and the rest sat, awkward and silent, even when they shoved out their horn cups to have the contents of the bottle splashed waveringly in it.

'Is Fitzwarin not joining us?' Hal asked politely and Bruce, his face pure as a priest's underclothes, announced that the Lord Fitzwarin was playing chess with Kirkpatrick. Hal did not say more; he knew already – as did everyone – that the haughty and annoying Fitzwarin, forever harping on about his kinship with De Warenne himself, grated on Bruce. No-one would be sorry to see the arse of him vanish over a horizon.

That ended conversation, all the same, and folk shifted uneasily, unable to speak.

'What is the German Method?'

It came, fluted as a bell, from the Dog Boy and cracked the strain of the moment like a stone thrown on an iced pool. Men chuckled.

'Aye,' Lang Tam Loudon enthused, the dam in him burst and spilling words. 'I heard your lordship say that about fighting yon Gascon. I am right sorry I missed it, too, for I am told it was a bonnie affair, as good as watching quines dance . . .'

He broke off, suddenly aware he was babbling, then stared, embarrassed, at his feet and finally buried his nose in his cup and slurped.

'The German Method,' Bruce said slowly to the Dog Boy, 'is how knights fight. One way. A Tourney way of fighting, though not much used, in preference to the French Method, which everyone seems to be at these days.'

He stopped, seeing the rapt, bewildered face of the Dog Boy, fixed on the words but understanding nothing.

'There are two ways of fighting for knights,' he went on,

drunken careful, speaking only to the Dog Boy though Hal saw every eye was on him. 'One is to train man and horse to charge straight at anything and bowl them over even if you miss with the lance. There are those who say that such a knight, on a proper horse, could burst his way through a castle wall.'

There were murmurs, half fearful, half admiring, from those who had seen heavy horse like this.

'That is called the French Method,' Bruce went on. 'The German Method is to ride a lighter horse, training it to avoid contact with the other mount. To skip to one side. To dance. Once your enemy has passed you, you ride after him and, before he can turn his great beast, you strike him from where he least expects it.'

There was a collective 'aaah' of understanding and folk nodded to one another.

'Like you did with the Gascon,' the Dog Boy added.

'Aye,' Bruce answered. 'I was trained that way by the Auld Templar. But the German Method is one for war, not the Tourney. So it is not much used now, because Tourneys do not like it. Not chivalric. They only call it "German" as an insult to those folk, because the real name should be "Saracen". Those are the folk who taught it to the knights of Christendom, and an expensive lesson it was, too, though only a few took it to heart, the Auld Templar of Roslin being one. Not the way a knight is supposed to fight – the *gentilhomme* prefers the French way, simply because it is French. *L'âne du commun est toujours le plus mal bâté.*'

The peasant donkey is almost always badly saddled – Hal wondered if he should translate it, but drink was creating a common tongue.

'Wallace doesn't fight like a Frenchie,' said a voice from the dark, and the others laughed.

'Sir William,' Bruce said, choosing his words as if he fished in a purse to find whole coins that were not pollards, 'is lately

297

come to the *nobiles*. It is to be hoped he learns the ways of a knight well enough – but not the French Method.'

'Is it hard to be a knight?' demanded the Dog Boy and there were a few chuckles as this, from those who only saw a boy asking endless questions. Bruce felt himself dragged in by those dark, liquid eyes, as if pulled towards some centre far away; he felt a sudden fear and thrill mixed, as if he was a fledgling on a high place, teetering on flight's edge.

'Have ye plans to be a knight?' demanded Will Elliott and, though the question dripped with ripe sarcasm, everyone was surprised when the Dog Boy shook his head vehemently.

'No. I leave that to Jamie. I will be a spearman. They are the lads who win fights.'

'From the mouth of a babe,' Sim declared portentously.

'Jamie?' Bruce asked and Hal told him. Bruce nodded owlishly.

'Young James Douglas in France, with Bishop Lamberton. He is now the lord of Douglas, though he is not of an age yet and Clifford now holds his lands.'

'Jamie will get them back,' the Dog Boy declared firmly. 'When he is a knight. Is it hard to be a knight, lord?'

'Hard enough, though the training for it is not the hardest part,' Bruce answered and found he was amazing himself with what he was saying. 'The hardest part is attending to the vows of it.'

'What vows, maister?'

The question arrived with the inevitability of a rock rolling downhill. Hal was on the point of interrupting, seeing the strange, half-stunned look on Bruce's face, when the earl spoke.

'What vows would you have a knight take?' he asked and everyone was silent, watching the Dog Boy intently, sensing there was something happening but not aware of what it was.

'Speak up,' Bruce demanded, staring round. '*Jamais chat emmitouflé ne prit souris.*'

The mice were safe enough, since all these cats remained muffled. Save one.

'To never lie,' the Dog Boy answered, screwing up his young face and remembering all the ones that had gone before – the one his ma had told him when she led him through the gate of Douglas Castle. 'Just for a wee while', she had said. 'I will be back.'

Men nodded and chuckled their approval, though they did not know the boy's reasons for the choice.

'To not pizen dugs,' the Dog Boy said and the murmurs were angrier, for all of the men knew his reasons for that one.

'To nivver violet a lady,' the Dog Boy declared, half remembering something Jamie had told him and suddenly, confusingly, aware of Agnes when Malise had come for her – and the Countess Isabel. There was a moment, a flash, of Agnes's foot bobbing, with the Countess's slipper trembling on the edge of falling.

'Nivver violet a lady,' echoed Bangtail and laughed. 'Is that the same as makin' yin a scarlet wummin?'

'Even proper said that's not a vow ye could hold to, Bangtail,' Will Elliott chimed and everyone laughed. Hal saw the Dog Boy scowl, not realising what he had said and thinking they were laughing at him. To his surprise, he saw Bruce had noted the same and reached out to lay a hand on the boy's hunching shoulder.

'To fear God and maintain His Church,' the earl declared, speaking to the Dog Boy and almost as much to himself. 'To serve the liege lord in valour and faith. To protect the weak and defenceless. To give succour to widows and orphans. To refrain from the wanton giving of offence. To live by honour and for glory. To despise pecuniary reward. To fight for the welfare of all. To obey those placed in authority. To guard the honour of fellow knights. To eschew unfairness, meanness and deceit. To keep faith. At all times to speak the truth.

To persevere to the end in any enterprise begun. To respect the honour of women. Never to refuse a challenge from an equal. Never to turn your back upon a foe.'

He stopped; the silence was a cloak.

'This we vow,' he ended, almost in a whisper, for the image of the Auld Templar swam in him and the face was his father's and he felt unmanned by the brimming of tears.

'Aye,' said Sim, bustling into the moment like a bull elbowing through a herd. 'Noted more in the breach than the observance these days, your lordship.'

'Sma' wonder only Wallace can lead us,' added Lang Tam Loudon sharply, 'if all the grand *gentilhommes* of the realm struggle to joogle that in the air daily.'

Hal said a sharp warning word and Lang Tam subsided, but Bruce had heard and Hal waited for the thrust of that truculent lip. Instead, he got a face, raised up from looking at the ground and as despairing as a thirsting flower in a desert.

'Aye,' Bruce agreed. 'It is to the shame of this realm that those charged with its protection have to lie and foreswear their vows to maintain their station and hold to the defence of it. And even that is sacrificed on occasion.'

He paused and raked them with a sudden glare and the wine-slack seemed to have fallen from him.

'Mark me,' he said. 'There will come a day when the knights of this kingdom find their vows. Then our enemies had best look to their lives.'

There was a pause, then a low burr of approval, a small growl of sound that left Hal as amazed as he was at Bruce's vehemence. Here was a Carrick he had not seen before . . .

'You should never lie,' the Dog Boy persisted and brought loud laughs that made him glare.

'Aye,' Bangtail declared, 'ye are young yet to appreciate the need for a good lie, wee yin.'

'Tell us,' Bruce invited and Bangtail frowned, wondering if

300

he was being cozened. But Bruce's face was open and smiling, his eyes bright with wine and the moment.

'Ach, yer grace – have ye never had a wummin come to ye with the ribbons ye bought her bound in her hair? Or a wee bit fancy cloth shawl? And she asks – how do I look in this?'

Everyone was nodding; even Bruce, whose smile was broader than ever.

'Well,' Bangtail went on, 'd'ye risk the quim and tell her she will be a fat milcher even with a sack on her curly pow, but she is the only wummin for miles willing to part one leg from the other? No. Ye tell her she looks fine, or ye temper your honour and remark on how nice the colour is and how is suits her – even if the plain truth is that it would gag a sow.'

The laughter was loud and long now.

'Now we ken why ye are named Bangtail,' Ill Made Jock shouted from the fringes of the fire.

'A glance at yer face,' Bangtail countered, swift and vicious, 'and we are in no doubt why ye are called Ill Made.'

'Bangtail counts cunny more than honour,' Sim declared, 'which everyone kens. This is his excuse for a lie – but it is still an excuse.'

'Ach, Sim,' Bangtail said, 'the world is not as divided, like the border atween this Kingdom and the English, where ye can declare "here we are and there you are and we are different from you". When it comes to the bit, though, ye cannae tell an English Dodd from a Scots yin, or a Kerr in Hexham from another in Roxburgh.'

'Ye can always tell a Kerr,' growled Sim, 'since all that breed are left-handed.'

Bangtail leaned forward, his sharp, fox face guttering with shadows and light from the flames. Hal saw that Bruce was fascinated, listening intently.

'Let me spier ye this, Sim Craw,' Bangtail went on. 'Is it good to misguide your enemy? To make him think, maybes, that ye are weaker than ye are, so that he makes a bad fist of attacking ye?'

Sim nodded, reluctantly.

'So it is fine to lie to an enemy,' Bangtail ended triumphantly and Bruce slapped one hand against the other with delight at Sim's scowl.

'By God's Grace,' he roared in English, 'I am truly sorry I never sat with Herdmanston men before this, for the entertainment in it is finer than a tumbler and juggling act.'

'Aye, weel, so ye say, your lordship,' Bangtail responded, preening, and Hal could not resist leaping in.

'Thanks to his lordship, we have learned a deal this night,' he declared, nodding deferentially to Bruce, who acknowledged it with an elegant, slightly mocking, one of his own.

'We have learned,' he went on smoothly, 'that Bangtail cannot judge which leg of a wummin is finer, the left or the right.'

Hal paused and let the puzzled frown of the man in question squeak on his forehead for a heartbeat.

'The truth of it for him is somewhere atween, of course,' he added and there was laughter at that.

'Abune all, there is the truth about lies,' Hal went on, warming to matters now and aware that Bruce was watching him closely. Never harms to stamp the mark of who leads Herdmanston, like a firm seal impress in warm wax, Hal thought.

'As I jalouse the workings of it, from his lordship and Bangtail here,' he continued, 'it seems that if a pig-faced friend appears with some pretty ribbons, ye crack their heart with the truth. If a pig-faced enemy appears with some pretty ribbons, ye tell them how wonderfully fine they look — an' strike from behind as they preen.'

Above all, Sim Craw thought as the laughter roared and circled like the wind round the fires, we have learned that young Bruce is also a man who can win the hearts of hard men of no station – the commonality of the kingdom who, until now, Sim believed to be the province of Wallace alone.

Here was a new thing, to find a man who was a powerful *gentilhomme* of the kingdom, yet who could share a cup, in companionable friendship, with a boy who did not even own a proper name.

Hexham Priory, Northumberland
Feast of St Donan the Martyr of Eigg, April 1298

Hal came up whooping and streaming water, dashed it from his eyes and dried his face on his serk, the sun warm on his back and a breeze with enough chill in it to remind him that this was the north in April.

He blinked back into the garth at Hexham, to the walls with their unpleasant stone the colour of dried blood, blackened here and there by fires set the year before – even Wallace had not been able to prevent the Galloway men's looting and arson, though he had hanged a few afterwards.

Hal saw Kirkpatrick staring at him intensely, a needle glare that almost made him recoil. Even when he stared back, the man's gaze did not shift and Hal grew irritated, both at the rudeness and the lick of fear the man's eyes smeared on him.

'If ye bring ribbons an' some decent wine ye might have a chance,' he snarled. 'Though I would not put much store by your supposed charm.'

Kirkpatrick blinked and flushed to the roots of his hair at the implication.

'Yon bauble,' he muttered. 'Round yer neck. Looked mighty fine, that is all. Where did ye come by it?'

Hal glanced down at the ring on the cord round his neck, a little surprised. Still flustered, he scowled back at Kirkpatrick.

'No doing of yours where this came from,' he harshed out and Kirkpatrick's face darkened even further, the eyes

303

narrowing. Hal cursed; his weapons lay three steps away . . . but a loud burst of shouting snapped the moment away and they both turned.

Fitzwarin, his face thick with flush, came storming out of the priory guesthouse, waving his arms and bellowing incoherently. Behind him came a flustered man-at-arms, making little bleats of protest, and, after that, Bruce himself, frowning darkly.

'Gone,' Fitzwarin roared, then strode on before the man-at-arms could reply. Then he stopped, whirling on the man as he trotted up, forcing him to skid to a halt.

'Gone,' he repeated and waved his arms wildly. 'To bloody Berwick. Are you entirely in your mind?'

'He is on parole, my lord,' the man-at-arms bleated. 'I sent two men with him – but if he wants to go to Berwick, there is little I can do save protect his person.'

Fitzwarin gave a final pungent curse and strode away, leaving the man-at-arms floundering in his wake, turning with a pathetic, appealing look to Bruce. The Earl of Carrick merely looked at him, shrugged and walked across to where Kirkpatrick and Hal stood, the latter climbing into his sweat-yellowed serk, aware of a sudden chill breeze.

'Sir Henry has taken himself to Berwick,' Bruce explained, his languid delivery belied by the grit of his teeth. 'Fitzwarin is less than pleased to be kept drumming his fingers here.'

'Berwick?' Hal demanded, bewildered. 'Why for?'

'A message, lord,' said the man-at-arms coming up to join them, his face anguished. 'I tried to tell the Lord Fitzwarin, but he would not listen.'

The man-at-arms was a captain from the braid in his belt and, in the next bobbing and deferential second Hal learned that he was Walter Elton, charged by Norfolk to bring Sir Henry Sientcler of Roslin to Hexham for the exchange.

'Then he had a message,' Elton went on. 'From a pardoner.'

'Message?' Hal demanded.

'Pardoner?' said Bruce at the same time and the captain's frantic eyes whipped between the two, then worked out that Bruce was an Earl and Hal of little account.

'By name Lamprecht,' he answered. 'Has a strange way of speaking, as if all tongues were used at once. French and Latin, I heard in it. Some of the Italies, too, by the sound and even words I do not know, though they might be from the Holy Land, which he has visited.'

'*Lingua franca*,' Kirkpatrick mused, 'which at least proves he has journeyed the lands round the Middle Sea, if nothing else.'

As have you, Hal suddenly saw and added a new dimension to the figure of the Bruce henchman.

'Oh, he is from the Holy Land,' enthused Elton. 'Has the shell to prove it and lots of relics and wondrous objects – here, look, noble sirs.'

He fumbled out a cord from round his neck to reveal a stamped lead medallion, a quatrefoil on one side and a fish on the other.

'Proof against evil spirits and wandering demons.'

No-one wanted to gainsay it, for demons existed, as everyone knew. Only last year one had been caught in the Tweed, a nasty black, snarling imp tangled in the salmon nets and beaten with sticks by the brave fishermen until it finally burst free and fled, shrieking laughter all the way back to the water. A bishop had written of it, so it must be true.

'Message?' Hal repeated and Elton blinked.

'Aye, sir. Came looking for Sir Henry by name. Said he had a message for him to get to the spital in Berwick. Life and death, he said.'

'Life and death?' repeated Kirkpatrick slowly, then curled his lip in a savage smile.

'Death, certes – the only spital I know of in Berwick is a leper house.'

'Christ be praised,' muttered Bruce, crossing himself.

'For ever and ever,' intoned the others and did the same.

'What could a leper house want with Sir Henry?' Bruce added, half to himself.

'A Savoyard,' declared Elton, nodding and admiring his lead amulet. It took a moment for him to realise the air had frosted and he looked up to see haar-harsh faces looking back at him and then each other.

'Savoyard,' repeated Hal in a voice full of tomb dust and echoes. Elton nodded uncertainly, the throat suddenly constrained.

'You are sure of this name?'

Again the nod. Kirkpatrick shifted and gave a grunt.

'Life and death,' he muttered.

Hal snapped from the moment and glared at him, all his suspicions flooding up in a rush.

'Aye, right enow – death for the Savoyard if ye get yer hand on him.'

Kirkpatrick's curse was pungent and the hand that flew to his dagger hilt was white at the knuckles. Elton gave a sharp cry and stepped back, fumbling for his own weapon – then Bruce slapped Kirkpatrick hard on the shoulder.

'Enough.'

He turned to Elton and thanked him for his information, then waited, saying nothing, until the captain took the hint and scuttled off, muttering. Bruce turned to where Hal and Kirkpatrick glared at each other like poorly leashed dogs.

'Sir Henry is in danger,' he said and Hal rounded on him, ruffed up and snarling, sure now that he was right, that Bruce and Kirkpatrick were responsible for the death of the master mason and that they done it to hide some other sin.

'Not him alone – d'ye kill us all, my lord earl, to keep your secret?'

'Hist,' said Bruce warningly, then let his glare dampen. 'Time ye were told some matters.'

'My lord,' Kirkpatrick said warningly and Bruce waved his hand dismissively.

'Christ's Bones, what does it matter now?' he declared savagely, resorting to French. Taking the hint, Kirkpatrick shrugged and fell silent.

Bruce looked around; they stood as a little knot out of earshot of everyone else. It was a sun-dappled garth, drenched with morning birdsong and bursting with budding life. Not the place for this, he thought to himself. This should be delivered in a tight-locked room of shadows and a guttering candle. He took a breath.

'When it was clear what Longshanks intended for John Balliol and this kingdom,' he began, 'myself and Bishop Wishart decided to forestall him. Edward planned to strip King John Balliol and the realm of its kingship and he managed the first well enough – so well that King John, shamed wee man that he is, never wants to return here even if we conquered the English tomorrow.'

You would wish, Hal thought. Better still if King John Balliol melted away like haar in sunshine, rather than hag-haunt the throne you want for yourself. He said nothing, simply tried not to tremble with excitement and apprehension while watching Bruce scowl and search for suitable words.

'Longshanks took the regalia of the realm,' Bruce went on, 'the Stone and the Rood and vestements for coronation. He broke the Seal into pieces.'

'We all saw it,' Hal declared, bleared with the sudden misery of remembrance. 'A harsh day for the kingdom.'

'Aye, well,' Bruce declared. 'He did not get the Stone.'

Hal blinked. Everyone had seen it, cowped off its twin plinths and sweated on to a cart to be taken south to Westminster. They had built a throne round it he had heard, so that every time Edward put his arse on the seat, he consecrated himself anew as Scotland's rightful king.

'You saw another stone,' Bruce declared and his face was bright with triumph. Hal felt Kirkpatrick's eyes burn on him, a clear threat; he preferred not to look into them.

'Wishart had the idea from the Auld Templar,' Bruce went on, 'who knew this master mason, a Fleming who had been overseeing work at Roslin until matters brought it to a halt. The mason went to work at Scone to wait and see if Roslin's ransoms left enough to resume rebuilding and was glad of the interest of a Bishop – glad, too of the promised purse, just for choosing a stone that looked the same as the one Longshanks planned to take. Then he used his Savoyard carver to make some of the marks expected and they switched it with the real one.'

'This worked?' Hal declared, astonished and Bruce's chin came truculently up.

'Why not? Few have seen the Stone up close and none of the English who took charge of it. They saw what they expected to see – a block of sandstone, with strange wee weathered and worn marks here and there, sitting where it was supposed to be.'

Right enough, Hal thought, his excitement rising. Which of those who knew would have risked speaking out?

'The master mason, Gozelo,' Bruce declared as if in answer, then continued: 'He, in company with Kirkpatrick here, took the stone to the Auld Templar at Roslin, where it would be secreted away until the day it was needed.'

The day you sat on it, Hal realised, seeing Bruce's face. The day you would need as much of the kingdom's regalia as you could recover, to make you legitimate, especially if John Balliol still lived, sulking in the protective shadow of the Pope. By God's Wounds, Hal marvelled, you had to admire the mountain of the man's ambition and the length of his plans – he would not even be eligible to be crowned until his own father died.

Then he went cold. The mason, Gozelo, had been killed; Bruce saw the look and transferred it, with a brief glance, to Kirkpatrick, who had the grace to flush slightly.

'The mason ran,' Kirkpatrick growled. 'An hour or two

from Roslin, he panicked and ran. He did not wait for any promised purse.'

'No doubt he thought you would pay him in steel,' Hal snapped, reverting to Scots.

'I had no such plans,' Kirkpatrick snarled back. Bruce soothed them both like a berner with hounds.

'No matter what was thought,' he added, 'the mason fled. Kirkpatrick had to take the Stone on to Roslin himself, where the Auld Templar and John Fenton took charge of it – the less folk involved, the easier the secret of it could be kept.'

'The Auld Templar gave me a horse and told me to go after Gozelo,' Kirkpatrick added sullenly. 'He pointed out – rightly, for sure – that once he thought he was safe away, the mason would look to recompense himself and the only way to do that was get reward from the English by telling them how they had been duped.'

The Auld Templar – had he persuaded Kirkpatrick to red murder, or had that been Kirkpatrick's own idea? Hal saw the truth of it, bleak as a wet dog, and remembered his father's advice on the day of the battle at Stirling's Brig: do not trust anyone, he had said. Not even the Auld Templar, who is ower sleekit on this matter.

Kirkpatrick saw the bleakness and shrugged.

'Mak' siccar, the Auld Templar said. So I did.'

Make sure. Hal glanced at the dagger hanging at Kirkpatrick's waist; fluted, thin and sharp.

'I took that ring from him,' Kirkpatrick went on, his stropped razor of a face pale. 'Took it back to the Auld Templar as proof the deed was done. He asked for such proof in particular.'

Hal glanced to where Kirkpatrick looked. The ring round his neck was Gozelo's own, plucked from his dead finger and returned to Roslin. An auld sin . . .

'Now you ken my interest in it,' Kirkpatrick added wryly. 'Rather than your dubious charms.'

'The mason is to be regretted,' Bruce broke in, frowning. 'He was never meant to be found either, yet up he popped, like a fart at a feast, on a day's hunting at Douglas.'

And there was the Curse of Saint Malachy at work, he added to himself, tangling my sin up with my own reins, to be hauled out for the world to witness.

Hal saw the Earl's face and wanted to believe the shame and regret he saw there. Regretted only because he did not stay decently hidden, Hal thought bitterly, rather than because you had to red murder him. Hal remembered the hunt where Gozelo had surfaced – recalled, too, where the body had been taken and marvelled anew at the width and breadth of Bruce.

'You persuaded Wallace to attack Scone, so you could go there and destroy the evidence,' he said, half in a breathy hiss of wonder. 'That's what Kirkpatrick was up to in Ormsby's room – but how will you persuade folk that the Stone you have hidden is the real one?'

Bruce nodded, as if he had expected the question.

'It does not matter – folk will believe it when the time comes. Will want to believe it – it only remains to ensure the secret of it is kept until that moment comes.'

Until you need to sit on it, Hal thought. To be crowned.

'Burning Ormsby's investigations should have been the end of it,' Bruce added bitterly. 'Save for the Savoyard stone carver we forgot about, because he was of no account.'

'And Wallace,' Hal added pointedly, 'who did not trust you. Does not still.'

Bruce shrugged.

'That is of no matter. Wallace is a brigand, for all his elevation. If he finds out, he will approve, in the end.'

Which might have been true enough once, Hal thought coldly, though while Wallace has changed the Kingdom, it has changed him, too. Wee Bisset and a Savoyard were two deaths that might not sit well with the new knight that was Sir William Wallace growing into his estate as Guardian.

He said as much and saw Bruce stroke his chin and admit it grudgingly.

'Bisset was no work of mine,' Kirkpatrick growled. 'That was yon ugly bastard Malise, seeking answers for the Earl of Buchan, who is no yin's fool.'

He broke off and looked sadly at Hal.

'You were too noisome in pursuing the Savoyard, too careless with yer use of Bisset, so that it did not take much for Buchan to latch on to matters. Particularly Bisset – Malise spoored after him from the moment he left your care. I came on it too late to prevent it.'

He paused, his eyes bleak.

'It was a charnel hoose,' he added, half to himself, and Hal was chilled at what the man must have seen to make such a wasteland behind his eyes. The stone of it sank into Hal's bowels; he had left a trail a blind man could follow, let alone the sharp-eyed, cunning Malise Bellejambe. He had killed Bartholomew Bisset as surely as if he had stuck the knife in himself.

Bruce saw some of that in Hal's face and laid the comfort of a hand on his arm, though the smile on his face did not reach beyond his too-tight cheekbones.

'This is an old quarrel of great families of this kingdom,' he said. 'It is always to be expected that, whatever I do, I will have a Comyn breathing on me to find out the why and where of it.'

'Now they have the Savoyard,' Hal said, seeing matters for the first time. 'Using him to lure you to them. And you need the Savoyard stone carver dead, of course, to preserve your secret.'

'Almost,' Bruce declared grimly. 'They have the Savoyard, for sure, but I do not wish him dead. I want him alive. He is the only one who possibly knows where the Stone now lies. Unless you do.'

Hal blinked – then saw it, as if a curtain had been raised.

The Auld Templar and John Fenton had taken charge of the Stone in Roslin and had hidden it – now both were dead and the secret with them.

Bruce saw the look and sighed wearily, passing a hand over his face.

'I see that the Auld Templar handed you the ring and no more,' he declared. 'So, unless the secret is with this stone carver, then all we have done is for naught – the Stone is hidden in Roslin and no-one knows where.'

He broke off and laughed bitterly.

'A stone lost among stones. There is some message from Heaven in this, is there not?'

From St Malachy, Kirkpatrick almost said, but clicked his teeth.

'We must get to the leper house,' he said instead and Hal felt a sudden thrill of fear.

'To a trap?' he said. 'Where the Earl of Carrick is faced with his enemies? We can scarcely ride the whole entourage into the town – the English still hold the castle of it – so we will be alone . . .'

Bruce smiled, suddenly, warmed, Hal saw, by this burst of concern. He reached out and clapped a hand on Hal's shoulder.

'Now you know the truth of matters,' he declared, 'yet you still, it seems, esteem me well enough to be concerned by my fate. I am glad of that for I would have you as a friend, young Hal. The Sientclers are noted for protecting kings, after all – did not one take an arrow for King Stephen?'

'Sir Hubert,' muttered Hal, remembering the family history dinned into him by his father. Young Hal – God's Bones, he had five, even six years on the Bruce and the man pats me like a new pup. He glared back at him and then at Kirkpatrick.

'I am no shield and ye are no king,' he replied and saw Bruce scowl at that.

'I esteem you well enough as a belted earl of the kingdom, my lord. Even if you were a poor cottar, I would not want

312

you walked into the teeth of your enemies. I cannot wish the same for your henchman, all the same.'

Kirkpatrick growled, but Bruce laughed, as mirthless as a wolf howl and both their gazes turned on him.

'It is not me they want,' he said and leaned a little into Hal's uncomprehending frown.

'They have the wrong Sir Henry Sientcler,' he declared and sent Kirkpatrick off to fetch horses while the haar of that settled like a raven on Hal's soul and a name thundered in his head like a great bell.

Malise Bellejambe.

CHAPTER TEN

Berwick
Feast of St Opportuna, Mother of Nuns, April 1298

They had the wrong Henry Sientcler. Malise would have split the little pardoner in two, save that he thought the foul little turd might still have a use. Now he and the thugs he had hired had to huddle in the leper house, holding to ransom monks already frightened by the deaths of Sir Henry's two escorts. For ease of guarding, Sir Henry had been put in the same room as the gasping Savoyard, the priest who was caring for him and the bewildered uncle.

'This is idiocy,' Henry Sientcler had puffed, when matters had become clearer to him. 'You will have the young Bruce down on you, not to mention Fitzwarin. Christ's Bones, man, if you do not let me go free, you will have the English and Scots lords both coming at you. Your head is already on a spike, though you do not know it yet.'

Malise, gnawing his knuckles, could believe it – the Red Comyn, entrusted by the Earl of Buchan with this mission, had sent Malise into Berwick to seek out a certain Robert de Malenfaunt and hand over the ransom for the Countess Isabel. He would not do it himself, for he feared capture by the English, being Lord of Badenoch in all but name, but he had curled a lip when Malise expressed the same concern.

'You are of no account to them,' he declared with cutting assurance. 'Take the Templar writ, hand it to Malenfaunt, take the Countess and return to me. This is a task a trained mastiff could carry out.'

Malise remembered the Red Comyn's sneer, smeared on his freckled, red-haired face. Like all the Comyn, he was short, barrel-bodied, with the sort of fiery red hair that would turn, like his kin the Earl of Buchan, to wheat-straw with age. Like all the Comyn he was full of himself.

The Earl was another problem, Malise thought moodily. Unknown to the Red Comyn, who had been waiting a while and would fret for longer, the Earl had given further, private instructions to Malise regarding the Herdmanston lord who had been escorting the Countess all over Scotland until he had lost her at Stirling.

'It is inconcievable, of course,' the Earl declared silkily, 'but even the rumour of a liaison is damaging to the honour of Buchan. Bad enough to have her linked to the young Bruce – but a ragged *gentilhomme* of no account? The Countess must be returned and shown the error of her ways. It is important that the lord of Herdmanston understand his own. Forcibly. And that the young Bruce, who is clearly this Herdmanston lord's patron, receives a message he cannot fail to understand.'

Berwick was, ostensibly, controlled by the English, but they huddled in the castle, the town going about its business with little hindrance, *couvre-feu* or even law. Malise had tracked the Savoyard to it and thought, at last, to put the stupid little chiseller to the question – only to find him sicker than Pestilence on his Plague Horse. The idea of using the man to trap Hal of Herdmanston here had been too good to pass up . . . save that an idiot pardoner could not tell one Henry Sientcler from another.

A shape slid into the seat opposite and offered a brown smile. Lamprecht; Malise regarded the little man with a mixture of awe and distaste, not knowing whether he really did have Christian relics of power, not liking him because he was a snail who left a trail behind him as he moved.

'My ripeness, my mouse,' Lamprecht lisped in what he fondly believed was the way of the court in France. 'I have my bargain fulfilled. *D'argent*, certes. *Bezzef d'argent, tu donnara.*'

It had been God's Own Hand, Malise had thought, that brought him to the side of Lamprecht, a man he had used in small ways once or twice before. Useful, he had thought at the time – now he looked at the pardoner with distaste, seeing how he might have been handsome once, though all his years had played hop-frog with each other and landed on an ugly heap on his face, which was venal and pouched. He had once had long, clean hair, but it had been too fine to last and was now plastered in a few greasy wisps on his skull, which he covered, when he was not wringing it in his hands, with a soft, broad-brimmed hat lauded with a pilgrim's shell.

'I know what you want,' Malise spat moodily, 'and you are as far from it as always. Sir Henry Sientcler of Herdmanston, I said. You bring me Sir Henry Sientcler of *Roslin*.'

Lamprecht's eyes never warmed to the smile he gave.

'*Non andar bonu*,' he began, then laboriously turned out the thick-accented English of it. 'It is not going well. This is no fault of mine. Henry Sientcler you demand. Henry Sientcler you receive. Please to pay me, as agreed.'

He saw the aloes look he had back and realised he was not going to get his money. It was not, he thought to himself crossly, his fault that he had been sent to fetch a named man from a place where all the people, it seemed, were called the same. Now this man with a face like a kicked arse was scowling at him and denying him fair payment; not for the first time, he wished he had never met Malise Bellejambe.

He was no stranger to abuse, all the same; everyone seemed to believe they could gull, con or spit upon the likes of him, for all his pilgrim's badge. You would think folk would honour someone wearing the shell that told of a trip all the way to the Holy Land and, to be fair, most of the simple folk did. The ones with some money and a little power always assumed he was a liar and had never been to the Holy Land at all, but had stolen the shell badge.

Which was not true, he thought indignantly to himself. He had traded for it – a tooth of the Serpent from Eden, no less, only slightly chipped but a fine specimen. Not as fine as the other three he had, admittedly, but a fair exchange for the shell of a pilgrim. And, if he had not been to the Holy Land exactly, he had been to the Sicilies – which still had paynim influences everywhere – and to Leon in Spain, which was the next room to the heathen Moors.

'*Dio grande*,' he said with weary bitterness to Malise. 'God is great. I carry out my task and this is my reward. *A esas palabras respondieron los ignorantos con decirle infinitas injurias como ellos acostumbran, llamándole perro, cane, judío, cornudo, y otros semejantes* . . .'

'Speak English,' Malise finally spat, irritated beyond measure, and Lamprecht shrugged, as if the man was a fool for not comprehending either the Lingua, or decent Castilian, tongues understood by every traveller around the eastern Middle Sea.

'The ignorant,' he said haughtily, 'reply by uttering numerous insults as they are accustomed to do, calling me hound, dog, Jew, cuckold, and similar epithets. *Mundo cosi* – such is the world.'

'Give me no airs, you purveyor of St Pintle the Apostle's ball hairs,' snarled Malise, angry now. 'I have known you for a time – long enough to know that you would steal the contents of a dog's arse and put it in a pie if you had found someone with a taste for such a thing and had a handy bag.'

He glared at Lamprecht.

'You would sell the stolen skull of an infant and claim it to be Jesus when he was a baby,' he added viciously and saw that he had stung Lamprecht, who did not like his wares denigrated.

'*Questo non star vero*,' he protested, then shook his head with exasperation and translated it into English. 'That is not true. *Que servir tutto questo?* You should not say such things, even in anger, for God is watching. *Dio grande.* Besides, *se mi star al logo de ti, mi cunciar . . . bastardo*. If I was in your place, I would wait. The other Sir Henry will come, certes, to see after his *amico*, and here you hold him. *Dunque bisogno il Henri querir pace. Se non querir morir*. So the Henry will want peace. If he does not wish to die. *Capir?*'

Malise understood and Lamprecht saw it. He yawned ostentatiously.

'*Mi tenir premura*,' he said. 'I am in a hurry. Let me dip my beak a little, then I go. *Mi andar in casa Pauperes Commilitones.*'

Lamprecht did not need to translate the latter, for he saw Malise had understood perfectly. The *Pauperes Commilitones* – the Poor Brother-Knights – was a name he calculated would make Malise think twice about keeping him here.

Malise knew what Lamprecht was up to, knew also that the pardoner was headed to Balantrodoch purely in the hope of persuading the Order knights there to add their seal to the provenancies of the relics he carried; the Templars made part of their fabled wealth from selling relics.

Malise glanced to where his scrip sat carelessly on a bench, the Templar writ snugged in it. He marvelled at how a piece of parchment with some seals and words could be worth the astonishing amount of 150 merks of silver.

The money, he knew, had been deposited at Balantrodoch and Malise wrestled dimly with the concept of how you could take the parchment to any Templar Commanderie, present

318

it – and be given the money, as if it had magically transported itself there while folk slept. He shivered; from what he had heard of the Templars, such a thing was not beyond them.

No matter – if Lamprecht had the divine favour and miracles of the Pope himself, it would serve him no better.

'You remain,' Malise declared curtly and Lamprecht managed an insouciant shrug and a smile, while inwardly seething. He had been doing well recently in a land turmoiled by war and the rumour of it, for people were eager for *quatrefoil* amulets of St Thomas and St Anthony, the former proof against just about everything, the latter particular to ague and fever.

These were just enough to afford him vittles, but not enough for the finer things. Lamprecht had a box filled with plenary indulgences, pinches of the ashes of Saints Martin and Eulalia of Barcelona, Emilianus The Deacon and Jeremiah The Martyr. He still had a tooth of the Serpent – actually, he had several such teeth – a portion of the robe of Saint Batholomew The Apostle, a pinch of the earth on which the Lord Himself had stood, plus many others.

He had his finest cache, which he hoped the Templars would buy – three fingernails of St Elizabeth of Thuringia, only raised to sainthood thirty-odd years ago, so her relics were powerfully potent.

He was no fool, as Malise had declared – though Lamprecht had to admit that trying to sell the likes of Malise the thong of Moses' sandal had been a bad error – but no-one who could afford it wanted plenary indulgences, or a thorn from Christ's Crown these days. They preferred earthly necessities, like food and fuel for fires. As usual, the poorest were the ones who sickened first and they could barely afford the lead *quatrefoil* amulets.

So he smiled, though the purse he had been promised seemed to fade slowly away and he knew that his best chance of salvaging anything from this was to remove himself, in

319

secret, far from the coming wrath of this wrong Sir Henry's friends.

Outside, it rained on the dark of a Berwick glazed with a few pallid worms of light, the rat-eyed red wink of the castle braziers squirming through the rain as the garrison kept watch. It wasn't the Scots they feared so much as the wrath of Longshanks if they lost the fortress.

For all the rain and dark, Hal thought, you could find Berwick easily enough by the smell, a heady mix of smoke, clot and rot that sifted out a long way, like the snake-hair of Medusa, barely shifted by a wind that was little more than a damp nudge.

They splashed across the ford with the old ruins of the bridge to their right, troll shadows in the dark. No-one challenged them and they came up through the repaired defences of wooden stockade, ditch and wall, under a gate that should have been guarded but was not – Bruce had predicted as much and garnered silent admiration from the others in the small cavalcade.

They climbed off the wet, mud-spattered garrons and led them up the sliding cobbles, ankle deep in fishbones and the old spill of dogs, pressed closer and closer by the leaning walls of the poorer houses, where the strewn rushes were never cleared and stank with the humours that brought on liver-rot, worms, palsy, abscess, wheezing lung and every other filthy ague.

Fitting, then, that this street, bordered by lurching houses that drifted like timber-rotted ships in a slow wind of alley, should puke them out at the leper house of St Bartholomew, a shrouded ghost of stone in the shadows – save for one area, spilling butter-yellow glow out through the cracks of great double doors that led to a garth and then under an archway to the street.

The dripping band stopped and Bruce offered a grin to the

Dog Boy. Dressed like the rest of them in plain tunic and rough cloak fastened with an iron pin, with no blazoned jupon or blaring heraldic shield, the Earl of Carrick looked like the Dog Boy's da and was clearly enjoying the entire event.

Unlike Kirkpatrick, who did not like the idea of the heir to Annandale and the rightful throne of Scotland dressed like a peasant and putting his life in such danger.

He had said as much at length, about the foolishness of an earl of the kingdom plootering about, risking his neck in a foolhardy adventure with a band of scum. The band of scum had growled back at him for that – Bangtail Hob, Lang Tam, Sim and Will Elliott, all scowling angry. Even Hal had curled his lip, seeing he was included in the insult until Bruce had told Kirkpatrick, in a voice like the flat slap of a blade, to keep his teeth together.

Now they handed the reins of their stolid, dripping garrons to Will and slithered wetly away to their assigned tasks. Sim and Hal took up positions on either side of the great doors; no-one spoke and the Dog Boy, a loop of rough cloth over his head as a hood, took a deep breath and moved forward.

Hal felt his throat constrict at the sight of the lad, looking smaller than ever against the great double door, heavy with beams and thick with studded nails. Beyond it was the cookhouse, the yellow-red glare of it unable to be contained even by a door like this, because it was the one part of the spital that never slept.

From somewhere in the town, faintly pressured by the limp wind, came the drifting sound of instrument and motet voice – *ahi, amours, com dure departie*. It spoke to Kirkpatrick, achingly, of ale and wine and warmth and fug – more than that, it spoke of Oc and what he had done with the Cathars there, so that he almost grunted with the kick of it. Suddenly, this unknown little pardoner Lamprecht seemed to have conjured up all the smoke-blackened memories Kirkpatrick had thought long since nailed up behind the door in his head.

The Dog Boy had known about cookhouses from his time in Douglas. The way to get in had been his idea and the only reason he had voiced it at all was because a great earl, an individual so far above him as to be lost in clouds, had shared a cup and his innermost thoughts one night. The Dog Boy had been his man from that moment and spilling out his plan to approving nods had filled him with a sudden flooding sense of his own new value, so that the rush of it left him reeling and light-headed.

He hammered on the door with his nut of a fist, then kicked it hard because he wasn't sure he had made enough noise.

Inside, the cookhouse sweaters paused as if frozen. Abbot Jerome looked at the helpers, lepers all in various stages of illness, yet with skills needed to bake bread and prepare food. The only cuckoo in the nest was the big-bellied Gawter, charged by Malise with watching this door and the kitchen staff. He blinked once or twice at the thump, but when it came a second time, he moved to the postern set into one of the huge gates and slid back the panel that let him look out.

At first he could see nothing, then a voice dragged his eyes down to where a ragged boy stood, hunched under a piece of sodden sacking, rain dripping off the end of his nose. Gawter had seldom seen a more miserable sight.

'Away with ye,' he growled, relieved to see it was only a laddie. 'No alms from here.'

'Beggin' only the blissen' of God an' a' His saints on ye sir,' he had back. 'I am here deliverin', not askin' – a good lady whose man has recently passed on delivers her grace on the spital, for the elevation of his soul.'

Gawter paused, licking his lips with confusion.

'A brace of lambs,' the boy persisted and Gawter turned in confusion to Abbot Jerome and had back an approving nod. The Abbot tried to make it all seem as natural as breathing, but the truth of the matter was that his heart leaped, for he knew a ruse when he heard one. The spital depended on donatives and was guaranteed a lamb and a pig every ten days, from the guild of merchants.

They were delivered, butchered and hung, since no sensible man eats freshly killed meat – and the last delivery had been four days since; the remains of carcasses hung and swung in plain view and his cook teams were, even now, slathering joints of it with fat, herbs and mint.

But Gawter did not know this and, though there was a chance that there really were two lambs from a grief-stricken widow, Jerome fervently prayed there was not, that this was help, by Divine Grace.

'Aye,' Gawter said, uneasy and uncertain, but aware that refusal of such bounty would arouse suspicion. 'That's brawlie, wee lad – be smart with it. As weel suin as syne, as my ma said . . .'

Hal heard the clack and clunk of the beam locks coming off, then the grunt as Gawter heaved the beam out of the supports.

'Bring in your lambs, then . . .' he began and the door heaved in on his face, crashing him backwards to slide across the floor into a cauldron, whose contents spilled and sizzled on his legs. Gawter yelled and scrambled away, beating uselessly at the scalding soak, staggered round and came face to face with a beard like a badger's arse and a great broad grin splitting it.

'Baa,' Sim said and punched Gawter in the ribs – once, twice, three times. Only on the third did Gawter feel the strange sensation which he instinctively knew was sharp metal sliding into his body but by the time he had started to reel with the horror of it, he was already dead. Sim was sliding him to the greasy straw and flagstones as Hal and the Dog Boy wolfed through the door.

'Christ be praised,' Abbot Jerome declared, almost sobbing.

'For ever and ever,' answered Hal automatically, looking from side to side for other enemies. 'How many and where?'

'Yin other and the leader himself' mushed a voice, coming forward so that Sim recoiled at the sight of the wasted ruin of a face. It grinned blackly at him, waving a ladle in one dirty, swaddled fist.

'Christ's Bones,' Sim yelped, 'keep your distance and your breath from me.'

'Where?' Hal demanded, ignoring the gravy baster. Jerome recovered himself enough to stammer out where the other guard was – watching the main entrance to the spital – and that the leader was in the Dying Room, with Henry Sientcler, a poor foreign soul giving himself up to God and said poor soul's Flemish uncle.

'God be praised,' Sim declared and was moving even before the rote responses had sighed to a finish, a grin splitting his cheekbones at the thought of coming face to face, at last, with Malise Bellejambe. Hal followed on – Bruce was at the main entrance, Kirkpatrick his ever-present shadow, while Bangtail and Lang Tam were prowling, looking for other doors.

It remained only to make sure that Sir Henry of Roslin did not die.

Lamprecht had gathered up his bits and pieces, the precious relics box slung over one shoulder – and the equally precious contents stolen from Malise, an act of savagely triumphant revenge that left the pardoner grinning like a rat as he slithered into the shadows of the spital. There were many of them, for even the cheapest tallow was too expensive for this place and only essential places were lit.

One was the barred door to the outside world, with the crop-headed, ox-muscled lout called Angus lounging under the light, yawning and exploring the painful rot of his mouth with one huge, filthy forefinger.

The pardoner grimaced at the sight. *Sensal maledetto* – there must be another way out of this festering place . . .

He was moving carefully away into the cloak of the place, folding himself into the shadows and away from the ox when the clatter and yells froze him to the spot. It came, he was sure, from the kitchens; he saw Angus shove himself away from the wall, pause with a great arrow of indecision between his eyes – then leave the light and head into the dark, towards the kitchens.

Si estar escripto en testa forar, forar, he thought – if it is written on your forehead that you leave, you leave. In another second he was at the door. In one more he had the beam in both hands and was levering it out of the retainers.

'Haw . . .'

The bull bellow nearly made Lamprecht shriek and it did make him drop the heavy beam, so that it clattered to his feet and made him dance backwards while it bounced dangerously near his toes. He looked up to see Angus staring black daggers at him and heading back towards the door.

Which burst in with a blatting crash and a gust of rain-fresh air.

Neither Bruce nor Kirkpatrick could believe their luck when they heard the door opening, having found it fastened tight. Bruce was not sure if Hal or one of the others had unlocked it, but the thundering noise of the beam hitting the flagstones persuaded him that there was trouble enough to go in hard and fast.

Angus skidded to a halt, his mouth wet and wide at the sight of two armed men bursting in. Kirkpatrick darted forward, Bruce on his heels, and both of them saw a weasel of a man festooned with bags and a box – and, not far away, a collection of muscles on legs like trees, his mouth drooped, yet hauling out a long knife from his belt.

'Aside,' Bruce yelled and Kirkpatrick cursed – then the weasel shifted for the door and sealed the moment; Kirkpatrick rounded on him, catching him by the strap of the box and hauling him backwards.

'Swef, wee man,' he said, his mouth alongside the man's ear and the long, slim dagger winking an inch from the side of one wild eye.

'Let me loose,' Lamprecht spat, struggling. 'Let me go. Or. Else. I am as good as a priest. I am under the protection of the Pope himself. *Bastonada, mumucho, mucho.*'

The familiar tongue trailed down Kirkpatrick's spine like a lick of ice. There was a moment of embers and shrieks before he actually realised what the pardoner had just said.

'You will beat me?'

Lamprecht heard the words and the chuckle that went with them. Then his captor, now with a hand at the back of his neck, firm as an iron band, spoke in his ear, the breath stirring the greasy grey tangles of his hair.

'*Si e vero que star inferno, securo papasos de vos autros non poter chappar de venir d'entro.*'

If it is true there is a Hell, for sure your priests will not be able to avoid going there. The words circled into Lamprecht's ear like the sensuous coils of a snake and he knew, with a sudden cold weight in the depths of his belly, that he was caught, for this was a man who had been places where he had gained fluency in *lingua franca* and – no doubt of it – done things which involved daggers. Or worse.

Kirkpatrick felt the little man go slack, heard his bitter muttering.

'*Si estar escripto in testa andar, andar. Si no, aca morir.*'

If it's written on your forehead for you to go, you will go. If not, you will die here.

Kirkpatrick kept the dagger point high enough, all the same, so that the little weasel could see it, while he tried to watch what Bruce was doing.

Bruce was discovering that he could not dance, that the German Method was of no use in a tight, dark passageway. The sword was too long and the knife man was good. Bruce saw the man come in, hunched and fast, with the knife held like a boar tooth, and he swung, caught the sword blade on an unlit sconce and the great ox, moving faster than his bulk promised, slashed a tavern brawl stroke which cut the home-spun under Bruce's heart and scored a fiery line.

Kirkpatrick yelled and almost let go of Lamprecht, but the pardoner sensed it and wriggled, making Kirkpatrick auto-matically clench the harder; the pardoner screeched.

Bruce, feeling the burn of the knife slash, saw the triumph in the slit eyes of his huge opponent, the realisation that the long sword was a hindrance.

Fear licked the earl, then, for he knew he was in trouble, so he did what a knight was supposed to do – took a deep breath, screamed 'A Bruce' until his throat burned, and hurled himself forward.

From the kitchens, turn right, Abbot Jerome had told them, and Hal and Sim did so, moving as swiftly as a watchful crouch would allow. They went past the doors to rooms which may have been priest cells, chapels or storehouses, but no light spilled from the chink of them.

Finally, they reached the end of the passageway, saw the door, limned in pale light which seeped through the bad fitting. Sim and Hal grinned at each other, then Hal, with a sudden leap, realised there were only two.

'Where's the boy?'

The boy had gone left, for he had paused to pluck the long thin dagger from Gawter's dead hand, as much trembling at that as the sudden sight of swaddled folk, like dead risen in their grave rags, who came to stare.

With a last wild look at the smiling Abbot Jerome, the Dog Boy flung himself after Hal and Sim, turning left and birling up the passage, trying to look back and ahead at the same time.

He knew he had lost them a few heartbeats later, but by then he heard the loud roar of 'A Bruce' and the bell clangs

327

of steel. He moved towards it, heard the grunts, came up behind the fighters and watched a huge man close in on a hapless victim, who could only wave a sword and back away.

He saw it was the earl and, beyond him and struggling with another man, the earl's black-visaged man, who was clearly not able to help. He did not hesitate – this was the great lord who had shared wine with him, who had told him the vows of knighthood.

Bruce, backing away, desperately wondering if he would reach a more open area, hoping to get to the door, even if it meant going outside, saw the ox with a knife was about to rush him and end the affair. The French Method, he thought bleakly . . .

Then a wildcat screeched out of the dark and landed on the back of the ox, so that he half-stumbled forward and yelled with surprise and fear. He whirled and clawed with one free hand up behind him, but the wildcat hung on.

The Dog Boy. Bruce saw the frantic, snarling face of the boy and, just as the ox thought of crashing backwards into a wall to dislodge him, the little nut of a fist rose up, stabbed once, then the boy rolled free, the long sliver of dagger trailing fat, flying blood drops.

The ox howled, clapped a hand to his ear, the blood bursting from between his knuckles. He turned, the savage pain and anger of his face turning, as if washed by it, to a bewildered uncertainty. Then he collapsed like an empty bag, the blood spreading under his head.

There was silence save for ragged panting. Bruce saw the Dog Boy, half-crouched on all fours, feral as any forest animal, dagger bloody in one fist.

'Good stroke,' he managed hoarsely.

Hal and Sim burst in the door of the Dying Room to a tableaux of figures frozen in butter-yellow light, the shadows guttering wildly on the wall as the tallow was blasted by the wind of their entrance.

A little priest was untying Henry Sientcler from a chair, while a third figure knelt by a truckle bed, cradling the head of a man who gasped and gargled. He raised a face, bewildered and afraid, at the new arrivals.

'Sir Henry,' Hal declared and the lord of Roslin flung off the last of the ropes and staggered upright.

'Hal – by God's Wounds, I am pleased to see you.'

'Malise . . .' Sim declared, for it was clear the man was not here.

'Gone, moments hence,' Sir Henry declared, rubbing his wrists. Hal cursed and Sim was about to fling himself out of the door again when Bruce came in, the Dog Boy behind him and, behind that, Kirkpatrick clutching a man by the neck like a terrier with a rat.

'Malise – did he pass you?'

'He did not.'

Hal looked at Sim and the man grinned, then loped out to hunt Malise down. Bruce came to the truckle bed and looked down.

'The Savoyard?' he asked and Hal nodded.

'I suspect so.'

'Malise knifed him,' the priest declared bitterly. 'Not that he would have lived anyway . . . this is his uncle.'

The man by the bed stood up and Hal saw that he had a fine tunic stained with his nephew's blood. His face was grimmed with weary lines of bitterness and resignation.

'He is alive still,' Bruce declared and knelt, shoving his face close to the dying man's. 'He is trying to speak . . .'

The man's mouth opened and closed a few times; Bruce bent closer, so that his ear was almost to the lips of the man, and Hal was shamed that the earl was so bent on uncovering the secret of his Stone that he defiled the last peace of a dying man.

329

Then the man vomited a last wash of blood, on which sailed the wafer of the Last Rite like a little white boat. Bruce sprang up, his face peppered with bloody spray, which he wiped away with distaste. The uncle bowed his head and knelt, while the priest began to intone prayers.

Bruce blinked once or twice, then flung himself out and Hal went after him. Kirkpatrick, his hand numbing from clutching the sagging pardoner, thought to make sure that the man was, indeed, the Savoyard they had sought and not some luckless leper.

'Manon de Faucigny?' he rasped.

The uncle raised his head from his pious revery, gently brushed the sweat lank hair from the dead man's paling forehead.

'Malachy,' he said and Kirkpatrick jerked.

'His name was Malachy de Faucigny,' the uncle went on softly. 'He thought that had too much Jew in it for an England where they were banned, so he changed it.'

Kirkpatrick's mouth went dry, then he shook the thoughts away from him. Best not to mention this, he thought.

Bangtail and Lang Tam were pitched into a nightmare. They had come up on a door, which did not yield, then ploughed on through the wet and the mud to stumble into the backcourt privy. Where there is a shitehouse, Bangtail hissed in Lang Tam's ear, there is a wee door to get to it.

They found it, a darker shadow against the black – and it opened smoothly enough. Bangtail grinned as he stepped inside; no man liked to have a barrier between him and emptying his bowels when it came to the bit.

The pair of them halted in the dark of what seemed to be a large room, a hall or refectory. The air was fetid and rank and the dark yielded up the contents reluctantly – the flags of the floor, vague shapes on either side; the rushes shushed as they stepped.

A bed with a bench at the end of it. Another. Yet one more on the other side of them.

The figures loomed up suddenly, vengefully, the stuff of nightmares.

'Ye baistits,' screeched a voice and a blow struck Bangtail on the arm. Another whacked his knees. He heard Lang Tam curse.

Then he saw what attacked them. Noseless. Festering. Some with rags binding the worst of their wounds, some fresh from their dormitory beds and unswaddled, the fish-belly pale of them smeared with the black stains of rot.

The lepers, whose touch was condemnation, whose very breath was death.

Bangtail howled like a mad dog then and fought through them, panicked and flailing. He heard Lang Tam yelling, felt his fists strike something that he did not even wish to see.

Light flared at the far end, silhouetting the mad horde of lepers, whose dormitory sleep Bangtail and Lang Tam had shattered. Bangtail saw it and plunged towards it, finding, like a miracle from Christ Himself, that those who had been snarling in front of him had vanished like snow from a sunwarmed dyke.

Then he saw the figure scurrying forward, the naked-fang gleam of long steel waving like a brand in the dark.

Malise knew he had escaped from the Dying Room with seconds only. He had snatched up his cloak and slung the scrip over his shoulder at the sound of the Bruce warcry, heading down the corridor that linked the Dying Room, conveniently, to the leper dormitory; from there, he knew, he could reach the outside. His plans were thrown in the air and there was nothing now but escape and the gibbering fear of what was plunging at his heels drove him on.

The riot inside confused him and he hacked his knife at the mass of figures until they scattered, then hurled himself through before they could recover enough to counter.

Suddenly, he was close to a face he knew, saw it was one of the Herdmanston men and lashed out with his other hand, a wild shriek of terror trailing it like flame.

Bangtail saw the blow only at the last, managed to duck the worst of it, but was still flung full length, stars whirling into him.

Lang Tam saw Bangtail fall and lunged forward, tearing free from the grasp of half-a-dozen hands. Kicking feet made him stumble as he roared forward and he was on his hands and knees when Malise lunged, kicked him savagely in the mouth, then slashed right and left with his knife, to keep the lepers away.

The last wild cut was just as Lang Tam surged back upright and he had time to marvel at the moment of it, the sheer bad cess of it, how poorly he stood in the grace of God. It was no more than a catch across his throat, a blow that made him gasp – but the roaring and the drench of blood down his front told him the truth of it. His eyes rolled and he looked at the astounded, frightened-pale face of Malise, the dagger dripping blood.

'Bugger,' Lang Tam wheezed wearily and fell full length, his head bouncing.

Malise leaped over him and made for the door, while the lepers fell over themselves trying to get away. Behind, he heard a man roaring pungent curses.

Bangtail, he remembered dully as he stumbled out into the rain.

Lamprecht knew that information was life. It was what he traded to Malise and, he admitted, was what he should have kept to instead of playing in this treacherous game.

Now he stood in a ring of folk he knew wanted to kill him, while they stood scowling and black-despaired by the death of one of their number. He knew he had limited options and thought he would begin by establishing his credentials.

'*Kretto a in deo patrem monipotante kritour sele a dera, ki se voet te tout, a nou se voet; e a in domnis Gizoun Kriston, filiou deous in soul . . .*'

'Enough,' Kirkpatrick growled, slapping him. 'It will not stand here – ye are spoutin' lies like a horse cowper.'

'What is he saying?' demanded Bruce.

'It is the Credo,' Kirkpatrick said and Abbot Jerome frowned. It did not sound like any Credo he knew and he admitted as much.

'The Greek way,' Kirkpatrick said. 'From Constantinople.'

'Christ's Wounds,' Sim said, raking through the box while Lamprecht hovered in agony, watching. 'Is this a wee toebone?'

'*Guarda per ti,*' Lamprecht pleaded. 'Be careful. *Chouya, chouya* – sorry, in English – gently. That is the toebone of Moses himself.'

'Away,' exclaimed Sim in amazement. 'Moses, is it? Now here is a miracle – if ye are to chain up all the toebones of Moses ye have in here, ye find the blessed wee man had four feet.'

'*Questo star falso. Taybos no mafuzes ruynes.*'

Kirkpatrick, grinning, turned to the frowning Bruce.

'He says is it is not true. All his wares are real.'

'Ask him where Malise has gone,' Hal demanded and Lamprecht winced at the eyes on this one. The others, even the one he now knew to be a great lord, were easier on matters, for they were reviling him. Lamprecht had found that those who paused to spit on him seldom, in the end, did him the sort of harm that balm and a decent arnica root could not cure.

Sim let a delicate sliver of white clatter to the flags and then ground it to powder, grinning – even that, though the pain of its loss hurt him to the soles of his own feet, would not have loosened Lamprecht's throat. The one who spoke the Tongue might, but he was leashed by the great lord, so Lamprecht had no real fear of him.

333

But the grey-eyed one with a stare like a basilisk was different and Lamprecht knew, when the question came, that he would answer it humbly and truthfully, in the hope that he could step along the razor edge of this moment without shedding any of his blood.

Kirkpatrick listened and frowned, but Hal had caught a few words, so he could not dissemble.

'He says Malise originally employed him to seek out a Countess. That one is in the nunnery near here, a place controlled by Robert de Malenfaunt. Folk send their unwanted women to it – unruly daughters, wee wives who have outlived their property attractions, widows fleein' from some man who wants to get his hands on their inheritance. This Malenfaunt keeps it as a *seraglio*, the pardoner says.'

'I have heard of this Malenfaunt,' Bruce mused. 'He is a minor lord of little account, but he serves in the *mesnie* of Ughtred of Scarborough. I hear he rode some decent Tourneys at Bamburgh one season.'

'What's a *seraglio*?' Sim demanded and Kirkpatrick curled his lip in an ugly smile.

'A hoorhoose.'

'And he holds Isabel to ransom in sich a place?' growled Hal.

'I doubt she has been dishonoured or harmed,' Bruce soothed, marvelling at the way of things, for it seemed this young Sientcler was smit with his Isabel – not *his* Isabel anymore, he corrected hastily, as if even the thought could reach the Earl of Buchan.

'She is too valuable,' he added, then clapped Hal on one shoulder. 'Betimes – we will get her away.'

Kirkpatrick sighed, for he could see the way of it – bad enough charging down on St Bartholomew's without thundering on to the nunnery at St Leonards. He said it, knowing it would make no difference.

'Aye – raiding lazars and nunneries is meat an' ale to the

334

likes of us,' Sim declared cheerfully and drew out the long roll of parchment. 'What is this?'

The truth was that Lamprecht did not know – he had stolen it from Malise for the dangling Templar seal – two knights riding a single horse. He considered that the most valuable item, since he could carefully remove it from the document and attach it to another, this one painstakingly scribed to provenance the relics of Elizabeth of Thuringia. A Templar seal was as good as truth and doubled the value of his relics.

Now he watched it unroll, saw the other seal on it, one he did not know, and wished he had had the time to study it more closely. Bruce plucked it from Sim, who only held it the correct way up because the seals were at the bottom.

'It is a *jetton*,' Bruce said, marvelling and squinting in the poor light. 'For a hundred and fifty merks.'

Lamprecht groaned at the thought of what he had just lost.

'Whit is a *jetton*?' Sim demanded.

'A wee tally note, stamped by the Templar seal and – well, well, the Earl of Buchan's mark,' Bruce explained, grinning more and more broadly. 'The Earl has clearly deposited the money at Balantrodoch and now anyone with this document can go to any Templar Commanderie from here to Hell itself and put a claim on hundred and fifty merks of silver. See? You mark off the sums given to you in these wee boxes. Like a chequerboard, which is how the Templars reckon up the sums. The *jetton* are really the wee counters they use to shuffle from box to box to keep track of it all.'

They all peered and murmured their awe.

'Usury,' Sir Henry Sientcler said, as if trying to spit out dung. Bruce smiled grimly.

'Only the Jews have usury, my lord of Roslin. The Templars say this is not money lent, but a person's own money, held in safety for him. Still – they make a profit on the transfer.'

'What is this *jetton* for?' demanded Hal, beginning to see the possibility. 'In this case?'

Bruce blinked, bounced the parchment in his hand and his smile broadened further.

'For the ransom of a Countess, for certes,' he said, then offered a wry smile. 'I have about four good warhorses that cost as much. Cheap for a Countess of Buchan.'

Hal began to smile, but Bruce saw the muzzle curl of it.

'Ransomed by this wee tait of writing back to her husband,' Hal said, with a slow, grim smile. 'By a man this Malenfaunt will never have seen.'

'What about Lang Tam?' demanded Bangtail, which sobered everyone in an instant.

'We will take care of him, if you permit,' Abbot Jerome declared. 'Both for your rescue and the fact that the folk here feel, in part, responsible for his death. They did not know who was who when they attacked, ye ken.'

'He had brothers and a sister at home,' Bangtail argued bitterly.

'We can scarce cart his remains, Bangtail,' Sim answered, but gently. 'Enough for his kin to know he has a Christian burial in a fine house of God.'

Bangtail looked at Sim, then away and shivered at the memory of the inmates of this fine house of God.

'Best make like a slung stone,' Sim declared, 'rather than stand here like a set mill.'

'I would be joining you for the fight of it,' Henry Sientcler declared mournfully, 'but I am under parole and so cannot raise a weapon against the English.'

'If it is done right,' Bruce said slowly, looking at Hal as he spoke, 'there will be no fight in it – but, by God, there will be discomfort for the Comyn. Isabel MacDuff will be freed and Sir Hal may take her into his care.'

He laughed with the sheer joy of it.

'Everyone is made happy,' he declared, beaming.

The sudden, sharp sound of pealing bells made them all freeze and cringe.

'In the name of God . . .' Sim began.

'The alarm,' Kirkpatrick declared, but Lamprecht, to everyone's astonishment, started a mirthless laugh and rattled off another sibilant trill of his strange tongue.

Hal only caught the word, repeated several times – *guastamondo*.

Kirkpatrick, his face pale and sheened in the flickering light, turned and translated.

'This Lamprecht came across to London from Flanders,' he growled, 'and hurried on north, to York and then here. To be first with his wares.'

He ripped a medallion from round the pardoner's neck, fierce enough to jerk the man and snap the cord.

'To peddle worthless shite such as this to the feared and desperate.'

'Swef, chiel,' Bangtail muttered uneasily, 'lest God takes offence.'

'This dog is an offence,' Kirkpatrick snarled, then wiped his sweat-sheened face as the bells hammered out in the background.

'He says he came across with someone named Guastamondo and has beaten the news of it by a week,' Kirkpatrick declared and would have said more, save that Bruce forestalled him.

'*Guastomondo*,' said Bruce softly. 'My father told me that was the name he had in Outremer. The Breaker of Worlds.'

Even the bells paused as he stopped and looked round them all, his face serious as plague.

'Edward is back in England.'

No-one spoke for a moment, then Sir Henry cleared his throat and touched Hal's arm.

'We had best stir ourselves. This will put a heart we do not need into the garrison.'

Hal did not reply. He was staring at the medallion swinging in Kirkpatrick's fist and reached out to grasp it. Then he fixed his stone gaze on the pardoner.

337

'This,' he said, holding the amulet up to dangle like a dead snake. 'Tell me of this.'

The pounding at the door was a great, dull bell that slammed Isabel from sleep, spilling her upright. The nun who had been assigned to sleep at her feet – latest in an endless rotation of watch-women – came awake as suddenly, whimpering and afraid.

Clothilde her name was. She was from France, part related to the kin of the Malenfaunts there and dispatched all the way from the warm dream of vineyards to the cold stone and damp of Berwick by a family who wanted rid of an unwanted child. What happened to her mother Isabel did not know, but Clothilde had been here almost all her life, as an Oblate. Isabel, who had been here for almost half a year, shivered at the thought of such a time trapped in this eggshell of stone and corruption.

'Men are coming,' Clothilde said in a small voice. Isabel knew the child – she could hardly see her, even at fifteen, as a woman – feared the arrival of men and the reason for their coming. Malenfaunt, Isabel knew, took money and favours for allowing a select few to plunder the delights of a nunnery and, though some of the women were willing and depraved enough, some were not and Clothilde was one.

'Come closer to me,' Isabel said and the little Oblate scurried to her. I am her prisoner, Isabel thought with a wry twist of smile, yet she cowers behind my nightdress. She saw the scarred forearms of the little nun, knew that the girl sat and crooned hymns and psalms to herself when she thought no-one could see, slicing her flesh for the glory of God and an offering to the Virgin to rescue her.

The door slammed open so suddenly that Clothilde shrieked. The Prioress stood like a black crow with a candle, the sputtering tallow pooling her in eldritch shadows.

'You are to come,' she said to Isabel, then frowned at Clothilde. 'Get away from there, girl.'

'Come where?' Isabel answered. The Prioress turned the scowl on her, but it was a pallid affair by the time it rested on Isabel's face; long weeks of realising that this Countess could not be cowed by words and was not to be beaten by sticks had sucked the surety from the Prioress.

'You are to be released.'

The words spurred Isabel into dressing swiftly, her heart and mind whirling. Freed.

She followed the Prioress through the dark corridors to the Refectory, which seemed to be full of men – her heart thundered at the sight of the tall, saturnine Malenfaunt, leaning languidly on the table and studying a document. He raised his head and was smiling when she came in.

'My lord earl – your wife, safely delivered.'

Bewildered, Isabel stared at Bruce, who stared back and offered a stiff little bow.

'Good wife,' he said blandly. Then Isabel saw Hal and her heart threatened to leap out of her throat, so that she flung one hand up to it, as if to trap it at the neck. She saw the warning in his narrowed eyes, saw the huge bearded face of Sim behind him and heard, like the tolling of a bell, the word 'rescue' clanging in her head.

'Husband,' she managed.

'So it is, then,' Malenfaunt declared in French, smiling with triumphant pleasure. 'We part amicably, so to speak.'

Bruce turned a cold face on him.

'For now,' he answered, then held out one hand. Isabel, half numb and stumbling slightly, took it in one of her own and was led out. Behind her, Hal draped a warm cloak on her shoulders and pulled the hood up against the cold benediction of rain.

In the darkness of the nunnery garth were horses and more riders. Isabel felt a hand haul her long skirts up above her knees, then Sim was lifting her up, with a muttered apology.

'No fancy sidesaddle, Coontess. Ye ride like ye usually do.'

His grin seemed like a bright light – then Hal was beside her and Bruce was leading the cavalcade away into the cobbles and ruts and stinking rubbish of the street, with the sea wind blowing clean and exhilerating through the bewilderment of her.

'Isabel,' Hal said and she leaned forward then, met his face in a fumble of salt and rainwashed lips, sucking as greedily as he until the horses parted them.

'Aye,' said Bruce wryly in French, 'do not mind my part in this, mark you, for such chivalry and bravery is old clothes and pease brose to the likes of the Bruces.'

Isabel, starting to laugh with the bubbling realisation of it all, turned to answer him and heard a voice from the dark, slight shape on a big horse nearby.

'Ye should nivver violet a lady.'

'Dog Boy,' she said and saw the great smile of him loom out of the dark. Then, sudden as a blow, she thought of Clothilde, trapped like a little bird and knew, for all she ached to free the girl, she could not persuade these men to risk it – nor should she.

She was crying so hard, the tears and snot mingling with the rain as Hal tried to get his horse close enough to comfort her, that she missed Kirkpatrick's bitter growl – though Hal didn't.

'There will be the De'il to pay when Buchan finds his wife has been lifted like a rieved coo and his siller spent for no return.'

Neither of them missed the rain-pebbled exultation that was Bruce, grinning as he turned to them.

'God's Wounds, I only wish I could see his face when he is told of it.'

His laugh drowned out the mad tolling of the bell. Breaker of worlds, Hal thought wildly.

CHAPTER ELEVEN

Herdmanston Tower
Feast of St Theneva, Mother of Kentigern, July 1298

She woke to the sound of birds and the soft scent of broom
from the fresh rushes, wafted from the tall window where
the shutters were open against the stifle of the night. It had
rained, though, so the heat had gone and insects buzzed in
and out. The harsh wickedness of woodsmoke scattered the
brief heaven of the moment.

Her leg was over his, the coverlet thrown back and he woke,
slowly, as she watched the pulse in his neck, the trough of a
slight pox scar dragging her eyes down to the muscled shoulder
and another scar, a deeper, pale cicatrice. Lance wound from
a tiltyard tourney, a mercifully glancing blow which, if it had
struck full would have ripped the entire arm off.

Isabel's flesh crept and tightened at the thought. Even in
such a short time, she knew this man's body almost as well
as her own, each mole and scar of it – there were a lot of
scars, she saw, and had mocked him for being careless.

'None on my face, lass,' Hal had answered, almost half-
sorrowful. 'Every man who is thought of as a great knight has
a face like a creased linen sheet as far as I can tell.'

He stirred awake to her playful fingers, finally grunting as she clasped the rise of him.

'Christ's Bones woman – are there not Church laws that govern this?' he growled throatily as she moved over him. 'If so, we are condemned.'

'Feast days, fast days and menses,' she murmured. 'Gravid, weaning and forty days after birthing.'

She stopped mouthing him and looked up.

'I know them all, since it enabled me to avoid my marital duties more than once a week by canon law and more than that by contrivance.'

'Condemned already,' Hal muttered weakly, 'so it would be a sin to stop now.'

'Sheldrakes,' she mumbled and Hal fought with his senses, eventually reaching the answer.

'A dopping,' he gasped and countered at once, before he lost it.

'Harlots.'

Isabel stopped then and ignored Hal's plaintive yelp of loss.

'Under the circumstances,' she declared primly, 'you might have chosen better.'

'You do not ken it,' he accused and she frowned, started idly back to what she had been doing, though he could tell it was half-hearted and that she was concentrating on the puzzle.

'A byre,' she said eventually and then screamed when Hal whirled her round and on to her back.

'No,' he said, adjusting the curve of his hips until she gave a little gasp. 'I win. It is a haras of harlots.'

A stud farm for stallions – apt, she thought, gasping as he began ploughing the long, deep furrow of her, and then her mind turned into white light for a long time. In the dreaming aftermath, the sweat cooling deliciously on her, there was a stamping and throat-clearing from below.

The lord's room at Herdmanston was the top of the square

tower block and the only thing higher than it was the narrow, crenellated walkway reached by a ladder. The lord's room had no door and was reached by a stone wind of stair from below, coming up to a solid fretwork of balustrade.

It had its own privy hole, a strong oak four-post bed with heavy, faded hangings – blue, with gold owls, she saw – a table, a chair, a bench and two large kists but, best of all for Isabel, it had one window as tall as a man, inset with seats where someone could perch and sew in the light and sun.

A woman had wanted that and she had it confirmed from Hal.

'My mother,' he said. 'She died when I was young, but even by then I knew my father could refuse her nothing – even the folly of such a window making a hole in a good stout wall.'

A fair hole it was, too, with cushions of velvet, faded from the original crimson to a dusted pink. It was also armed with stout shutters for those days – more often than not – when the rain lashed the Lothians.

Below, at the foot of the top landing, the Dog Boy slept like a guarding hound and, if he heard their frantic gasps and her squeals it scarcely mattered, for this, to Isabel, was more privacy than she had known and more, she thought, than she deserved.

Beneath that was the main hall and the main entrance, fortified with a steel yett and a thick door, twenty feet up the thick wall, reached by a cobbled walkway and, at the last, across a removable wooden platform.

Deeper yet were the under-levels, two deep floors of cool, dark storage and, surrounding the thick square of it was a barmkin wall four feet high, enclosing stables, a brewhouse and the bakehouse and kitchens among others. Nearby was the stone chapel, isolated save for the tall cross beside it.

The throat-clearing got louder.

'Come up, ye gowk,' Hal growled, already into tunic and hose and casting a warning glance at Isabel, who pouted at him and drew the sheet up just as Sim's great tousled black head rose above floor level.

'Ready, Lord Hal? Ye wanted an early start, ye told me,' he said, then nodded and grinned companiably to Isabel.

'Coontess,' he added with a nod. 'I see why he is laggardly.'

'Cannot send my man off to war half-cocked, like a badly latched bow,' she replied as lightly as she could manage and had the gratification of a Sim laugh, a bell of sound from his flung-back throat.

'Weel said, Coontess,' Sim declared and dropped out of sight again.

She watched Hal drape all the panoply round him, from maille to jupon – freshly sewn by the two main women of the place, Alehouse Maggie and Bet the Bread – and finally turn to her, awkward and tongue-tied.

'Ye need to break your fast,' she chided and he nodded like a child.

'If trouble comes,' he began and she placed a finger on his bearded lip.

'I am safe here,' she said, 'whether it be the English or the Scots of my husband. Ye have left me Will Elliott, who is a fine man – not to mention the Dog Boy.'

They both paused at the name. The Dog Boy looked the same, yet both Hal and Isabel knew he was not, that the killing of the man in the lazar had snapped something of the boy away and the man replacing it was not yet comfortable with the slaying. They had heard him yelping in his sleep like a troubled pup; it had been the main reason Hal had decided to leave him behind.

To his surprise, he found he had not thought of John for a long time, nor his wife for longer than that; the knowledge flushed him with shame. Yet he had more on his mind these days, he said to himself by way of excuse. He was Lord of Herdmanston now, summoned to war by Bruce to serve in the host commanded by Wallace.

Longshanks was here, rolling north like a storm, and Hal had delayed, selfish as any callow youth, because of Isabel. He had missed joining the Roslin men under Sir Henry, released back into the love of wife and weans only to go off yet again, as a rebel.

Now Henry was with Bruce in Annandale, cut off from the main host under Wallace – and the Sientclers of Herdmanston would ride north to find the host, near Falkirk, before the English arrived in a tide that would cut Hal off from everyone.

The first lappings of that tide were already here – English under Bishop Bek, sent like the first blast of Longshanks' wrath, were rampaging through Lothian, set on taking the rebel-held castles of Dirleton and Tantallon. Roslin was too strong for them and Herdmanston too little a bother so far; Will, Dog Boy and old Wull the Yett were enough to keep the tower safe.

But it was not Bek and *herschip* raiders Hal feared. Buchan was leashed by the fact that Herdmanston was on the same side as himself, but that was a thin cord – if he snapped it and came for his vengeance, there would be no half-hearted exchange of bolts and arrows and taunts. Buchan would bring the deep hate of the robbed and cuckolded, the unrelenting vengeance that had made him send Malise after Isabel in the first place.

Hal heard the Auld Sire's voice, as if he was at his elbow – he will come at you sideways, like a cock fighting on a dungheap. Even from the dark . . .

And he might not be here to defend her. The thought embered up into his eyes and she saw it and balmed it with smiles and calm.

'Besides,' she added lightly, 'who would dare take on Maggie and Bet and hope for life?'

Hal smiled, remembering how she had taken them on herself. Alehouse Maggie ran the brewhouse, with arms muscled as

345

hams from stirring her vats, an arse like the quarters of a *destrier* and breasts, as Sim had mentioned, that you could see Traprain Law from if you reached the top. Once she blew the froth off her moustache, he added, she was a rare rattle on a cold night.

Bet the Bread ran the bakehouse and did the cooking for all in the Keep. Chap-cheeked, breasted like a pouter-pigeon, she had hair so long covered by a tight headsquare than no-one could swear to the colour of it – not even Sim since, as he had once confessed, it was the only thing she never took off.

They had sniffed a little, like bitches round a strange animal, when Isabel had first arrived, then given it a day or two before testing the steel of her. Alehouse Maggie had begun it, when Hal and Isabel had gone to the stone cross, ostensibly for him to pay his respects to the Auld Sire and, she knew, in some weird way, present her to the other occupants that lay beneath.

Isabel had stood beside him in the shadow of the great stone column with its coffin bell and chains – disconnected, she knew, after a violent storm had set the heavy bell ringing in the night and brought everyone to trembling wakefulness – and hoped to feel something from the mound.

There was nothing but wind and the wheep of birds, no word of greeting or condemnation from the dead, not even from the newest, the Auld Sire himself, who had winked and leered at her that day in the makeshift chapel on Abbey Craig.

Then Alehouse Maggie had lumbered up with a brown, glazed jug in one hand and, to Isabel's questioning eyebrow, lowered two of her own.

'First of a new brew,' she rumbled, 'goes to the Auld Sire.'

She was intrigued and shocked when Isabel reached out, took the jug and gently but firmly plucked it from her hands, then handed it to Hal.

'First of a new brew,' she said as Hal, taking his cue, drank

346

and handed it back to her, 'goes to the lord of Herdmanston. After that, you can water what graves you choose.'

Hal smiled at the memory of it, then uncurled one fist and held up an amulet on a leather thong; Isabel arched a quizzical, mocking eyebrow.

'Did that wee pardoner promise redemption, or just the Hand of God?' she demanded and he looped it over the tousle of her hair, then kissed her soft on the lips.

'We are all in the Hand of God,' he said and she clutched him. The Kingdom was a guttering candle in the high wind of Edward Plantagenet and Hal knew that the next few days and weeks would make or break it. I would not leave here for anything less than this, he said to himself, but he did not need to say it to her.

Yet, even now, he knew that Buchan would be scheming harder on how to bring down one wee Lothian lord than all the Plantagenets in Christendom; he threw the thought from him with a flick on the medallion.

'That holds the secret of making a king,' he said to her, smiling. 'Keep it safe. Give it to The Bruce if . . . matters turn out badly. Serve him right to have to uncouple the puzzle of it, as I did.'

She did not know what he meant, but clutched the lead medallion in one hand as he turned away, clumping and clattering carefully down the worn stone steps in his hobnailed shoes. She heard the shouts and neighs and armour clatter, finally dragged the coverlet tight round her for modesty and went to the great window.

Below, Hal and Sim were mounted and surrounded by a score of riders, all local men come to join him. I have to go, Hal said to himself, feeling the heat of her eyes on his back even after the curve of land hid the tower from view. There is no other Sientcler to do it.

With luck, he thought to himself, there will be no battle and the English, half-starved and thirsting, will be forced to abandon their campaigning for another year. Wallace was no fool and was not about to give Longshanks the battle he craved – particularly as the English king had finally reached Scotland with the largest army anyone had ever seen, with hundreds of heavy horse and a great mass of foot, almost all of them Welsh, or Gascons – even some Germans.

Isabel watched the Lothian men cavalcade away, the younger ones on their first such great endeavour, whooping for the joy of it. She felt the lead settle in her heart for the life that might be ripped away from them all.

And afterwards . . . the chill of that sleekit a way in to her, unwanted and unloved, so that she could not ignore it.

Afterwards, there would be sunshine and a gentle life with a man I have come to hold dear, as much a surprise to me as it is to him.

Even as she warmed herself at the idea of it, she knew it was a lie. Afterwards, win or lose, would come the reckoning – and she was not sure she wanted to visit on Herdmanston such a hatred as Buchan would wreak.

Yet, for now, there was the hope of something else, forlorn and ragged though it was.

'Aye,' said a voice, 'it is a hard matter to watch yer man ride away to war, Lady.'

She turned to see Alehouse Maggie and Bet the Bread at the top of the stairs, the former holding a limp swatch of cloth.

'You'll be missing Sim,' she managed and saw the pair of them smile and look at each other.

'Pleased to see the back of him,' Maggie declared. 'He has wore us both out, the muckhoond.'

They did not look worn to Isabel and she did not want another game of tests with them. To her surprise, Maggie held out her arms, full of the limp cloth which Isabel saw was a dress.

'We made ye this,' she said awkwardly, 'seeing as how ye came with no furbishments and have, we heard, refused to wear the mistress's auld cloots.'

Isabel's gaze flicked to the chest that held the clothes. It had not been hard to refuse the offer: she did not want to parade in his dead wife's leavings.

She took the dress, which she knew would fit perfectly. It was good linen, dyed the colour of sky, festooned with ribbons and frippery and she dropped the coverlet under their gaze and slipped it on.

'Bigod, Lady,' sighed Maggie wistfully, 'I wish I had yer slim. I did, a long time since. But too many bairns has ruined it.'

'Ye never did,' Bet replied scornfully. 'Ye were a byword for sonsie, you – and every laddie for miles came to get a grip of some, which is why ye have had too many bairns.'

Maggie laughed, so that bits of her trembled like a quake, and admitted she had not been short of suitors. Then she saw the bleak of Isabel's eyes and realised, suddenly, that this woman would trade slim for bairns at the cock of a head; her heart went out to her in that minute.

'It is very fine,' Isabel said slowly and Bet nodded.

'Needs an underkirtle, mind. I have one which will fit – and some small clothes as well. Now your man is away ye might get a chance to wear them.'

Both women started to laugh, shrill and loud and Isabel, after a pause, saw there was no malice in it and joined in. Then she looked wistfully at the dress.

'The ribbons and some of the frippery will have to go,' she said, 'for all your good work and fine words, I am more mutton than lamb like this.'

'Aye,' Maggie answered with serious and surprising agreement. 'I was hoping ye had no grand airs, Coontess or not. I was right about that, eh, Bet? The ribbons are easy removed, your ladyship.'

349

A sudden breeze brought the strong smell of char, raising Isabel's head like a hound on hare scent.

'Well,' she said, stripping it off and fetching the old dress she had arrived in. 'This must do for now – I will keep yours for good. There is work to be done, is there not?'

The English had raided for food, right up to the barmkin and the garth it enclosed, where cattle and desperate, frightened folk had huddled while men shot bolts and arrows at the enemy and had them back, with thrown torches besides. In the end, the alehouse and a couple of other buildings had burned but, as Maggie declared in her booming voice, 'Ye cannot burn my vats.' Nor could you, for they were made of stone and only the enclosing building had flamed.

It was that, in part, which had kept Hal here – though Isabel smiled at the lie that nestled at the heart of it. He stayed because he wanted her, as she wanted him, sucking the most joy they could from the time they had left.

Now she had to see to the ruin of what was left – in every sense. The debris around Herdmanston had been cleared out, the stone thatch weights found and rescued. Now a new building would be constructed round the brewing vats, but waited for labour now that men had gone to war.

'We'll get no help from Dirleton or Tantallon,' Isabel declared, 'for Bishop Bek has shown his Christian charity by burning them out.'

Maggie and Bet looked at one another; they had not known this, for Hal had only heard the night before and told Isabel of it just before they drifted off to sleep.

'So,' Isabel said grimly, 'there is only us. I am no expert in making buildings, but I daresay there are folk, yourself included, who can weave the wattle. And I can at least tread mud and dung and straw in a bucket.'

They followed her down the steps, tame and admiring as sheepdogs.

Temple Liston, Commanderie of the Knights Templar
Feast of St Theneva, Mother of Kentigern, July 1298

His army was sliding away like rendered grease and the expensive loss made Edward grind his teeth. Dog turd Welsh, he thought to himself, though he had to admit that bringing some several thousands of them had been the only option to overawe the Scots, who had had a year to preen and laud themselves for having won a victory.

Victory, by God – I will show them victory, Edward thought, even if good Englishmen had long since given their forty days of service and would not be persuaded further.

Yet the elaborate supply of what army he had was broken like a bad bowstring. Ships coming up the Forth had failed to arrive, forage had scrabbled what it could, but this Wallace was as smart an enemy as any Edward had faced and had left scarcely a cabbage or an ear of rye. There were precious few carcasses of livestock, either – save for a rotted pig shoved down a well. How could you hide so many cows and sheep?

He strode out of his elaborate panoply and stood under the banners in a deliberate pose, facing the assembly of lords. The pards of England drooped wearily above him, tangling in the golden snarl of wyvern that everyone knew as the Dragon Banner, which signified no quarter. To left and right hung the banners of Saint John of Beverley and Cuthbert of Durham – for you could not have enough holy help in the endeavour of red war. He rubbed his arm, where the poisoned dagger of the *hashashin* had all but killed him save for the Grace of God.

Sixteen years ago, he realised and hardly a night when he did not wake, slick with sweat and hagged by the wild-eyed dark face of the Saracen he had strangled with his bare hands. God's Own Hand had been over him then – though He might have tempered the months of crawling sickness that followed that single nick.

He looked at the sweating assembly. God's Holy Arse, how he hated most of them – and how they hated him. Each time he looked at a sullen face, he wanted to humble it, bring the great lord to his knees. Norfolk, Lancaster, Surrey and all the others who thought themselves greater than the king, the scions of the families who had tried to shackle and then subvert his father's reign, plunging them all into a long, bloody business. Not content with that, they tried with me, too.

Percy and Clifford especially, he thought savagely, who thought themselves God's anointed in the north, together with all the lords scrabbling for his favour and their lands in Scotland, yet prepared to break their oath as soon as his back was turned.

He was too kind, that was the problem. Even the young Bruce was not to be trusted, but that was almost certainly the fault of his whingeing father and the influence of that relactricant old schemer, his grandfather. He liked young Bruce – there was something of himself at that age in the Earl of Carrick, he thought.

If he can be bent to forgetting this foolishness of a crown, he added to himself, for there was only one ruler in Scotland. And England. And Wales. And Ireland. By God's Holy Arse he would bring this Wallace to the quartering and the headsman and the country to the knowledge that there was only one king and that was Edward, by the Grace of God an Englishman.

For what? The thought always slid in there, like Satan at his elbow. For his son, he replied by rote, though he winced. Fifteen. Young yet and the only survivor of the brood. Left too long alone after the death of his mother . . . as ever, the memory of Eleanor rose up, the death of her taking him in the throat. That long mourn of a journey, the hole in his life where she should be still black and infinitely deep, unable to be filled by any amount of stone crosses raised in her honour.

Let the boy have his thatching and ditch-digging a while longer, but in the end, he would buckle to the dignity, to what it means to be heir to the Crown, or, by God's Holy Arse, Edward would make him . . .

The truth of it was that he knew God had a Plan for him and that it was to rescue the Holy City. With the Welsh and the Scots securing his north and west, he could turn his will to Crusade; the thought drew him up into the glory of it, though the reality of God's Paladin was not what he thought.

The assembled lords saw the unnaturally tall, slightly stooped figure, long-armed and lean, his hair, once a gold cap, now swan white and straggling out of the customary coiffure of curls round his ears, his beard curving off his chin like a silver scimitar. His eyes were pouched and violet-ringed, because his dressers had all their paste and powder arts in a lost sumpter wagon and so could not produce the illusion of his health and vigour.

Now everyone could see that the skin of his face had sunk and seemed to want to peel back over the cheekbones, while the one drooping eye gave him a sly look, as if he was about to visit some corner of Hell on them all. Which, thought De Lacy, might well be the truth.

'You wish congress, my lords,' Edward said flatly and his dislike of it was plain.

De Lacy cleared his throat. The Earl of Lincoln was the closest thing to a confidant Edward had, yet even he was not sure how far friendship stretched.

'The army is starving,' he declared. 'Desertion is rife. The Welsh are . . . fretful.'

Someone sniggered and Edward could hardly blame him for it. Fretful was a serious understatement for what those black dwarves from the mountains had perpetrated, even on each other. For a time it had seemed as if the only battle fought on Scottish soil would be between drunken Welshmen and everyone else they staggered across. In the end, English knights had charged the worst of them down and killed eighty; now the Welsh were muttering about going over to the Scots.

Which had all been his own fault. A ship arrived and those expecting food had found its cargo to be wine. To offset the disappointment, Edward had issued it to the army, the Welsh had sucked it up and, on empty bellies, had gone fighting mad – he'd had to let Aymer de Valence lead a charge of horse to bring order back and Welshmen had been killed. Now the rest were sullen.

The Devil with them all, Edward thought savagely. Let the Welsh desert to the Scots – at least then I will know the enemy and can shove them back into Satan's arse, where they all fell from in the first place.

First – find your enemy.

'No news, my Earl of Lincoln?'

De Lacy heard the mocking tone, but also the underlying desperation in it. If the Scots army was not found, and quickly, they would have to leave for the south and do it all again next year. The realm of England and its king, De Lacy knew, could not afford that.

'Sir Brian de Jay and his Templars seek them out, my lord king.'

That, at least, was a fillip for the Crown – a handful of English Templars, seeking royal favour, had come to join Longshanks using the excuse that their actions had separated the Scots rebels from the community of the Church. Handily, Bishop Bek had readily agreed – though not many had been persuaded and the Scots Templars had been even more reluctant recruits, for all that their Scottish Master, John de Sawtrey, was with the army.

It did not matter – the Templars brought a fearsome reputation far in excess of their meagre numbers and, with two Masters riding at their head, brought God Himself to the side of the English host, now slathered round the lands of the Temple Commanderie at Liston, waiting for news of the Scots.

354

Yet the army, expensively and painstakingly gathered, was melting as fast as the costs were mounting, Edward thought – Christ's Wounds, he had summoned men as long ago as February, while he was still conducting a war in Flanders, and sent them north to bolster De Warenne. There had been 750 lances and 21,000 foot at Christmas – and only 5,000 by the end of March, so that the whole business had had to be done again, using Welshmen and foreigners.

He wanted it done. He had a wedding to attend and it had cost him dear – a truce with Philip of France and a sixteen-year-old bride called Marguerite. Christ, he was nearly sixty – yet she had come with the real prize, a cartload of gold and the key city of Guienne, so he could afford to ignore the sniggers. Behind his back, of course, never to his face – but he heard them, all the same,

'I will decide on the morrow,' Edward said, disgusted at his compromising tone, turning away before any of the lords decided – foolishly – to press the point. Back in the cool of his panoply, he slumped in a curule chair, took wine and slopped it into his mouth.

All through the rest of the day, heavy with heat, hazed with woodsmoke, leather, horse dung and shit, the army sat and muttered, or dreamed of food.

Riders came and went; the sun slithered wearily to a glorious death and insects started to sizzle and die in the sconces.

Then, like the balm of rain, riders came out of the dark, forcing slope-necked horses wearily up to the king's tent. They were Scottish and the guards were wary but, in the end, the leaders they escorted were presented to the king's person and stood, stained with the sweat of hard travel.

Earl Patrick of Dunbar and Gilbert D'Umfraville, Earl of Angus, were Scottish *nobiles* who professed to be as English as Edward himself but he looked at them balefully, since he distrusted everyone. They saw the violet cast round his eyes, the sinister droop of one lid, and did not prevaricate.

'Thirteen miles away,' Dunbar declared.

'In the Wood of Callendar,' added D'Umfraville. 'Beside Falkirk.'

Edward permitted himself a smile. Treachery, as ever, worked its wiles and he had found Wallace.

CHAPTER TWELVE

The woods at Callendar, near Falkirk
Feast of St Mary Magdalene, July, 1298

They were singing, which reminded Hal of the last time he had heard voices glorifying God – at Stirling, when they had been raised sweetly over the smell of churned earth, the stink of fresh blood, shite from horses and men and the high, thin acrid smell of fear.

'Brabancons,' muttered Sim knowingly. 'Celebrating Mass.'

The whole English army was celebrating mass in the midst of some colourful tentage, as if there was no hurry. They had arrived like a great, slow wave that radiated power and numbers, so that Hal could see men near him shift in their saddles, looking uneasily from one to the other. Strathearn and Lennox, he saw, Mentieth and the Stewards, all trying to make their mouths summon up some spit.

There were retinues from Carrick and Comyn here, too, Hal noted – but no Earl of Buchan or any Badenoch or Bruce with them. Wallace saw the strained look on the Lothian lord's face as he glanced at the small – God's Hook, pathetically small – *mesnie* of Scots horse.

Aye, well may ye worry, young Hal, he thought bitterly.

357

They all had good reasons for being elsewhere, none more so than Buchan, who had brought his men personally weeks ago, riding like a sack of wet grain and waspish as a damp cat.

'I am with ye in spirit, Sir William,' he had announced, 'but I go to keep the north in order.'

'Does it need so kept?' Wallace countered and Buchan had merely smiled and flapped a dismissive hand.

'It always needs order,' he answered politely. 'God keep you safe – and the English at a distance. Where are they anyway?'

'Under the smoke they make,' Wallace had answered laconically and had then watched Buchan ride away, looking right and left constantly. Looking for the Lothian lord, Wallace thought, So I know what business Buchan has and where. At least his quarrel with his wife and her new wee lover is a genuine, if selfish, excuse and not some callow tale like others presented to justify their absence.

But their lack had been noted by those of the *nobiles* who had turned up, sitting in their fine trappings on barded horses – few of them the fearsome and expensive *destrier* – feeling their bowels turn to water.

> *Nun bitten wir den Heiligen Geist*
> *Um den rechten Glauben allermeist*

It drifted on the wind, sometimes louder, sometimes fading, but a constant reminder of what Longshanks had brought. Thirty thousand, some said he had gathered – the largest army ever seen. Not now, the sensible heads pointed out, for there is less than half of it left.

But even that was more than enough and Hal could see the *nobiles* knew it. Brabancons, Gascons, Welsh spears and bows, the scouts reported with assurance – and, above all, three thousand heavy horse. We have ten thousand men, Hal thought bleakly, with only five hundred of it horse and not all of that fit to match the English knights if his own men were anything to judge – twenty hard fighters on tough little garrons, with latchbows, Jeddart staffs, daggers, little axes and less armour.

Dass er uns behüte an unserm Ende,
Wenn wir heimfahr'n aus diesem liende.

'Christ, I wisht they would be doucelike,' said a voice, thick with fear. Hal swivelled; Sir William Hay of Lochwarret, desperate to wipe his mouth and face, kept raising his hand, then remembering his steel-segmented gauntlet and letting it fall again.

'What are they chantin'?' demanded Ramsay of Dalhousie, his bascinet-framed face the colour of spoiled suet.

Kyrieleis!

'I do not ken,' Wallace answered languidly, grinning, 'but I jalouse they are done, so it matters little.'

'Ye mun find,' said a gruffer voice, 'that they are calling on the Holy Ghost to protect them. It is also the first of several verses, so they are not done with it yet.'

Hal knew the grizzled Robert de Ros of Wark by sight, though he had not known the man was any expert on the Brabancon. Wallace, however, resplendent in his Guardian's gold jupon, blazoned with the red lion of Scotland, did not seem surprised. He had cut the tangle of his hair into a style more suited for the Guardian of Scotland and clipped his beard short and neat – but the man beneath had not been changed one whit.

'Aye, weel,' he said, turning from one to the other of the clustered knights, a grim, lopsided grin twisting his face. 'It is a nice tune. I have brought you to the ring, *gentilhommes*. Now ye dance if ye can.'

He nodded to Hal and then jerked his head to send him and the hobilars, the light horse, far out to the right flank, into the trees to hide and watch and, hopefully, fall on the rear of English knights once they had fallen foul of the great ring of men which stood there.

Wallace watched them go. He liked the new lord of Herdmanston and wished him well – the man had uncovered the business with Bruce and the Stone with skill and stuck to his word, though Wallace did not know what to do with the knowledge of it.

On the one hand, a valuable relic of the realm had been saved. On the other, red murder had been done, by Bruce and the Comyn. If we still stand by the end of the day, he thought, I will have to think more on it.

He shifted and looked right and left at the *nobiles* of Scotland. Steady as an egg on a stick, he thought morosely, and those who are not thinking on how to get advantage over their immediate neighbour and enemy are wondering how to hang on to their lands and titles.

They will run, he thought.

Sim thought so, too, and said as much, though Hal tried to ignore him. It was that Sim Craw rasp, perhaps, that prompted Nebless Clemmie to force out from the ranks and alongside, turning his ruin of a face towards Hal.

It was not entirely true to call him Nebless, since he had half the proboscis left, though the wen that had caused the loss had left a disturbing hole. For all that, it was an honest face and a Herdmanston one, which was the meat of his words.

'The lads,' he said to Hal in his rheumy voice, glancing back over his shoulder to make sure they were still agreed, 'wish it known that they are all proud to be at yer stirrup, my lord. Ye ken us and you are auld in the horn when it comes to red war.'

Hal blinked, a little stunned by this. Since he had been old enough to know his place, he had taken his rank as a given, however slight it may be in the eyes of greater lords. Riding a shaggy pony across to a rickle of sticks with the Herdmanston oxen in tow for some poor plough got him a knuckle on a seamed forehead from a peasant who relied for his life on the loan of the beasts.

Rattling around with the Henry and others, Hal had even abused his rank, only sometimes realising that the food and drink he and his band took from a blank-faced family was more than they could afford.

Even later, into the full of himself, there had been times when he considered that his fruitful raiding into the English Borders had been the saving of Herdmanston in lean times. Later still, of course, he had come to realise that it was his father's constant, sure and steady stewardship which provided.

Now it was his hand. The Lord of Herdmanston – in time, he thought, I might have become the Auld Sire of Herdmanston save that a covetous king and a beautiful wummin got in the road of it and placed it all at hazard.

He shook the mordbid thoughts just as a rider came up, with men at his back; he did not need Sim's warning growl to know who it was – the red lion shield told him and sent a block of ice into his belly.

MacDuff of Fife, Isabel's kin, his florid face and wisped hair like autumn bracken in snow, a distant ghost of herself.

'Herdmanston,' MacDuff called out and Hal stopped. Behind the man was his *mesnie* of men-at-arms, a dozen men in maille and surcoats and lances, lacking only the slap of a sword on shoulder and a decent horse to rank them beside any knight on the field.

'Ye impugn my honour, sirra, and I am Fife. Ye have been gallivanting with the Countess of Buchan, I hear. Bad enough that her name should be tied with The Bruce, but he at least is an earl. You are of no account at all.'

That was flat out as an unsheathed blade and Sim's eyes narrowed.

'Have a care...' he began and Hal laid a hand on his arm to silence him. He was fighting for words and against angry ones when a shadow fell on them both, making them turn into the blazing blue of Wallace's eyes.

'Ye are not Fife,' Wallace said and, though it was low and

361

soft, everyone heard it grating across the pride of MacDuff like an edge on maille. 'The Lord of Fife is a wee laddie, held by the English these last dozen years. Fife is now the provenance of the Crown until he is returned to it − and in the absence of a king, it is held by the Guardian. Who is me.'

He leaned forward a little and MacDuff, before he could resist, leaned back.

'So who is Fife, my wee lord?'

There was silence and Wallace smeared a savage smile on his face and slapped his jupon.

'It is me.'

He waved a hand behind him, never taking his eyes from MacDuff's pallid face.

'Down there, beyond the pows and a burn or two, is the enemy. Turn your ire on them, my lord, not yer own.'

He nodded to Hal.

'On yer way, as commanded.'

Hal kicked Griff and moved under the scowl of MacDuff, his men trailing after him like a snow wind. It took MacDuff a yard or so before he recovered his voice and enough anger to substitute for courage, though he glared at Hal's back first, before he dared turn it on Wallace.

'This is what we have become then,' he snarled, reining round. 'Petty lords and brigands rule in these days. It will not stand, sirra. It will not stand.'

Neither will you, Wallace thought bitterly.

Hal and the hobilars rode away from it, feeling the imagined heat on their backs, past the right flank, upwards of a thousand men in a ring that was being called *schiltron*. It was a word from the old time and the north that meant Shield Troop, though half of the men in it would not know that and the other half would not care much: they were busy hammering stakes all round themselves, out to four or five feet distant, linking them with a tangle of ropes.

There were four such rings in a line, with at least a thousand, not more than two, in each one. In between, the tall, muscled Selkirk men waited quietly, bows still unstrung, checking arrow flights and trying to ignore the galloping of their commander, Sir John Steward, riding up and down with instructions, exhortations, a manic energy that would not let him or his slathered horse rest.

'They will run,' Bangtail muttered and Hal realised he was talking of the knights, glanced back to the shift and stamp of Scotland's finest.

No Bruces, or Balliols, or a single Comyn lord; for all they had sent men they stayed away because they would not be second to each other and certainly not to the upstart Wallace. Knighted or not, they sneered – though never to his face – he is still a brigand of little account.

At least, that would be the excuse of it, Hal thought, but the lie in it was more to do with their terror of Longshanks and what they could do to placate the beast.

They will run, Hal said to himself and the dull cold of it sifted into his belly, chill as wet rock.

The cloy of the communion wine, too sweet for Edward's taste, made his mouth feel thick. His ribs hurt where the fool of a groom had let his own warhorse step on him the previous night – it gave the king no comfort to know that the groom was nursing his own ribs and most of his striped back.

If truth was told, Edward thought moodily to himself, his ribs only ached worse than the rest of him – sleeping like a spearman on the wet ground, wrapped in a cloak, may perform wonders for his image but it did nothing for his joints.

Stabat Mater dolorósa, iuxta crucem lacrimósa, dum pendébat Fílius.

The Templars, on this day dedicated to their favourite, the Virgin Herself, were almost as ecstatic as the crazy Brabancon, Edward thought, and smiled grimly. Good – let the Mournful Mother weep at her station by the Cross if it left Sir Brian de Jay and Frere John de Sawtrey rolling-eyed with martial fervour.

They, brilliant in their white and black and red, would turn Scots bowels to water when they charged with their retinues, small though they were — but that black-barred Beau Seant banner was worth another five-score knights, without a doubt.

The distant bleat of shouts from the rebel ranks wafted to him and he did not need to hear it clearly to know what it was they bellowed.

Berwick.

As if he had perpetrated some sort of bloody massacre — only a few hundred had died after all. A thousand at most and that was no more than any other stormed town in a red war suffered, and rightly, for resistance. Hardly the lake of blood the Scots painted the affair with . . .

Raised voices shook him from his revery and he found the Earl Marshal arguing with Surrey; it had reached the leaning and pointing stage, but they subsided, glaring and panting, as Edward clumped up, his prick-spurs rasping the muddied grass.

'My lord king,' said the pouch-eyed stare of Bigod, the Earl Marshal of England. Beside him, sullen as thwarted babes, Hereford and Lincoln dripped poisonous stares and coloured finery.

'What?' demanded Edward savagely and had the satisfaction of seeing them wince and shuffle like boys.

'I thought to allow the men to take some sustenance before we attack,' growled Bigod and saw the droop-eyed scowl that made his belly curl.

'Foolish,' De Warenne interrupted, drawing on his full dignity as Earl of Surrey, his white arrow of beard quivering above the steel gorget. 'A thin stream barriers us from the rebels — what if they come down on us while we sit on our arses chewing?'

Edward felt the press on his temples, as if the gold circlet was tightening on the maille coif. Christ's Holy Arse – was he the only one with any sense here?

'It is a Holy Day,' he said to Bigod, soft as silk, and those who knew him braced themselves. 'So mayhap the Virgin will summon up the miracle of a loaf and some fishes – otherwise, my lord Marshal, what God's Anointed sustenance are you suggesting the men take?'

The Earl Marshal opened and closed his mouth a few times, but Edward had already started to savage the triumphantly smiling De Warenne.

'As for you – you need not grin like a mule's cunny pissing in a heat-wave,' he snarled. 'It is a great pity you did not have this caution the first time you encountered this Wallace, else we would not be in this mess.'

The Earl of Surrey glowered, his face turning dark with suffused blood, which brought a savage leap of exultation in Edward's heart; he twisted the knife harder.

'He will not, of course, come down on us here, for we are not hemmed in on three sides as you contrived at Stirling.'

'We will attack at once,' the Earl of Lincoln said swiftly, with a neat little bow from the neck. Edward saw the smoothly transmitted warning from De Lacy and reined himself in; it would not do to antagonise every great lord of his realm on the morning of battle.

'Of course you bloody will,' Edward growled, waving to his arming squire to bring up Bayard. 'Over there is the ogre we have spent weeks on empty bellies to find. Now slay the beast, in the name of God and all His Saints, and let us be done with this business once and for all.'

'Amen,' said Lincoln and reined round.

The army shifted, like a huge stone trembling at the top of a mountain.

Addaf felt it, even in a belly as clappit as his, where his belt buckle rattled against his spine. Buttered capons and golden, crusted pastries rich with mushroom and onion, soups

365

luxurious with eggs and milk – if you are dreaming of food it is always better to dream large, rather than of rye bread and pease brose.

'Captain Heydin.'

The voice bellowed out from a splendid figure, all red and gold on a barded horse. His banners and accoutrements were all marked with a golden flower and a studding of little gold daggers on a bright red background; as Heydin Captain said, he would not be missed at a thousand paces, would the Lord FitzAlan of Bedale.

In the retinue of Bishop Bek, he had been appointed *millinar*, the command of the foot and took the task seriously.

'Captain Heydin,' he said in careful English, his helm tucked under one arm, the other fighting to control the warhorse, which wanted to be away with all the others riding ahead. 'Watch your station and do not get between the horse and the enemy. Mark me, now.'

'Yer honour,' Heydin Captain replied and put a fist across his chest in salute as the knight rode away, then turned to the other Welsh archers, a wry smile plastered on his face.

'The mannie wants us to stay out of the way of those caperers on their fat ponies,' he boomed in Welsh. 'Let the proud folk have their fun and then we will win the day for them. *Nyd hyder ond bwa.*'

There is no dependence but on the bow. The Welshmen all growled and grinned at that, while Addaf checked his flights. It had taken him a long while to make new arrows with fine peacock flights to replace the ones he had thrown away at Stirling – the memory of that floundering panic of a day, when he had hauled himself out on the safe side of the river like a half-drowned dog, made him shiver.

He had lost his bowbag and arrows, his shoes and a good gambeson that day, a hard loss for a man with little enough; he touched the new leather shoes – hung round his neck like an amulet, for you never risked their loss on a field cut with

366

sucking streams and churned mud. He would not lose this time. This time, he would gain.

The knight of Bedale forced a way through the throng of spears and bows, repeating his message to those he had found spoke English, though he was not sure whether some were cozening him with that or not. The Welsh nodded and saluted and watched him ride off; he was not a bad commander for an Englishman, but he was still an Englishman, who had asked Heydin Captain why his name was round the wrong way.

It was not, he was told. For over there was Heydin ap Daffyd and there was Heydin, nicknamed Gwrnerth Ergydlym, or Powerful Sharpshot since he was the worst archer of them all, barely putting six out of ten in a palm's width at a hundred paces. Then he had to explain to the bemused lord that it was a jest, just as Rhodri was called Gam – Squint-Eyed – because he was the best shot of all, even to putting it round corners and killing a bear with a straw arrow, it was rumoured.

In the end, just as Heydin was patiently explaining that Gwynned ap Mydr was nicknamed One Eye though he actually had two – he could not close his aiming eye and had to have a black patch placed over it for shooting – the Lord of Bedale had held up one hand.

'He is the best shot of all, look you, my lord,' Heydin Captain tried to add as the knight rode away, still unsure whether he was being made a fool of. 'He can shoot the wren through his claw, from Caenog, in the Vale of Clwyd, to Esgair Vervel in Ireland . . .'

Now the Lord of Bedale put his great bucket helm on the saddle bow and leaned on it, looking wistfully after the knights of Bishop Bek's command, the Second Battle all riding ahead to join the heavy horse of the king himself, the combined Battles forming the hard right hook of the army. He wanted to be there rather than the *millinar* of foot, trying to herd the great body of spearmen and archers, gabbling in their own foul language and ploughing harsh furrows over Redding Muir down to the Westquarter Burn.

Addaf did not care what the Lord of Bedale felt, only what he belly felt. Away to his left, he saw a magnificent galloper, bright in horizontal stripes, tippets flying from the dome of his sugarloaf heaume; he and other archers who saw him growled deep in their throats, for this was De Valence, who had charged down good Welshmen not long before – eighty were dead of it.

One or two of the archers aimed their unstrung bows at him in future promise, then hurried on when a knot of bright riders surged up past them, thick with banners and purpose. The king himself . . .

One arrow, Addaf thought. One good peacock-fletched shaft with a bodkin point at the back of that red jupon with the three gold pards and Llewellyn is avenged, Ylfron Bridge's ghosts laid to rest, Maes Moydog and Madog ap Llewellyn paid for. Yet no-one shot more than surly looks, just kept their heads down and slogged on.

Edward saw them, all the same, and both parties would have been surprised to find they were thinking of Maes Moydog, though for differing reasons.

Like the Welsh then, Edward thought, the Scots are trying great bands of spearmen to resist the knights. Well, we shot them down with Gascon crossbows at Maes Moydog and we will do so again here – there will be no repeat of the idiocy at Stirling. The idea cheered him – even if Maes Moydog had been the victory of the Earl of Warwick – and he raised a hand to wave to delighted youngsters, who had never been in great battle before and were bright with the thrill of it all.

'*Dieu vous garde.*'

'*Felicitas.*'

'*Dieu vivas.*'

They threw greetings like gaudy tokens to lovers and

Edward watched them, wondering where his own fire for this had gone, thinking savagely to himself that they would find the truth of it all when the spear points tumbled them and their expensive horse to the mud and the shite rolled fearfully out of them as they scrabbled to be away. In the end, he knew, the Gascon crossbows would decide it. And the Welsh bowmen if they stuck to the task of it.

Maes Moydog . . .

He saw Sir Giles D'Argentan ride up, splendid and grim and was cheered by the sight of the second-best knight in Christendom, admitting in his inner heart that, since the foremost knight was himself in his better days, the laurels had shifted a little to a much younger man.

Alongside D'Argentan was an even younger squire, riding easy and lithe and splendid, his hair like fine gold mist wisping from under the coif and his helmet tucked under one arm so that he could drink in all that was happening around him. With a shock, Edward saw that this was a boy, no older than his own son.

D'Argentan reined in and bowed his inhuman, barrel-heaumed head, then removed it to reveal his beaming, scarred face. He saw the king was looking elsewhere and turned to the squire.

'Do you not know your king, boy?' he said. The squire bowed at once. No scowl or resentment, Edward thought; this boy knows the dignity of knights and how to behave as one, which starts with obedience. My own son is as tall and as strong and rides the lists as well – but this one knows the style of his profession, as surely as little Edward fails to grasp the dignity of the Crown he must one day wear. Thatching and ditch-digging; the thought made him scowl.

'If your grace permits,' D'Argentan declared, 'may I present Piers Gaveston, esquire. I have been given him for the instructioning.'

'Gaveston,' Edward repeated slowly. Son of Sir Arnaud, he

369

recalled suddenly, the Gascon I used as hostage with the French twice. He remembered welcoming Arnaud into his household after the man had fled France.

The boy had a smooth, beardless face, innocent as prayer and capped with an angel's gold hair. Like mine once was, the king thought wistfully.

'How old are you, boy?' he demanded.

'Fourteen years and two months, if it please your grace.'

The answer was steady and not in the least overawed by the stern old ogre king, Edward thought. This lad is good material and of ages with my own son.

'Keep him safe,' he said to the smiling D'Argentan. 'I may have uses for this lad.'

He watched them ride off, pleased to see the straight back of the boy and the easy way he controlled a *destrier*. Perhaps an example like this, he thought, would turn Edward to kingly matters. Thatching and digging ditches, by God's Arse. Mimers and mummers and naked swimming in rivers . . .

'*Quod non vertat iniquita dies*,' said a sonorous voice and Edward knew it was the Bishop of Durham before he had even turned his head.

And so it comes, the wicked day – typical of the round-faced little cant, Edward thought sourly. Yet Bek was another of those necessary evils of ruling, a churchman of power, armed, armoured and resplendent in red with his ermined cross and his pudding-bowl tonsure.

'*Regis regum rectissimi prope est Dies Domini*,' he rasped back. The day of the Lord, the rightful King of Kings, is close at hand – let him chew that one over, Edward thought with savage humour. '*Virtutis fortuna comes.*'

Fortune favours courage was what folk took it to mean – but the *comes* in it originally referred to the elite Roman horsemen and Bek knew the king had made a clever wordplay on the knights of his own army. Since the king's jests were few, Bek never faltered or frowned, offering a small, admiring smile instead.

'Very good, my liege,' he said, then glanced up the long roll of slope and dips to where the faint line marked the enemy. 'Do you think they fear us yet, sire?'

Wallace felt the fear behind him, washing like stink from a shambles as the coloured skeins of armoured horsemen advanced over the meadow, careless and bright as trailing ribbons. A Battle, forming the left of the English line, it was a dazzle of fluttering pennons and banners that Wallace knew well and he smiled grimly to himself. De Warenne again . . .

The Van, pushing forward to the right of De Warenne, were singing, the voices faint and eldritch on a fickle wind: *Quant Rollant veit que la bataille serat, plus se fait fiers que leon ne leupart.*

When Roland sees that now must be combat, more fierce he's found than lion or leopard – Wallace knew that *chanson de geste* to Roland well enough and screwed half round in his saddle, into the drawn, pinched grimness behind him.

'Have we no voices, my lords?' he demanded in halting French.

A high, clear voice started it and Wallace thanked God for his kin – Simon, his cousin. The other two, Adam and Richard, joined in almost at once, for they had been known as the Unholy Trinity since they had started to tear around together, causing mischief. You would not know that now from their angel voices and the thought made him smile, even as other throats, gruff, out of tune, trembling, rose to join in.

Hostem repéllas lóngius, pacémque dones prótinus; Ductóre sic te praévio, Vitémus omne nóxium

Drive far away our wily foe, and Thine abiding peace bestow; If Thou be our protecting Guide, no evil can our steps betide.

In the tight ring of dry-mouthed spearmen, men unflexed

371

a hand from the shaft and crossed themselves. Even if they did not understand the Latin of it, they knew it was a call to God to hold His Hand over them as the coloured talons scarred towards them, paused, then started to coalesce into fat, tight blocks of silver-tipped dazzle.

Deep in the forest of spears, someone was sick.

Peering through the leaves like an animal, Hal saw the horse of the Van gather like wolves, the great bedsheet banners of Lincoln and Hereford smothering the host of lesser pennons of their retinues. They were planning to fall on the centre and Hal grinned through the sweat as he saw the sudden flutter in them; the Selkirk archers had released.

The horsemen bunched; commanders galloped back and forth and, in the still, fly-pocked swelter of the woods, men who knew the muscled sign of it grunted expectantly as the huge blocks started forward at a determined, knee-to-knee walk.

'Not long afore they find oot,' Bangtail shouted with glee and was shushed for his pains. Still, the joy of it was hard to keep from bubbling up, Hal thought and almost let out a sharp yell of triumph as the splendid, implacable riders came up over a slight lip – and found the great slew of boggy loch they had not seen before, spread out like a moat in front of the first two *schiltron* rings.

Confusion. Milling. The Selkirk men let loose again and horses were goaded to plunge and buck, flinging men to the ground with a noise like falling cauldrons. The faint sound of cheers washed up the Hal's ears, followed by the great tidal roar . . .

Tailed dogs.

Slowly, painfully, the commanders galloping and yelling – even striking shields, Hal saw, so that the whole straggling mass started to turn to the left, towards the Battle of De Warenne, their unshielded side to the arrows as they circled

372

the long strip of muddy marshland that had balked them. Many of them had not put on their full-face helms and were hunched and turned from the arrows as if in a snow storm.

It was a moment to savour – yet Hal saw that all this did was concentrate all the force from the centre to the right of the Scots line, where he and the other Herdmanston riders huddled in the trees.

'Watch to yer right, lads,' Sim growled and the men crouched on the patient garrons as De Warenne's knights came up, wheeled into formation and started in towards the great shield ring – and the Scots knights that blocked the passage between it and the woods. They would pass close to Hal, he saw, funnelled by wood and *schiltron* spears to a mass the Scots knights could match for frontage – and Hal would lead his twenty riders out into their flank, hoping the flea bite would be enough to unnerve the crush of English knights.

'God preserve us,' muttered Ill Made Jock.

'For ever and ever,' came the muttered rote response.

'*Lente aleure.*'

The cry came, faint as lost hope, from the English commanders of the *echelles* as, one by one from the right, these sub-units began to move off, lances raised.

'*Paulatim.*'

The pace picked up slightly, the huge mass of mailled men churning forward, horses snorting and calling out in high-pitched squeals of excitement. Griff shifted under Hal, for he smelled the rank battle stink, felt the tremble – as they came level, the great quake of it came up through the saddle into Hal's belly. Leaves shook; a twig fell.

'In the name of all God's Saints . . .' someone whimpered.

'*Pongnié.*'

One by one the units obeyed and spurred, the great warhorses churning up the ground, the riders bellowing. Yet they were so closely pressed that they could not manage more than an ungainly half-canter, half-trot and still remain knee to knee.

'Now,' Hal hissed, watching the distant block of horse, the figure of Wallace head and shoulders above the tallest in it, watched him raise that hand-and-half to arm's length over his head . . .

Someone broke from the back ranks, speeding off into the woods like a pursued fox. Another joined him. Then another. Wallace brought the sword down and surged forward, trailing a knot of men – twice as many hauled their mounts round and bolted.

The *nobiles* of Scotland had run after all.

To fight and win was now a dream. Hal saw it even as he saw Wallace and the pitiful knuckle of remaining knights slam into the great chest of English lances. The only sensible thing to do was run – the sudden rush of that made him jerk Griff's head back – but, in the same moment, he saw the horse fall, saw the red and gold giant vanish into the mass; Hal raised his sword, kicked Griff hard enough to make the garron squeal and every man at his back surged out of the wood, screaming, 'A Sientcler.'

They ploughed into the flanks of the struggling knights, just at the point they piled up like water at the dam. Hal cut and thrust and heard his sword bang like a hammer on a forge, felt the shock of it up his arm. A figure in stripes loomed; Hal cut and the man's armoured head snapped back like a doll, his helmet dented on one side. A blow smacked Hal's shield, reeled him so that he had to hang grimly on, while Griff spun in a half-circle.

He saw Nebless Clemmie hook his Jeddart staff in a knight's fancy jupon, then spin his horse and ride off, dragging the knight to the ground with a clatter, where Ill Made Jock, elbow working like a mad fiddler, rained a flurry of furious stabs until the battle surged his plunging garron away.

The dam broke; the great mass of armoured horse rode over

the remains of the Scots knights, who were either unhorsed and dying, or fleeing for the woods. Hal knew that his own attack had achieved only a moment of surprise and now the English were cursing and turning to fight. He saw Ill Made Jock's garron, Wee Dan, smashed in the chest by the fearsome hooves of a warhorse, go down screaming – Hal lost sight of Jock in the whirl of hooves and legs and spuming blood.

Corbie Dand, on foot and with his face all bloody, was screaming and wielding the remains of his Jeddart, splintered down to a short-handled axe; the blow that crushed his head, kettle hat and all, came from a knight in blue and gold.

'Wallace . . .' yelled a voice and Hal turned into it, ducked a mad axe-cut at his head, took a mace on his shield and slashed back. He registered Sim as a flicker, on foot, open-mouthed and pointing; Hal spun Griff, felt the animal stumble, cursed and flogged it with cruel heels.

Wallace, off his mount, stood like a tree in a flood, the sword in both hands now and the added power hacking Hell into his enemies. Horsemen struggled and fought to get to him, for they saw the red lion rampant blazing on his chest and knew who it was, could taste the glory of it – but he stood there, a roaring giant, more ogre than man.

He turned briefly as Hal surged Griff up on one side, not even sure of what he was doing or why – then he saw the sheer joy of Wallace, the great beatific smile.

He is prepared to die, Hal thought, stabbed with sudden wonder. He is not afraid at all . . .

Sim staggered out of a ruck, slashing right and left, and stood on one side of Wallace, so that Hal found himself on the other, feeling Griff stagger and buckle.

'Make for the ring,' Wallace yelled and they did so, moving as swiftly as they could. Hal suddenly felt Griff sink and managed to kick free and drop; the snapped lance shaft was deep in the animal's chest and, even as Hal cursed himself for not having seen it – when had it happened, in the name

375

of Christ? – he heard the animal blow a last bloody froth and die.

'The ring,' yelled Sim, grabbing an elbow – a horse slammed into them, splitting them apart and sending Hal over in a dizzying whirl that left him dazed and looking at calloused, filth-clogged feet; when he rolled over, trying to get his eyes in focus, he saw the hedge of shafts over him.

Then a hand grabbed his surcoat, dragging him backwards; he heard the cloth tear and thought, mad as gibbering, that Bet the Bread would be furious at the ruin of her sewing.

A figure floated in front of him, a hand came forward and he felt the blow only faintly, then the second, sharp as a bee-sting. He flung up a hand to ward off a third and saw Wallace, his face streaked with blood, grinning at him.

'Back with us? Good – there is work yet to do.'

Hal had lost his sword and his helmet and there was something wrong with the coif, which seemed to be flapping loose on one side. A mad-eyed figure with hair bursting out from under a leather helmet shoved a long knife at him, grinning insanely. Hal took it, looked up and round, feeling the shudder through the nearest shoulders and backs as English knights tried to force into the hedge-ring of grim men, standing like a single beast at bay.

The riders circled, frustrated and hurling curses, maces, axes, the remains of their lances and – now that the Selkirk bowmen had been scatteered and ridden down – their huge barrel helmets. The spearmen thrust and slashed, panting and snarling, and the great horses died, spilling the proud blazon of their riders into the crushed grass and bloody mud, where men in dirty wool came from the back ranks of the ring of spears, squirming between legs and feet to scuttle out and pounce on the trapped, or those too slow to struggle away on foot.

'No' chantin' noo, ye sou's arse,' howled one, leaping like a spider on a black and silver figure, crawling wearily on hands and knees away from the kicking shriek of his dying

376

horse. The thin-bladed knife went in the visor and blood flooded out the breathing holes – then the spider was back beneath the shelter of the spears, breathing hard and smiling at Hal like a fox fresh on a kill.

He wiped the dagger on his filthy, ripped braies and Hal saw it was Fergus the Beetle, black-carapaced in his boiled leather and grinning with blood on his teeth. He winked, as if he had just spotted Hal across a crowded alehouse.

'Aye til the fore, my lord.'

Hal blinked. Still alive. Beyond the safety of the spear rings, the Scots archers were being ridden down and killed in a running slaughter and he wondered what had happened to Sim.

The Bishop's horse limped and his surcoat was torn open under one arm, so that it flapped like the wounded wing of a red kite. Behind him stumbled a knight on foot, helmet and bascinet both gone and his maille coif shredded; there was blood on his face and a great spill of it down a once-cream surcoat, almost obliterating the two ravens blazoned on it.

Addaf did not need to hear Bek to know his anger, for it was plain in the wild, red-faced hand-waving he did at the knight in red and gold stripes, who sat sullenly on his expensive warhorse. It was draped in pristine white barding scattered with little red-and-gold-striped shields, each one ermined in the top left quarter; Basset of Drayton, Addaf had been told after the first angry encounter between the knight and the Bishop.

That was when Bek had tried to check the knights of his command and wait for the king before attacking, but this Basset of Drayton had arrogantly pointed his sword at Bek and told him to go and celebrate Mass if he wished, for the knights would do the fighting. Bek's retinue heard it and took off in a mad gallop, a great metal flail that splintered itself to ruin on the nearest Scots ring of spears while the Bishop beat his saddle with futile anger.

Now the survivors of it, their horses dead, staggered away – and Addaf knew that Bek was scathing Basset because neither he nor any of his two bachelor knights nor nine sergeants had ridden anywhere near the Scots.

'This horse is worth fifty marks,' Basset argued, scowling as Addaf and the other archers came level with the arguing pair.

'Then point it and spur – it should charge home,' Bek snarled back, 'even if the rider does not care to.'

'By Christ's Wounds,' Basset bellowed, his beard bristling. 'I will not take that from the likes of a tonsured byblow . . .'

'Neither will you charge home,' bellowed a new voice and everyone turned as Edward and his retinue came cantering up. Eyes went down; no-one wanted to look at the furious, droop-lidded lisping rage that stormed out of the king's face.

Especially not Basset, who went as white as his horse barding and started to stammer.

'Quiet,' Edward ordered, then surveyed the wreckage of staggering, unhorsed knights, trailing back like drunks from an alehouse. A groaning knight in green, torn and spattered with mud and blood, was helped by two others; his left hand was hanging from a bloody mess by a few last fragments of tendon and flesh and someone had tied his baldric round the forearm to stop him bleeding to death.

'My Lord of Otley,' Edward said, nodding to the green knight as if they had met in cloistered court. The green knight moaned and another limped out behind him, bare-headed and leaking blood; he paused, looked up at his king and bowed.

Edward returned it.

'My good lord,' he said blandly. 'You have lost your horse.'

Voiced as commiseration, it had a vicious twist to it – Eustace de Hacche had refused to sell his splendid charger to the king and now the beautiful bay with one white sock was lying, screaming in a tureen of its own entrails.

De Hacche turned away, nursing his ribs and more bitter

about the horse than the spear which had burst him open; he did not want to have to remove his maille and gambeson for fear of what might tumble to the ground. I will look like my horse, he thought.

Esward watched him stumble off, his face a dog's dinner of anger, then turned his droop-eyed fury on Bek and Basset.

'Neither of ye have the sense of an egg,' he growled and watched them bristle, mildly curious to see if they would spill it over to argument. They winked on the brim of it — then puffed it away and Edward sat deeper in his saddle, slightly disappointed but not surprised.

Christ blind me, he thought, good men have died because this Basset fool has a head fit only for carrying a metal helmet and as empty. Not that he is alone in it, he added bitterly, else I would not have to be here, completing the task I set for the Earl of Surrey and others.

'If you have finished squandering the chivalry of England,' Edward growled at the pair, 'perhaps we can return to completing this affray?'

He gave a signal; a horn blew and Addaf heard the Lord of Bedale shouting at Heydin Captain, who, in turn, roared out orders in his sonorous Welsh for the war-winners to step on this bloody stage.

Addaf rolled his shoulders expectantly, then looked right and left, dismayed. Around him, the Welsh archers, watching the expensively hired Gascon crossbowmen trot forward and start rattling shafts, twisted smiles of braided scorn on their faces. The Welsh spearman butted their weapons and leaned on them insolently.

Addaf's heart sank — the sullen hatred for the English was more to the Welsh than honour and, though they would not change sides, they did not want to participate further, a defiant response to the slaughter perpetrated on them earlier.

The archers stood, stolid faces blank, one horned nock of their unstrung bows on the instep of a shoed foot to keep it

379

out of the mud, the other clamped between two fists as they leaned gently, pointedly going nowhere.

Like all the other *millinars*, Bedale yelled and galloped back and forth, but it was Heydin Captain and all the other captains of a hundred who persuaded the reluctant Welsh of his command into the business, with a combination of scathing curses on their bravery and wheedling promises of being first at the plunder.

That lashed them to action and they moved forward, knowing that each step took them closer to the part that mattered – the plundering of the bodies when the field was won. Yet Addaf was aware of the low mumured growl of all the other Welsh, conscious of the burn of their eyes on his back.

It was not Bedale or even Heydin Captain – for all their shouting and waving – who did the serious work for Addaf and his fellows: that task belonged to Rhys, the Master. Mydr ap Mydfydd, they called him – Aim the Aimer – and with good reason.

He brought them to within a hundred paces, while the remaining knights circled aimlessly round the thicket of spears, waving weapons and trying to dart in now and then and stab with their lances – though most of them had thrown them down. They saw the Welsh archers come up and frantically spurred or staggered away from the *schiltrons* as if the men in them had plague; they did not want to be anywhere near the arrow storm when it fell, for they knew the Welsh would take as great a delight in killing English horse as the enemy.

There were no more enemy bowmen left, Addaf saw, peering through the two ranks ahead of him – all scattered and cut down. Yet someone snugged in the ring of spears had a crossbow and was shooting it at that portion of the line where Addaf stood; he did not like the angry whip of the bolts.

Aim the Aimer ignored them as if they were spots of light rain, strolling down the front ranks, his own bow raised, judging wind and distance from the red and green ribbon fluttering from the end. The Gascon crossbowmen, sweating and sullen at being left to do the work on their own, belly-hooked their bows to the latch, firing in slow, uncontrolled flurries and the Welsh curled a lip at them.

'Nock.'

There was a rustle as the long arrows snugged into braided string.

'Draw.'

The great creak of tensioned wood was like the opening of a heavy door.

'Shoot.'

God ripped the sky as if it were cheap linen and the spear-ring began to shriek. The real killing had begun.

It was like a giant wasp byke someone had kicked, a mad, black, humming mass that fell on them. The cry went up when the arrows were loosed and Hal saw the man nearest him, a whey-faced boy, turn his face to the sky to try to find them.

'Get yer head down, Tam ye arse,' his neighbour hissed and the boy saw that everyone else was hunched up and staring at the ground, as if their eyes could dig holes in the mud and blood. Those with steel helmets hunched up as if to climb inside them, those with leather or none instinctively covering up with their arms; spears rattled and clacked like a forest of reeds in a high wind. Hal braced, feeling his flesh crawl, ruching up tight as if hardening against the impact.

The wasps buzzed and zipped. Tam thought it sounded like the gravel he had thrown against the wattle wall of Agnes's place when he had been trying to entice her out into the night. Instead, he remembered, her da had stormed out and told him to bugger off . . .

He straightened, turned to Erchie to thank him for the good advice − Christ, yin of those in the eye would have ruined

381

my good looks, he started to say. Then he saw the feathers perched incongruously in the side of Erchie's neck, like some wee bird. When he realised it was all that could be seen of the yard of metal-tipped wood that had gone in the top of Erchie's shoulder and was slanted down into his kneeling, still upright body, he gave a wail.

Hal saw the whey-faced boy weep and start to pat his neighbour as if he was an injured dog. He wanted to tell the boy that his friend wasn't injured, was certainly dead for no man could survive what that arrow had done to his insides. But he thought the boy probably already knew all that.

There was no time to tell him much, for the second sleet was lancing on them and Hal saw three shafts spit the turf at his feet. In front, a man reeled with the deep spanging bell of a hit on a steel plackard and the arrow splintered sideways in ruin. Yet the man fell like a mauled ox, gasping like a fish from lungs collapsed by the shock of the impact. Even without penetrating, Hal saw, fighting the rising panic in him, their arrows are killing us; he was not alone in the thought.

'They will shoot us to ruin,' Wallace bellowed. 'If we are here to allow it. Time we were away, lads. Step now, in time. Towards the woods. Now – step. Step. Step.'

Towards the woods. A short walk across a litter of dead horses, groaning men and the bloody dead. You could pick your way into the trees in five minutes, Hal thought, unless you were in an ungainly ring of men all trying to move in the same direction and keep some semblance of a shape. Thirty minutes if we are lucky, he thought mournfully – any longer and it will not matter much.

The wasps arrived again, a fierce, angry sting. Men shrieked and screamed and fell, clattering into their neighbour, to be pitched away with a curse. Slowly, like a huge dying slug, the *schiltron* lurched towards the trees, spitting out a slime-trail of bloody dead and wounded.

*　*　*

382

'One wants Wallace, my lords,' Edward rasped, listening to the thrum and rasp of his archers at work. Like music, he thought. The song of battle, as the monks' chant is the song of the church.

'One wants the Ogre,' he repeated and the Earl of Lincoln, spattered with mud and blood, grinned, saluted him with his sword and clapped down his fancy new pig-snout visor.

'The cruel Herod,' he bellowed, metallic and muffled, 'the madman more debauched than Nero. He will be brought to Your Grace's footstool.'

Hal knew the knights were circling like wolves on a stag, waiting for the moment of supreme weakness to pounce – it would not be long, he thought. He did not know how the other rings fared, but the one he was in was a nightmare of sweat and fear and bloody dying.

It stretched slowly, became egg-shaped and halted on one side for the ranks to re-form. It thinned – the space in the middle was larger, so that Hal could walk now, helping those shuffling backwards to negotiate the dead horses, the still groaning men, some of them pleading to be taken – all of them disgorged with no mercy.

They stumbled over things that cracked out marrow, skidded in fluids and slithered entrails, heard the last, farting gasp of the dead they stepped on and had breath themselves only for a muttered '*Ave Maria, Gracia plena . . .*'

Hal saw a sword, bent to pick it up and looked into the unseeing bloody remains of MacDuff of Fife, a great blue-black hole in the side of his head like a blown egg. He blinked once or twice, thoughts whirling in him – so MacDuff had not run after all and paid the price for it. Then Wallace knelt suddenly and, for a shocking moment, Hal thought he had been hit. The arrows were coming in flocks like startled starlings out of a covey, steady and fast from practised hands.

'Ach, Christ's Mercy on him,' Wallace said, rising up, and

Hal saw the bloodied face and battered, muddy ruin that had been a cousin – Simon, Hal remembered, the sweet-voiced singer.

'Keep moving,' bellowed a file commander. 'Not far now.'

Far enough, Hal thought. It had taken an eternity – but the trees were closer, tantalisingly within touching.

The singing brought sweat-sheened, crack-lipped faces up, red as skelpt arses, with tight white lines of fear round mouths and eyes.

> *Alma Redemptoris Mater, quae pervia caeli*
> *Porta manes, et stella maris, succurre cadenti,*
> *Surgere qui curat, populo: tu quae genuisti,*
> *Natura mirante, tuum sanctum Genitorem*

The song rolled out from triumphant throats away to their left, and everyone who heard it knew that the spear-ring there was shattered and gone – that both the other *schiltrons* were broken, with men shrieking and scattering, to be chased down and slaughtered like fleeing chicks.

> *Loving Mother of our Savior, hear thou thy people's cry*
> *Star of the deep and Portal of the sky,*
> *Mother of Him who thee from nothing made.*
> *Sinking we strive and call to thee for aid*

'The Auld Templar will be birling in his grave,' Wallace growled to Hal and then turned left and right into the grim faces around him, who had spotted the black-barred banner of the exultantly singing Templar knights.

'Why do they do this?' Hal asked, plaintive and bewildered. Wallace braided a half-sneer of grin into the sweat-spiked tangle of his beard.

'Because we are the only heathen they have left to fight, young Hal. They need us to dangle before God and the Pope, as proof that they have purpose.'

His teeth were feral as the grin widened and he hefted the long, clotted sword.

'Weel – much can break in the proving, as any smith will tell ye,' he added, then raised his chin and raised his voice to a bull bellow.

'Hold,' he roared. 'Never be minding the Bawsant flag and their wee chirrups. They are heavy horse, same as ye have been ruining all the day, my bonnie lads. Stay in the ring . . .'

The Templars came on, across the field where they had ruined the left *schiltron*, ignoring the mad, fleeing screamers of the other two, leaving them to the snarling, vengeful spears and swords of the plundering Welsh and Brabancons. They came after the final spear-ring, the one they knew must have Wallace in it; there were a handful only, but seemed a grim black cliff of *serjeants*, with two white streaks marking the true knights. Above it, like an accusing stare, streamed the black-barred Beau Seant banner.

The Order have ruined themselves, Hal thought, wild and sad. Ruined, as sure as if they had cursed God and spat on the Pope – what merchant, lord or priest, after this, will believe the word of a Templar, entrust his riches to the care of a brotherhood dedicated to saving Christians and who now prey on them?

They were a tight black fist aimed at the last mis-shapen ring of spearmen, the two white knuckles of Brian De Jay and John de Sawtrey blazing in the front. Like a long-haired star, the black-clad *serjeants* of the Order trailed other knights after them like embers, but these could not move with the arrogant fast trot of the Templars.

Poor knights, Hal thought bitterly, supposed to ride two to a horse – yet even the least of the Templars had *destrier* that were better than some ridden by the chivalry, who were stumbling over the dead and dying at no better than a walk.

The Templars trotted, the highly trained warhorses delicate as cats. It took five years to train the best warhorse, Hal recalled

385

wildly, almost hearing his father's voice in his head. From two, before it can even be ridden, until the age of seven when, if you have done it properly, you have a mount which will charge a stone wall if the rider does not flinch. With luck, the beast will survive to the age of twelve, when it will be too old for the business of war and you put it out to breed more of its kind.

No sensible horse will suffer this, so what you have is a mad beast on four legs – and if you add a rider who fears only displeasing God you have a combination fit to punch a hole through the Gates of Hell.

The mad beasts broke into a canter; someone whimpered and Hal saw that it was the whey-faced boy, his filthy face streaked with tears.

'Stay in the ring. Hold to the ring.'

Wallace's bellow went out on a rising note, growing more shrill as the ground trembled; the last file captains beat and chivvied their men, the last men-at-arms, the armoured *nobiles* who had opted to fight on foot, braced themselves and hunched into their *jazerant* and maille.

'Hold to the ring.'

Beyond, the black tide curled on them, their iron-rimmed kettle hats painted black round the rim, white on the crown and with a great red cross to the fore. Their reins were loosed entirely, leaving both hands free, and the crosses on their black shields were like streaks of blood.

'Hold to the ring.'

Deus lo vult.

The Templars throated it out on the last few thundering strides and came in like a ram, knee-to-knee and at a rising canter where, all day, no horseman beyond the first clatter of them had managed better than a fast walk.

There should have been a great shudder, a splintering of spears, a loud lion roar of desperate, defiant Scots – but the ring, too thinned by bolts and arrows, too worn by fear, shattered like an egg hit by a forge hammer.

The whey-faced boy was plucked from Hal's side and torn away with a vanished, despairing shriek as a lance skewered him; the rider swept past Hal like a black wind. On the other side, a great shaft went over Hal's head, slamming into men like a swinging gate – Hal fisted his battered shield into the rider's armoured foot, braced straight out and high on his mount's shoulders and the man reeled wildly, then was gone, tilting and crashing into the mass of men.

The Templars carved through the struggle of foot like claws through an apple, bursting out the far side, lances splintered or tossed aside, their great warhorses rutting up the blood-skeined turf in ploughed riggs as they fought to turn. The riders hauled out swords or little axes.

'Run,' yelled a voice, but Hal was already moving. A lumbering bear he seemed, his limbs moving as if he was underwater, fighting a current – yet he remembered hurdling a dead horse, remembered the whip and smear of thin branches, the collision with a tree that spun him half-round and lost him his shield.

Then he was on his knees spitting blood, the world a whirl of sky and trees and torn earth that smelled of autumn.

'Up,' said a voice, as mild as if lifting a bairn from a puddle. Hal leaned in the iron grasp, looked up into the blood and mud of Wallace's face and had back a grin.

'Aye til the fore,' the Guardian said, then glanced back over his shoulder, to where the milling riders were slaughtering the slow. 'Into the woods.'

No sensible knight risked a good warhorse by forcing it into a tangle of undergrowth and trees, where his vision, already no more than a narrow slit, was arrowed down to nothing by leaves and branches, so that it was impossible to resist the temptation to rip off the heavy constriction of helm. Vulnerable, slow, unable to use weight and power, a man in his right mind knows woods are not for heavy horse.

Hal knew, as soon as he heard the great crashing, that

387

sanity had run from this part of the world, with a frightened look over one shoulder at the madness of God which rode in to replace it.

Hal, following the stained gold surcoat with the red lion snarling defiantly, turned to see a white *camilis* billowed, ripping apart on the snatching talons of tree and bush as Brian De Jay, Master of the Templars and righteous with the power of the Lord in him, closed with a triumphant roar on the running fox of Wallace, that offence to God.

Hal did not think. He turned, stepped to one side as the warhorse plunged, De Jay reeling in the saddle, half pulled out by the snag of the treacherous white robes. The German Method, Hal heard himself say aloud, though the voice did not seem to be his at all − then he half crouched and spun, putting all the weight in a backhand cut, the sword grasped in both hands.

It broke the warhorse's hind leg with a crack like a snapping branch and the shriek of it falling was high and thin, piercing as any blade. Brian De Jay went out between the ears of it, smashing into the mulch and the briars, rolling over and over until he slammed into a tree with a sound like an acre of tin kettles falling off a cart.

Pulled off balance by his blow and the weariness of a hard day, Hal tipped sideways and fell his length, then started to scramble up. De Jay, struggling weakly, also started to rise, bellowing rage and pain out in bloody froth; then a shadow fell on him and he looked up.

'Ye were seeking a wee word with me?' Wallace asked mildly and De Jay tried a cut, so weak that Wallace only had to put his sword out for the Templar blade to ring a soft chime, then fall limply to the ground.

'Aye, weel,' Wallace said softly, 'here I am, my wee lord. May God forgive ye for what ye have done to Templar honour this day − argue your case when ye see Him.'

The hand-and-a-half, clotted to the hilt already, came round in a vicious two-handed swipe that took De Jay badly.

388

It was meant to be a neck kill, a single-stroke beheading that men would later marvel at, but rage and fear and the black howl of defeat made Wallace poor with it; the blade slammed into the Templar Master's expensive, new-fangled plate gorget and skittered upwards, taking the man in the jaw and carving through into the tree beyond, where it stuck.

With a pungent curse and a frown, Wallace put his foot up – he had taken off his boots, Hal noted dazedly – on De Jay's chest and began to work the blade out, his toes flexing in the vomited mess flooding from the Master of Templars' ruined face.

The forest crashed and a new rider, like the ghost of De Jay himself, came bounding out like a stag on the run. Hal, half-way to his feet, saw that Wallace was trapped, saw the Guardian let go of the wedged sword and whirl, fumbling for a dagger.

Brother John De Sawtrey, his white robes shredded and stained, his helmet and bascinet, maille coif and all flung away, whirled a little fluted mace in a circle and his purpled face under a thorn-crown of sweat-spiked tonsure was a vicious snarl.

He saw the fallen De Jay and howled at the outrage of it until his throat corded. His head was a storm of vengeance and he dug in his spurs; the warhorse's great rump bunched and it squealed – Hal levered himself to his feet, knowing he was between Wallace and this charging knight.

He tried to brace, but his legs trembled and his arms felt as if they had two anvils on the end; De Sawtrey rocked as the great warhorse shot forward – four strides and it would plough Hal into the forest floor.

One stride. Hal saw small twigs and acorns bounce up off the ground with the powered weight of each hoof.

Two strides. Something flicked at the corner of Hal's eye, but he could not turn his head from the sight of the warhorse's snarl of yellow teeth, the angry pink flare of nostrils and the great, slow-motion rise of massive feet.

Three strides – something went between Hal and the great loom of beast and rider, whirring like startled bird. John De Sawtrey flung up one hand as if arrogantly dismissing the world and then vanished over the back of his cantled saddle.

The warhorse, veering, slammed a shoulder into Hal and there was a moment of flying, a great tempest of leaves and earth that left him breathless and sprawled. Gasping and desperate, he struggled to rise, to find his sword – MacDuff's sword, he remembered wildly. He staggered and weaved, then a shape lurched into trembling view, the crossbow across one shoulder. Beyond, John De Sawtrey lay with the black leather fletches of a bolt perched like a crow in his eye.

'Aye til the fore,' said a familiar voice. Hal's head wobbled on his neck as he looked up into Sim's badger-beard grin and, beyond, other faces he knew, twisting and sliding like heat haze in the dappled, dying light of the forest – Ill Made Jock, Dirleton Will, Sore Davey, Mouse . . .

'Aye til the fore,' echoed Bangtail Hob from the filth of his face and stuck out a hand to haul Hal back to his feet. 'Time we were not here.'

The fires were piled high, as if to ward off all the bewildered ghosts who wandered that field and, in the dark, the moans and cries of those still alive crawled on everyone's skin.

Edward sat in his curule chair, sullen and droop-lidded, looking at the stained, bloody rag they had brought to lay at his feet. Red jupon with a white lion, someone had pointed out; you could see it if you squinted, Edward thought, but even this man's own mother would not know him now.

'The Wallace arms, I am told, your Grace,' De Warenne declared proudly, his Saracen beard a quivering silver curve as he smiled.

'The Ogre,' Edward declared sarcastically, 'seems to have shed the arms of Scotland which I was reliably informed he wore at the start of this affair – yellow-gold, my lord of Surrey, with a red lion rampant.'

De Warenne's eye flickered a little.

'Also,' Edward went on savagely, 'even allowing for the exaggerations of the fearful, this giant ogre Wallace seems to have diminished. I have a court caperer whose little bauble is taller than this.'

With a sudden, sullen twist, De Warenne signalled for the body to be removed and followed it, stiff with indignation. De Lacy leaned forward, his face bloody with torchlight.

'Possibly a cousin, your grace,' he said softly. 'I heard there were three such in the field here. The search goes on . . .'

'He is gone,' Edward muttered and gnawed a nail. Gone. Wallace was gone, into the damned forests where had had come from, where he fought best.

There was a slew of bloody grass studded with Scots dead like winnowed stooks – and only two English deaths of note, Sir Brian De Jay and John de Sawtrey. The Master of England's Templars and the Master of the Scottish Templars – there is a harsh justice in that, Edward thought, chilled by the presence of the Hand of God.

He did not bother with the tally of lesser lights, dead Welsh, Gascons and foot, for they were mainly men of little or no account – but the victory he'd had here was no more than possession of a blood-slimed field near Callendar.

Wallace was gone. Nothing had been resolved.

CHAPTER THIRTEEN

Herdmanston
Feast of St Merinus, September 1297

She stood between the merlons and looked out and down to where the riders sat, patient as stones, while a crow circled like a slow crucifix in the grey-blue. The rider in the centre looked up as it racked out its hoarseness and, even from this height, she saw the red-gold of his beard and hair. She knew who he was and glanced sideways at Bangtail Hob.

'Ye were right, Hob,' she said.

'No' me, Lady. Sir Hal sent me to warn ye this might occur – him and the rest of the men are running and hidin' with The Wallace.'

He was matter-of-fact about it, but Isabel knew that the running and hiding he spoke off hid a wealth of hurt, fear, blood and rough living. The fact that Bangtail Hob had managed to slither his way unseen to Herdmanston with the message was not the only miracle in it.

Below, the man with the red-gold head waved.

'I can shoot the een oot of his head from here,' muttered Wull The Yett, nocking an arrow to the hunting bow and getting a scathe of glance back from Bangtail Hob.

'Away. Ye could not hit a bull's arse at five paces when ye could see clear, Wull The Yett. Ye have not seen clearly the length of your own arm in years.'

'Go down and tell Sir John Comyn he can come up to the yett,' Isabel said. 'Then escort him into the hall.'

Wull shot them both a black scowl and slid the arrow from the string.

'Oh aye, no bother,' he declared bitterly, hirpling his way to the stairwind. 'Open the yett to our enemies — let the place scorch betimes, for it seems there is no respect left for a hauflin' like myself, the least of a clekkin' of bairns to a poor widow wummin . . .'

They ignored him, as folk always did, while his long, bitter murmur trailed behind him like damp grey smoke.

The Red Comyn heard the invite and dismounted, then handed his sword to the nearest of his men, smiling back into their warnings and anxiety. He went up the steep, cobbled incline, across the laid plank bridge and into the short arch with its opened, iron-grilled yett. There was the scent of woodsmoke and new-baked bread fighting with the headiness of broom in his nose.

Briefly, in the dim of the small hall, he was blind and took a few breaths to accustom himself before following the shuffling old servitor to where the lady sat in the high seat, as neatly arranged in Lenten grey and snowy barbette as any nun, while the glowing brazier of coals and freshly lit sconces bounced the light back off the too-brilliant gentian of her eyes.

But her hair and skin were damp from fresh grooming and her rings were loose enough on the fingers he kissed for him to know she had thinned, while the marks of sleeplessness told him much.

'Countess,' he said, with a formal bow.

'My lord.'

The voice was steady, even musical, but the strain was

393

evident in it and the Red Comyn was suddenly irritated by the whole business – he had more to do these days than play advocate in the life of his kinsman Earl of Buchan and his wayward wife.

'I am told your father is unwell.'

The solicitous inquiry stumbled him off the track of matters, but he recovered, swift as a russet fox.

'His humour is turned overly choleric,' he declared, which was a bland description of the paralysis which had twisted one side of the Lord of Badenoch's body and exchanged his power of speech for a constant drool from one side of his mouth. His own temper, folk said, that had given him the name Black John, had finally choked him – but his son knew better and his voice was thick and bitter when he said.

'Imprisonment in the Tower did that.'

'He is fortunate, then,' Isabel replied steadily, 'since most of those sent to the Tower never come out alive at all.'

She was baiting him, he knew, but he held himself in check and nodded to the man at her side.

'I do not know your man, there,' he said in sibilant French, 'but I know what he is, so I am certain you have been told of the events that bring me here.'

'His name is Hob,' she replied and felt Bangtail's head come up at the name, the only part he understood. She switched to English, deliberately to include him.

'MacDuff is dead, Hob tells me,' she said, the harsh crow-song of it raking her, for all that she had disliked the man.

'Bravely,' Red Comyn replied, also in English, 'together with others. Wallace is fled and resigned his Guardianship. New Guardians have been appointed by the community of the realm.'

What was left of a nobility not scrabbling to kneel at Edward's footstool, she thought. Yet the way he said it made her breath stop a moment.

'Yourself?'

He acknowledged it with a haughty little nod and, at last, she realised the duty that had brought him here. Not just for the Earl of Buchan's pride, then.

'The Earl of Carrick is the other,' he declared and she almost laughed aloud but he saw her widening eyes and her lip-biting and smeared a wry twist on to his face.

'Aye,' he admitted. 'The Bruce and myself. Unlikely beasts in the same shafts, I will allow – but the Kingdom demands it.'

'Indeed,' Isabel replied softly. 'To what does Herdmanston owe for the honour of your presence here?'

He grew more irritated still, at her presumptious sitting there as if she was lady of this pawky manor, as if she spoke for the absent lord of Herdmanston as a wife.

'Ye know well enough,' he replied shortly. 'I am to return you to the good graces of your husband, the earl.'

'Others attempted that,' she retorted bitterly. 'One in particular decided force was best. Is that in your instruction from my husband?'

'If necessary,' he replied bluntly and leaned his short, barrelled body towards her a little, so that Isabel felt Bangtail start to bristle like a hound.

'The lordship of Fife is invested in your wee brother, currently held by the English – so Fife has reverted to the Crown, lady,' he said coldly. 'In the absence of a king, it reverts to the Guardians – namely myself and the Earl of Carrick. Your presence with the Earl of Buchan is now desirable less for reasons of his passion than reasons of Comyn honour, dignity and estate. I am here, as a Guardian of Scotland, to impress upon you the need for it. You should know also that my lord earl wants the bladder that is Hal of Herdmanston dipped in dark water.'

She looked at him, this stocky, fiery wee man; his boots had high heels and that little vanity robbed him of some of his menace. God's Wounds, he had enough of it just by looking like a smaller version of Buchan.

It was undignified, she thought, sitting here within sight of this small, blurred image of her husband, so like him in colour and temper and discussing her intimacies. She had known her husband's rage was enough for him to injure her but lately had hoped that it was enough for him just to detach from her.

Now, eyes blank and fogged, she saw the stupidity of that. He had been cuckolded, made a fool over the business of ransom – when he need not have ransomed her at all – and now needed to stamp the imprint of the Buchan lordship firmly on the lands of Fife. With a wife who was the last noble MacDuff in Fife and the backing of his kinsman, an appointed Guardian, he would be able to gain control.

Shame and anger flushed her, sank into her belly and twisted all the weary organs. Like beads on a rosary, all the slights she had given her husband, small and large, winked in her memory. Worse, with a chill that flushed goosing on her skin, she thought of the grim little Comyn of Badenoch's words regarding force. If necessary.

There was no way out of it. It was no longer a wayward wife Buchan wanted, but the key to unlock the rents of a powerful earldom and he would not let Isabel or Hal alone. If she remained, Herdmanston would feel the wrath of Buchan and she knew, as she knew her own palms, that Bruce would not prevent it – even if he felt like it – for he would be persuaded that Hal of Herdmanston was not cause enough to break the uneasy pact with the Comyn.

'A bladder may be dipped,' she said flatly, 'but not drowned. I will have your word on that.'

The Red Comyn shrugged; he did not care one way or the other and said so.

'Betimes,' he added with a wry twist, 'I would not put yer faith in the wee lord of Herdmanston. I hear he's eating grass and living like a slinking dog in the wild. The Plantagenet has punished him for his rebellion and appointed these lands to one of his deserving others – a certain Malenfaunt, who was lately your . . . host. He has a way with the vicious that you cannot help but admire, has Longshanks – have you heard how they are calling him Hammer of the Scots now?'

'Malenfaunt's is a parchment gift,' she replied stonily and he acknowledged that much; Longshanks had parcelled out a deal of lands belonging to rebellious Scots, but with no way to enforce their titles, the new owners were left clutching a roll with seals and were no better off than before.

He saw the thin hemline of her lips and allowed his temper a slip of the leash.

'Regardless of the fate of this fortalice, lady, my task is to impress on you the necessity of the inevitable – Christ's Wounds, woman, ye sit in this mean hall as if you were married on to its owner. Have ye no shame?'

She had not.

'I will have your word on matters. You are Guardian. You can persuade my husband not to exercise the full of his anger on Sir Hal of Herdmanston and, if the Bruce agrees nothing else with you, he can be persuaded to add his weight to this. Have I your word on it?'

He was struck, then, by what it revealed of her feelings. It does not matter, he thought to himself, if Buchan has her body back, for someone else has her heart. Usually, that would not matter to a powerful lord only interested in lands but Badenoch knew that it mattered to the Earl of Buchan. There would be more trouble over it, he knew – but he was sick of the business and had more important matters than arguing with a well-bred hoor. It was a deal of persuasion – but he was flattered that she thought him able to fulfil it, so he spoke the formal words she wanted and saw her jaw knot.

'Have you a spare mount?' she managed, the words ash in her mouth.

'Ach, no – coontess . . .'

Bangtail was silenced by the bright-eyed stricken look she

turned on him. The Red Comyn, wise enough to stay silent, merely inclined his head.

'I shall make arrangements,' she said and he nodded silently again, turned and clacked his high-heeled way back to the yett.

'Mistress,' Bangtail began desperately, but stopped again, for the upright lady had slumped and buried her dissolving face in the sieve of her loose-ringed fingers.

Roslin
Feast of St Andrew Protoclet, November 1298

They watched the long-haired star throwing off beams to the east and, for a long time, no-one spoke. Then Bruce hunched himself into his fur collar, his breath a white stream.

'The Blessed St Andrew sends a sign,' he declared portentously. Kirkpatrick nodded and agreed with a smile, though he had to bite his tongue to stop himself, viperishly, from suggesting that it was probably more of a sign from St Malachy.

'Let us hope this means that Hal of Herdmanston's news is good,' Bruce added and Kirkpatrick shivered.

'My teeth are chittering,' he said in a passable imitation of the the Lord of Herdmanston, who rode far enough behind them to be out of earshot. Bruce grinned whitely at him; they moved on up the road to Roslin's shadowed bulk, the Carrick entourage falling in behind with a clatter of hooves and metal.

The great black storm of Longshanks had finally blown itself out. Roger Bigod, the Earl Marshal, had taken his forces home, as had Hereford, and, though they were entitled to do it, having served their tenure for king and realm, Edward was brooding foul over it.

Forced to turn south himself, he came howling through Ayrshire, sacking towns and villages — save for Ayr, which Bruce burned for him, in order to prevent any aid from it.

Spiteful as an old cat, Longshanks, with the staggering remains of an army already eating its own horses, took the Carrick holding at Lochmaben. Then, with a graceless final swipe of his claws, Longshanks spoiled Jedburgh and reeled off back into England, already summoning troops for a new campaign in the summer.

It had all, Bruce thought, been ruinously expensive – for both sides. Thousands of Scots had died at Falkirk, among them some of the best of the Kingdom's community – Murray of Bothwell, Graham of Abercorne, the MacDuff of Fife. It was no way to fight the power of the English and had been a bad slip by Wallace to try to do so. Moray would not have been so foolish.

Yet matters had not turned out badly, he added to himself. His father's influence exempted Annandale from punishment by Edward, so only the Carrick lands suffered. Wallace was discredited and, though he had to walk in a trace with the hated Red John, Bruce was a Guardian, a step nearer the seat he craved and, at last, a power in the land.

Enough of one to pluck Hal from the outlaw wilderness and back under the Bruce wing and Herdmanston remained in his hands simply because Edward's new appointment to it, Sir Robert Malenfaunt, did not have the force to impose the royal writ against a Guardian of Scotland.

Or the balls, Bruce thought. He glanced towards the hunched shadow that was the Lothian lord. I need this wee Herdmanston man and everyone knows my interest in him, so that even Buchan balks. You would think, he added bitterly, he would at least smile over it.

Hal's world was all bad as spoiled mutton as far as he was concerned, so that he said nothing at all on the long ride to Roslin. Once in the hall, he squatted like a brooding spider, while Henry Sientcler chattered and his children played and his wife, Elizabeth, drifted gracefully, moving like a swan to prepare for the visit of the Earl of Carrick.

All of it, Sim knew, only added to the loss of her and he felt alarm, more than he had done in the days after his lord had lost wife and bairn. Then he had offered Hal what he had always offered – a stolid friendship, a loyalty he could trust and an expertise with horse and weapons that allowed them in and out of trouble. In return, Sim got the only home he had ever known and the only man he felt he could call a friend, despite the difference in their station.

It nagged now that none of it was of any use – Isabel had gone like a morning mist and they had only found out after months of slipping and slithering round the forests and hills, avoiding the English – and Scots in their pay – who hunted Wallace.

The arrival of Bruce's messenger to pluck them from Wallace's last remnants came as a blessed relief, tinged with shame at feelin it.

Wallace himself, disgraced, discredited and with the old brigand settling back on him like a familiar cloak, simply shrugged and wished them God speed. Not long after, they had all the news of what had happened, at Herdmanston as well as elsewhere.

'An ill-favoured chiel came for her,' Bangtail told them. 'The wee Guardian, the Red Comyn himself. Her uncle was slain at Falkirk and it made the difference.'

Hal had known it, of course, in the aftermath of the battle, in the sweating, fevered nights when he had woken from the spill of dead, white faces, the screams and the steel. MacDuff was dead and he had been the Buchan link to a say in the control of the Fife estates.

'She told me to say it was no use,' Bangtail went on, his face twisted with grief. 'She said her husband would not let matters stand still now and that Herdmanston was in danger.'

Hal acknowledged Bangtail's words and the man went off, droop-shouldered at the loss and angry at his own impotence in the matter. Hal stood there, numbed by it; Isabel was gone back to Buchan.

Ironically, he knew that, even as she returned to her gilded prison, she was safer than before and had leverage of her own – he had no doubt that part of the price for her compliance would be that neither he nor Herdmanston would suffer.

But the price was high and, even when he returned to Herdmanston to prove to all there that it was his yet, he felt the bitter cost of it every time he looked at the lonely tower chamber, the dress folded neatly, the bed – and the pardoner's medallion she had left on the pillows.

Bruce, of course, offered sympathic noises and was struck by the darkness in Hal. Who would have thought Isabel could engender that? He had seen her, too, when Red Comyn and the Buchan had come to the Parliament at Scone to oust Wallace and redesign the power in the Kingdom.

The florid Earl had brought the Countess with him, flaunting her like some stag with a returned hind. Bruce had noted the hawk-proud bearing of her and the despair behind her eyes and felt a stab of anger – there was no doubt Buchan had burned his mark anew on his wayward wife. Yet there was defiance there, too – and loss. Who would have thought the likes of Hal could bring out that in her?

Because of what they had once been, he could see the clench of her and felt a wash of sympathy at her plight – yet the love in it was a mystery he dismissed with a head shake. Almost as much a mystery as the one which had married him and the Red Comyn to Scotland's fate. The only reason the wee popinjay had been so elevated was because he held a claim to the Kingdom's throne and the Comyn wanted to wave him as a taunt to Bruce.

Still – he was glad Hal had not been there to see Isabel with Buchan, for blood would have been spilled

'A strange marriage that,' Henry Sientcler offered as they

ate, and Bruce, still thinking of Red John, acknowledged it with a wave of one hand.

'Wishart says God may still make it work,' he said with a wry smile. 'I had word from him in his Roxburgh prison.'

Sir Henry shifted and made a moue.

'He has more ken of the mind of woman than I gave him credit for then,' he replied and, for a moment Bruce's food hung, half chewed in his open mouth.

Kirkpatrick chuckled.

'I believe the lord of Roslin was referring to the marriage of the Buchans,' he answered, 'rather than yer hand-fasting to the Red Comyn as joint Guardians.'

'Ye are unlikely to plough a straight furrow with that wee man at your shoulder,' Hal suddenly declared. 'A more mismatched brace of oxen it wid be hard to find.'

'Indeed,' Bruce offered with a fixed smile, neither liking the comparison with an ox or the flat-out brooding moroseness of the man.

'Are you enjoying the fare, my lord earl?' asked Elizabeth, anxious to sweeten the air. Bruce nodded graciously, though the truth of it was that he thought the Lady of Roslin too pious for comfort – especially his. Broiled fish and lentils with oat bannocks might be perfect Biblical food for the occasion, reminding everyone that St Andrew was the patron saint of poor fishermen, but it was marginally better than a fast and no more.

He managed to keep the smile on his face, all the same, while he watched Sir Henry and his wife exchange loving glances. Well, Kirkpatrick thought as he witnessed this, you arranged for this loving reunion and I daresay you thought to get effusive thanks and pledges for it – at the very least a decent meal. More fool you, my lord earl . . . there are too many folk who still regard you with suspicion.

'Where is Wallace?'

Hal's voice was a knife through the soft chatter.

'Gone,' Bruce replied shortly.

Hal lifted his head.

'Gone where?'

'France, I hear,' Kirkpatrick said and Bruce nodded, chewing.

'Fled,' he managed between forced swallows of clotted bannock, and Hal frowned. Fled did not sound like Wallace and he said as much, though he was surprised by the thoughtful nod he had back from Bruce. He had been expecting the sullen lip and the scowl.

'Indeed. The Red Comyn is ranting about him not asking permission of the Guardians – namely himself, of course – to quit the realm after he resigned the Guardianship. I suspect this is because he has designs on Wallace holdings.'

'Resigned,' Sir Henry said with a twist to his voice which was not missed. When he caught Bruce's eye, he flushed a little.

'Hardly freely done, my lord earl,' he added.

'They forced him out,' Hal said, blunt with the black-dog misery of what he had heard of it. 'The bold *nobiles* in conclave at Scone. Not content with runnin' like hares at Falkirk, they then turn on Wallace, as if it was all his doing. Betrayed because he was not the true cut of them. Now ye tell me they squabble over his wee rickle of lands.'

'I trust,' Kirkpatrick said sharply, 'ye are not casting anything at my lord earl. Your liege lord.'

'Now, here, enough,' Sir Henry bleated and his wife stepped into the breach of it, bright and light as sunshine.

'Frumenty?' she asked and, without waiting, clapped her hands to send a servant scurrying. Bruce grinned, half-ashamed, across at Hal.

'Scotland betrayed itself,' Bruce answered flatly. 'Ye all ran at Falkirk, even Wallace in the end. That's the fact and the shame – and the saving grace of it, for if you had stayed and fought, you would be dead. In my own defence, I had business enough in Ayrshire to keep me occupied – but I would have galloped from that field, same as everyone else.'

Hal felt the sick rise of it in his gorge, knowing he was right and having to admit it with a curt nod. They had all run and, because of it, proud Edward had his slaughter, but no real victory. The Kingdom had its back to the wall more than ever before, but though the struggle was more grim, the realm was no more subjugated than before.

Now the resistance was what it had always been – strike from the forest and hills, then run like foxes for cover. Bruce had occupied the English in Ayrshire with the tactic and showed a surprising aptitude for the business. He had learned well from Wallace, it seemed to Hal, and, by the time had finished, a desert seemed like a basket of cooked chicken compared with the desolation he made.

This was a new ruthlessness, which allowed Bruce even to destroy his own holdings if it hindered the enemy – he had burned Turnberry Castle to ruin and Hal well knew he had loved the place, since he had been born there and it had been his mother's favourite. There was new resolve and a growing skill in the man, Hal saw, and his next words confirmed it.

'Wallace fled to France,' Bruce added, frowning at the bowl in front of him, 'because he could not be sure that he would not be betrayed by his own. There will be no peace for Wallace. Edward will have his head on a gate-spike.'

Hal regarded the Earl of Carrick with a new interest, seeing the sullen face of two years ago resolved into something more stern and considered. There was steel here – though whether it would bend and not break alongside the Red Comyn was another matter.

Bruce stirred and looked up at Sir Henry, then pointedly at Hal, who nodded and levered himself wearily up from the table.

'It is time.'

Sir Henry stood up and a flutter of servants brought torches.

They left Elizabeth and the servants behind, moving into the shifting shadows and the cold dark of the undercroft, descending until the stairwind spilled them out into the great vaulted barrel that was Roslin's cellars. Their breath smoked; barrels and flitches gleamed icily.

'This has been finished a little, since I was last home,' Henry Sientcler mused, holding up the smoking torch.

'As well your Keep is now stone,' Hal said. 'I would do the rest, and swift, my lord of Roslin, now that your ransom money is freed up – if Edward comes back, Roslin's wooden walls will not stand and that Templar protection we Sientclers once enjoyed is no longer as sure as before.'

Henry nodded mournfully while Bruce, his shadow looming long and eldritch, waved a hand as if dismissing an irrelevant fly.

'Castles in stone are all very fine – but only one stone matters now,' he said, then turned to Hal. 'Well, Sir – ye claim to have the saving of us. Do you ken where Jacob's Pillow lies?'

Hal fished out the medallion and handed it to the frowning earl, who turned it over and over in his gloved hand.

'A medal of protection,' he sniffed. 'Sold by pardoners everywhere. Like the one we took from yon Lamprecht fellow.'

Hal watched while Kirkpatrick and Sim, suitably primed, moved down the length of the vaulted hall, shifting bundles and barrels, peering at the floor and tallying on sticks. Bruce and Sir Henry watched, bemused.

'It is the very one,' Hal said, watching the two torches bobbing across the flagged floor. 'It was the pardoner explained the significance of the marks.'

Bruce turned it over and over, then passed it to Sir Henry, who peered myopically at it.

'A fish?' he hazarded and Hal fumbled out the ring corded round his neck.

'The same one is on this,' he declared, 'which the Auld Templar bequeathed me on his deathbed. An auld sin he called it.'

Bruce looked steadily at Hal and he was struck, again, by the absence of the sullen pout, replaced by a firm, tight-lipped resolve and an admitting nod. Sim appeared and shook his head; Hal felt his stomach turn.

'Reverse it,' he said and Sim nodded. The torches started to bob again, the tallying began anew.

'A mason's ring,' Hal went on. 'Belonging to Gozelo, who worked here before he became involved in your . . . scheming, my lord. And died for it.'

'Yes, yes,' Bruce muttered as he frowned, muttering half to himself. 'If he had not run . . . a sad necesssity for the safety of the Kingdom. The ring went to the Auld Templar and then to you. It is the Christian fish symbol from ancient times – what has this to do with locating the Stone?'

Henry, who had only recently been told of all this, blinked a bit and shook his head with the sheer, bewildering stun of it all. Plots were nothing new in this Kingdom, nor the killing that invariably went with them, but, even so, the careless way the Earl of Carrick dismissed a murder was disturbing.

The torches bobbed to a sudden stop and Sim and Kirkpatrick both cried out.

Hal moved swiftly, the others following, drawing into a breathless ring round a single broad flagstone, the faint chis-elled mark gleaming in the torchlight.

'A fish,' Hal said pointedly and Bruce agreed, then pointed to his left.

'There is another. And one over there. Every flagstone is marked – there are scores of them.'

'Just so,' Hal said. 'Gozelo's mark, which all masons leave behind – if it seems he was excessive fond of making it here, he had reason, my lords.'

Sim and Kirkpatrick, their breath mingling as they strug-gled, shoved pry bars into the grooves of the flagstone as Hal spoke.

'Not an original mason's mark,' Hal said, speaking in rapid

French, spitting the words out as if they burned him. 'Gozelo was not that imaginative and thought to find a good Christian symbol of this land, to suit the tastes of his customers. He took the fish mark from the same place the makers of wee holy medals took it and for the same reason – to impress and because it is simple to make.'

He held up the medallion.

'Taken from the Chalice Well in Glastonbury,' he said as they peered at it. 'See – the circumference of one circle goes through the centre of the other, identical circle. The bit in the middle is called the *vesica piscis*, which is the name of the mark.'

'Bladder of the fish,' Bruce translated thoughtfully. 'Of course – I had forgotten the Chalice Well had it.'

There was a grating sound and the flagstone shifted, the two men sweating and panting to slide it with a long grinding slither, leaving a dark hole. The dank of it seemed to leach chill into Hal's breath of relief.

'The Holy fish symbol of Christians from the times of the Romans,' Hal explained. 'Lamprecht knows his business and told me the Holy nature of it – and it became clear why masons fancy the symbol. I am no tallyer, nor was he – but he knows his relic business well enough and the holy fish measures a ratio of width to height which is the square root of three – 265:153. The number 153 is the amount of fish Our Lord caused to be caught in a miracle, so there is the work of Heaven in it.'

'Gospel of St John,' Kirkpatrick breathed, astounding everyone with that knowledge, so that he blinked and bridled under the stares.

'Two hundred and sixty-five fish-marked stones one way, a hundred and fifty-three the other and you have this,' Hal said and held the torch over the hole, allowing the light to fall, golden as honey on the ancient sandstone snugged inside.

'The Auld Templar's secret place,' Hal said, then glanced

at Henry's open-mouthed stare. 'I hazard there are deeds and titles and Roslin secrets you will want from there, Henry – but first you will have to lift a heavy cover.'

'The Stone,' Bruce declared and gave a sharp bark of delight.

'Not easily moved by two men – but done all the same,' Kirkpatrick added and there was a pause as they saw how the Auld Templar and Roslin's Steward, John Fenton, had struggled the Stone into the undercroft and hidden it.

'Yon Gozelo was a clever man,' Sim offered and glanced into the scowl of Kirkpatrick. 'Just not very fast on his feet when it came to the bit.'

'Aye, well,' Bruce said and straightened. 'Once you have taken what you need, Sir Henry, cover it up anew.'

He glanced round at the faces, all blood-dyed in the light, their breath like honeyed smoke.

'Here we all are, then, party to the future of the Kingdom,' he said. 'In the absence of Bishop Wishart, I call upon us all to kneel and pray for the strength to hold to our resolve, to keep this secret until the time is right.'

This piety took even Kirkpatrick by surprise, but he dutifully sank to his knees. Bruce and Hal were the last to descend to the chill stones and looked at each other for a moment over the heads of the penitents. When the time is right, Hal echoed silently. The time for Bruce to make his move.

'Welcome to your Kingdom,' Hal said to him, savage and morose. 'A bloodier place these days, my lord earl.'

The sun of Bruce's smile was a bright uncaring knife that cut through Hal's bitter grief and the Kingdom's turmoil of pain.

'*Hectora quis nosset, si felix Troia fuisset?*' he answered, leonine with new dreams, and then added, in perfect English:

'Who would know Hector if Troy had been happy?'

AUTHOR'S NOTE

In light of the collective nouns used in this book, I should add another which is particularly apt – a roguery of historians.

Unlike the earlier Dark Ages, there is no paucity of sources for the Scottish Wars of Independence, or the lives of Wallace and Bruce – what there is instead is a contradiction of times, dates, places and people, sometimes accidental, more often deliberate, from those being paid to enhance the reputation of their subjects.

That, coupled with the general attempts to revise history in favour of the various protagonists, has polished the personae of Edward I, Wallace and Bruce almost beyond recognition, while creating the impression that the war which culminated in the battle of Bannockburn was one of the freedom-loving Scots against the tyranny of England.

Ask any Scot in a pub and they will tell you chapter and verse on Bruce and on Wallace – they may even pour scorn on Mel Gibson and *Braveheart*, while admitting that they thoroughly enjoyed the movie, even the pseudo-kilts, face-painting (now almost *de rigueur* at any Scottish event) and waggling of bare arses at opponents.

The truth is harsher and more misted. *Braveheart* is a

dubious interpretation of already dubious history, while relative sizes and composition and exact location of the armies at Stirling Brig and Falkirk is supposition and best-guess, depending on whom you read.

There is no doubt that the major protagonists were genuine heroic figures to a large body of opinion, in their own lifetimes and since. Equally, they were regarded as the blackest of terrorists to much of the rest of the population of both Scotland and England.

The legend had made Bruce into the hero king, liberator of Scotland, and any grey areas of his life have been airbrushed. Wallace, of course, is painted in easy black and white, as the giant with an anachronistic two-handed claymore, fighting to the very end and never giving in.

The truth – or what can be seen of it now – is different, but open to interpretation. This period was Scotland's civil war more than anything, with the powerful Comyn, Buchans and Balliols against the determined Bruces for the possession of the Kingdom of Scots. Edward, the opportunist, tried to muscle in and soon realised his expensive mistake, for both sides used him unashamedly to further their own ends.

Nor is he the out-and-out villain, the 'proud Edward sent hame to think again' about trying his tyranny on the Scots; to the English he was one of the best kings they ever had and they feared – rightly – his passing, knowing the son was not the father.

I have tried to give Bruce and Wallace and Edward I back their original lives, after a fashion, to show them against the backdrop of the times while also unveiling some of the people, great and small, fictional and historical, who struggled to live in that emerging Scotland.

There are those I have maligned, or used for my own ends. Isabel MacDuff, Countess of Buchan, for one. All that is known, for certain, is that she existed, was married to the Earl of Buchan and, at one crucial moment in history, deserted marriage and party to side with her husband's enemies, by becoming the hereditary MacDuff, Crowner of Scottish kings, and helping to legitimise Bruce.

She suffered for it, being subsequently captured and imprisoned in a cage on the walls of Berwick. Her later life is debatable, the best theory being that she was huckled off to a nunnery, her husband, the earl, having died.

The rest is my intepretation and invention – even her age is a confusion of accounts; her marital status is based on the evidence of her turning her back on her husband in favour of the Bruce faction. That and her lack of children told me much about her personal relationship with Buchan. Her supposed love affair with Bruce is mentioned as a rumour in some sources, probably scurriously anti-Bruce propaganda; her love affair with Hal of Herdmanston is pure invention.

Kirkpatrick is another invention and, though I have based him on the real Sir Roger Kirkpatrick of Closeburn, I have deliberately made him a fictional figure, since the real one crops up, irritatingly, on the English side far too often to be the firm Bruce henchman I needed for the story. Until, that is, he appeared on the scene to complete the murder of the Red Comyn in Greyfriars Church. That killing persuaded me of his darkly murderous character, though he is invention, as is his counterpart, the vicious Malise Bellejambe. Another villain, Malenfaunt, is a legitimate family name, but the saturnine and dubious Sir Robert does not exist.

Hal of Herdmanston, of course, is also fiction – though the Sientclers (or St Clairs, St Clares, Sinclairs or any other variant spelling you care to dream up) are not. They and Roslin became renowned, not least for Rosslyn Chapel – but Herdmanston, though it existed, is now no more than a rickle of unmarked stones in a field in Lothian. The other Sientclers are real enough, save for the Auld Templar, who rode into my head at the start of this tale and was just too magnificent to wave on.

411

Why the Sientclers at all? Because I needed a powerful Lothian family who could be opposed to the dominant force in the area, Patrick of Dunbar, who, with his son, was a committed supporter of the English right up until the aftermath of Bannockburn. Why Lothian? Because that was the battle-ground of the Wars of Independence, more so than any other part of Scotland.

There are other lights, lesser or greater, who may or may not be fictional – I hope I have written this well enough to leave the reader guessing most of the time.

Lastly – Edward I was never known as Hammer of the Scots in his lifetime. That name was given to him in the sixteenth century when it was carved on the unsubtle square slab of his tomb. Yet I prefer to believe that it did not spring, full-formed at the time, but came from all the whispers that had gone before.

The start of this is purportedly written by an unknown monk in February of 1329, three months before Robert the Bruce is finally acknowledged as king of Scots by the Pope – and four months before his death.

Think of this as stumbling across a cache of such hidden monkish scribblings which, when read by a flickering tallow candle, reveal fragments of lives lost both in time and legend.

If any interpretations or omissions jar – blow out the light and accept my apologies.

LIST OF CHARACTERS

ADDAF the Welshman
Typical soldier of the period, raised from the lands only recently conquered by Edward I. The Welsh prowess with the bow and spear was already noted, but the true power of the former, the Crecy and Agincourt massed ranks, was a strategy still forming during the early Scottish Wars. Like all of the Welsh, Addaf's loyalty to the English is tenuous.

BADENOCH, Lord of
Any one of two, father and son. Both called Sir John and both members of a powerful branch of the Comyn, they were favoured because, after John Balliol, they had a legitimate right to claim Scotland's throne as good if not better than the Bruce one. The Badenochs were known as Red Comyn, because they adopted the same wheatsheaf heraldy as the Buchan Comyns, but on a red shield instead of blue. Sir John, second Lord of Badenoch, was also referred to as the Black Comyn because of his grim demeanour – a former Guardian of Scotland, he died in 1302, leaving the title to his son who was known as the Red Comyn. Despite being married to Joan de Valence, sister to Aymer De Valence, Earl of Pembroke, John the Red Comyn was a driving force in early resistance

to Edward I – and truer to the Scots cause than Bruce at the time. He was murdered by Bruce and his men in Greyfriars Church, Dumfries in February 1306.

BALLIOL, King John

A member of one of the more powerful families of Scotland and backed by an equally powerful one, the Comyn, John Balliol was elected to the vacant throne of Scotland by a conclave of Scotland's nobility and prelates, a conclave chaired by King Edward I of England. By the time the Scots discovered they had been duped by Edward, it was too late and subsequent attempts to exert their independence resulted in invasion, defeat and the stripping of the regalia of the kingdom – the Stone of Scone, the Black Rood and the Seal – and also the public humiliation of King John Balliol. His royal coat of arms was torn from his tunic, leaving him with the name that still resonates down through history – Toom Tabard, or Empty Coat. The Balliol and Comyn were arch-rivals of the Bruces.

BANGTAIL HOB

Fictional character. One of Hal of Herdmanston's retainers, a typical Scots retinue fighter of the period. Mounted on garrons – small, shaggy ponies – they are armed with Jeddart staffs, a combination spear, pike and hook, and are not cavalry, but mounted infantry. The English counterparts are called 'hobilars' because they are mounted on small ponies known as 'hobbies' (hence the term hobby-horse). Bangtail and the likes of Tod's Wattie, Ill Made Jock, Will Elliott and others are the common men of Lothian and the Border regions – the March – who formed the bulk and backbone of the armies on both sides.

BEK, Anthony, Bishop of Durham

Commander of one of the four knightly 'hosts' at Falkirk, he led some 400-plus heavy horse.

414

BELLEJAMBE, Malise
Fictional character, the Earl of Buchan's sinister henchman and arch-rival of Kirkpatrick.

BISSET, Bartholomew
Fictional character. Notary clerk to Ormsby, Edward's appointed justiciar of Scotland. His information leads Hal and others on the trail of the mysterious murderers of a master mason found near Douglas.

BRUCE, Robert
Any one of three. Robert, Earl of Carrick, later became King Robert I and is now known as Robert the Bruce. His father, also Robert, was Earl of Annandale (he renounced the titles of Carrick to his son when they fell to him because, under a technicality, he would have had to have sworn fealty to the Comyn for them and would not do that). Finally, there is Bruce's grandfather, Robert, known as The Competitor from the way he assiduously pursued the Bruce rights to the throne of Scotland, passing the torch on to his grandson.

BUCHAN, Countess of
Isabel MacDuff, one of the powerful, though fragmented, ruling house of Fife. She acted as the official 'crowner' of Robert Bruce in 1306, a role always undertaken by a MacDuff of Fife — but the only other one was her younger brother, held captive in England. In performing this, she not only defied her husband but the entire Comyn and Balliol families. Captured later, she was imprisoned, with the agreement of her husband, in a cage hung on the walls of Berwick Castle.

BUCHAN, Earl of
A powerful Comyn magnate, (the Red Comyn Lord of Badenoch was his cousin) he was the bitterest opponent of the Bruces. Robert Bruce finally overcame the Comyn,

following the death of Edward I and a slackening of English pressure, in a campaign that viciously scorched the lands of Buchan and Badenoch in a virtual Scottish ethnic cleansing of Bruce's rivals. Defeated and demoralised, the earl fled south and died in 1308.

CLIFFORD, Sir Robert

One of Edward I's trusted commanders, he and Sir Henry Percy were given the task of subduing the initial Scottish revolt and negotiated Bruce and other rebel Scots nobles back into the 'king's peace' in 1297, but could not overcome Wallace. Clifford also brought a retinue to fight at Falkirk which included knights from Cumbria and Scotland – one of the latter being a certain Sir Roger Kirkpatrick of Auchen Castle, Annandale, and the 'real' Kirkpatrick who murdered the Red Comyn.

CRAW, Sim

A semi-fictional character – Sim of Leadhouse is mentioned only once in history, as the inventor of the cunning scaling ladders with which James Douglas took Roxburgh by stealth in 1314. Here, he is Hal of Herdmanston's right-hand man, older than Hal, powerfully built and favouring a big latchbow, a crossbow usually spanned (cocked) using a hook attached to a belt. He is strong enough to do it without the hook.

CRESSINGHAM, Sir Hugh

Appointed by Edward I as Lord Treasurer of Scotland, he was disliked by his English colleagues as an upstart and universally detested by the Scots, whom he taxed. His attempts to curtail the expense of the campaign of 1297 fatally compromised the English army at Stirling Bridge, where Cressingham himself was killed leading the Van. Famously, legend has it that he was flayed and strips of his skin were sent all over Scotland, one being made into a baldric for Wallace.

DE FAUCIGNY, Manon

Fictional character, a stone-carver from Savoy brought into a conspiracy from which he has subsequently fled. Now all factions are hunting him out for what they believe he knows.

DE JAY, Sir Brian

Master of the English Templars, he brought a force to Falkirk in the service of Edward I, thus pitting the Templar knights against fellow-Christians, to general odium. With Brother John de Sawtrey, commander of the Scottish Templars, he pursued Wallace into a thicket, where both Templar commanders were killed – the only 'notable deaths' in the entire affair according to the chroniclers.

DE WARENNE, Sir John, Earl of Surrey

Long-time friend and supporter of King Edward, De Warenne was already in his sixties when Edward appointed him 'warden of the land of Scots' and had served in the Welsh campaigns of 1277, 1282 and 1283. He hated Scotland, complaining that the climate did not suit him, and attempted to run the place from his estates in England. Finally forced to do something about the rebels, he brought an army to Stirling Bridge and was famously defeated. Fought again at Falkirk, commanding one of the four 'hosts' of heavy horse. He died, peacefully, in 1304.

DOG BOY

Fictional character, the lowest of the low, a houndsman in Douglas and of ages with the young James Douglas. Given to Hal as a gift by Eleanor Douglas to spite her stepson, the Dog Boy finds that service at a Herdmanston at war brings him to rub shoulders with the great and the good and invests him with a new stature he would not otherwise have enjoyed.

DOUGLAS, James

Son of The Hardy by his first wife, a Stewart, whom he simply sent off to a convent in order to marry his second, Eleanor de Lovaigne. After the death of 'Le Hardi', Eleanor and her two sons, James's stepbrothers, were packed off south to a convent and the Douglas lands given to Clifford. James went to Paris under the auspices of Lamberton, Bishop of St Andrews. He returned as a young man just as Bruce became king and joined him, rising to become one of Robert the Bruce's most trusted commanders.

DOUGLAS, Sir William

Lord of Douglas Castle in south-west Scotland, father of young James Douglas, later to be known both as The Black Douglas (if you were his enemy and demonising him with foul deeds) and The Good Sir James (if you were a Scot lauding the Kingdom's darling hero). It is clear nicknames ran in the family – William was known as The Hardy (which simply means Bold) and was a typical warlord noble of Scotland. Sent to defend Berwick against Edward I in the campaign that brought John Balliol to his knees, William Douglas was finally forced to surrender and watch as Edward ravaged the town in a slaughter which became a watchword for the Scots and their later revenge. Douglas agreed to serve Edward I in his French wars, but absconded as soon as possible and joined Wallace's rebellion. Taken into custody – in chains – after the convention of Irvine, he was imprisoned in the Tower and died of 'mistreatment' there not long after.

DUNBAR, Earl Patrick

The most powerful Baron of the Lothians, Dunbar was a staunch supporter of the Plantagenets right up until 1314, when it was clear he had to submit to Bruce or suffer. He is, technically, the lord to whom the Sientclers owe their fealty – and the one they continually defy by joining with the cause of the Scots. Together with Gilbert D'Umfraville, another lord with extensive holdings in Scotland, he brought the news of Wallace's Falkirk location to Edward just when it seemed that the English would have to give up and retreat.

EDWARD I
King of England. At the time of this novel he has only recently conquered the Welsh and has a vision to become ruler of a united Britain before returning to his first love, a Crusade to free the Holy Land. He sees his chance to take over Scotland when the nobles come to him, as a respected monarch of Christendom, to adjudicate in their attempts to elect a new king of Scots from the many factions in the realm. His subsequent attempts to impose what he sees as his rights inveigle both realms in a long, vicious, expensive and bloody war that lasts for decades. Much maligned by Scots, for obvious reasons, he was beloved by the English, who were mournful about what would happen to their realm under his son, Edward II – and with good reason.

GAVESTON, Piers
Seen here briefly as a young squire at Falkirk, Gaveston was actually picked by Edward I as a suitable companion for his son, in an attempt to give the Prince some sort of benchmark for how to conduct himself with the dignity and honour of his station. This fatal error resulted in an unhealthy relationship between the two men which eventually brought both Edward II and his kingdom to ruin.

KIRKPATRICK, Roger
Fictional character, but based on the real Sir Roger Kirkpatrick of Closeburn, whom I have as kin to the fictional one. This is because my Kirkpatrick is a staunch Bruce supporter from the outset and the real Sir Roger was not – he even fought for Clifford in the English retinue at Falkirk. My Kirkpatrick

419

assumes the mantle of Bruce's henchman, prepared for any dirty work on behalf of his master's advancement, including murder.

LAMPRECHT
Fictional character, a pardoner and seller of relics from Cologne, a sometime spy and agent of those who pay most, he becomes involved in the Buchan plot against Hal of Herdmanston.

MALENFAUNT, Sir Robert
Real family, fictional character – a knight of dubious renown who captures Isabel at Stirling Bridge and is then duped into handing her over to what he believes is her husband, the Earl of Buchan, by Bruce and Hal.

MORAY, Sir Andrew
He raised the standard of rebellion in the north of Scotland in 1297, then joined forces with Wallace and, arguably, provided an acceptable commander for the nobility to rally to rather than the 'brigand' Wallace. Arguably, too, he provided the military skill of handling an army – but was badly wounded at Stirling Bridge and later died, leaving Wallace to organise subsequent events with disastrous results.

SIENTCLER, Sir Henry of Herdmanston
Known as Hal, he is the son and heir to Herdmanston, a lowly tower owing fealty to their kin, the Sientclers of Roslin. He is typical of the many poor nobles of Lothian who became embroiled in the wars on both sides of the divide – but Hal has fallen in love with Isabel, Countess of Buchan, and their ill-fated affair is shredded by war and her husband's hatred. Hal himself is torn by doubts as to whom he can trust, even between Wallace and Bruce, in a kingdom riven by family rivalries and betrayals. The Sientclers of Herdmanston are a

little-known branch of that family, appearing prominently for one brief moment in fifteenth-century history. Herdmanston is now an anonymous pile of stones in a corner of a ploughed field and any descriptions of it are pure conjecture on my part.

SIENTCLER, Sir Henry of Roslin

In reality, held as a hostage for ransom by the English, with his father, William, also held in the Tower. Here he is grandson of the Auld Templar and eventually ransomed by Hal and Bruce. In reality, he was also ransomed and later fought in the Battle of Roslin Glen alongside Red John Comyn and Sir Simon Fraser and against the English of Segrave and others, a famous victory for the Scots in 1303, when victories were scarce.

SIENTCLER, Sir John of Herdmanston

Fictional character, father of Hal, the Auld Sire of Herdmanston is captured by Sir Marmaduke Thweng fighting at Stirling Bridge and dies before he can be ransomed.

SIENTCLER, Sir William of Roslin (the Auld Templar)

Fictional character – the 'Auld Templar of Roslin' has been allowed back to Roslin by his commanderie because both his son and grandson are prisoners of the English. The real Sir William Sientcler (here described as the Auld Templar's son) is already in the Tower by the opening of this story and destined to die there.

THWENG, Sir Marmaduke

Lord of Kilton in Yorkshire, a noted knight and married to a Lucia de Brus, distant kin to Bruce himself, Sir Marmaduke is the accepted, sensible face of English knighthood. A noted thief-taker – bounty hunter – in his own realm, he was also part of the tourney circuit with the young Robert Bruce.

Fought at Stirling Bridge and was one of few to battle their way back to Stirling Castle, where he was eventually taken prisoner. Took part in subsequent campaigns against the Scots including Bannockburn, where, in his sixties, he fought until he could surrender personally to Bruce and was subsequently released without ransom.

WALLACE, William

The legend who led Scottish forces to victory at Stirling Bridge and defeat at Falkirk, was forced to relinquish his Guardianship and eventually betrayed to the English. That at least is the myth, but the man behind it is more elusive – described as a 'chief of brigands' at the time of the rebellion, he was barely of the nobility of Scotland and accepted by them unwillingly and only while he was winning. He was, however, the only one of them all who never gave in, or changed sides.

WISHART, Robert, Bishop of Glasgow

One of the original Guardians of Scotland following the death of King Alexander III – and partly responsible for inviting Edward I to preside over subsequent proceedings – Bishop Wishart became the engine of rebellion and a staunch supporter of first Wallace, then Bruce. He and Lamberton, Bishop of St Andrews, were instrumental in bringing support to Bruce even after he murdered his rival, the Red Comyn – Wishart went so far as to absolve Bruce for the affair. The Bishops' reasons for rebelling were simple – the Scottish church was responsible only to the Pope, who appointed all their senior prelates; they did not want the English version, where the King performed that function, and could maintain that difference only if Scotland remained a distinct and separate realm.

GLOSSARY

ALAUNT
Large, short-coated hunting dog of the mastiff type, used for bringing down large game.

AVENTAIL
Neck guard on a helmet, usually made from MAILLE.

BABERY
Term for any ape, but applied to the carvings on the eaves of churches – which were wonderful confections of people, beasts and mythology – apes featured prominently, frequently wearing the garb of bishops and priests as a sly joke by masons.

BACHLE
Untidy, shabby or clumsy. Can be used to describe bad workmanship, a slouching walk, or simply to insult someone as useless and more. Still in use, though more usually spelled *bauchle*.

BARBETTE
Women's clothing – a cloth chin strap to hide the neck and chin, to which was attached a variety of headgear, most commonly

the little round hat known then as a turret and nowadays as a pillbox. Compulsory for married women in public and still seen on nuns today.

BASCINET
Open-faced steel helm, sometimes covering down to the ears. The medieval knight or man-at-arms usually wore, in order from inside out – a padded arming cap, a COIF of MAILLE, a bascinet and, finally, the full-faced metal helmet, or HEAUME.

BATTUE
A hunt organised as if it was a melee at a TOURNEY, usually involving indiscriminate slaughter of beasts driven into an ambush.

BLACK-AFFRONTED
Ashamed. A Scots term still in use today and probably derived from the act of covering your heraldic shield (*affronty* is a heraldic term) in order not to be recognised. Scots knights did this as they fled from Methven, in order not to be subsequently accused of being supporters of Bruce.

BLIAUT
An overtunic worn by noble women and men from the 11th to the 13th century, notable for the excessively long drape of sleeve from the elbow in women, from mid forearm on the male version.

BRAIES
Linen, knee-length drawers, as worn by every male in the Middle Ages. Women had no true undergarments, though 'small clothes' were sometimes worn by gentlewomen.

CAMILIS
The, usually white, flowing overtunic worn by some knights. Despite military sense dictating the use of tight-fitting clothing

in close-combat, the urge for display frequently led to extravagant and impractical garments and headgear.

CATERAN
Originally a term to denote any fighting man from the Highlands, it became synonymous with any marauders or cattle thieves. See also KERN.

CHARE
A narrow, twisting medieval alleyway. See also VENNEL.

CHAUSSE
Legging, originally made like stockings until eventually joined in the middle to become trousers. MAILLE chausse were ring-metal leggings including the foot and with a leather sole.

CHIEL
Scottish term for a man. See also QUINE.

CHIRMYNG
Charming – most commonly used (as here) as the collective noun for finches or goldfinches.

CHITTERING
Scots for chattering.

CLOOTS
Scots word for clothing and still used today for any old rags. The term 'auld cloots and gruel' used in the story means 'of no account' or 'everyday'.

COIF
Any hood which covered the head and shoulders. Usually refers to one made of ring-metal and worn like a modern balaclava.

COMMUNITY OF THE REALM
Medieval Scotland being enlightened – this referred to the rule of law by all the kingdom, not just the king. However, it *was* the Middle Ages, so the Community referred to was one either with land and title, or rich merchant burghers from the towns. The commonality – peasants – of the realm still had no say.

COTE/SURCOTE
Old English and French for men's and women's outergarment. The male cote was a tunic varying in length half-way between waist and knee, sometimes slit for riding if the wearer was noble and almost always 'deviced' (ie bearing the wearer's heraldry) if you're someone of account. The TABARD was a sleeveless version. King John Balliol, whose ceremonial tabard was ritually stripped of the heraldic device, became known as 'Toom Tabard' (Empty Cote) forever after.

COWPED
Scots word for tumbled.

COZEN
To trick or deceive.

CROCKARD
The stability of Edward I's coinage had the unfortunate side-effect of allowing merchants to take the silver penny abroad as currency. This enabled unscrupulous Low Country lords to mint a debased version, which became known as a crockard. See also POLLARD.

CROTEY
The dung of hare or coney (rabbit). See FIANTS.

DESTRIER

Not a breed, but a type of horse – the warhorse of the Middle Ages was powerful, trained and cosseted to the point where it was to be used, at which point, depending on the importance of the affray, it was considered expendable. Destrier is from the Vulgar Latin *dextarius,* meaning right-handed, either from the horse's gait, or that it was mounted from the right side. Not as large, or heavy-footed as usually portrayed they were about the size of a good riding horse of today, though more muscled in the rear. They were all stallions and each one, in 1297, cost as much as seven ordinary riding horses.

DRIECH

Scots term to describe a dull, grey day where it never actually rains but you still get wet from an unseen drizzle.

EECHIE-OCHIE

Neither one thing nor another.

FASH

To worry. The phrase never fash means don't worry.

FIANTS

The dung of the fox, wolf, boar or badger.

FOOTERING

Fumbling.

GAMBESON

Knee-length tunic, sewn with quilted flutes stuffed with wool if you could afford it or straw if you could not. Designed to be worn over or under MAILLE to negate blunt trauma but frequently worn as the sole armour protection of the less well-off. A lighter version, brought back from the Crusades, was known as an aketon, from the Arabic *al qutn,* or cotton, with which it was stuffed.

GARDECORPS

A cape-like overtunic with a slit under the armpit so that you could wear it sleeveless, its shapelessness appealed to those of a larger size. As if to compensate, many such garments were given BLIAUT style sleeves, sometimes with long tippets, or dagged hems, while the collar and cuffs were trimmed with expensive fur.

GARRON

Small, hardy Highland pony used widely by the HOBILARS of both sides, though more favoured by Scottish foot. It enabled them to move fast, raid like cavalry and yet dismount to fight on foot if faced by the knight on his heavy horse – and no archers to hand.

GLAUR

Scots word for sticky mud.

GRALLOCH

The contents of a stag's stomach which has been 'unmade' after a kill. The gralloch, in medieval times, went to the hounds as a reward.

GUDDLE

Scots terms which, as a verb, means to grope blindly. As a noun it means mix-up or confusion.

HAAR

One of the many Scots words for rain – this refers to a wet mist.

HEAUME

Another name for the large medieval helmet. More properly, it was given to the later TOURNEY helmet, which reached and was supported on the shoulders.

HERSCHIP
From hardship, a Scots term for vicious raids designed to lay waste and plunder a region to the detriment of the enemy.

HOBILAR
English word for light cavalry, recruited to counter the Scots raiders and so called because they were mounted on large ponies called hobyn. This gives us the modern child's toy, the hobby horse, as well as the generic name for horses everywhere – Dobbin.

HOOR
Scots pronunciation of whore.

HUMFY-BACKIT
Scots term for hunchback.

JACK
Origin of our word jacket, this was a variation on the aketon or GAMBESON and usually involved the addition of small metal plates sewn to the outside. Also known as *jazerant*.

JACOB'S PILLOW
The Stone of Scone was popularly believed in Scotland to be the same one consecrated to God by Jacob in the Book of Genesis, following a vision while he slept.

JALOUSE
The original Scots meaning was surmise. Some time in the 19th century, the English adopted it but, mysteriously, used it as jealous. It is used here in its original sense.

JEDDART STAFF
More properly known by this name in the 16th and 17th century Border country (the Jeddart refers to Jedburgh), the weapon was essentially the same – a reinforced spear which

also incorporated a thin cutting blade on one side and a hook on the other.

JUPON
A short, closely-tailored arming cote worn over MAILLE in action, to display your heraldry.

JURROCKS
Lowlife servant.

JUSTICIAR
An official appointed by the monarch, from the time of William Rufus, son of William the Conqueror, to ease the burden on overworked SHERIFFS.

KERN
Irish/Scots soldiery. Later, it came to refer to the Gallowglass warriors of Ireland.

KINE
Scots word for cattle.

KIST OF WHISTLES
Scots term for a covered, boiling cauldron or kettle, kist being any kind of container, from clothes chest to tomb.

LATCHBOW
Originally, a light crossbow with a simple latch release, it came to be a common term for all crossbows and arbalests.

LAW OF DEUTERONOMY
Specifically Deuteronomy 20, which states: *And when the LORD thy God hath delivered it into thine hands, thou shalt smite every male thereof with the edge of the sword: But the women, and the little ones, and the cattle, and all that is in the city,*

even all the spoil thereof, shalt thou take unto thyself; and thou shalt eat the spoil of thine enemies, which the LORD thy God hath given thee. Used by medieval Christian commanders to justify the sack and slaughter of any city which did not yield before a siege ram or ladder touched the walls.

LIMMER
A low, base fellow – also a prostitute.

MAILLE
The correct spelling of mail, which is also incorrectly referred to as chainmail and should be properly termed ring maille. The linked metal-ringed tunic worn by warriors since the early Roman period. By the 13th/14th century, these had evolved – for those who could afford it – into complete suits, with sleeves, mittens and integral COIF, or hood.

MAK' SICCAR
Make certain. A famous phrase uttered by Bruce's loyal follower Sir Roger Kirkpatrick of Closeburn shortly before he returned to Greyfriars Church to ensure the death of Bruce's rival, the Red Comyn. It became the motto of the Kirkpatrick family, under the crest of a bloody hand holding a dagger.

MESNIE
Can refer, loosely, to a medieval household, but more usually to the trusted group of knights who accompanied their lord to war and TOURNEY.

MILLINAR
Any knight or SERJEANT appointed to command a band on foot.

MOUDIEWART

Literally, a mole, but frequently used as an insult.

NEB

Scots word for nose.

NOTARY

Nowadays it is a person with legal training licensed by the state to perform certain legal acts, particularly witnessing signatures on legal documents. In the Middle Ages it was a man who could read, write, take notes and acted as clerk to a JUSTICIAR.

ORB

Scots word for young bird. See also SPEUGH.

OS

From the Latin, a mouth or opening – usually applied to the female parts, whether human or animal. In some cases, the os of hind was considered a delicacy.

PACHYDERM

Medieval classification usually applied to elephants, but which also included pigs and wild boar.

PAPINGO

The popinjay or parrot – any brightly coloured bird, or person who resembles one in dress or manner. Can also refer to an archery competition, where such a live bird was placed on a pole and used as a target. It still pertains to the present – there is an annual Papingo Shoot at Kilwinning Abbey – but the papingo target is no longer a bird, live or otherwise.

PAYNIM

Medieval term for heathen, particularly Muslims.

PLENARY INDULGENCE

The remittance of sins, granted by the Catholic church after confession and absolution. However, these could also be sold as a sort of cheque drawn on the Treasure House of Merit, an abuse which was widespread in the Middle Ages.

PLOOTERING

Scots word meaning to walk carelessly, with the added connotation of splashing, as through puddles or into marsh or mud.

POLLARD

A fake silver penny of Edward I's reign, so called either because of the miscast head (poll) of the monarch or because it had been clipped (pollarded) of some of its metal, making it smaller.

POW

Scots word which can either refer to the head (as in 'curly pow') or an expanse of water meadow cut up with small pools.

POWRIE

Scots Fairies which, as you might expect, are not ethereally-pretty winged creatures. They are short and wiry, with ragged pointed teeth and sharp claws like steel. They wear a red bonnet on their heads and are generally bearded with wrinkled aged faces. They kill by rolling boulders or tearing at people with their sharp claws. They then proceed to drink the blood of their victims and dip their hats in it, giving rise to their other name of Red Caps. In particular they haunt castles with a reputation for evil events in the past. Also known as Dunters.

PRIGG

Scots word meaning to beseech or plead.

QUINE
Scots word for a woman or a young girl. See CHIEL.

RIGG
Scots word for a strip of ploughed field.

SCAPULAR
Large length of cloth suspended from the shoulders — monastic scapulars originated as aprons worn by medieval monks, and were later extended to habits.

SCHILTRON
The first mention of the schiltron as a specific formation of spearmen appears to be at the Battle of Falkirk in 1297. There is, however, no reason to believe this is the first time such a formation was used and there are references to the Picts using blocks of spearmen in such a fashion. The name is thought to derive from the Middle English for shield troop.

SCRIEVING
Scots word — to move swiftly and smoothly.

SCRIVENER
Medieval term for anyone who could read and write.

SCULLION
Servant performing menial kitchen tasks.

SERJEANT
The armed 'middle class' of medieval England, only differing from a knight in that they had not been recognised as such. Equipment, training and skill were all more or less the same.

SERK
Scots word — originally Norse — for a shirt or undertunic.

SHERIFF

A contraction of the term 'shire reeve', he is the highest law officer in a county. A term and idea which has spread from England to many parts of the world, including the US and Canada. In Scotland, English sheriffs were particularly hated, none more so than Heselrigg, Sheriff of Lanark and the man Wallace famously killed to begin his part in the rebellion.

SKITE

Scots word meaning to slip or skate.

SLAISTER

Scots word meaning a dirty mess, or slovenly work.

SLEEKIT

Scots word for crafty or sly.

SLORACH

Scots word for a wet and disgusting mess of anything.

SNECK

Scots word for a bolt or latch on a door. Still in use today in the Borders and north of England in the term 'sneck lifter' – the last coin in a man's pocket, enough to let him open a pub door and buy a drink.

SONSIE

Scots word for a woman with a generous, hour-glass figure.

SPEUGH

Scots word for baby sparrow.

SPIER

Scots word meaning to inquire after, to question.

SPITAL

Medieval short-form of hospital, which was any place – usually in a monastery or abbey – which cared for the sick.

STAPPIT

Scots word for stuffed full.

STOOKS

Scots word for sheaves.

STRAMASH

Scots word for a noisy disturbance.

STRAVAIG

Scots word meaning to wander aimlessly.

STUSHIE

Scots word for being in a state of excitement. Also for a shouting argument.

SWEF

Medieval bastardised French for gently or softly.

TABARD

Medieval short tunic, sleeveless, or with shoulder pieces, designed to show a noble's heraldic device or arms – hence the term cote of arms. Still seen today on ceremonial heralds.

TAIT

Scots word for a little item or a small portion.

THOLE

Scots word meaning to suffer or to bear.

THRAWN
Scots word for twisted or misshapen, which can be applied equally to a tree, a face or a disposition.

TOLT
Medieval word for a tax, usually on wool.

TOURNEY
Simply put, this was the premier entertainment and sporting pursuit of the medieval gentleman. It involved, usually, the Melee, a mass of knights fighting each other. A Grand Melee could involve several hundred and be fought over a large distance – it was not a spectator sport. The object of the Melee was to unhorse your opponent and take him for ransom – as was expected in a real war – though the weapons were blunted for the Tourney and no-one was expected to die or get hurt (though, of course, some did). Latterly, the one-on-one joust became more and more popular, simply because it *was* a spectator sport and everyone could see your skill.

TRAILBASTON
Medieval term for the itinerant judicial commission ordered by Edward I to combat outlaws and brigands, it became the name for the perpetrators themselves.

VENNEL
Scots word for alleyway.

WHEEN
Scots word for many, a lot.

YETT
Scots word for a door, originally applied to the grilled inner gate of a fortress.

AND FINALLY

There is a short scene in chapter four which is designed to show how the broadest of Scots is virtually incomprehensible even to other Scots and certainly to French-speaking nobles.

Delivered from one Fergus, a man from the north of Scotland, it runs:

'*Atweill than,*' Fergus declared to the haughty rider, '*this wul dae brawlie. Gin ye haed spoke The Tongue at the verra stert, ye wad hae spared the baith o us aw this hatter. Tak tent ti whit Ah hae ti say an lippen ti me weill – ye maun bide ther until I lowse ye.*'

The rider, mailled and coiffed, flung up his hands, so that wet drops flew up from his green-gloved fingers, and cursed pungently in French.

'*I am Sir Gervaise de la Mare. Do you understand no language at all?*'

'*Ah prigg the blissin o the blue heivins on ye,*' Fergus scowled back. '*There are ower mony skirrivaigin awhaurs, so bide doucelyke or, b'Goad's ane Wounds, Ah wul . . .*'

'*Fergus,*' Hal said and the dark man fell back and turned, his black-browed face breaking into a wary grin.

'*Yersel,*' he greeted with about as much deference as he ever gave and then jerked his head contemptuously at the rider.

'*This yin an' his muckle freends came sklimming the heich brae, aw grand an' skerlet and purpie. Luikin to spier you somewhiles.*'

For those who haven't worked it out, here's what Fergus was really saying:

'Well then. This will be fine. If you had tried to be understood from the start you would have spared us both a deal of trouble. Pay attention now and listen to me closely – you have to remain here until I permit you to pass.'

The rider, mailled and coiffed, flung up his hands, so that wet drops flew up from his green-gloved fingers, and cursed pungently in French.

'I am Sir Gervaise de la Mare. Do you understand no language at all?'

'I beseech the blessing of the blue Heaven from you. There are too many people wandering everywhere, so stay here quietly, or by God's Own Wounds, I will . . .'

'Fergus,' Hal said and the dark man fell back and turned, his black-browed face breaking into a wary grin.

'Yersel,' he greeted with about as much deference as he ever gave and then jerked his head contemptuously at the rider.

'This one and his great friends came gliding over the high hills, all grand and garishly dressed. They are searching for you in particular.'

And now you know!